Also by Deryn Collier

Confined Space

PRAISE FOR *CONFINED SPACE*

"An intelligently conceived, suspenseful, and elegantly written story . . . [Collier] knows just how to insert into her story the right hints of menace to keep readers in a state of iffy balance."

—*Toronto Star*

"A nice mystery with good characters in a well-developed setting . . . the series has promise." —*The Globe and Mail*

Collier "doles out ingredients in an appealingly low-key fashion and paces the book and clues at a steady clip." —*National Post*

"While it's often noted that getting a female character right can be tough for a male author, the reverse is equally true. Collier manages this with sympathetic poignancy." —*Winnipeg Free Press*

"A great debut novel. *Confined Space* perfectly captures the unique beauty of the Kootenay area of British Columbia as it introduces two conflicted, engaging, completely realistic characters. I'm looking forward to meeting Evie and Bern again soon."

—Vicki Delany, author of *A Cold White Sun*

"Fans of Dana Stabenow and Deborah Crombie, rejoice! Deryn Collier's maiden outing is superbly written, densely layered, and marvelously suspenseful. *Confined Space* is a tour-de-force heralding an explosive new series guaranteed to please the traditional mystery lover."

—Julia Spencer-Fleming, *New York Times* best-selling author of *One Was a Soldier*

"An enigmatic coroner with a deeply layered past. Believable characters and a multilayered plot. Deryn Collier's debut novel keeps you up late reading to find out more. A thoroughly enjoyable read."

—Peggy Blair, author of *The Beggar's Opera*

OPEN SECRET

Deryn Collier

PUBLISHED BY SIMON & SCHUSTER CANADA

NEW YORK   LONDON   TORONTO   SYDNEY   NEW DELHI

Simon & Schuster Canada
A Division of Simon & Schuster, Inc.
166 King Street East, Suite 300
Toronto, Ontario
M5A 1J3

First Simon & Schuster Canada edition April 2014

SIMON & SCHUSTER CANADA and colophon are registered trademarks of Simon & Schuster, Inc.

For information about special discounts for bulk purchases, please contact Simon & Schuster Special Sales at 1-800-268-3216 or CustomerService@ simonandschuster.ca.

Manufactured in the United States of America

10 9 8 7 6 5 4 3 2 1

ISBN 978-1-4767-1680-0
ISBN 978-1-4767-1681-7 (ebook)

For Ron

St. Brigid's Reserve, 1981

The dining set arrived at night, delivered by two shifty-eyed teenagers. As soon as the table's curved legs touched the floor, she scooted underneath it. It was the cleanest thing she'd ever seen.

"Say hello to your cousins." His voice cut through her daydream of making a world for herself under there. Her own room.

"Hello, cousins," she said to the strangers as she slid out again. She didn't like to lie; maybe they were her cousins. She seemed to have so many.

"Show respect."

So she'd stood still and quiet because showing respect meant standing still and not saying anything. She stood still while the cousins brought the chairs in and while they sat down on them and drank a few beers.

"What are you staring at?" he asked. "Idiot kid."

The cousins laughed. So she moved away to the other side of the couch, where there were piles of papers and dirty clothes and a sticky mess on the carpet that she didn't like. She spun circles and practiced her jumps as quietly as she could, careful not to bump into anything. She was going to be a figure skater one day.

She had just landed a double axel when a hand reached out

and held her extended foot. She had to hop up and down in place to keep from falling over.

"You've got good balance," her cousin said.

He had black hair, like hers, but his eyes were pale blue and mean. Except when he was smiling, which he was now.

"What's your name?" he asked.

Before she could answer, the others stood up from the table. He dropped her foot so suddenly that she stumbled onto her hands and knees. In one swift motion he was down next to her, his eyes mean again.

"I said, what's your name?"

"Cindy," she replied.

He smiled then and reached out to touch the collar of her dress. "Cindy," he said. "That's not much of a dress for a pretty girl like you."

She didn't know what to say, so she stayed perfectly still and said nothing. Show respect.

"What are you doing?"

"Skating." She whispered the word.

"I'm going to come back one day and bring you a skating dress," he said. "And skates. Do you have skates?"

She shook her head.

"Have you ever even been to the rink?"

She shook her head again.

And then he was out the door. Both cousins were gone and she was alone again with her father.

"Good-bye, cousins," she said quietly as she scooted across the sticky floor to her sanctuary under the table.

1

"Just going to the Home Depot to pick up some paint." Gary Dowd practiced saying the words out loud. He sounded tense. "Going to pick up some paint. Good day to paint the garage." *Better.*

There were four cars ahead of him at the border. At the front of the line a logging truck idled. Behind it sat a motor home with Canadian plates—snowbirds making an early trip south for the winter. Gary pictured himself following them down the highway, leaving it all behind. He hit the CD player and the sound of children's music filled the van so loudly, he jumped in his seat. He twisted the knob to turn the volume down and switched over to the radio. The tin beat of pop music worked its way out through the speakers. In the rearview mirror he could see Geoffrey's car seat. Empty, or so it seemed at first glance. But Gary knew better.

Just in front of him a run-down Nissan hatchback stalled and started up again. Gary's knee started bouncing. *I've got to calm down.* He made a bet with himself: the US guards would give the Nissan such a thorough going-over that when Gary pulled up they would just wave him through.

He caught a glimpse of himself in the rearview mirror. Eyes, shit brown. Hair, shit brown and thinning. God, he hated that fact. His face was smooth and he knew he looked younger than his thirty-two years, but his retreating hairline gave away the secret: he was an old man waiting to happen.

He tried to draw a breath down into his abdomen, just as they'd showed him in the prenatal class his wife had forced him to take. Michelle had been the model student, but Gary hyperventilated every time he tried to take a deep breath. In the delivery room she ended up calming him down between her own contractions. His lungs expanded in anticipation, but when no air got to them, a panic spread to the tips of his fingers and he felt an urge to run. On one of his many walks around the perimeter of the hospital, sucking cold mountain air through his wide-open mouth, Natasha had come into the world.

Four years later, Michelle was still mad about that. "It's like you forget everything. When you get like that, nothing matters at all," she'd said. As usual, she was right.

The logging truck pulled forward. Gary took in the scenery. There wasn't much difference between Canada and the United States, so far as he could tell. The same chain of smoky mountains linked the two sides of the border. Once across the line he would be in Idaho, in a tiny finger of that state that spread its way to the border of British Columbia. Barely fifty miles to the west a person would cross into Washington. To the east, it would be Montana. But Gary was headed to Idaho, through what was considered to be the loosest border crossing along the forty-ninth parallel. *That's why Seymour picked it,* he thought. The station house before him was a simple two-room brick hut with only two guards on duty at a time. Traffic was so sporadic that the crossing closed completely at night.

Seymour had shown up a month ago. That day, it was Gary's turn to come home and cook, and Michelle's turn to pick the kids up at day care. He loved those nights, when he could leave his office at the mill a little early and have a beer and an hour of quiet before his family got home.

"Hey, man, can I help you with that?"

Gary had recognized the voice at once. Seymour. He froze midstep, holding a tray of burgers.

"Don't look so worried, my man." Seymour slid open the screen door and came right inside. He took the bottle of beer that dangled from Gary's fingers and laughed. "Let me help you with this." He took a deep pull from the bottle.

The words Gary should have said did not come. "Get the hell away from me and my family" might have been good. Or "Go back to wherever you've been hiding for the last fifteen years." Even a simple "get out" would have done it. But instead what came out was "What are you doing here, Seymour? It's been a long time." His words were easy, cool. But the tightness in his chest was already making it hard for him to breathe.

Seymour looked just the same as always. Hair black and shaggy, and as full as it had been in high school. His slight figure was still girlish in tight black jeans and a long-sleeved white T-shirt. The black leather vest seemed new and made him look like a biker, though it didn't have any patches, so it could have been for show. His hand was delicate and white as it held Gary's beer.

"Just passing through, passing through." Seymour's eyes were almost black. Gary wondered if the girls still went crazy over him, like they had in high school. In elementary school.

Seymour took another sip of beer and held up the half-empty bottle. "You got another one of these?" he asked.

"Yeah, sure," Gary said.

"Here, let me put those on the barbecue." Seymour reached for the tray. "You go get your old friend a beer, Gar. And bring out some mustard and ketchup. I'll put some special sauce on these babies."

And so Seymour was invited for dinner. When Michelle came home, he talked her into letting him stay for a few days by offering to help paint the garage. He played snakes and ladders with Natasha for a full hour before bedtime and tickled Geoffrey until he squealed.

In bed that night Gary stroked Michelle's blond hair, letting his hand fall to her shoulder. "Thanks," he whispered.

"Just don't lend him any money," she said, and turned her back to him.

Back at the border, Gary's gaze fell once again on the rear seat. He tried to block out the image of an enormous spotlight over Geoffrey's car seat. A spotlight aimed at the elastics that held the seat padding to the molded plastic frame. Lift those elastics away from the little hooks, move the padding, and a person would find a tight bundle wrapped in black plastic, about the size of a paperback. Gary didn't know what was in it. *I don't want to know.*

Yesterday had marked a full month since Seymour's arrival. Gary had walked down the steps to the basement holding a garbage bag. He ran his hand down the paneled walls, carefully painted sage green on instructions from Michelle. She had stenciled golden fleurs-de-lys over top, at intervals so exact it looked like wallpaper.

Seymour was asleep on the pullout couch. The place smelled like the one damp towel left at the bottom of a laundry basket. Seymour's clothes were piled on the floor, even though Michelle had cleared out a dresser for him. Gary nudged Seymour's foot and cleared his throat.

"You need to get out of here. Today. Now."

Seymour opened his eyes but did not move.

"I need more time, Gar," he said. His voice was that same wheedling whine that had punctuated Gary's childhood. "Just a few more days. Like I said, I've got something big going down."

"Look, Seymour, you're ruining everything." Gary blew out his breath and ran his hands through his hair. "Michelle says she's going to move out with the kids if I don't get you out of here. I know we used to be buddies, but this is my life."

The mattress squeaked under his weight as Seymour sat up and leaned against the woven back of the couch. His black eyes moved from side to side. Gary knew that look. Seymour's voice got quiet and the words seemed to slide out of his mouth: "Is that all I am to you? A guy you used to be buddies with?"

"Don't be like that. I've got a family—a wife—now. It's not like the old days."

"A wife. Sure I noticed that, Gary. Pretty little thing she is too, the lovely Mrs. Forsberg-Dowd." He spoke quietly, but the threat in his voice was impossible to miss.

Gary tried to speak but all that came out was a croak.

"Forsberg. Now where have I heard that name before? Think I should ask her about that?"

Gary found his voice. "You wouldn't."

"Why not? The way you keep trying to kick me out has got me thinking that maybe we're not such good buddies after all. And if that's the case, maybe I just feel like talking about this secret I've been carrying around all these years." Seymour was smiling now, watching Gary through his hooded eyes.

"Look, I'll get you a motel room, okay? I'll pay for it for a few weeks—a month, even. Just get the hell out of my house!" Even as he said the words, he knew it was too late. React, and Seymour goes in for the kill. Gary knew this like he knew his times tables.

Angry now, and careless, he opened the garbage bag and

started shoving Seymour's clothes into it. He grabbed a handful of shirts, a pair of jeans scabbed with dirt, and an undershirt that felt oily in his fingers. When he came across the kit he froze.

Seymour was watching him, his hand rubbing absently across his chest, white hand against white T-shirt. "Does she know you're a user?" he asked with a sad shake of his head.

"I'm not a user. I haven't touched that shit in years," Gary said. He couldn't pull his eyes from the tiny plastic bag. The green lighter. The spoon.

"Not a user? Look at you. You're jonesin', man!" Seymour laughed.

Gary saw that the spoon, bent and blackened at the bowl from a month of being heated with the lighter, was one of their good ones, from the set that Michelle's grandma had passed along to them on their wedding day. He looked up at Seymour, lying so casually on the very same couch that had been in Gary's rec room when he was growing up. The same couch that Seymour had inhabited every day after school, every weekend, every holiday—until one day late in their junior year, when he'd just slid away and disappeared.

"What will it take to get you out of my house?" Gary asked.

"One simple thing," Seymour replied.

Gary knew he would do it, whatever it was. Anything to get Seymour out of his life for good.

Gary snapped back to the here and now when the black Nissan rattled forward. The driver's hand flashed out the window as he offered up his passport. Gary practiced the words out loud again: "Canadian citizen. Just going over to pick up some stuff at the Home Depot." His voice croaked. He leaned back in his seat, trying to make more room for his lungs. Trying to let the air in.

The Nissan roared away without the driver even being asked

to open the trunk. Maybe it was an easy guard. Would Gary be as lucky? The band of steel around his chest tightened even further as the guard motioned to him. An enormous American flag waved crisply over the roof of the station house as he inched the van forward, rolling his window down. The flag passed from his view until he could only hear its sharp flapping in the fall wind.

"Nationality?" the guard asked. He held his hand out the window automatically, reaching for Gary's passport. He looked to be in his early twenties. His uniform was pressed, his tanned biceps flexed as he flipped the passport open deftly with one hand. A tag on his chest pocket said that his name was Weir.

"Canadian," Gary replied. It came out like a pant. His slick hands slipped from the steering wheel and he held them in his lap. He pushed down on his right knee, which had started bouncing up and down again.

"Where are the kids today?" Weir asked, jutting his chin at the car seats in the back.

"At home, with my wife," he answered. "I'm just going to Ho-Home Depot." The words rushed out before he could stop them.

Weir puckered his dark eyebrows at Gary and tapped something into the computer. "Wait here," he said, and slid the window closed.

Gary could not remember if he was inhaling or exhaling. His mind fogged with the effort of breathing. A buzzing began in his ears and he closed his eyes momentarily. When he opened them he could see a formation of geese in the patch of sky that was not blocked by the roof of the station house. Whether they were practicing for their flight south or had started on the actual journey, he could not tell.

Three minutes passed. Four. Gary tapped the stereo and the

canned beat from the radio stopped. In the silence he could hear that his breath was coming in ragged gasps. He had to get out.

Weir's back was turned and he was talking on the phone. He looked back at Gary once, then sat on the counter, hooking the receiver between his ear and shoulder. Gary glanced in the rearview mirror. There was no one behind him.

In one quick movement he unlatched his seat belt and slid his hand beneath the padding of Geoffrey's car seat. He closed his fingers around the package and slid it out. Each movement propelled from the last in an inevitable momentum. He crawled over the emergency brake, opened the passenger door, and slipped down onto the pavement. An electronic chime sounded and Gary froze. He had been caught. He almost laughed when he realized it was from the open door of the van. He did not dare close it.

Crouching below the height of the van, Gary sprinted away from the station house as fast as he could. The blowing air filled his lungs. He expected the shot to come at any moment, but soon he reached the end of the pavement and rolled down a grassy slope. Scraped up but not hurt, he began to run again. There was a strip of thick forest just in front of him and he raced through it, dodging trees, jumping over shrubs and fallen branches. He stopped only once, to shove the package into his back pocket. He listened but could hear only the sawing of his own breath. It flowed easily once again, sweet mountain air, in and out, without his having to think about it.

He crouched lower and aimed his body to the thickest part of the forest. Toward the base of the mountains, where there was nothing but space and air.

St. Brigid's Reserve, 1981

A white lady came and brought a book. She walked right up to the door in her buttoned coat and shiny shoes and pounded on it. When no one answered, she opened it anyway.

Cindy, who had been watching her approach from the window, shook her head at the lady, wide-eyed.

"Well, hello there," the lady said. "What's your name?"

Cindy didn't answer. She couldn't. She just shook her head fast and glanced at the couch.

"You look like you're about ready to start school. Is that right? Are you five?"

Cindy nodded quickly.

"Would you like a book? To help you get ready for school?"

Cindy inched closer to the door and took the book from the lady's hand. It was shiny and on the cover was a picture of a cow, smiling at her.

"She's not going to school." Her father's voice rumbled up from the couch, where he'd been sleeping. His voice was mean enough to make the white lady's smile flop right off.

"Don't you want to go to school?" the lady asked Cindy with what was left of her smile.

Cindy nodded faster and faster. She stood as still as she could and nodded up and down, up and down. She had to show respect to the white lady, even though she wasn't a cousin. Show respect. So she didn't jump up and down and yell, "Yesyesyesyes!" Which is what she really wanted to do.

Her father stood up then and walked over to them. The lady kept right on talking. Cindy should have told her that wasn't a good idea. She should have said something.

"It's a program called Early Start," the white lady said, to her father now. "To help kids on the reserve get ready for school."

Her father grabbed the book out of Cindy's hand. He ripped it in two and threw it. It smacked the door hard, just as the lady was closing it.

Cindy watched the two parts of the cow's face flutter to the floor.

2

Now that it was finally time to replace the fence, Bern Fortin could not bring himself to do it. He had wanted to mend the falling-down structure ever since he moved in last spring. The soldier in him liked straight lines and tidy rows; the rest of his garden was a testament to that fact. But even Bern Fortin, former commander of the Canadian battle group in Afghanistan, could not stand up to his neighbor, the formidable Mrs. Kalesnikoff.

"Wait," she'd said last spring. Soon after, the sweet peas had grown up both sides of the fence, their riot of blossoms lasting well into fall. Only last week, once Mrs. K. had clipped the last of the fading blooms and collected their seeds into a large paper grocery bag, crinkled from reuse, did she grant him permission to do the job.

Now that the time had finally come, however, Bern found himself putting off the task. There was only a small window after the sweet peas stopped blooming and before the ground froze, and yet for some reason he could not do it. Not today.

Mrs. K. and her grandson Brian would be expecting him to join them for breakfast soon. They followed the same dance steps every day, and though Bern loved some parts of the routine—especially working side by side with Brian as they stacked Mrs. K.'s winter woodpile—he was starting to find it hard to sit still at the breakfast table. And he was struggling to keep quiet when Mrs. K. told him, as she did every day, that he drank too much coffee. She'd started serving him tea instead.

From his perch on the back deck, Bern could see the tidy pile of fence posts awaiting him. He heard the plunk of Brian's bike as the teen dropped it on the strip of grass between the two houses. At the sound of the first slice of the boy's swing through the morning air—the thwack of the ax on that first piece of wood—Bern went inside.

There, the laptop admonished him. He had not opened it in days. Messages would be waiting for him. From Alais. From that reporter, Troy Thompson, who had been emailing and calling his cell phone nonstop. From a growing number of others who had found him and were asking questions. Bern—who had only gotten the computer to shop online for seeds and learn how to garden—was regretting his choice.

Of course, the computer was a lifeline to his job. The multiple forms he needed to fill out, the correspondence, the reports, his many duties to the dead in his role as coroner to the community of Kootenay Landing—all relied on that tiny folded rectangle of white that lay unplugged, battery drained, on the plane of wood that was his desktop.

Bern stood in the middle of his small house. His stomach felt empty and sour: too much coffee, not enough food. He made an assessment of operations to date. Seven months into deployment, he'd won the hearts and minds of the locals. Logistics and matériel were on track, perimeter well on its way to being secured. Supply stores were filled; they would get through the winter warm, dry, and ready for the next season of ops, when Bern was determined to grow a perfect crop of tomatoes. On good days, he allowed himself to imagine winning the special ribbon for his tomatoes at next year's fall fair.

What more could he need? Yet this anxiety trailed him and whispered: be ready. Mrs. K. would tell him what he needed: more food in his belly, less coffee. He needed to swing an ax or a sledgehammer. To split logs or pound fence posts into solid earth. She would be right, of course, but at the moment he felt unwilling—perhaps even unable—to take these steps.

He was already dressed: jeans, thick wool socks and tightly tied leather hiking boots, a navy-blue flannel shirt. He pulled on a thin down vest and put a wool cap over his dark, curly hair. In his kitchen, spotless as always, the espresso maker called to him. Just one more. One for the road. A triple.

Coffee made, he turned off the machine but did not wipe it down. One drop of grainy brown liquid remained on the counter and he forced himself to leave it there. At the front door, his cell phone waited. As the coroner, he needed to be reachable at all times, but he was tired of this tether. The only person to call him in days was that blasted reporter. The man was closer to breaching the perimeter every day.

What were the odds that someone would die on a sunny fall morning? On a Sunday morning? Most of the community would be at church. He'd be back before the ladies' auxiliary finished serving lunch.

He closed the front door firmly and then locked it, as though shutting out the protests he imagined coming from the abandoned phone.

Juniper Sinclair tapped at her soft-boiled egg. She shook some seaweed-flavored salt replacement into her palm. She missed salt; it was just one of the many concessions they'd had to make to illness.

Gia was looking at her, so she kept her focus firmly on sprinkling the seasoning evenly over the runny yolk.

"You'll have to say something eventually, you know," Gia said. "You can't stay quiet forever, Juniper."

When her egg was just right, Juniper picked up her spoon again and stirred the fake salt into the yolk. She didn't look up. She knew what she'd see: Gia, as regal and calm as ever, her rather plain face framed by that damned white turban she insisted on wearing—*helps divert negativity, makes my aura strong*—like nothing had happened.

Of course, given what *had* happened, it was a good thing she had that turban, and that she'd been wearing one for years. No one would notice a thing.

Juniper stole just a quick look now, while Gia doctored her own egg. She'd seen her share of challenges, Juniper knew. But in this house, the mountain sun came in at angles and washed everything clean: the cedar logs, the wide pine floorboards, the solid furniture spaced widely to accommodate a wheelchair. It seemed to wash the memories away. There were stories that Juniper knew she would never hear, no matter how long she stayed in the other woman's home. But there. *There.* Was that something? A line between her eyebrows. Was that new?

People reacted differently to trauma. Juniper knew this too—it was something she told her patients all the time. Just last week, a woman had stared at her stone-faced as Juniper had given her a diagnosis of breast cancer. The woman's husband had looked on, a little smile on his face, and hummed—yes, he'd hummed—as though they had stopped for a chat about the weather while he was on his way to the post office. Even this was a normal reaction. Gia's steel-rod calm should really not come as a surprise. But it did.

Juniper managed to squeeze out a few words. "Where's Lennon?"

Gia didn't answer right away and Juniper looked up at her. The older woman's eyes were brown, intelligent, kind. The eyes of a friend. Even now.

"I think he went in to work. Not sure, though." She hooked her strong hands over the rims of her wheelchair and backed away from the table. Her legs were thin now as the multiple sclerosis claimed one muscle at a time.

"I failed you," Gia said.

Juniper shook her head. "There was nothing you could have done."

"If only—" She lifted one wasted thigh in both hands and let it drop back into the seat of her wheelchair.

"Don't."

"But—"

"Just don't. You're not at fault here. Neither am I."

"You think it's Lennon's fault."

"I never said that. Did you hear me say that?"

Now it was Gia's turn to be silent.

"Look," said Juniper, making up now. "Let's not argue, okay? I've got an ER shift starting tonight. I'm going to go for a walk first. Why don't you come?"

Gia winced and pointed at her legs.

"We'll stick to the road, and we don't need to go far. Come for some fresh air." *We can't let them know they've gotten to us,* she wanted to say but didn't.

The older woman shook her head, her turban crossing a ray of sun coming in through the window, so the sun flicked in and out of Juniper's eyes. "I won't walk. But when you get back, let's spend a few hours cleaning up the studio. I can help with that."

With that she spun her wheelchair around and rolled up to the window. She liked to sit in the sun like a cat. It was something Juniper often teased her about.

Juniper stood and walked over to her. She put her hands on her friend's shoulders and pressed softly, unconsciously checking muscle tone. She stopped herself, but not before noting the strong and defined shoulder muscles. There was still time. Together they looked out over the hundreds of hectares of marshland that spread out below them. In the distance the Kootenay Landing town site glittered on its hillock in the sun.

"I don't think I can go back to the studio. Not yet anyway," Juniper said. "Look at those geese."

They watched in silence as a skein of geese brought themselves into formation and headed on a test run south toward the border.

"They'll be back. It's too soon yet," said Gia. "Look at that little straggler. Catch up, buddy! You can do it."

As they watched the stray goose did catch up with the others.

"There, I knew you could do it," Gia said, satisfied that her encouragement had made all the difference. Then to Juniper, her voice firmer: "You have to get back on the bike. Get back to work. It's important."

Juniper let her hands fall from her friend's shoulders to the handles of the wheelchair and then down to her sides. "Is it? I'm not sure anymore."

Gia nodded. "It is."

"You're so certain."

"People are counting on you."

She pictured the studio in her mind. The converted woodshed, once her sanctuary, came to her now as a slick of melted beeswax caked with pellets for the woodstove, the whole mess hardened to the wide wood boards of the floor.

"For the next thirty-six hours, if they are lucky, people can count on me to keep them from dying in the ER. That's all I can promise."

"But you know that's not where healing happens."

Juniper stepped away now. "Do I? Do I really know that?" She picked up the breakfast dishes and brought them to the counter. Gia would want to do them as part of her exercise, so she left them there. "I'm not really sure what I know anymore," she said, more to herself than to her friend, as she headed out the door for her walk.

St. Brigid's Reserve, 1981

Auntie came. She swept in and brought sunshine and a bag of candies, each wrapped in paper like a jewel, the whole bag tied with a purple bow.

"Fucking head case," her father muttered, loudly enough for Auntie to hear. "Like she could help anyone."

The girl hid the candies under the corner of the blue foam camping pad that served as her bed, her movable bed that traveled from room to room, depending on how many cousins were visiting.

Auntie pushed the hair out of the girl's eyes and said her name.

"Cindy," she'd said. "I see you there."

Auntie swept in with smiles and swept out all the unsmiles. All the gray and crunch underfoot, the sticky mess on the kitchen floor, the jumble of papers and plastic—she bagged it all up and piled it neatly in one corner. Cindy worked with her, stuffing garbage into bags and bags and bags.

"We can't put it outside. Not yet. Not until Wednesday, when the garbage truck comes. Can you remember Wednesday? Don't put it out before or the dogs will get it."

Cindy nodded. "Wednesday. I'll remember." But even as she

promised it, she realized she was not sure which one of the days was Wednesday. And anyway, she didn't like to go outside. The dogs on the reserve wandered in packs and made a home wherever they could find food.

When Auntie leaned right over to help Cindy undress for the bath, she smelled like cigarettes and gum. At the bottom of her purse she found a mini bottle of shampoo that smelled like sunsets. She used it as bubble bath. "It's from a hotel," she said as she rubbed the dirt and grime from Cindy's body.

"That one doesn't come off, Auntie. That dirt won't come off. What's a hotel?"

"A place where you can go to sleep," she said as she examined the black bruise on Cindy's arm. "You pay money and you get to sleep in a bed. It's always quiet and clean. The more money you pay, the quieter and cleaner it is. The sheets are white and the blankets are soft and the bed feels like a cloud."

It sounded nice. Cindy wasn't sure why Auntie was crying.

"And they give you shampoo? I want to go to a hotel."

Auntie helped her out of the bath and rubbed her dry with her own T-shirt. It was the cleanest thing she could find. She was ever so gentle, dabbing softly to absorb the droplets of water over the girl's bruised shoulders, the bracelet of finger-shaped bruises on her upper arm, the blackened crescent moon on her hip.

"How did you get this one?"

"I was in the way."

Auntie whispered before she left, "I'm coming back for you. As soon as I get my shit together, I'll come back and get you out of here. Okay?"

"Can I go to school?"

Auntie hugged her. "Yes, yes. You can go to school. Of course you can go to school. You are my Cindy."

Not used to hugs, Cindy stiffened. But she let the words in. *You are my Cindy. You are Cindy.*

"I am Cindy."

"Yes. And remember: garbage day is Wednesday. Every Wednesday. I left you extra bags, okay? So you can do a little every day."

"I promise," she said.

But what she didn't ask was, How will I know which day is Wednesday?

3

The two civilian receptionists were the only other females who worked at the station. In some odd form of competition that Constable Maddie Schilling did not understand, they tried to outdo each other by restocking the women's washroom with hand cream, molding hair gel, and antiperspirant. Schilling could not fathom using another woman's deodorant, but today she was grateful for the inventory of female products in the cupboard under the sink.

She wasn't supposed to get her period for another week, and the accompanying cramps felt like they were going to rip her pelvis in two. She leaned her elbows on the counter and bent forward, allowing her hips to sway from side to side. It felt like her insides were trying to wring something out but had gotten stuck midmotion. The squeeze without the release. It was a pain that could last for days, and it was showing up way more frequently than promised by her phys ed teacher in junior high.

"Constable Schilling? Maddie?" Kelly John's voice was as hesitant as her knock on the door.

"Be right out!" It came out too loudly. Maddie closed her eyes and stifled a moan. Kelly knocked quietly again.

"It's just . . . there's a call from the border. They need you to go out."

"Okay! Be right there!" She stood, bracing herself on the counter. Her face in the mirror looked mottled, her eyes too small in her bloated skin. People sometimes called her pretty, but Maddie knew they were lying. There was nothing pretty in her square face, her mousy hair that always looked the same no matter what she did to it. Her high school boyfriend—her only boyfriend—had said her dark eyes were remarkable. But when she got her period, which was practically all the time these days, her face puffed up like a blowfish and swallowed her eyes until they were just slits in her blotchy skin.

There was only one thing that seemed to help. She took a small brown jar with a white lid out of her makeup kit. Victoria's Remedy, the handwritten label read. Her only friend in Kootenay Landing had given it to her. "Gets rid of cramps like that," Aimée had said with a snap of her fingers, her other arm wrapped around her sleeping son's body. "Herbs. It's all natural. There's only a little left, but you can have it."

All natural. Maddie had her questions about exactly what that meant, but they'd have to wait for another time. Right now it felt like her service belt was tied over a balloon. She loosened it and spread a tiny amount of the dark green, buttery cream over her stomach and hips. She rubbed the remainder on her temples, leaning against the counter so her pants didn't fall down. Whatever it was, it seemed to get rid of headaches too.

She put her uniform back together and slapped on her game face. The pain would go now, in just a few more minutes. She screwed the lid back on the almost-empty jar. She'd have to ask Aimée for more.

Kelly John stood a respectful distance down the hall, practically wringing her hands. Her tentative eyes scanned Maddie's face. "You okay?" she asked.

Maddie wrinkled her nose in annoyance. Kelly would never ask a male officer that, and it occurred to Maddie that the other woman would know how many pads she went through on shift. Someone had to keep that box full.

"They need you out at the border right away. Something about a guy who abandoned his minivan. Sounds like it might be Gary Dowd."

Maddie furrowed her brow at Kelly, then stopped when she thought what she must look like. Her eyes were already small enough. "You ran the plates?" she asked.

"No, no." Kelly shook her head, her hair flying around. She'd recently had it cut in a complicated, midlength do with layers and highlights. Kelly was what, midforties? Married for twenty years already. Time for a change, Maddie supposed. She'd changed how she dressed too—the flowered turtlenecks and corduroy jumpers that had been her trademark were just gone one day.

Now it looked to Maddie like Kelly had taken some bad advice from a bored clerk in the department store. She started each day in carefully matched separates: trousers and a cardigan over a silky blouse in some pattern that would be too much if you had to look at the whole thing. But by midday the whole outfit had usually fallen apart. As much as she hated her uniform, Maddie was glad she didn't have to put together a civilian outfit every day.

"They didn't give me the plates. I just thought—from the description of the van," she said. "A sparkly purple. Gary and Michelle Dowd are the only ones in town who have a van like that, and I saw him drive off in it this morning on my way to work."

Maddie rubbed at her lower back. There were so many things wrong with that assumption—with making it, with saying it out loud like a statement of fact—but there was almost no sense explaining that to Kelly. She put her arm out to the wall and sucked in her breath. As she leaned forward a spasm clamped her spine. Beads of cold sweat broke out on her forehead. That always happened with the cream. A final, wringing cramp before the relief came.

"Can you radio back and get the license plate, then run it?" Maddie asked when she could speak again.

Kelly nodded, her eyes owl-like behind her glasses, which had not been updated with the rest of her look.

"Can you go now, please?"

Kelly nodded with those huge eyes again, then peeled herself away from the wall. Maddie watched her walk away in her navy slacks and belted cardigan. She wore navy pumps like a stewardess's. She wasn't used to walking in them and with each step her right hip hitched, dislodging the slippery fabric of the blouse beneath the cardigan. By the time she'd reached the door to the staff office, a strip of paisley swirled silk was busy making an extra clump around her waist.

As soon as she was out of sight, Maddie straightened up slowly. The cream had done the trick again. The pain was almost gone already and she knew she'd be fine for hours now.

He slowed down once he got to the river. He could breathe again, deep gulps of air. It no longer felt like his lungs would explode on each inhale. With the relief, reality set in.

"You stupid, fucking idiot." Michelle would say it, so he said it for her. "You've really done it this time."

He had run through a strip of forest next to the border, and then between the rows of a harvested field of hops that stretched in a thin line between highway and river. He'd ended up in a copse of trees by the riverbank. An unstable-looking grassy over-hang dropped off suddenly to the black water below.

He sat on this overhang, his feet dangling over the edge, and looked across at the opposite bank. He'd never been to this spot before, but he knew exactly where he was, and just as suddenly he knew exactly where he'd go. Directly across the river, which was not wide at this point, was the edge of a farmer's field. And beyond that was the marshland, hundreds of acres protected against development, where birds and other animals could safely live and breed, and stop on their migratory routes.

He allowed the roaring in his ears to subside and the ac-tual sounds that surrounded him to come to the fore: the wind rustling the drying birch leaves, the gentle lapping of the river as it claimed more of the muddied bank, the distant squawk of the flock of Canada geese, which had evidently circled back, not quite ready to migrate yet.

What he did not hear: search dogs, helicopters, sirens, gun-shots. Not yet anyway. He sat under the golden leaves of a birch tree, the smoky afternoon haze of the mountains all around him, and felt oddly at peace. Michelle would be furious. He could pic-ture how her brow would furrow, and how she'd try to smooth it so she wouldn't get a permanent crease.

He should have known that he'd never be able to make her happy. Should have known that the whole situation was impos-sible and he'd never be able to set it right. But by the time he'd met her parents it was already too late. Somewhere in the deep recesses of his mind—his stubborn place, as his mother used to call it—he'd already decided to marry Michelle. If there had been any wavering in him at all, he would have called it off after that first Sunday dinner with her family.

To start with, they had been late. Rather, Gary was late. He'd run to the mill to solve some crisis and then lost track of time, which was easy to do at month-end—something that even in those early days Michelle did not understand. She was waiting for him on the front lawn of her parents' house wearing a pale-yellow dress with frills around the collar that made her look girlish. It was summer and her legs were bare and tanned. Lean then, but without the sculpted muscles she had now. Slim legs in a yellow dress and a pair of flip-flops that to his mind ruined the look.

He'd brought wine, which she pulled impatiently out of his hand as he bent to kiss her cheek.

"Hurry," she hissed, pushing him to the door. "My mom's a little uptight about Sunday dinner. It's kind of her thing."

"Her thing?" Gary asked, confused. Michelle was behind him and he turned. "Okay, just hold on a sec." He wrapped his arms around her waist, started to pull her toward him, the little-girl dress a turn-on all of a sudden.

"Oh my God! What have you got on your shirt? Is that coffee?"

"That?" he asked, pointing to a tiny droplet on his sleeve.

She nodded.

"I spilled a little coffee at the office." He shrugged. "I got held up, month-end. It's a big thing every month right now, getting this new system in. It won't always be like this."

"Let's just hope she doesn't notice. But who am I kidding," she muttered, almost to herself. She looked at him—those hazel eyes and that heart-shaped face—and at that moment any doubts in his mind resolved forever. Whatever it was, he would protect her, keep her safe. He'd change his shirt five times a day; he'd never be late. Goddamn it, he'd learn to play golf.

"Let's go inside," he said, placing his hand on the small of her back.

Everything was calm at first. Mrs. Forsberg met them at the door, and though it was a little weird to Gary that she was wearing the exact same dress as her daughter, she seemed okay otherwise. She took the wine with a smile and shook his hand with an awkward left-handed grip, then led the way to the main part of the house.

It was a ranch-style house, much like the one Gary and Michelle would buy when they married a year later. Eerily similar, Gary thought now as he swung his legs and looked around the riverbank. That should have been a clue.

A rumble in the distance—a truck, or maybe a four-wheeler—pulled Gary out of his reverie. Whatever advantage surprise and confusion had given him, it was gone now. He had to get moving. Luckily Gary knew the land across the river well. As a child he had followed his own mother through the meandering dikes and pathways that wound their way through the marsh. He knew it as surely as he knew the geography of his children's faces.

The most important thing is not to get your shoes wet. It was his mother's voice now, much gentler than Michelle's. *If your shoes get wet, you're toast.*

He unlaced his sneakers and pulled them off, placing them next to him on the bank. Next, his socks. They were the thin black polyester socks that he wore to work.

Black socks with sneakers, he could hear Michelle sneer.

But then another voice: *No, those are good. They are thin but warm, and will dry quickly if they get wet.*

Michelle and his mom had never met. He often wondered what they would have thought of each other. With her windowsills filled with cobwebbed birds' nests, bits of rock, and weathered beach glass, Gary's mother would no doubt have become a pet project for Michelle.

The engine roared again. Closer this time.

Are you just going to sit there and wait for them to catch you? Michelle. But again, his mother's voice: *The marsh is a sanctuary for all.*

He rolled his socks into a ball and stuffed them into the toe of one of his sneakers, then held the shoes and Seymour's package together and jumped down from the bank. The water took him in, beyond cold, each step forward immersing him back into the past.

That Sunday night over five years earlier, Duke Forsberg had been sitting on a recliner in the living room and had shifted his bulk to get up and shake Gary's hand. "You're more our Cindy's age, aren't you?" he asked. "Do you know Cindy?"

Gary's mouth went dry and he took a step back to lean on the edge of the couch. Somehow he hadn't expected the question, straight out like that.

"We—" he stuttered. "We . . . uh, had some classes together. In high school."

Mrs. Forsberg handed Gary a glass filled to the brim with white wine and disappeared back into the kitchen. He took a big gulp.

Duke grunted and was easing himself back into his chair when Michelle hissed at him. "No, Dad. Dinner's on the table. Go sit."

He heaved himself up again, his bland features reddening from the effort. The slick of hair that covered his bald spot flopped in front of his face.

"Dinner's ready!" Mrs. Forsberg called.

Gary followed Michelle to the formal dining room, which was open to the kitchen. The heavy china cabinet, ornate with circa-1970 carvings, had been pillaged to set the table. Every platter was groaning with food: roast beef, mashed potatoes,

gravy, Yorkshire pudding, beans, beets, and oddly, a tray of sandwiches.

The table was set for five. The four of them sat and started
piling their plates with food. As Gary filled his, he noticed that
no one touched the sandwiches. They were almost directly in
front of him, and even over the aroma of the roast beef and gravy,
he could smell that they were tuna. Not his favorite, but he took
one, just to be polite.

Gary's mom had raised him well. He knew to wait when he
ate at a new place. Maybe they'd say grace, or maybe they were
the kind of family where the man of the house took the first bite.
With his stomach grumbling and his plate full of delicious food,
he fingered the beveled edge of the polished silver fork at his
place setting and waited.

No one spoke. Duke cleared his throat. Mrs. Forsberg made a
little mewing sound and looked meaningfully at the empty seat
next to Gary. Michelle looked at Gary, her eyes wet and blinking,
her face doll-like.

"She could be running late. She knows dinner starts at six,"
Mrs. Forsberg said.

Gary gulped the last of his wine and looked around the table
for more. The bottle was not on the table and he noticed he was
the only one drinking wine. Everyone else, even Duke, had a little
cut crystal tumbler filled with what looked like cherry Kool-Aid.

"Who are we waiting for?" He smiled as he asked it, as if that
might lighten the suffocating tension.

"Cindy," Michelle hissed.

And then he understood.

Gary watched the gravy congeal in the porcelain gravy boat.
He saw the steam from the dainty casserole dish of beets slow
and then fade away. He watched the smile on Mrs. Forsberg's

face freeze and then thaw and then disintegrate into a wrinkled
frown. Duke had his head down like he was praying, hands on his
lap, face impassive, eyes closed. After a few minutes, Gary wondered if the man had fallen asleep.

All the while Michelle looked at him across the table with
those *do something* eyes. Gary fingered the stem of the wineglass,
the growing heaviness in his chest making it difficult to breathe.

He stared at Michelle in that ridiculous dress and picked up
his fork.

"Mrs. Forsberg, this looks delicious," he said. "I'm digging
in." And with that he sliced a corner of cold beef, swirled it in a
thickened blob of gravy, and took a bite.

The cold river drew him back to the present. With each step
the tingling in his feet grew until sharp tendrils of pain shot up to
his ankles. He held the package and his shoes above his head and
kept walking, balancing on the occasional rock between stretches
of soft, murky sand.

At the deepest point he was up to his chest, and while his
body was a frozen block of ice, his lungs, for once, seemed to be
working at an optimal level. The air came in easily as the sounds
of engines circled closer, bringing with them the knowledge that
he had turned some corner and there was no going back.

Bern allowed the shade of the birch and aspen trees to draw
him in, to swallow him and make him invisible to the civilized
world. Once his camouflage was complete, he turned uphill and
followed an animal trail deep into the woods and high up the
mountain. Every so often he took a sip of coffee, ignoring the
gurgles of protest from his empty stomach.

When he finished his coffee, he left the stainless steel mug at the base of an enormous fir tree. He'd collect it later, maybe on another day. He'd taken little from the truck when he parked it below: his coffee, his knife, and a set of binoculars, which bounced against his chest from the string around his neck. He felt alert; he could not resist the rush of purpose that adrenaline allowed him. He pushed himself forward.

The animal trail soon angled into a single-track mountain bike trail—one so steep it would only be possible to ride downhill. Bern pushed himself up at a stiff clip. The branches brushed his tuque and the sun reached through gaps in the tree canopy to warm him. He ignored the heat, along with any sensation in his body. He was not his body but part of the woods, part of the brush of branches and the turning fall leaves. He became part of the steady forward pace of his boots, reaching toward whatever lay ahead. Though his rational mind told him there was nothing to fear, he knew deep in his core that horror could meet him at the turn of any corner, anywhere in the world. There was no space for thought. Only breath and step, breath and step, and the undercurrent of hurry, of anxiety, of rushing to prevent some awful eventuality from happening.

He reached the top of the bike trail and paused, but only for a moment. The trail was not wide enough to afford a view. When he looked back the way he'd come, all he could see was the occasional glimpse of valley between thick tree trunks and branches. He had to go farther.

The bike trail turned and soon opened up to a forest service road, which rose at a more manageable angle. Bern picked up the metronome pace of his boot beats and, with more space now, began to swing his arms.

The road was nothing more than two tracks of dirt with a

strip of weeds and quack grass growing between them. His mind wandered back to Mrs. K. and Brian. They'd be finished breakfast now. Since it was Sunday, she would have baked something—cinnamon buns or some kind of loaf. His absence would have been noticed by both but not commented on by either.

Bern allowed his pace to slow as the road climbed and curved. He was almost at his destination. The trees began to thin out and he continued until he found a break between them. A trail. He followed this, moving toward the open sunshine he spotted just beyond. The trail ended at the edge of the mountain.

Bern scrambled over an outcropping and pulled himself up onto a flat rocky ledge that was backed by a boulder. His throne, he called it. But he wasn't the only one who knew about it. He often found beer cans and the remains of campfires nearby, though he'd never seen anyone else up here.

He sat on the ledge and leaned back on the boulder. His boots hung off the edge of the rock, and it looked as though, if he leaned forward, he would pitch right off the edge and parachute into the abyss below.

Below him the Kootenay Landing valley spread itself out like quilts drying in the sun. First the marsh, a precious band of wetlands that frogs, river otters, and an endless variety of birds called home. Past this was the river, winding its lazy way toward the American border. And then the fields, square upon square in shades of brown: dark and rich for those just tilled, light and golden for those where the final cut of hay had just been harvested. Beyond this was the town itself, framed by mountain ranges on both sides.

When he raised his binoculars he could see the cluster of houses and businesses hugging a small treed hill, mostly green, but with fiery crests of gold—stands of larch and birch among the evergreens. He could make out the Bugaboo Brewery, with its empty parking lot and chained gates, a major employer recently shut down. He could follow the tracks from there to his own backyard, where, though he could not see them, he knew the fence posts waited. How small everything was from this vantage point; how little it mattered. How little any of it mattered. What matters is the people, he reminded himself.

Bern trained the binoculars on the bird tower directly below him. On a sunny Sunday hikers and walkers would be out in force. He followed the marsh trail that led away from the bird tower until he saw a woman walking slowly. She looked familiar somehow, and Bern adjusted the lenses until he could see her more clearly. Ah, Dr. Juniper Sinclair. The lovely Dr. Sinclair. He took in the sight of her. Lost in thought, she looked serious, as she tended to do.

Bern went back to looking at the valley, swiveling back now and then to follow her progress. She was indeed a lovely woman, tall and slim, with long legs. He was watching those long legs move toward him when the shot rang through the air. In one movement Bern was off the boulder and crouched behind it, reaching for his rifle, which of course was not there. He breathed heavily, his body tensed for action, every sense attuned to movement.

The echo of the shot bounced off the mountains and lifted up to the trees, where it was diffused and released to the sky. Below him, a marsh full of birdlife called and flapped and settled back down again. The danger had passed.

Bern was left with only his shame. Dr. Sinclair, on the trail below, was much closer to that shot than he was, perched on the safety of his woodland throne. He wondered if she'd been braver than him. He climbed back up to the boulder and focused the binoculars again.

Juniper Sinclair was nowhere to be seen.

St. Brigid's Reserve, 1981

Auntie came back in a coffin.

"There she is, back for you just like she promised." He said it in his mean voice—the one that told her it was time to hide. Then he looked right at her. He never did that. "Don't ever trust a junkie," he said.

Later she would remember it was the only advice her father ever gave her.

But then she was good. She washed her own hair with a bit of laundry soap that she found, and even though she couldn't comb it out as nice as Auntie did, it was clean. One of the elders brought her a dress, a bit frayed on the hem but with a soft blue frill at the collar. Cindy waited until the going-away ceremony to put it on. After that she wore it every day for six months until the same elder noticed and brought her something else to wear.

At the going-away ceremony, there was a feast and drumming and singing. And a fire. A big fire outside the tipi where Auntie waited. There were tears too, wailing and sadness like a curtain from the grannies.

"How many? How many?" one had cried.

Cindy's own granny was long gone, but her granddad had

traveled a long way to be there. He sat in a folding chair, closer to the flames than the others. He drank beer and fed Auntie's clothes and shoes and papers to the hungry fire.

"Hi, Granddad," Cindy said to him.

His eyes were brown, like hers and her father's and her auntie's. Like everyone's really, except for the white lady who brought the book and the cousin who brought the table. But where some people had mad eyes, Granddad's were sad with their puddle of water around the brown pupil as though he were saving up all his tears to cry later.

He did not recognize her.

"It's me. Cindy."

She burrowed right down into Auntie's things, which were piled high as three lawn chairs. Her tunnel smelled like Auntie— like sunset shampoo and cigarettes. She could hear the crackling of the fire and the shuffling of Granddad's feet. He did not seem to notice her there, or if he did, he didn't mind.

There was drumming until late. Drumming and talking. Cindy stayed in her quiet place until Granddad's hands reached her. Then she sat up and helped him, handing him Auntie's precious things for the fire. Cindy wanted to keep a blouse—satin and soft with lace at the collar and sleeves—to remember Auntie by. But Granddad said no. We don't want anything to hold her back from her journey.

In the silhouette of trees in the evening sky two eagles watched and waited. She watched them back until she was tired, and then she lay on the ground and went to sleep, her tummy stretched from eating fry bread.

She woke up in the dark, with only the red glow of the fire. Granddad was asleep in his chair, the pile of Auntie's things all burned. There was drumming still, quieter now, and hushed, expectant murmurs. In the light from the trail of a flying spark, she saw that the eagles still waited.

Cindy walked away from the fire and ducked into the tipi where Auntie waited too, alone in her box on a long table.

"Auntie?" Cindy asked. "Can you hear me?"

Auntie's hair was as soft as ever. Cindy pinched some between her fingers and lifted it to her nose, then rubbed it onto her cheeks. She touched Auntie's cold, empty hand. Her coffin was empty too, except for her leather-wrapped medicine bundle. Nothing from this world to hold her back. Nothing.

She seemed so sad and alone, this body that was not Auntie. Cindy desperately wanted to give her something. A gift to take with her on her journey. A barrette. A candy wrapped in crinkly purple paper and tied with a ribbon. A tiny bottle of shampoo. But she had nothing to give.

"Auntie, I got a new dress," she whispered.

She did not know if Auntie heard her, but one of the grannies did and she steered Cindy back outside with a shush. In the light before dawn the girl pointed to the eagles, still there and waiting. With the granny's hands on her shoulders they watched together as the eagles waited and the fire died down. Just as a ray of sun climbed the eastern mountains and shot like an arrow across the valley, the eagles took flight. Heading west, they escorted Auntie to the spirit world.

4

The sound drew Dr. Sinclair forward. Somewhere between a moan and a whimper, it became more distinct as she got closer. Her mind landed on individual details, pulling them together to form a tilted picture.

First: his truck. She recognized it immediately. There would be no forgetting that truck, which had roared into their little homestead last Thursday and ripped apart their very existence.

Second: his body. He had fallen backward, his arms splayed, fingers open to the sky. His hands were white and looked almost dainty, but she knew this to be a deception. Those hands were ropelike in their strength. Or had been. They were unmoving now.

Third: the sound. It drew her closer still. The gurgling cough of a man drowning in his own blood. *I need to turn him.* She crouched down to him and put her hands on his shoulders.

The other hikers, the bird-watchers—where had they gone?

"Help!" she called out. She was utterly alone.

The bullet had blasted a hole through the center of his face.

"Seymour?" Pupils fixed and dilated. His T-shirt was the same one he'd worn the week before—it had that same greasy feel under her fingers. He wore the same black leather vest as well.

She also recognized the track marks on his arms and hands—layers of old healed scars, and newer infected puncture holes between his fingers. A biography written on his skin.

She steeled herself to this thought: her tormentor was now her patient. The irony of it bloomed, but there was no time for emotion or questioning. He was an airway that needed to be managed. Nothing more.

She needed a trauma team, a surgeon. She needed gloves, a mask, a kit, a pocketknife. She had none of these things.

She remembered the words of her emergency medicine preceptor: *If you cannot establish an airway, there is nothing more you can do. The estimated time of death is ten minutes.* She could almost hear his lilting Jamaican accent. He had survived by never getting overly worked up about any one patient. She'd always hoped some of his detachment would rub off on her. It hadn't.

She turned Seymour on his side. He coughed and spluttered blood into the dirt. He gasped once, then his breath slowed and calmed for a minute before he gasped again. *Airway, breathing, circulation. ABC. The alphabet of emergency medicine.*

His breath had slowed to rare sips of air. She needed IV fluids, steroids, a neurosurgeon. What could she do? Just sit there and wait for him to die?

With helplessness driving her on, she rolled him onto his back again. She cradled his neck in her hand and tilted his head back until his lips parted.

He'd done the same to her, had he not? Forced her mouth open, forced his lips over hers, forced his tongue into her mouth. She pushed these thoughts away. HIV, hepatitis—she pushed these thoughts away too. In the case of this patient, she'd already been exposed.

Not now. Not now. These are just lips. It's just breath. He's just an

airway to manage. I am a doctor. This is my patient. I cannot just sit here
and watch him die.

She steadied herself with a breath and leaned over him. She
formed a letter O with her lips and, pressing them to his, began
to breathe her life into him.

Constable Maddie Schilling rang the doorbell and stood, ready to
take charge of whatever she might face, just like she'd been taught
at RCMP academy. Maybe Gary Dowd was the dangerous ter-
rorist that the US border patrol agent seemed to think he was.
Maybe he'd managed to somehow get home by now. He could
be armed and Schilling needed to be ready for that, but she found
it hard to believe that anything untoward could happen at this,
the most ordinary-looking house in the world.

Below the gray stucco, wide slate-blue boards covered the
bottom third of the house. The aluminum-framed windows were
bordered by shutters painted the same slate color. The front yard
was littered with just enough toys to make the place look lived
in but not untidy. Every available surface—from the ornamental
tree at the exact center of the yard, to the ornate fake ironwork
of the miniature streetlamp at the head of the path, to each tread
of the concrete steps—was draped with Halloween decorations.

A wooden planter, also painted slate blue and filled with still-
blooming red geraniums, took up almost half the front stoop.
From inside, Maddie could hear the sound of a vacuum cleaner,
which seemed to bump up against something hard every few seconds. A glow-in-the-dark ghost dangled from above the doorbell,
which the constable now pressed again.

The vacuum noises finally stopped. The woman who answered

the door had the polished look of an actress who vacuumed in a television commercial. Her blond hair was artfully shaped in a chin-length bob, a look Maddie had tried for dozens of times, but one that never lasted longer than the time it took her to walk from the salon to the car. Her face was lightly made up and she separated her rather thin lips to smile briefly at Maddie through two lines of pink gloss.

"If you're looking for that asshole, he's not here. I kicked him out," she said.

"Mrs. Dowd?" Maddie asked. She could hear kids in the background, one of them shrieking.

The woman nodded. "I go by Forsberg-Dowd. But sure, that's me. Look, there's nothing to talk about. We don't know anything about what he was up to. He left this morning. I kicked him out. Just a minute," she said. She swung the door partially closed and said, in a voice that was firm but laced with threat, "Natasha, leave him alone. Don't touch his trains, or there will be consequences." She swung open the door again and kept talking to Maddie as though there had never been an interruption: "Happy to see the back of him, creepy idiot."

The two women stared at each other for a quick second, and then Mrs. Forsberg-Dowd started talking again. "We're getting ready to go out. So if that's all?" She started to close the door.

Maddie found her voice again. "No, no, that's not all. Sorry. Are you talking about your husband. Gary Dowd? You kicked him out this morning?"

The woman's eyes narrowed. "Gary? No, I'm not talking about Gary. He's gone to get paint." She looked impatiently at her watch. "Shit, and if he doesn't get home soon, he's not going to get any painting done before we go for Sunday dinner. Shit."

Maddie took a deep breath and found her authority. "Mrs.

Forsberg–Dowd," she said. Then looked down at her notebook to find the woman's first name. "Michelle. Can I come in and sit down for a minute? We've got to talk about a few things."

Bern jogged along the strip of road between the waterfall trail and the marshland trail. He found Dr. Sinclair in front of a bright blue truck, kneeling above the gunshot victim, performing mouth-to-mouth. Even from where he was standing, he could see that the man was fatally wounded. He would be dead soon, if he wasn't already.

Bern dropped into the moment and scanned the landscape, looking for movement in the reeds of the marsh, in the trees at the base of the mountain. Looking for anything out of place. Looking for the shooter.

Only when he was reassured that Dr. Sinclair was not in danger did he approach. He moved slowly, so as not to surprise her.

Her eyes locked on his, registering him. "Help me!" she cried to him between breaths to the dead man's bloodied lips. Her cheek was stained with his blood. "I need you to call nine-one-one. Get an ambulance. Then come help me."

He moved toward her, but not quickly enough, it seemed.

"You need to help, Coroner. He's not yours yet! Don't just stand there." Her voice was surprisingly strong.

He kneeled down next to her, placing his hands gently over hers. Blood spilled from the wound and pooled in the dirt of the trail. The man lay silent, motionless; the wound split a hole between his eyes, which were still open but no longer seeing. She breathed into him again with a tenacity that surprised Bern. Surely she could tell this patient was beyond help?

Bern shifted so he could hold her gaze. He flattened his hands gently over hers until she stopped at last.

His voice was soft as he said, "I believe he is—as you say—mine now."

She pulled her hands away and shook his off. She stood and took two steps away, turning her back to Bern and the dead man.

The sight of the man tore straight through him. His body was thin in the way of drug addicts, his skin already graying. Black jeans covered his painfully thin legs. His feet, incongruously, were bare, his toes slowly turning purple. Over his T-shirt, which had once been white but was now rimmed with blood, he wore a black leather vest.

Bern heard a sound behind him, something between a choke and a sob. He turned to see Dr. Sinclair, holding her bloodied hands out before her.

"Are you injured?" he asked. He'd seen her face multiple trauma patients in the ER with more equanimity.

She shook her head, eyes still glued to her hands.

"Have you called anyone?"

"I wanted to get away. Just for a walk. I left my cell at home."

Bern stood and reached for his own cell phone, then stopped midmotion when he remembered he had done the same. *"Eh bien,"* he said. "So did I. We will have to rely on the kindness of passersby."

The sounds of the marsh asserted themselves around him. The long trail that stretched through the wetlands percolated with wildlife: river otters, beavers, snakes, and all manner of ducks and geese and other birds. People, however, were few and far between.

She went to run her hands through her chestnut hair, then

stopped herself. "Oh, God. Can I wash this off?" She held her shaking hands out to him. Her fingers were long and smudged with the man's blood.

He put a firm hand on her shoulder and turned her away from the dead man. As horrific as the sight was, he knew she had to be reacting to something else. Something from the past. It was a problem he knew only too well. Guiding her toward a tributary of the marsh, he kneeled at the edge of the muddied water and hoped she would follow suit. She did, scrubbing her hands as though prepping for surgery.

When she was through, she held her clean hands up and he hesitated before pointing at her cheek. With another cry she leaned farther into the stream and washed her face clean.

"Okay?" she asked.

The blood was gone, and rivulets of brown water dripped down her cheeks in its place.

Bern could hear the birds, trumpeting their interrupted symphony. From this angle he could only see the tops of the reeds and the cattails and the sky. He could not see the mountains, the cottonwood trees, or the corpse. He felt the small openness the past weeks had carved around his heart close abruptly by the force of the duty that lay before him.

He stood and held his hand out to her. As he captured her long fingers, cold from the marsh water, he looked down at her. Their gazes held—his eyes dark, hers an almost see-through green—and with that look, he knew she felt the burden too.

"Did you see what happened?" he asked. "See who did this?"

She shook her head. "I heard tires squeal."

"So the shooter is gone?"

She nodded solemnly, biting her lip. "I assume so."

He gestured in the direction of the dead man. "Do you know

who he is?" He knew she needed time to recover, but there were questions that had to be asked.

They'd reached the trail and the man's bare feet were once again within view. "I've seen him before. I recognized his truck."

"Do you know his name?"

She pressed her palms against her eyes. "His first name is Seymour. I don't know his last name."

"Did you hear anything else?"

This time she shook her head and waved a hand toward the trail behind them. "I was way over there, by the bird tower. I heard the shot." She paused, dropped her arm. "I—I thought it was hunters."

There was nothing more they could do now but set the wheels of the investigation into motion, Bern thought. "We will need to go get help. Are you okay to flag down a passing car? One of us should stay here with the . . . the victim."

Without further prompting, she stepped gingerly around the dead man—around Seymour—and walked past the truck. She turned left at the road, not right.

Bern waved his hands in the other direction. "Head toward the highway!" he called to her. "More traffic there. I'll wait here until you come back."

But she ignored him, walking along the center line in the opposite direction.

CHILD PROTECTION SERVICES

REPORT OF SUSPECTED CHILD ABUSE OR NEGLECT

Reported by: Ms. S. Wakely—Aboriginal Early Intervention Worker for Kootenay Landing School District

Date: April 21, 1981

Name of child: CINDY JOHN (surname unconfirmed)

Date of birth of child: Unknown (Age: 5 years)

Current whereabouts of the child/children or young person(s): Rural Route No. 4, Kootenay Landing (commonly referred to as Indian Road). House has no fire number. Third driveway on left from highway. Small shack in the trees, cannot be seen from the road.

Name (and aliases) of parents/guardians and contact details: Father is living in the house (RUPERT JOHN—name not confirmed).

Name of known siblings: Unknown

Nature of abuse and neglect: Child is living in extreme poverty. House in a state of disrepair. (Ms. Wakely witnessed: broken windows, mold, strewn garbage, lack of furnishing [beds?], dining table covered in liquor bottles and possible drug paraphernalia.) Child appeared to be hiding in a corner, extremely fearful of adult (assumed to be father) who was sleeping on the couch. Child accepted book from Ms. Wakely. Then father woke up. Stated forcefully that the child would not be going to school. He then tore the book and threw it at Ms. Wakely.

Date of alleged abuse/neglect: During month of February 1981.

Details of how the person making the report became aware of the information: Ms. Wakely visited the home believed to belong to RUPERT JOHN in mid-February, as part of her annual visits to preschool-aged children on the reserve. It was at this time that Ms. Wakely observed the events listed above.

Re: reporting delay. Ms. Wakely was not certain if her concerns merited reporting. After considering the matter and reviewing her files, she determined that the torn book was "too much to bear." A death in the JOHN family (child's maternal aunt) and subsequent funeral service further delayed investigation.

Description of any injuries seen: Ms. Wakely believed that the child may have had bruises on her upper arm, but she was not able to get close enough to confirm.

Attitude of the carers of the child/children or young person(s) to the injury/incident: Adult present (believed to be RUPERT JOHN) unconcerned about state of home and child. Belligerent toward Ms. Wakely.

Known supports to the child/children or young person(s): Home is on the St. Brigid's Reserve. Tribal elders may be able to support or identify supports for this family.

Are the parents/guardians aware that the report is being made? No.

Is the child/children or young person(s) aware that the report is being made? No.

What action is the reporter expecting from Child Protection Services? Follow up to ensure safety of child.

5

He was alone with this one corpse now, but the memories of a thousand others pressed against him. He held them in check by naming what he saw. *Cattails, horsetails, cottonwood trees.*

He walked as close to the body as he dared and mentally checked off each observation: flattened grass, angle and direction of the body, footprints. He kept his eyes peeled for a spent cartridge but did not see one. Finally, he moved his gaze to the body and started naming aloud, as though the sound of his voice would hold the memories at bay. "Black hair. White skin. Bullet wound. White T-shirt. Leather vest. Thin arms. Scars on inner arms, look like track marks. Black jeans, no belt. Bare feet."

He wondered about this last detail and scanned the trailhead for shoes, but didn't see any. He noticed that the man's toenails were long, and he appeared to have an ingrown nail on the big toe of his right foot.

"That looks like it would hurt," Bern said out loud.

He continued this perusal for quite some time, taking in details about the landscape, the victim, and the interplay between the two. Time was suspended in this exercise, this macabre lullaby. The last man standing in a field of death always asks the same question: *Am I the only one left alive?*

And then the inevitable: *Why me?*

And finally: *Why did my instinct not warn me?*

For Bern, this last question weighed heavily.

He focused on the gunshot wound and continued his grim list: *Severe burning of the skin at the edges of the wound. Black flecks of gunpowder.* He leaned closer now, noticing the dark clotting at the edges of the wound, where the blood had begun to dry.

Bern crouched and placed his hands on one of the man's shoulders and lifted him slightly to see the exit wound. Except there was no exit wound.

The coroner stood and checked his watch. What had become of Dr. Sinclair? It had been more than ten minutes. He stepped around the corpse and walked past the truck, careful not to touch anything. He could hear cars on the highway in the distance, but no cars passed in either direction on the access road. He could not see Dr. Sinclair.

Surely, wherever she had gone, she would call the police, as they had agreed?

He walked back down toward the scene. He found a tree stump in the shade with a view of the body and waited with the dead for the long accounting to begin.

Schilling followed Michelle into a living room fit for a show home. The woman leaned down and gracefully swooped up a few stray toys. She dropped them into an artful glass bowl on a kidney-shaped glass coffee table, neither of which had any business being in a house full of toddlers, as far as Schilling was concerned.

Maddie sank gratefully into a deep armchair, while Michelle Forsberg-Dowd perched on the edge of a white couch across from her.

"Feels good to sit down. It's been quite a day."

"You said you wanted to talk to me about Seymour?" Michelle prompted.

"Seymour? I'm sorry, I don't know who Seymour is, or what he has to do with what happened today at the border."

"At the border? Oh, I don't know about that. But if there was trouble, you can be sure Seymour had something to do with it. There's no doubt about—"

A boy and a girl ran into the room, both of them shrieking. The girl held a stuffed toy over her head. The boy, wearing only a diaper and a T-shirt, followed in a lopsided baby gait, arms high in the air, yelling, "Mine!"

"Natasha," Michelle said in a voice so firm and quiet the girl stopped dead. "Give it back. Now. Is the TV still on?"

The little girl lowered the toy—which Schilling could now see was a stuffed frog—and turned to her mother, nodding. Michelle pried the frog from her hand and handed it to the boy. Then she said in a singsong voice, "You get an extra show today. One extra. Off you go."

Just like that they were gone.

"Now, where were we?" Michelle asked.

"I guess you were going to tell me about Seymour," Schilling said.

It took a while for the story of how Seymour had moved in uninvited, and stayed on and on until that very morning, to tumble out. Schilling wrote a few notes in her notebook, mostly to look like she was doing something. She jotted down Seymour's last name—Melnychuk—and the fact that he'd been close to Michelle's older sister, who had disappeared without a trace sixteen years earlier. She wrote down Michelle's sister's name, Cindy Forsberg, and put a little star beside it, thinking she'd look up the case file one day on a slow shift.

"Gary was so useless about the whole Seymour thing," Michelle said, her voice sharp with resentment. "He wouldn't make him leave. Wouldn't stand up for us, his own family. I thought I was going to have to move out with the kids to get Gary to pay any attention at all."

"What did Seymour do that was so upsetting?" Schilling asked, more out of curiosity than anything.

Michelle closed her eyes and shook her head. "That's just it. It's nothing you can put your finger on. He was just *there*. And it was creepy. You feel like you can't go into your own basement when he's around. And when he's not around, which is pretty rare, you don't want to go down there. All his stuff is in a little pile in the corner—and he never makes the bed. And there's this smell. I can't quite describe it." She sniffed at the air and crinkled her nose. "Can't you smell that?"

Schilling sniffed and got a lungful of the boxed-flowery smell of chemical air freshener. "I don't really smell anything."

"You know, after Seymour had been here for two weeks, I finally made Gary go down and change the sheets. That's just gross, don't you think? I've had the fans going all day and I'm going to book the carpet cleaner first thing tomorrow. Get my house back."

Schilling looked around at the framed prints, the pristine furniture, and the wall-to-wall carpeting with fresh vacuum tracks across it and said, "It looks like you've kept things pretty clean around here. My place never looks like this and I live by myself."

Michelle seemed to perk up. "You should see my mom's house. According to her I live in a pigsty."

She was about to say more, but Schilling cut her off. No sense getting into two generations of neuroses when none of it would have any impact on the news that Schilling still had to break to her.

"So I understand you've had some trouble with this Seymour fellow. And if he comes back, my suggestion is not to let him in the door. But I'm here to talk about Gary."

Michelle's pink-glossed lips parted. "Gary?"

"Do you know where he is?"

She wrinkled her brow, then gently stroked it with her thin fingers, as though smoothing over creased fabric. Schilling noticed the flash of her wedding and engagement rings with their interlocking diamonds the size of a small beetle.

"He went to the Home Depot in Sandpoint—you know, across the line in Idaho? He was getting paint for the garage. That's why Seymour stayed, you see. He was going to paint the garage for us while he was here. But he never did anything. Gary never even bought the paint until today, when I told him he needed to get that asshole out of our house and paint the garage himself or we were out of here. Sometimes you have to be tough with these guys or they'll spend their whole fucking lives on your couch drinking beer and leaving the bottles lying around for you to pick up. Ever notice that?"

Schilling shook her head and did not say that she'd never had the opportunity to notice that. "So Gary was going down to Idaho to buy paint. And you were expecting him back when?"

Michelle looked at her watch. "Well, I guess I was expecting him back a while ago. But I got so busy with the kids and with cleaning out the basement." Her voice faded out. "He'd better come back soon or he's going to be late for Sunday dinner at my parents' place. My mom freaks when we're late."

"Mrs. Forsberg-Dowd, Gary's got a lot more to answer for than being late for dinner." Schilling looked down at her notes, though she knew perfectly well what they said. "This morning at approximately eleven fifty-five a.m. he ran away from his van when he was stopped at the crossing into the US. He escaped into the bush and no one has seen him since. There has been a manhunt going on for hours. I came by to see if he had maybe come home or has been in touch. Have you heard from your husband since he left this morning?"

Michelle was staring at her, mouth open. She'd crinkled her forehead unattractively and made no move to smooth it out. She looked suddenly like a mean and somewhat plain girl.

"Michelle? Have you heard from Gary?"

She shook her head, looking down. "No. No, he hasn't called. He hasn't been home."

"Do you know anything about why he ran away?"

"No! No, I don't know anything. But you have to understand: this is Gary. Whatever he did—if he did anything, and I'm not saying he did—it's Seymour's fault. Don't you see? Gary can't decide anything on his own, and he gets all freaked out by things. That must be what happened. He has these panic attacks; he can't breathe and he has to get out. He gets them when he's under a lot of stress."

The TV show must have been wrapping up: Schilling could hear the crescendo of the kids again in a faraway room. Soon they'd be squabbling and she felt exhausted just thinking about it. The effort of pushing her body through the treadmill of her day had finally worn her out. Gary Dowd would probably crawl home with his tail between his legs before too long. No doubt his wife would turn him in for questioning—if she didn't kick him out on the street first.

Schilling's radio squawked and the noise made her jump. "Unit Three, can you RTO?" *Return to office.* So close to the end of her shift, Schilling knew this couldn't be good.

"Unit Three, copy that. ETA five minutes," she replied.

Schilling stood and turned to Michelle. "I've got to go," she said. "Look, I'm sure you're right. There's probably a reason why Gary ran away from the border. But you have to understand: the American border patrol takes this kind of thing very seriously. And so do we. You need to help us find your husband." She handed Michelle her card. "If Gary comes home—day or night—I want you to call me. Promise me, okay?"

Michelle nodded, then stood as well. The movement seemed to fill her with anxious energy all over again and she started chattering. "I'm sure it's a misunderstanding. It is. He's just so hopeless, you know? He panics. It's happened so many times. Oh my God, we've got to go. I've got to get the kids cleaned up and ready for Sunday dinner, and look at me!" She pointed to her pressed pants and spotless T-shirt. "I'm a mess!"

Schilling closed the door on Michelle's anxious monologue and made her way to the patrol car.

To Ruben, the line was meaningless, invisible. As easily as a bird, a bee, a caterpillar, he slipped across the longest unsecured border between two sovereign states. It meant nothing. Consequences were for those who got caught. To get caught, he would have to be seen, and Ruben was invisible.

In all the years he'd lived in Ciudad Juarez he'd never been caught crossing into the promised land of Texas. He would slip back and forth across the hole in the barbed wire, between patrols, as indistinct as a tumbleweed blown by the wind. First he was smuggling goods, stolen from the maquiladoras and sold for a fraction of the retail price on the US side. Later it was people. Finally it was drugs.

When that got too hot, he came north as an agricultural worker. For as long as he could remember, it had been about survival. About keeping on. Pleasure? Sure, there was some of that. But if he found peace, it was only for moments at a time— those moments after the crop was in, when the cerveza bottle was passed hand to hand, the joint mouth to mouth. And the ideas and laughter and songs shared among brothers. Between those moments there was only work, and schemes to make things better. The schemes always fell flat, but not this time.

The good doctor would help him succeed this time. *La doctora*. Lovely, she was, with dark brown hair and eyes the color of the cream she spent hours concocting and putting into brown jars. Brown jars that everyone wanted.

It was not far from the invisible border to *la doctora*'s house and the small outbuilding she'd converted to do her work. Not far as the crow flew and as the Mexican hops picker walked. Ruben could make it easily in under an hour. It took a little longer at night, or if he stopped to pick some vegetables along the way—beans or squash or tomatoes to sell to the roadside market, to add a few dollars to his monthly packet home.

The cream might be big enough to put an end to those envelopes filled with American cash. It would certainly put an end to his secret bean picking, to his long days of picking hops for the rich American farmer. He just needed to watch. And wait for the opportunity that was sure to come his way.

"Aw, shit. What the hell?"

Bern knew it was Resnick before he could see the man. He was driving his own pickup truck, not a police cruiser, and he had parked it behind the slain man's truck. The coroner stood and watched as the RCMP officer made his way down the short roadway to the scene, swearing all the while. When he saw Bern, he swore even louder.

"God love a duck, Fortin. You're in a hurry, aren't you? I don't even know if there's a body yet."

He passed around the gate that marked the trailhead, swatting at the tall grasses. His uniform looked as though it might have been recycled from the day before. His buzz cut was a little longer than normal. Other than these small details, Staff Sergeant Alvin Resnick looked the same as he always did: short, frustrated, and stubborn.

"Jesus H. Christ, I got a call that Schilling's busy with some screwup at the border, no one else can come, and some guy has got himself shot. I turn up and what do you know? The coroner is already here—" The head of the Kootenay Landing RCMP detachment stopped midsentence when he saw the body. "Aw, shit." He blew out his breath, then looked at Bern. "Well, there's one less criminal for us to track down."

"You know him?"

Resnick crouched a few feet from the body, his beady eyes scanning the length of the corpse. "Seymour Melnychuk," he said, still shaking his head from side to side. "Knew he was up to something, couldn't prove it. As usual. What happened?"

"I was hiking, up there"—Bern waved in the direction of the mountains that buttressed the marsh—"when I heard a shot."

Resnick's eyes kept up their scan of the body. He did not appear to be listening at all. "So you came running down here? Thought you'd get an early start on the investigation?"

He raised his shoulders an inch in reply, but the movement was lost on Resnick.

"What do you say, huh, Fortin? You're not turning funny like that fire chief on the coast? The one who set fires so he could put them out?" He leaned back on his heels, hands on his knees.

"*Pas du tout.*"

"Don't pull that froggy shit on me. I know you speak better English than the Queen. What happened here?"

Bern raised an eyebrow. "I only know what I saw."

"So tell me what you saw."

"I was at the lookout on the waterfall trail. The one almost at the top, above the hunting cabin. I was looking through my binoculars, and I saw someone down here, on this trail."

"You saw someone down here? Was it the shooter?"

"No, no. It was Dr. Sinclair."

"Dr. Sinclair? The family doc? Did she have a gun?"

"She didn't do it."

"What do you mean she didn't do it? What, you're her alibi now?"

"Sure, I can be her alibi. I was watching her through the glasses when I heard the shot. She didn't do it. She was just walking along." He didn't add that she was looking worried, and a little sad. He wanted to ask her about that himself.

"You were watching her," Resnick said. "Okay, I got it. She's something to look at. I got that part. Something we can both agree on for once." He looked up and chuckled. "Dr. Sinclair, hey? Well, good luck with that. Okay, so you were watching her when the shot went off. But you say she wasn't holding a gun?"

Bern took a step forward and crouched down next to Resnick. He looked straight into the other man's tense, dark eyes. "Two things," he said, holding up one finger. "First, she did not have a gun. She was walking when the shot occurred, with both hands in her pockets. I was watching her walk, yes."

"And what did she do when the shot went off?"

Resnick did not look away from the coroner's gaze. Bern took in the heaviness of the officer's brow and how it formed almost a small shelf along the upper third of his face. He wondered how he had never noticed it before.

"Fortin, what did she do when the gun went off?"

He allowed the sensations to overtake him again: the thwack of his binoculars as his body hit the ground, the hyperfluttering of his heart that felt like the noise of a thousand children screaming, the roaring in his ears that drowned out all other sound. "I—I don't know. I hit the ground. Instinct, I guess."

"You guess," Resnick repeated.

"When I got up and looked, I couldn't see her or anyone else. I thought *she'd* been shot. I got down here as fast as I could."

"Next time I need an alibi, remind me not to ask you." Resnick shook his head. "Okay, so you got here and what?"

"Dr. Sinclair was there—" He waved toward the gash that made up the dead man's face. "She was trying to resuscitate him, but it was too late."

"And then?"

"And then she went to get help." He didn't state the obvious: that she never came back. "And then you arrived."

Resnick coughed. "Small detail, but where exactly did the good doctor go?"

Bern shook his head but held the man's gaze. "She was pretty upset."

"So you're saying she went home?"

He shrugged. "She seemed to suggest she lived not far from here. I don't know. I was a little surprised when she didn't come back."

Resnick looked out over the marsh. "She lives just over there," he said, gesturing toward the road, away from the highway. "Had an eye on that house for a long time."

"Why's that?"

"You really should get out more, you know that, Fortin? Let's just say the good doctor is not just another pretty face. Waste of a good pair of legs, if you ask me." Resnick rubbed at his wrinkled shirt. "I'll go by and talk to her, if I can ever get a team over here to take over the scene. Won't have to call the coroner, so that's one less thing on my list." He gazed out at the marsh. "So what was the other thing?"

"What other thing?"

"You said there were two things," Resnick reminded him.

"Oh, yes, of course." He pointed to the bloodied tissue that made up the wound. "There's no exit wound," he said. Without touching the man, he traced a circle an inch away from his head with his open palm.

The officer's eyes darted to the ground, just as Bern's had. "No cartridge?" he asked.

"Not that I could see."

Resnick took this in, then moved away. He walked around the truck and up to the road, where he paced, waiting for the ambulance. As was his habit, he took out a cigarette and chewed on the end of it. Bern sat back down on his stump and stared out at the marsh, where life had already returned to normal for the birds, insects, and small ground animals. For him, there would be no return to normal. This was his reality now: this caring for the dead; this accounting for each detail; this attempt, however unworthy, to name, catalog, impose reason, and bring understanding to each death in the greater Kootenay Landing region. This was his duty.

The edginess that had driven him to the woods that morning was back and made more acute now by hunger, fatigue, and a deep unwillingness to perform the tasks ahead. He looked at his watch. It was well past lunchtime, and he had not eaten yet that day. Mrs. K. would have something to say about that. At the thought of his neighbor, and how he'd slipped out to avoid her that morning, the sourness in his stomach turned over.

He stood and took in the body again. There was something sad about the man lying there, something pathetic and small; he looked like a child, skinny in those black jeans and dirty shirt, with those painfully thin arms. A child-man, robbed in death of his identity, his face a gaping hole of blood, bone, and tissue. Bern was past the point of being sick at the sight of a body. He found his reaction now was a steely coldness in his core, a shutting down, a locking out. And a knowledge that before he could look after the dead, he needed to look after himself, if only for an hour.

He moved past Resnick along the road, calling out instructions on his way. "Once you get a team here, see if they can find that cartridge. Knowing the type of weapon will be our starting place."

"What? Are you telling me how to do my job?" Resnick called after him. "Wait a minute. Where are you going?"

Bern picked up his pace and called over his shoulder. "It's your scene, Resnick. I'll be back in an hour." He reached a curve in the road and broke into a jog. It was only once he got to his truck and started it up that the engine drowned out the sound of Resnick yelling at him.

St. Brigid's Reserve, 1981

The cousin with the mean eyes came back. He cleared off the table and the floor. He took out the garbage on Wednesday and he chased away the dogs. He fixed the hot-water tank and the broken windows and wiped everything clean.

Cindy helped him, practicing her spins as she wiped the spray of tomato ketchup from the wall. He didn't seem to mind if she talked, so she talked to him about figure skating. And hotels.

"This place is going to be as clean as a hotel."

He didn't answer, didn't say much at all. Her father was quiet too, and when he got mad he went outside. He'd sit on the swept-off back step and smoke and look out at the woods. One time he threw a beer bottle at a tree and it smashed into a hundred pieces.

Cousin Jared said something then: "Clean it up. She could cut her feet."

And her father did.

Jared brought her a skating dress. Fuchsia, with sequins on the shoulder. It was too big, so he folded the strap and pinned it with a safety pin, careful not to poke her skin.

He took her to the rink. On the first day, and the second, he walked in a circle around the ice while she clutched his arm, the dull blades of the rented skates squeaking beneath her turned ankles. On the third day he sat in the penalty box and watched her, arms crossed, until she could skate one whole time around without falling. Then he smiled and she felt happier than she ever had.

When she could skate five whole times around the rink without falling or stopping, he said, "It's time." When they returned to the rink, it was for figure skating club.

The first day, a white girl with yellow hair and a satin skating dress with sequins in the shape of leaves sniggered and whispered, loud enough for Cindy to hear, "That used to be *my* dress."

That night Jared made spaghetti with his special sauce and combed out Cindy's hair. "You're going to show all those girls. You'll see," he said, tucking her into her bed. She finally had a bed—one that didn't move from room to room depending on how many cousins were visiting. Cousins didn't visit anymore. Just Jared.

Her bed had sheets. The sheets were yellow, not white, but she didn't mind. Her sheets were mostly clean, but they did not smell like sunsets. They smelled like Jared.

"I'm going to show you so many things," he said. "You'll see."

6

Bern found the driveway without any trouble. A faded wooden sign on a rotting post read Hinton and beneath it a newer sign, not quite as faded, read Sinclair. Who was Hinton? he wondered. Boyfriend? Partner? Landlord? Neighbor? He prepared himself for anything.

But he was not expecting a woman in a wheelchair on the rough-built porch, aiming a rifle at him.

"You want something?" she said flatly as he got out of the truck.

Her body looked wasted by disease but her demeanor exuded strength. He could not tell the color of her hair—her whole head was intricately wrapped in a white turban. Bern looked past this distraction and saw her headgear for what it was: a frame for a serious and rather practical face. She had likely never been called pretty but there was something appealing about her. He allowed a smile to spread across his own face.

"I survived the killing fields of Rwanda, witnessed the genocide in Bosnia, and made it through Afghanistan without getting blown to pieces," he said. "But I guess my luck has run out."

He approached the porch. As he got closer, he could see that she was older than she looked at first. Or perhaps it was the disease that made her look older, the lines of pain etching deep grooves from her nose to her lips and down to her chin. He raised his hands in the air.

"Still, if I have to go, I'd like the deed to be done by a woman with intelligent eyes." He stood still, arms open in invitation. "Go ahead, if you like."

She continued to stare at him, their eyes locked in a duel. During the staring match Bern came to understand something of her. She had perhaps not seen as much horror as he had, but she had been impacted just as deeply by what life had brought her way. He looked away, and when he looked back, she had lowered the rifle to her lap.

"You the coroner?" she asked.

He nodded.

"Juniper said she ran into you. She's pretty upset. Got cleaned up and went straight back out to the woods to walk it off. Work it out, you know?" Her voice had a gravelly quality of a life well lived. "She won't want to talk to you."

"Can I wait?" Bern asked. "I have a bit of time before the RCMP start a manhunt for me."

She narrowed her eyes at him, taking measure. "You can come in, I suppose."

He took the porch stairs in one bound and held the door for her as she wheeled through it, rifle still on her lap. Inside the enclosed porch a path just wider than her hands on the wheelchair had been cleared through an inventory of rakes and shovels, snowshoes and waders, fishing nets, walking sticks, a metal cane, and gardening boots. A stacked washer and dryer churned in one corner. A long bench held a stock of egg cartons piled so high they almost toppled. Next to this was an old fridge with a sign hanging from it: "Eggs $3.00 a dozen. Leave your money or your name." Bern opened the door to the fridge and plucked out a carton of eggs.

"Can I ask your name?" he said as they made their way through the debris. "I'm assuming you know mine already."

"Gia," she said.

It was a simple, beautiful name. "Gia, if I buy this dozen eggs from you, will you let me make us an omelette? I make a good one, if I do say so myself. And I'm starving."

When Gary finally reached the cabin, he was huffing and grunting from the climb and beyond caring who heard him. He'd had more close calls than he wanted to think about on his journey—a miracle, really, that he'd made it this far. The familiar sight of the cabin was a comfort. It looked exactly as it had the last time he'd been there, over fifteen years before. Its rough-hewn logs had likely been felled and peeled right there before being squared into place. The single-pane windows, the stone floor—the whole structure, in fact, was shifting and settling into soil that, Gary knew, was rockier than it appeared to be.

The cabin faced a grassy field, and beyond that, a stream. Taken together, cabin, meadow, and stream made the perfect resting place for a hunter, a snowmobiler, a man on the run.

He pulled the door open with his left hand and slipped inside, where the temperature dropped a good few degrees. He leaned his back on the door and, in the dim light that filtered in through the cobwebbed windows, inspected a gash on his right palm.

That might need stitches. You're really in for it now. How'd you get that anyway?

He wished he knew. From the moment he got out of the

river, everything was a blur. He remembered the farm. He'd had
to hide in the barn until the tractor went past. And then he'd seen
Seymour on the marsh—what the hell had he been doing there?

That ditch between the farm and the road. Was it there?
Barbed wire, maybe?

Barbed wire? Next to a farm? That's going to get infected for sure.

Yeah, thanks, Michelle. What would she be doing now, anyway? The sun had already begun its final descent behind the west-
ern mountains. Almost dinnertime. Would they sit at the table
tonight even though he wasn't there? Sometimes when he was
out, Michelle let the kids eat in front of the TV, and when he got
back he could tell that she'd had white wine instead of food for
dinner. Would they be wondering what had happened to him?
He took a breath of stale cabin air and knew the answer: they
would be at Michelle's parents' house, eating tuna sandwiches.

Look what is around you. Nature always has an answer. His mother.
Always so calm.

He pressed the gash into a corner of his shirt and took a quick
inventory: shelter, food, water. Shelter was good enough; he had
his choice of dry beds on the main floor or up the ladder in
the loft. The roughly built shelves under the window held a few
cans of food, a roll of paper towel, and a sealed plastic container.
Through the filmy casing he could see the familiar face of the
oatmeal man and several boxes of macaroni and cheese. Good
enough for now. A tin pail for water; a wood-burning stove, if he
dared light it; a small ax; and a coffee tin full of matches.

Water first, he decided. He dropped Seymour's package on
the plywood counter and fashioned a bandage out of paper towel.
Then he grabbed the pail. Water before dark. He headed back out
into the last strains of light. If he had not known where it was, he
probably would have missed the trail to the stream, hidden as it

was in the tall grass. At the bank he filled the bucket and headed back in the dark. He deposited the bucket, then headed out one more time, to the outhouse, which he found just where it had been fifteen years earlier. It was new then, but now it showed decay and emitted a stench that nearly sent him back outside.

So many luxuries, his mother had always said about their house: a dishwasher, laundry, hot water whenever they wanted it. *Best not to get too used to them.* Sometimes he would find her washing dishes by hand. *Just a habit.*

Back in the cabin he rubbed his hands and cleaned the cut as best he could with some sterilizer he found in the plastic container. He was cold, but a fire was more than he could risk. At least not for a few days. He found an enamel bowl and poured in a little oatmeal. He decided to take his chances with the unfiltered water and poured it in too, letting the mixture sit for a few minutes while he sipped more water from an enamel mug.

As he ate he kept his thoughts from his situation. It was too much to take in all at once. He wiped his bowl clean and sealed the food container shut. Then he lay down on the cot by the woodstove and pulled a thin wool blanket over his body to keep warm.

Just like you to go to sleep and pretend nothing is wrong. Michelle. *Rest now. Everything will look better in the morning.* His mother. He could only hope his mother was right.

Gia watched him from the dining area as he made himself at home in the kitchen.

"Not much to go with this," Bern said. "Doesn't anyone get groceries for you?" He held up a heel of cheese. She was staring steadily at him, one of her thin legs shaking up and down in the chair. If he hadn't suspected some wasting disease, he would have thought it was impatience. Maybe it was.

"You'll find there's no shortage of vegetables and herbs." She waved a hand back the way they had come. "In the garden. The greenhouse. The root cellar. Go out the side door."

He went back out to the mudroom and found something that might be called a side door. It was wider than the others and opened to a wooden ramp. At the bottom of the ramp and off to the left was a rough outbuilding buried half in the ground. *Root cellar.* Past this, a fenced-off area and a low building of grayed boards. *Chicken coop.* Farther along, a greenhouse beckoned. It was just like the one he dreamt of building for himself someday. Beyond this, an elaborate garden called him forward.

He stood under a wide archway made of driftwood and surveyed the garden. It was exquisite. At first glance it was similar to his own—similar to any garden at the end of season: beds turned and covered in straw, herbs trimmed back. Blankets lined the edges of some beds like shed skin, ready to cover the remaining plants in case of frost. There was nothing tangible about its beauty, just a feeling of fleeting perfection that he wanted to grasp and hold in place.

He breathed in the familiar scent of rot mixed with growth, of turned soil warming in the last of the fall sun, of hay starting its slow metamorphosis back into soil. There was a spicy scent to the air and he followed this to a bed of greens. Chives, spinach, hardy lettuces, and kale were plump and happy in the dark soil. Using the tips of his index finger and thumb, he plucked a few leaves of each. The chives protested, but the spinach surrendered at once.

Crouched there in the remnants of the garden, he felt a presence. A human presence, not a plant one. He was instantly on alert, scanning the perimeter. Whatever had disturbed him had come from the direction of a bed of black-eyed Susans, the centers of the blossoms dark, in contrast to their brilliant yellow petals. He turned his head an inch, focusing his gaze on the spaces between the foliage and the flowers. There, he saw a variation—black as the stigma, darker than the leaves. He could feel eyes looking back him, unblinking as his own, dark as the hearts of the flowers. Bern felt a prickle at the base of his hairline and reached for the familiar comfort of his rifle. But where he expected the smooth, cool haunch of molded metal and plastic, he found only hard-packed dirt and the greasy feeling of an edge of cardboard slick with mud.

A sudden crash and his quarry was on the run. Bern caught a flash of dark shirt and dark hair—or was it a baseball cap?—and then his target was gone, swallowed by the trees and brush that pressed up against the edge of the property. Bern was on the move just as quickly. He hopped the fence and dodged into the trees in pursuit. A single-track trail led uphill, and Bern followed this, quieting his own footsteps so he could listen for the other's.

The trail ended at an opening in the trees—a meadow of tall grass with a raised hillock at its center. Bern circled the edge of it, searching for his prey, or for some opening in the perimeter that would show where the trail continued. There was no sign of either.

He was left with his breath, quick and shallow, the sound of his heartbeat echoing in his ears, and the caw of a crow, disturbed from its dining table over the slatted compost bins.

He steadied his breathing, his heartbeat, and the tremor in his knees. The fistful of herbs and greens in his palm let out a spicy breath as Bern shook the uneasiness away. He circled the clearing once more, then followed the single track through the woods back to the garden. The invasion into the peace that had swaddled him only moments before had shaken him more than he wanted to admit.

He climbed the fence, then turned to look back at the woods once more. He kept his gaze low along the base of the trees in the distance. Satisfied that whoever it was had now gone, he made his way to the greenhouse to see about finding a tomato to round out his omelette.

"Constable Schilling? You in there?" This time it was Chantel Postniuk, the afternoon shift receptionist, knocking on the door.

"You need in here?" Maddie tried to make her voice sound normal over the pain. It was time for more cream. How did the guys manage? There were way more of them. One female officer and two civilian staff and she could never have even one moment's peace in the bathroom.

"You okay?"

"Yeah. Just be a minute."

"Staff Sergeant Resnick called again looking for you. He wants you to head over to the scene ASAP."

"'Kay. Be right there."

For the second time that day she looked at herself under the bad lighting of the police station bathroom. This time she leaned right up to the glass so she could see her small eyes pressed into her doughy skin.

"Twenty-four," she whispered. "I'm only twenty-four. Why do I feel like I'm seven hundred years old?" She stood again, pulled the little brown jar from her makeup bag, and scraped her fingernail along the very bottom to get at the last of the cream.

She rubbed it on her belly and closed her eyes to inhale the sharp smell, like mown alfalfa with something sharper and something sweeter thrown in. "Herbs and stuff" is what Aimée had said. Schilling did her best not think too much about the "and stuff" part. How bad could it be? Nothing else worked. And besides, it was only a few days a month.

Schilling shook her head to clear it. Two thoughts: she needed to get back to work, and she needed more cream. And then a third: she wanted to go to bed. And one more: she should go to the doctor.

"Pull. Yourself. Together," she whispered viciously to her reflection.

Unlike Kelly, the afternoon receptionist did not stand outside the bathroom door waiting for her. Instead, Chantel sat coolly at her desk. She wasn't filing her nails, but she may as well have been for the nonchalant look she tossed at Schilling.

"Headed there now," Maddie called as she breezed by.

A cramp almost stopped her at the door but she prevailed. "I am in charge," she muttered. "Damn it. I'm twenty-four years old. I am in charge of this body."

The last cramp, the one that always took hold just before the cream finally started working, hit her as she got back in the cruiser. She leaned against the steering wheel and breathed deeply. Then it passed and she knew she'd be fine for a few hours. With luck, she'd be able to get through her overtime and swing by Aimée's for more cream before the cramps took hold again.

Back in the house Gia was nowhere to be seen, so he set to work on the omelette. He sautéed a crushed garlic bulb in olive oil, then beat the eggs in a metal bowl and swirled them around the heated pan until they clung to the edges. He chopped the tomato and the sad bit of leftover cheese and waited for the moisture of the eggs to reach the exact point where it would meld with the other ingredients without overcooking them. When he determined that point had been reached, he slid in the chopped tomato and cheese. He put the pan down and turned to see Gia watching him from the doorway.

"Find everything you needed?" she asked.

He nodded at her but kept his eye on the surface of the omelette, waiting for the moment just before it was cooked through—when he could layer the herbs on top.

"A little more than I expected. I scared someone off." He looked at her as he said the next words. "Have you been having trouble with intruders?"

Her eyes held his. The only change was a slight sucking in of her right cheek. A cheek biter, he thought. Everyone has her thing.

"Why do you ask that?"

He shrugged, looking back at the pan. It was time. He moved fast, sprinkling the chopped chives, parsley, and spinach. Then, with a quick flip of the spatula and a shake of the pan, the omelette was ready.

"Just connecting the dots. Even here, in the backwoods of Kootenay Landing, it's pretty rare to be greeted with a shotgun. Come and eat," he said, as he slid the omelette onto a platter.

She rolled up to the place at the dining table that did not have a chair. "Get a plate for Juniper too," she said. "She won't be much longer."

"How do you know? Did she call?" he asked, as he reached into the cupboard for another plain white plate.

"She has this unbelievably accurate food radar," she said. She jutted her chin toward the extra plate. "Go ahead and serve her as well. She'll be here before it's cold. And sit down and eat, for God's sake, before you fall over."

Bern filled the remaining two plates and chose the chair that seemed least likely to be someone's regular seat. It was across from Gia and backed on a window with a spectacular view of the distant mountains. The flash of marsh he saw as he turned to sit made him think of Resnick, the ambulance attendants, and the scene-of-crime team, all waiting for him.

He forced the thought out of his mind. He would be useless to them until he'd had some food. Nodding at Gia, he muttered, *"Bon appétit,"* and began to eat.

When the omelette was still piping hot, he heard the metallic flap of the screen door and Dr. Sinclair's voice, more relaxed than it had been that morning.

"Christ, that smells amazing. I'm just starved. Did the—" She came into the room and stopped short when she saw Bern. Her brows knitted together in confusion, or perhaps annoyance; Bern did not know her well enough to tell the difference. "Oh," she said. "I can come back."

"Come back? What the hell are you talking about, Juniper? You live here." Gia's voice was as gruff as a man's. "Just come sit down. He makes a mean omelette." Bern saw Juniper wince again and look down. His thought—she's trying not to cry—surprised him. She went to the kitchen sink and washed her hands in that same careful way he'd seen her do at the stream. By the time she joined them at the table, her features were composed.

She sat down next to him with a sideways glance, as though assessing how dangerous he might be. He smiled up at her, taking the last bite of omelette. She was obviously hungry. Her low-peaked hairline dipped down toward her plate as she started in on her meal. Her glossy hair fell in front of her face like a privacy screen. He watched her intently, and she ignored him with as much intensity. He would have to take care; he would have to come back. He would not get far with her today.

"I didn't expect you to run away," he said.

"And I didn't expect you to just turn up." She looked up at him suddenly, her eyes defiant. She'd showered—the hair that she flipped back was still wet at the ends and around her ears. She was wearing a waffle-knit cotton shirt, white and clean, and jeans that were more faded than the ones she'd had on earlier. Her fingers, he noticed, were stained green at the tips, which he used to think meant smoker, but now knew could equally mean gardener.

One question. He'd allow himself that. He could hardly hold it back.

"Did you know him?" He asked it as innocently as possible. She stiffened visibly and looked over at Gia. He watched the silent, complex exchange between the two women. Then Gia gave the tiniest of nods. Permission granted, apparently, though only so much.

"We knew who he was. Enough to know he meant trouble."

It was not much, but it would have to be enough for now. "The police will be here. They will ask you more," Bern said.

Gia's hoarse voice from across the table severed the fragile connection he'd made with the young doctor.

"Will you be there too? Keep them in line?"

Bern bowed his head slightly. "I can be. If you request it." He directed his words to Juniper. "I'll come if you ask me to."

She looked back at him with indifference. "I've got an ER shift starting in an hour. I won't have time to talk to anyone until that's over."

He pushed back his chair and stood, turning to take in the marsh, in shadow now as the sun made its way behind the mountains. A pair of binoculars sat on the windowsill, but even without them he could make out the white square that was the ambulance parked at the trailhead.

"When will that be?" he asked.

"Sometime on Tuesday."

Resnick would have something to say about that, no doubt. But it was not Bern's responsibility. He stepped away from the window to take in the warmth of the log home. Every corner spoke of settling in, of comfort and long term, of commitment. Recent changes spoke of lives adjusting to illness: the wide spacing of the furniture did not quite suit the rooms; an open door off the kitchen looked to be a bedroom, rather than the expected study. And yet, what an odd couple they made. The older woman: rough, handicapped, and yet in charge, emanating a raw kind of beauty. The younger woman: fresh as the petals in the garden and too young for the responsibility heaped on her.

"They'll be waiting for me," he said as the slam of the metal door echoed again.

"Mom! Did you hear? The bastard is dead!" This was followed by a whoop and a laugh, and then a young man appeared before them. His guileless face hesitated for only a moment when he saw Bern. Unusual in one so young, Bern thought. He did a quick scan of the young man's compact build. He'd make a good soldier.

The young man grinned at him. "I'm Lennon," he said, holding out his hand. He was darker in complexion than his mother, but with those eyes there was no doubt he was Gia's son.

His grip was firm, confident, cheerful even. Bern could not help but smile. "I'm Bern. The coroner. Here about the dead guy."

If Bern was expecting this to pull the boy in line, it didn't. Lennon just laughed. "Well, what do you know," he said. He went and stood behind his mother's wheelchair and hugged her. "That looks great. Any left?"

Gia slid her half-eaten meal over to an empty spot at the table. "You can finish mine. I'm full." With that, a circle seemed to close around the three of them. A circle that excluded Bern. He acknowledged the change with a simple nod.

"I'll see myself out," he said.

CHILD PROTECTION SERVICES

NOTE TO FILE: Report of Suspected Child Abuse or Neglect

Date: May 31, 1981

Re: Follow-up Action Taken

In response to a report of suspected child abuse and/or neglect submitted by Ms. S. Wakely, Aboriginal Early Intervention Worker, with the Kootenay Landing School District, the following action was taken:

- CPS staff met with band elders to discuss Ms. Wakely's concerns about CINDY JOHN. (Specifically re: neglect, possible physical abuse, emotional trauma, and father's stated refusal to allow Cindy to attend school.)
- Tribal elders assured CPS staff that they were well aware of Cindy's situation and were working to stabilize her home life.
- Visit by CPS staff to the JOHN residence showed substantial improvement from the situation reported by Ms. Wakely. The household was tidy and free from debris. There was sufficient food in the cupboards and refrigerator, including milk and cheese.
- CPS staff visited Cindy's room and spoke with the child. She appeared to be in good health and good spirits, was communicative and well cared for. She was excited at the prospect of starting school and said she was learning to figure skate.
- Elders noted that a family cousin (paternal second cousin) had recently moved in and was helping to stabilize the situation. The cousin was hired as a loader operator at the log yard on

the reserve. His income would provide steady financial support to the family.

- No evidence of physical abuse could be found.

Recommendation: Continue to monitor the situation, in cooperation with social workers and elders on the reserve.

7

Bern looked away from what was left of the man's face and out to the broader landscape: marsh grasses, open sky. In the distance, mountains in the fading light. Closer by, the three scene-of-crime officers that Resnick had managed to rustle up on a sunny day at the tail end of elk-hunting season scoured the trail and the edge of the road for clues.

He knew he needed to find a place of equilibrium, solid ground on which to perform the tasks ahead of him. Logic was failing him. He knew, could see with his very eyes, that he was not alone in a world taken over by death. Count them, he said to himself, turning back. One dead. One, two, three officers, plus Resnick. Two paramedics. Six living. Seven, if he counted himself. And yet the feeling persisted: he was alone in the world. He was responsible and lacked the tools for the job.

In the shadow of the late afternoon the thought came to him: What had he done? What had he done, swaggering into this town, a retired soldier who knew a little about a few things and nothing at all about gardening? He'd answered the classified ad for the on-call coroner position and bought an acre of land. The ease, almost thoughtlessness, with which he'd taken on these two major commitments now filled him with dread. What had he been thinking? That the dead would slide easily from his grasp? That the soil would yield to his paltry efforts?

Who was he to walk into this new life, as if the past did not matter and would not follow him? And yet there it was, evident in this skewed logic, this very denial of reality, this fear. With every death he witnessed, it became clearer to him that he could not escape his past.

Constable Schilling was heading his way through the growing number of police and emergency vehicles along the side of the road. She was short and would tend to stocky if she wasn't careful. Her mouse-brown hair was cut in a plain bob and her expression was serious to the point of severe. Bern's sense of her was that she had good instincts but was unsure of herself. She never seemed at ease in uniform, and she didn't seem to like being a police officer. Or maybe it was just Staff Sergeant Resnick she didn't like.

"What have we got?" she asked. Her voice was strung taut as razor wire.

Bern jutted his chin at Resnick, who was walking toward them along the marsh trail. "Your boss will want to give you the official version. Basically, this unfortunate young man got himself shot in the face."

Schilling crouched down before the corpse. Bern saw her grimace with the effort. She whistled softly, but showed no other emotion.

Already, Bern thought. He'd been with Schilling at her first homicide scene, just a month and a half before.

"We've got a witness telling us his name is Seymour Melnychuk," he said out loud.

"About time you got here," Resnick's voice boomed at them across the marsh.

"There's no exit wound," Bern said to her in a voice too quiet for Resnick to hear.

She stood at attention as her superior officer approached, and Bern watched her get her reaction under control.

"I was delayed by the incident at the border," she said.

"Well, obviously we've got bigger fish to fry now," Resnick said. "Coroner's here, after all. Something big going down, right?"

Bern shifted uncomfortably and looked off in the middle distance.

"Bern—I mean, Coroner Fortin said that this is Seymour Melnychuk?"

Schilling was still crouched, staring at the bullet wound. Bern looked over at Resnick's tapping foot and followed the yellow line on the leg of his uniform up to his clenched fist, his frustrated face.

"What else did he tell you? Let me guess: no exit wound, right? And so far no shell, and no discarded weapon. But we've still got three hundred seventeen or so acres of marshland to search and—"

"Sir?"

"What?"

"Sorry to interrupt, sir. It's just . . ." She hesitated.

"What is it, Schilling? For Christ's sake, we don't have all night. We've got a murder to investigate here."

"If you were one of my men you'd be polishing boots right now, Resnick. I bet you ten bucks that if you listen to her, she'll save you from making an ass of yourself."

Resnick's eyes slid over to Bern and narrowed even further. "Twenty," he said.

Bern shrugged. "Sure, if you want to lose that much."

"Spill it, Constable," Resnick said.

She pulled herself taller and gave a succinct, professional report.

"As you know, sir, earlier today a man named Gary Dowd ran away from the border, leaving behind an abandoned van, complete with car seats and a Barkyardigans CD. When I went to check his residence in Kootenay Landing, I found his wife, Michelle Forsberg-Dowd, in a fit of housecleaning, trying to get rid of the bad smell left behind by an unwanted houseguest named Seymour Melnychuk." Schilling checked her notebook. "Her exact words to me were: 'Whatever happened, it's Seymour's fault. Gary's a useless idiot.'"

Bern cocked an eyebrow at Resnick. "I'll take that twenty dollars in credit at the Kootenay Landing Hotel."

"Shit, yeah, I bet you will. Okay, so we've got one idiot running away from the border. Was he armed?"

Schilling shrugged. "His wife says Gary doesn't have a firearm. But who knows?" She gestured to the dead man. "Seymour could have brought one into the house without the wife's knowledge."

"What do we know about this guy, anyway?" Resnick asked.

"Dowd or Melnychuk?"

"Dowd, Dowd. Melnychuk has been on the radar for ages. Known associate of the Hells Angels. Runs drugs and keeps people in line—or so we think. Up north mostly, but he came this way about a month ago and we got a heads-up from the drug squad in Prince George. But I never heard of Dowd before you said his name."

"Gary Dowd seems like just a regular guy. He's the comptroller for the mill. An accountant. His wife works out too much, his kids yell at each other. And they're little, under five," Schilling said.

"Well, it's a lead anyway. I'll give you that. What time did he run?" Resnick asked.

Schilling flipped a page in her notebook. "Just before noon."

Resnick nodded at Bern, who answered his unspoken question. "Shot was fired at twelve forty-three."

"Plenty of time to run from the border to the marsh. But then where is he now? And is he still armed?"

None of them had an answer to that question.

The man walked in right around the ten o'clock lull—that time of a Sunday night that separated the true drinkers from the family men. Those who stayed had put out of their minds everything they had to lose by staying: wives, lovers, and children; homes and cottages; dually trucks pulling quads; RVs and snowmobiles; jobs that they had to go to the next morning. All that was left for them was the promise at the bottom of the bottle.

In the six weeks since the brewery had shut down she'd seen the number of stragglers growing—Sunday night and every night. Those who hadn't had all the life sucked out of them had headed north to the oil patch, east to the mines, or west to the smelter. Two weeks on, two weeks off, they'd come back between shifts to torment the guys left behind with their new trucks, with the fact that their wives could still play golf, with the reality that they hadn't had to snap up the last of the retail jobs to make mortgage payments.

There was an intake of breath, a barely perceptible pause, when the man walked in, as though the crowd had collectively spotted him, assessed him as an outsider, decided to ignore him, then carried on.

There was something uptight about how he stood in the doorway and scanned the room. Something in the way he held his shoulders. His complicated blond haircut said city. His beard looked scruffy, but no doubt it took work to contain that perfect symmetry between the lines of his jaw. He was the only man in the bar wearing a cardigan.

He slid into a stool at the bar and nodded at Leigh. She nodded back but did not smile, kept polishing the already spotless glasses.

"Get you something?" she asked.

He grunted. "Will I get beat up if I order something other than beer?"

Despite herself she barked a laugh. "Better make it rye or scotch. Vodka or gin might cause trouble."

"Scotch it is. On the rocks," he said. He slid a leather satchel onto the stool next to him and she felt his eyes on her as she poured his drink. Blue eyes, clear like a young boy's, and she suddenly saw the reason behind the haircut, the goatee, the cable-knit sweater, and the professor's satchel. They were statements: I'm a grown-up.

She placed the drink in front of him. "Just passing through?" she asked.

He swirled the glass. "Remains to be seen," he replied, then looked up at her with his little-boy eyes. "I'm waiting for someone."

Now that she was staring right at him she saw another reason for his beard: it camouflaged his crowded teeth and a sharp nose that conspired to give him the look of a rodent. Better viewed from a distance, she thought.

"Aren't we all?" she said. She scanned the bar and nodded at the hand that waved at her. She picked up a pitcher and started filling it with beer. "You going to tell me who?" she asked.

He didn't reply.

She delivered the pitcher and made another tour of the room, taking several more orders and settling an argument over whether the new beer tasted like cat piss. When she got back to the bar he appeared not to have moved, though his glass was empty.

"Another?"

"Kind of expected he'd be here. It's his kind of a place."

"Who you looking for again?"

"Retired Canadian Forces Lieutenant-Colonel Bern Fortin." He looked up from his empty glass as he enunciated each syllable. She got the tense shoulders then too. Soldier.

"Huh," she said. Cautious now. Bern was a gentle man, finding his way. This man-boy would be trouble for him, she had no doubt. She filled four pitchers with beer, lining them up on the bar, then refilled his glass and put it in front of him.

"You know him?"

"Leigh! Hurry up! Where's our beer?" Someone called from the crowd.

She grasped two pitchers in each hand and delivered them. Taking her time. She adjusted the volume on the sports network and fiddled with the cable for the keno game. That was one machine she wanted to throw right out the window—nothing ruined a man faster than gambling, so far as she could tell—but the revenue was good for the owner. She went to the other end of the bar and called her son, reminded him to go to bed.

The man's glass was empty again when she got back.

"One more?" she asked.

"You never answered my question." Those eyes again. Like a toddler's after a tantrum.

"If I see him, who should I say is looking for him?"

He tried to stare her down, but in a matchup between a soldier and a bartender, Leigh knew who would come out ahead.

"Troy Thompson," he said.

"And where can he find you?"

"Right here. You rent rooms, right?"

She nodded.

"Fine. I'll sleep upstairs, then sit on his bar stool until he shows up."

She laughed again, despite herself. "How did you know that's his seat?"

She thought she saw a smile under the fur around his lip.

"It's the only seat in this shithole a soldier would choose."

It was just before midnight when the ambulance pulled away from the scene, Resnick following in his truck. Seymour would spend the night in the morgue at the Kootenay Landing Hospital before being transported to Kelowna the next morning. As the first officer on the scene, Resnick would follow the ambulance the whole way.

Bern started up his own truck and turned onto the highway. His duties done for the night, he set a pace that matched the progression of his thoughts. He allowed them to wander and followed willingly, noticing after a while that they always came back to the same question: Why had he not felt anything in the moment before Seymour was shot?

His whole life he'd had an uncanny ability to sense when disaster was coming. A priest at the English Catholic school he'd attended in Montreal had first pointed it out, in front of the whole class. Bernard's desk, he noted, always seemed to be clean on the mornings the sisters inspected them.

At cadet camp, those who caught on would take extra care

to polish their boots and fold their sheet corners when they saw Bern doing the same. But it was in the field that this soldier's instinct really shone through. He could feel a tingling at the base of his hairline, a slight tightening behind the retina of his eye, whenever danger was near. He learned too that if he squinted his eyes slightly and scanned the landscape—be it the jungles of Rwanda, the rolling hills of Bosnia, the mountains of Afghanistan—the source of the impending danger would make itself known to him. Crazy sixth sense, Colonel Sauvé called it. Ungodly, the priest had said.

Whatever others thought of his ability, Bern began to see it as a simple truth he could rely on to keep him alive. And it had— often at times long past the point when he wanted to live.

Of all the lingering symptoms of the trauma he'd witnessed, the warping of this secret sense was by far the worst. Sometimes it was still intact—as it had been with the intruder in Gia's garden—but other times, this sense failed him. The uncertainty left him unanchored and tentative.

He reached the Kootenay Landing town limits and navigated the sleepy streets. At the intersection where he would normally turn toward home, he headed straight instead. His truck seemed to turn of its own accord and there he was, in the parking lot of the Kootenay Landing Hotel. A double whiskey and a visit with his favorite bartender would be just the thing.

Don't go in there.

Bern froze at this clear order that came from inside his own head. What danger could there be in a small-town bar an hour before closing on a Sunday night? But this was the thing: his sense had always been right—at least until it started to be wrong. He had always listened to it before.

Don't go in there.

But where had it been this morning, when there was real danger? And how many times over the past weeks and months had he sensed danger when there was none to speak of?

He closed his eyes and pictured a glass of golden liquid sliding along the bar in front of him. He pictured Leigh's strong hands, her smooth-skinned arms and round shoulders. He saw her smile that said hope, though life had taught her to expect otherwise. What danger could there possibly be?

He stepped in the back door of the bar and hesitated before opening the inside fire door. The danger signal clanged. *What the hell was this?* He stopped to breathe, hand on the door. *This is not real. It is the burden of the past. That is all.*

He fought the panic and the hesitancy and pulled the door open.

Something was off. He could tell from his sweep of the room that something in the upper left corner was not right—that something was about to happen. He saw a blond head sitting in his seat. He saw the brace of the shoulders, and he knew. *A soldier.*

Just then a group of regulars made their way out of the bar, pushing past him, and Bern let their momentum carry him into the cool fall air.

He slid back into his truck and leaned his head against the headrest for one weary moment. The past had found him. As he started the ignition to drive the three blocks home, he knew he could not run any longer.

Quebec City, 1993

Bern made his way down the historic street, pressed with graystone on all sides. Fingers of cold reached into the depths of whatever they encountered—the layers of cobblestone, the shadows of leafless trees, the cracks in the centuries-old homes, the soul of a young officer on an unknown mission—and held fast.

He passed a still-open restaurant promising raclette and warmth and he had the foolish thought of inviting the general's wife back there, to sit together over bowls of sharp melted cheese and soft, fresh bread.

"Damned if you do, but damned even worse if you don't," the major in the mess hall had whispered to Bern, after she'd called and asked for him by name. "Just be discreet. It won't last long. It never does with her."

He knew who she was, of course. Everyone knew Mme. LeClerc. Everyone knew that General LeClerc had recently taken a position in New York, overseeing joint peacekeeping operations in far-off places. His wife would join him soon, ready to apply herself to advancing her husband's career in the wider world of the United Nations and New York City.

Bern had seen her just recently, at the send-off parade for her husband. General LeClerc had inspected his troops and in return they'd inspected his wife with quick darts of their focused eyes. Three-sixty, they called it. A good soldier knows what's going on all around him. Insurgents, snipers, a gorgeous woman—no matter.

Bern looked only once but the image still burned in his mind. Her skin was perfectly white, the only color from two tiny rosebuds of cold on her cheeks. Her hair was black and thick and fell in a rich smooth cape to the shoulders of a charcoal-gray wool coat. Belted tightly at the waist, it could not hide the sensuality of the body beneath. Her lips were full and deep red, and he had the urge to crush them under his own. With that unexpected thought he looked quickly to her eyes, and they surprised him too: pale blue and almost translucent. She smiled. She'd been looking right at him.

She had waited a full week to call. A Sunday, and Captain Fortin just starting two days' leave. Did she know this? Would she have known that he was at loose ends in the officers' barracks, in the mess, in the rec room?

He pressed on now and reached the large stone house that served as home to the presiding commander of the regiment. A snow-covered shovel stood sentry by the door. Bern climbed the steps two at a time and began clearing them from top to bottom, using the flat end of the shovel to scrape off a treacherous patch of ice that must have been there for some time. When he reached the bottom, he continued, clearing the snow to the corner. It felt good to be moving, to be warm. When he finally turned back to the house, she was standing with the carved wooden door open wide to the cold, watching him.

"*Merci,*" she said, pointing to the shovel.

He leaned it back where he had found it, against the quarried stone of the façade. "*De rien.*"

"This doesn't mean I have to go out, you know," she said. The crushed petals of her lips spoke the words and then she turned and walked inside.

He followed. "But now you have the option. And it's always good to have an escape route."

The foyer was no warmer than the outdoors. He closed the door behind him and the sound echoed between the marble floor and the open space around the grand staircase. He could have sworn he saw the crystal teardrops of the chandelier dip and clink in response to her laughter.

"You see? I told my husband: 'I need a soldier to look after me when you are gone.'"

He stood to attention and saluted. "At your service, *madame*."

She narrowed her eyes as though inspecting him. She was wearing that coat again, charcoal wool covering her from neck to toe, but still she could not mute her curves. "I need a fire," she said. She turned on her heel—she wore sheepskin slippers as elegantly as a pair of high-heeled shoes—and headed into the drawing room.

Bern untied his boots and followed, his wet socks suctioning footprints across the floor. The soft white carpet before the hearth was only slightly warmer than the marble beneath his feet. He kneeled down to find a grate full of half-burned newspaper over a pile of cold ashes.

"It must have been going pretty good to make a pile of ashes like that," he said.

"*Le général* made a fire before he left," she said from behind him. Then she paused and inhaled sharply. With a long, slow exhale the smell of cigarette smoke reached him. "But a fire lasts only so long, no?"

It took him a few minutes to shovel the ashes from the grate, find the healthy stack of wood that was piled neatly outside the back door, and build the fire up again. It was only then that he took in his surroundings.

It was a grand old room, the ceilings as high as the room was wide, the moldings deep and thick with cream paint, the plastered walls still holding a blush of color from some long-faded fresco. In that room she had placed a low modern couch and settee and a teak table on which sat a hand-carved chess set.

The room was already beginning to warm up. Madame LeClerc had taken off her wool coat and beneath it she was just as he expected—a pile of curves in layers of cream-colored silk and pink cashmere.

Bern crossed the white shag carpet again and closed the French doors to the foyer to keep the heat in. Then he closed the door to the kitchen to do the same. He came back to the now-warm hearth, and to keep from looking at her, he kneeled and gave the log another shove with the poker.

He turned to face her and stood at attention again. He kept his gaze on her toes. She was curled up on the couch now, hugging her knees to her chest. She'd kicked the slippers off and her feet were swathed in cream silk stockings. Her toenails were as small as a child's and painted bright red.

"Madame LeClerc, will there be anything else?" he asked.

She took a drag of her cigarette and then lifted her head to the ceiling to let the smoke out, exposing her long neck from the point of her chin to the place where her breasts met under the silken robe.

"I need you to keep it lit," she said. "Cold night like this, I could freeze, no?"

Bern knew what he should do. He should put on his wet boots, zip up his parka, and head back out into the cold night. He should walk quickly, or better yet run, back to the base, where he belonged. Watch some TV and drink a beer and forget the whole thing. *Damned if you do, damned even worse if you don't,* the major had said. And Bern knew that the damage had already been done, that the rumors had started circulating the moment he'd hung up the phone. The second she had called and asked for him—or even the moment she had first laid eyes on him—was when his fate was sealed. There was nothing he could do now, and so he just nodded.

"*Bien*. In two days, the movers will come and pack my things and some other woman will come with her own *général* and live in my house. So listen, Fortin, I need you to keep me warm for two days and two nights. Can you do that?"

He could feel his feet, still frozen in their wet socks. He could feel a pricking of sweat under his armpits in his parka. He could feel the ends of his fingers, the very edge of his skin as he was pulled into her orbit.

"I'm on leave. For two days." And when the words came out, he realized that she knew this already. She knew the rumors would have started. She knew perfectly well the situation she was putting him in. None of it mattered to her.

And still, he did not leave.

Her fingers were small and smooth and white. They gestured to him now, cigarette in hand. "Do you play chess?" she asked.

8

He woke up in the dark, the air thick around him. The pressure on his chest was too much to bear; he hurtled out of the cabin and sat gasping on the stoop. A cluster of stars blinked at him through an opening in the canopy of trees.

Cindy. It was like she was there with him. Her skinny arms marred by scars, like a child with mosquito bites; her legs in too-tight jeans, wrapped around Seymour's waist; her caramel breasts floating under a baby-blue tank top. He pushed at the air as though to push them away, once and for all. Seymour and Cindy had haunted him for too long.

His chinos were rumpled now, his polo shirt not warm enough for the mountain air. He grabbed the thin blanket from inside and wrapped himself up in it. *Birds don't worry about what comes next,* his mom had told him once. *They follow their instincts and go back to the same places.*

Like a migrating bird, Gary had returned to the place where things had changed irrevocably. In the deep of the mountain night, as he waited for morning, he started an inventory of what he needed to preserve from his old life.

• • •

Mrs. K. was already in her going-to-town clothes.

"Groceries today," she said, as he walked in. Her flowered dress ended just below the knee and she wore thick woolen stockings and sturdy shoes. Next to a sliced loaf of zucchini bread on the wooden worktop lay her enormous purse and an empty string bag.

"Can I pick you up after? So you don't have to walk home with groceries? We could go for coffee," Bern said. He walked in with his boots on—she insisted—though he expected that to stop when the snow started. He made his way to his usual seat, to wait, which was also expected.

"Four-dollar coffee," she scoffed. "I can feed a family for a whole day for less than four dollars." She filled the kettle and turned it on as she spoke. The teapot was already out, next to "his" mug.

"Where's Brian today?"

"Basketball practice," she said. It came out in the same scornful tone she always used, but with a lighter undertone. "Monday and Wednesday mornings." She started placing things in front of him on the table: zucchini loaf, stewed cherries, a hard-boiled egg, a small earthenware bowl full of butter, another full of homemade jam. "Did you eat anything at all yesterday? No breakfast. Gone all day."

"I had an omelette."

She put a full-sized dinner plate in front of him and made a tsking sound. "Not much food, an omelette. Eat."

They fell silent as he filled his plate and started in on his food. When the kettle boiled she went through her usual series of efficient movements to make the tea. She placed the sweetened cup before him, then poured her own and sat across from him.

"Someone was looking for you yesterday," she said.

"Oh?" said Bern, taking a sip. He didn't tell her about the triple espresso he'd had before making his way from his garden to hers.

"I didn't like him," she said, eyeing him over the rim of her mug.

He smiled at her scowling face. "Why is that?"

"Are you making a joke?" she asked.

He shook his head. "No, no. I'm not making a joke. I'm perfectly serious when I say that I'm glad you were here. Because I have no doubt you stood up for me better than I could have for myself."

"That's right! I told him he looked like bad news. I told him you already had plenty to do, and you do not need some nosy person like that sneaking around."

Bern spread butter on the zucchini loaf and took a bite. When she didn't continue he prompted her. "Sneaking?"

She nodded seriously. "Went right into your garden like a raccoon! I chased him off with my hoe."

Bern bit back a laugh. "Thank you," he said simply. "That was the right thing to do."

She narrowed her eyes at him. "Who is he?"

Bern shrugged.

"I need to know," she said.

"In case you need to get out the rake?"

She nodded. "I think maybe the shovel."

He laughed. "I saw him only for a second last night before I went into deep cover. But I think it's Troy Thompson. I used to know him as Private Troy Thompson. Taught him to be a soldier. Now he's a journalist."

"Huh," she said. "No gratitude."

He shrugged and sipped some tea. "I left a whole world behind when I came here."

She stood, rubbing her dry, strong hands together. "You are only one man," she said. "Don't forget that part." She surveyed the table and, satisfied that he'd eaten enough, started clearing things away. She left his mug of tea, which she refilled from the pot. "And the man in the marsh? What about him?"

Bern smiled tightly and waited. He was not allowed to share information about an active investigation. But if he waited, he knew Mrs. K. would tell him what she knew.

"Fine," she said after a moment. "I heard Seymour Melnychuk. No good when he was a kid and back now to cause trouble."

"And?"

"And nothing. Not my kind of people," she said. "Except . . ."

"Yes?"

"Except for Mrs. Forsberg. She's good people."

Bern swallowed a sip of tea. "Mrs. who? I don't think I came across her yesterday."

"You will. And then remember: she's good people."

Bern nodded. "I'll remember. I'd better go see what I can find out. But I can still drive you home with your groceries if you want."

She shook her head. "I'm meeting my daughter. For coffee. She'll drive me home."

Bern raised an eyebrow. "Brian's mom? Is this a reconciliation?"

Mrs. K. shrugged. "For sure she's paying for the coffee."

He was tempted to hug her. To wrap his long arms around her hunched shoulders. To pick her up and spin her around and set her down again. But he didn't. "Thank you for breakfast," he said simply.

She nodded and patted the air dismissively. "Go. Figure things out. I'll get the shovel out, in case the journalist comes back."

• • •

Mountain Station was busy, but she sensed a pause in the action when she walked into the crowded café in her uniform. As usual. Conversations stopped and then started up again, more quietly. The pause lasted barely a second and then she heard Lennon's voice call above the crowd, "Hide your stash, folks! The fuzz is here!" He followed this with his cheerful laugh, and then said to Schilling, "Your regular?"

Maddie nodded. She found a recently vacated table and sat down, pulling over the latest edition of the *Main Street,* Kootenay Landing's weekly paper. This issue featured a photo of the mayor standing on the steps of town hall with the director of the chamber of commerce. Together these two beacons were going to revitalize the local economy and attract new business and industry. "We are not a one-company town," the mayor was quoted as saying. "Even if we are feeling the recent loss of the Bugaboo Brewery, we will find our way back to prosperity. The answer is in attracting new light industry." Maddie set the paper aside with a snort.

"Not liking what the mayor has to say, Constable?" Lennon asked as he placed a tall mug in front of her.

Schilling took a slurp before the caramel and chocolate toppings had time to slide too far into the whipped cream. She closed her eyes and inhaled, then smiled up at Lennon. He was dressed in his usual fashion: pinstriped trousers with a pocket watch chain snaking into his front pocket; a ribbed white T-shirt that hugged the curves of his body; a little peaked bowler hat covering his dark hair.

"You make the best coffee," she said.

He slid onto the bench across from her. With her eyes she

traced the movement of his abs under his T-shirt, the muscles of his arms. She counted the reasons why this handsome boy was all wrong for her: He was Aimée's boyfriend. He flirted with everyone. He was probably a drug dealer. All very good reasons.

He smiled that sweet smile of his now. "C'mon, Constable. Don't change the subject. What's the mayor said that makes you laugh?"

She smiled back at him. "He thinks that the biggest industry in Kootenay Landing is gone now that the Bugaboo Brewery has shut down."

"Ah," said Lennon, nodding.

"But we both know that's not the case, don't we, Lennon?"

He wiped the table around her coffee with a bar towel. "Do we, now?"

Maddie took another sip of coffee. "You could make my job a whole lot easier."

He raised his eyebrows and grinned at her. "That would be no fun at all," he said. Then his face turned serious. He leaned closer and spoke quietly. "The Bugaboo Brewery may not have touched the biggest industry in town, but things are going down, you know?"

She nodded. "We noticed. Dead guy in the marsh yesterday. Know anything about that?"

Lennon's friendly face turned hard. "He was one bad dude. I can tell you that much."

"Nothing more?"

"Nothing more."

"Other stuff going down?"

Lennon's eyes shifted and he didn't answer.

His parents had owned Mountain Station for years. Word was that his mother was now in a wheelchair and his father was serving a twenty-year sentence in the US for pot trafficking. Americans took their marijuana seriously. Not that the RCMP didn't—especially in a border town like Kootenay Landing. Schilling was beginning to form her own opinions, though. She was starting to think that cultivating good relations with some key people might unlock the whole drug puzzle for the region. And Lennon Hinton and his family were marijuana royalty in town.

Of course, she kept these thoughts to herself.

"So nothing you want to talk about is what you're saying. Or not saying." She took another sip and watched him. The fact that he was still there, listening, spoke volumes. "It's all outside my beat anyway. I'm just a rookie cop, right? But here's my thought: big shit like this goes down and those little guys on the fringes—the guys who grow a little dope, maybe share it with their friends?— they're the ones who get hurt."

Lennon just stared at the table. She'd never seen him so quiet.

"Guys like that have nowhere to turn when something happens." She played with the edge of the mug. She'd taken a step down a new road, and she wasn't at all sure where it might lead. It felt a little dangerous. Resnick for sure would not like it, but she kept going anyway.

"Game's changed, Lennon. Since your parents started out. Since you were a hippie kid, potty-trained by mother nature, clipping bud before you were old enough to read. It's a whole lot more dangerous now," she said.

He looked up at her, his eyes enormous. "I know."

"You've got Aimée and Gabriel to think of now."

"Believe me, I know." He whispered it this time.

"Aimée here today?" she asked, lightening her tone.

He stood and nodded. "In the kitchen. Go on back."

She found Aimée in the kitchen, stirring a huge bowl of batter with her skinny, tattooed arms.

"Hey, Maddie, how are you?" she asked. Her English was rounded and halting. Like the coroner's, Maddie thought, and wondered if the two French Canadians had met yet.

"I'm okay. Where's Gabriel today?"

Aimée nodded to the screen door that led to the back patio. "He's out there. Probably making a mess for me to clean up. Work twice as hard when I bring him with me," she said as she scooped batter into a muffin tin.

"I can imagine," Maddie replied, though really she couldn't. She couldn't imagine being as tall and as effortlessly glamorous as Aimée. She couldn't imagine being a single mom, working in the business owned by the family of her child's father. She couldn't imagine letting Lennon, gorgeous as he was, play hot and cold with her life while he flirted with every rock climber and fruit picker who came into the coffee shop. She couldn't imagine any of it.

"I'm getting cramps again," she said. "The sage cream really helped. Do you have any more?"

Aimée looked up sharply. *"Déjà?"* she asked.

"What?"

"Sorry. Already? You just had it."

Maddie nodded. "I know."

"But, Maddie!" It came out like *Maddeeee*. "It's too much! Too . . . too often! The cream is just for once in a while. It doesn't solve anything serious."

"I know, I know. But I just need to get through today. Have you got any more?"

Aimée tilted her dainty head toward an enormous quilted bag by the back door. "There's a little in there. Go ahead and take it. But are you sure?"

"Yes, I'm sure."

"You know there is more than sage in there, yes?"

I don't want to know, Maddie thought. She heard a giggle from outside as she dug through the bag for the little brown glass jar. "Yes, of course there is. All natural, though, right?"

"*Oui,*" said Aimée. "Natural, but—"

"Natural is good," said Schilling, cutting her off.

"But promise you'll go to a doctor. Promise me, Maddie. *C'est pas normal.*"

Even Maddie, farm girl from the Prairies, could get that much French. Not normal. Damn straight. The screen door squeaked open and four-year-old Gabriel appeared in the doorway, a small wooden box clasped to his chest. He was blond where his parents were both dark-haired, his features a perfect blend of Aimée's and Lennon's.

"Hey, my little man," his mother said as she slid a tray of muffins into the oven.

"*Regarde, maman,*" he said, holding the box out to her.

Schilling tucked the little jar into the pocket of her uniform pants and looked down to see his offering—a box of soldier figurines.

"Where did you get those?" Aimée asked sharply.

The boy looked back out the screen door, confused. "*Le monsieur,*" he said. "Outside."

"A man outside?" Aimée rubbed her hands on a towel and stepped toward her boy.

"Let me go see," Schilling said. She patted the boy's head as she walked around him and pushed the screen door open.

The patio was built around the trunk of a tree, its foliage brilliant orange and ready to fall. The sheltered café tables and chairs were all empty of patrons. A rolling pin and a bread pan filled with a loaf of Play-Doh marked the boy's spot. The alley was deserted, except for a few parked cars.

A shot of pelvic pain accompanied Schilling back inside. "No one there," she said. "Do you want me to—"

Just then Lennon breezed into the kitchen. He rustled Gabriel's hair as he walked by and jutted his chin at the soldiers, which the boy was taking great care to line up on the stainless steel work surface. "Hey, squirt, nice soldiers." He called back to Aimée from the door, "I've got some stuff to go do. Cover the front, 'kay, babe?"

Aimée crossed her arms and shifted to one hip, a gesture lost on Lennon, who was already out the door and headed toward a truck parked in the alley. Aimée sighed.

"It's okay," she said, waving Schilling off. "I'll just keep him inside. Now go. Get to work. And promise me you'll go to the doctor soon, okay, Maddie?"

"Promise," Schilling said. Cream in her pocket, she headed straight to the café bathroom. Somehow her cramps felt better already.

Dawn was making her presence known when Gary finally raised himself from the stone stoop. The birds flitted from tree to tree, heralding morning as noisily as any rooster. He moved slowly, his legs and hips aching from the hours of sitting in the cold. None of the faint morning light had made its way into the cabin yet. He finally broke down and lit a candle, to keep the memories from closing around him in the dark. Next to the candle on the plywood countertop was Seymour's package, still sealed.

He picked it up and turned it in his hands. He wanted to

think that his life had fallen apart because of this little packet wrapped in black plastic and sealed with parcel tape, but he had to admit that the frays had already been there. This parcel was the one long thread that had caused everything to unravel. But without that early tearing at the fabric of his existence, a little parcel like this could have done no harm.

What was in it? What did the final straw look like? He pawed through a small box of utensils on the counter until he found a paring knife. Ever so carefully he ran the tip of the knife along the seam of tape and through the first layer of plastic.

Dry marijuana buds broke through the surface and scattered on the counter. The smell was unmistakable. He pulled the package to his nose and inhaled deeply. His mouth watered, setting free a longing he'd held in check for years.

His fingers found their way through the inevitable next steps and he had no trouble performing the long-remembered movements in the shadowy light. He ripped a small rectangle of newspaper from the damp pile next to the stove, filling it with crumbled weed. He'd have to make do without tobacco. He ripped a piece of matchstick and folded it to form a makeshift filter. Then he rolled himself a fat joint.

He played with it for a minute before lighting it. He rolled it along the countertop to even out the buds and balanced the ends between thumb and forefinger. Then he tapped the filter end on the counter exactly four times and placed it between his lips.

The newspaper was damp and it took a minute for the grass to ignite. He puffed to get the joint going, then inhaled deeply. Stifling back a cough, he held the smoke in his lungs as long as he could, then let it go in a long, slow exhale. With it went the tension from his shoulders and between his eyebrows, the heavy tightness in his chest, and the wiry energy in his limbs that had kept him awake much of the night.

Two more puffs and he felt the memories receding: Michelle and her anger, Cindy and her tragic wildness, Seymour and his neediness. They all left him. He was alone in the cabin at last. Alone with the reality of the four log walls and the morning light through the grimy windows. Just outside was a great sanctuary, ready to shelter him for as long as he needed.

He finished the joint and butted it out on the top of the woodstove. Then he crawled into the cot and, ghosts now gone, buried himself in the blanket that still somehow smelled of Cindy.

Kootenay Landing, 1984

Everything in her new room was white. Everything.

At first she was scared to go in, but her new father gave her a little pat on the back and she stepped around the white rug and over to the bed. She touched the satin coverlet and let her hands roam over the masses of pillows. She'd never seen so many pillows.

They were watching her from the doorway, waiting for her to say something.

"Will I sleep sitting up?" she asked.

Her new mother came in then and showed her a pretty basket in the closet where she could put the pillows when she went to bed. There were dresses in the closet. Five of them. And skirts. Her new mother showed her these too.

"We got you just a few things to start with. We'll take you shopping soon so you can pick out what you like."

She showed her something called a dresser, which was filled with socks and underwear, tights, T-shirts, and sweaters. The middle drawer was full of outfits for skating and dance classes.

The baby—her new sister—woke up just then. New Dad ran out and New Mom looked in a hurry.

"You must be hungry, dear. Are you hungry?"

Cindy stood in the space between the edge of the carpet and the bed and tried not to get anything dirty.

"After we have some dinner, what would you like to do?"

Cindy stared down at the bed.

"Sorry, honey, did you say something?"

Cindy pointed at the bed.

"You want to go to bed?" New Mom asked. "But it's so early!"

"It's just so pretty," Cindy whispered.

New Mom clasped her hands and sighed. "It is, isn't it? Well, that's just fine. I understand perfectly. How about we have some dinner, and then you can have a nice bath with lots of bubbles, and then let's call it a night."

Down the hall the baby wailed even louder. "I'd better go see to that babykins. We're having tuna sandwiches. Do you like tuna?"

Cindy had never had tuna before. She nodded.

Later, washed in white bubbles and with her hair combed smooth (she could comb her own hair now—she was eight, after all), she put on a *nightgown* from the *dresser* and lined up the *throw pillows* in the basket. She said these new words to herself as she slid into the bed.

New Dad tucked her in and read her a story from one of the books on a shelf next to the bed. Then he patted her shoulder and stood up.

"Light on or off?" he asked.

She widened her eyes at him.

He waited.

"Off," she whispered.

"Door open or closed?"

"Closed," she said.

"Good night."

She lay there in the dark, the only sound the wails of the baby from down the hall. Her baby sister. She'd had lots of cousins, but she'd never had a sister before.

She lay there and let the smell of the sheets surround her. They didn't smell like sunsets. They smelled better than sunsets. They didn't feel clean. They felt cleaner than clean.

She lay there in her own room, with the white sheets that were clean and smelled better than sunsets, and she didn't dare move—in case it was a dream.

9

He woke to the sun streaming through the grimy windows. He was too warm, sweating under the thin blanket. His mouth was dry and tasted like something left over, but his limbs were relaxed and he felt calm.

Thoughts came clearly, and the one that presented itself most persistently was this: Why would Seymour go to so much trouble to smuggle such a small amount of pot over the border? It was nothing. Hardly worth ruining Gary's life over—not that Seymour would care about that. But hardly worth the bother to anyone.

There had to be something else. Gary got up from the cot and took the two steps to the counter. He picked up the package and opened it a little further. More pot spilled out and he caught it in his other hand, making a pile on the countertop. Then he put the package down and took up the paring knife again. He sliced open one side of the parcel and folded back the plastic.

Under the weed he found half a dozen tiny brown glass jars with white plastic lids. Gary picked one up. It was labeled with an oval-shaped sticker, the kind Michelle used on the jars of antipasto she made to give away at Christmastime. Each one was hand-printed with the words Victoria's Remedy.

He opened one of the jars. In it was a cream that looked like green petroleum jelly. Gary rubbed his finger along the inner edge of the jar and brought the cream to his nose. Then he laughed. Pot cream. *Well, well, Seymour. What a brilliant idea.*

He scooped a little more onto his finger and then rubbed it on the skin of his cheeks, which were dry and scraggly with the shadow of a beard. He tried some on the cut he'd got the day before. *Nature always has the answer.* Maybe his mother was right after all.

Schilling knew she had to go in and type up her notes from the day before. The scene-of-crime officers and the coroner would be waiting for them, and if she delayed much longer she'd hear from Resnick about it. But his instructions had been clear: Go through Gary's life and find every intersection with Seymour's and follow it. *I know you can be a bulldog when you put your mind to it, Schilling. So go ahead, be a bulldog with this.*

It was as close as Resnick would ever get to a compliment.

The Kootenay Landing coffee klatches had had an early start. If she was to retain any element of surprise, she needed to start talking to witnesses right away. Michelle was first on her list. Maddie would break the news about Seymour and gauge her reaction.

But when Schilling reached the perfect family house on its street full of perfect family houses, Michelle Forsberg-Dowd was nowhere to be found. The toys from the day before had been cleaned up from the yard. The potted plant on the stoop was freshly watered. The hallway, when she peeked through the space between the curtains, was as clean as it had been yesterday. No one answered her ring or subsequent knocking.

She headed out to Kootenay Lumber next. The road to Gary's place of employment was well known to her. The mill was surrounded by a network of tumbledown houses, all owned by the same cousins who owned the mill, and these were rented by workers when they first arrived in town and needed a place to stay. Some got stuck in that miserable valley with the mountains backing them on one side and the mountains of logs on the other. Perpetually dark and always a little wet, Lumberville, as she thought of it, was an RCMP training ground in the art of handling a drunk and disorderly or a domestic incident.

Schilling drove past the little strip of misery. Pickup trucks squatted as close to the back doors as their drivers could get. The houses crouched together, the washing line of one hooked to the roof of the next, tying the inhabitants together in a long chain of survival.

She pulled into the parking lot of the mill and opened the door of the squad car to the sound of grinding machinery. A front-end loader roared by carrying a mouthful of trees. She followed the signs that said Office and opened the flimsy door to what was little more than a shack. When she closed it, the door barely kept out the sounds from the log yard.

A young woman sat at the reception desk. There were a half-dozen other desks in the room—all of them empty. Two doors led off the main office area, and one of these opened now.

"Where the hell is he? How the hell can he just not show up?" a man hollered.

The young woman ran a hand through her dark hair and smiled at Schilling. She had dark thick eyelashes, the kind that never needed to see a mascara wand.

The man looked over at Schilling. "Are you here about him?" he asked.

Schilling raised an eyebrow. "About who?"

"My goddamn cousin. Hasn't shown up for work. Says he gets equal inheritance, but he's a lazy ass just like his father always was. Supposed to run the goddamn log yard. I've got a fucking conference call to Japan, and he just doesn't show up. So unless you're here to tell me he's dead . . . Are you?"

The man stopped talking so suddenly that Schilling shook her head to clear it before she could speak. "Are you talking about Gary Dowd?"

"Gary?" His eyes shot over to the neat desk in the corner, the only one to look out on the mountains, not the log yard. "Huh." The man was suddenly quiet. "Where the hell is Gary anyway? He's supposed to do this call with me. Holler when he gets here, will ya?" he said to the girl. "What did you say your name was again?"

"My name is Karma," the receptionist answered.

He looked up at Schilling and winked. "Of course it is, sweetheart. Okay, I'm going to take that call now. Get the officer here whatever she needs and send Gary in as soon as he gets here." He closed the door with a slam that shook the walls.

"Is this your first day?" Schilling asked her.

The young woman shook her head and blinked her perfect eyelashes. "I've been here awhile. But they go through so many receptionists, I guess they don't always learn their names right away."

Maddie nodded as though this made sense. "So I'm here looking for Gary Dowd. Have you seen him?"

Karma pushed her chair back from her desk and crossed her legs. "Well, here's what I heard," she began. "I haven't told Mr. Bellinger yet, because without Gary this whole place will fall apart, but I heard that he"—she paused here, stretching out the

moment as though she were sucking on something delicious—
"ditched his wife and kids and took off."

"Took off?" Schilling asked.

"Yeah, he, like, took the minivan and just headed down to the
States. Then he ditched that van, must have got in some getaway
car, and now he's gone. One thing for sure: Mr. Bellinger is going
to freak if he was stealing money from here. What do you call it
again?"

"Embezzling?" Schilling asked.

Karma snapped a finger and pointed at Maddie. "Embezzling—that's exactly it. Anyway, it's no surprise. I was a year behind Michelle Forsberg in school and I can tell you she is one
bee-itch. I'm surprised Gary lasted as long as he did. She never
has a nice word to say about anyone. Oh my God, and were
we all surprised when she got hooked up with Gary right out
of high school. Turns out they were dating secretly when she
was, like, seventeen. Came out when she graduated, and a year
later—boom!" She clapped her hands together. "Married, house.
Michelle got a job at the clinic and the next thing you know,
kid one, kid two, and now this." She leaned forward and spoke
quietly. "I didn't want to be the one to break the news to Mr.
Bellinger."

"Break the news about what?" The new voice surprised them
both.

Karma sat up and flashed a brilliant white-toothed smile over
Schilling's shoulder. "Mr. Bellinger! Good morning! The other
Mr. Bellinger was looking for you—something about a conference call to Japan?" She smiled at him again, and played with a
curl of her hair. "Oh, and the mayor called. About your tee time
this afternoon? He's going to be a few minutes late, but he said to
let you know he'd be there."

Schilling turned to see a man in his thirties wearing loose-fitting jeans and a golf shirt. His curly brown hair was thinning and his eyes were glassy, but he clung to the roguish young man look.

"Good, okay. Thanks, Karma." Then to Schilling he said, "Excuse me," and pushed past her. If he noticed that she was a policewoman, he certainly was not the least bit curious about it. He went to the twin of the door that the other Mr. Bellinger had slammed, opened it, and closed it behind him.

"He's kinda cute, don't you think?" Karma whispered this, then took a breath and continued her story as though they'd never been interrupted. "Anyway, if he did do any embezzling it will take them forever to figure it out. Gary practically runs the place. No one else knows where anything is. These guys? They're just the owners, you know? And what I heard is that Gary has got this secret life, with drug dealing and smuggling stuff across the border."

"Did you ever see any evidence of something like that?"

Karma looked surprised. "You mean here? At work?"

Schilling nodded.

Karma sucked on a lock of hair and thought for a minute. "He's just a quiet guy, you know? Sits at his desk, works all day. Some days he comes in early, though—before anyone else gets here. And then he leaves early, dot of four o'clock, no matter what else is happening or who is yelling. He just leaves." She shook her head as though this explained everything.

"Who works at all these other desks?"

Karma spun around in her chair, her eyebrows arched as though surprised to see she was all alone in the main office. "Oh—well, that's Gary back there. These three are logging supervisors—they're all out in the bush until after lunch. This one is for visitors—we hardly ever have any. And this one is for the main secretary, except she quit just before I started and they haven't replaced her yet."

Schilling surveyed the grouping of desks. Most were controlled chaos—piles of papers and binders, a telephone on each. Gary's was the only desk that had anything personal on it. She wandered over to it. There on the windowsill, below the view of the mountains, was a framed photo of his family. Schilling leaned closer to look at it. The rugrats she'd seen the day before were even smaller in this photo. The boy was just a baby, hitched to Michelle's skinny hip. Schilling was no judge of kids' ages, but he looked like almost a newborn, which made the photo at least a year old. Maybe a year and a half. It was safe to say that Michelle was one of those annoying women who kept her svelte figure, even in pregnancy. Schilling was sure that if she ever had kids, she'd balloon up like a cow and gain a dangerous amount of weight. Not that she was ever likely to get pregnant, because for that to happen, first some guy would have to look at her twice. *Face it,* she thought, *you live in a different world than women like Karma and Michelle.*

She focused in on the photo again, this time looking at Gary. Staring back at her was the most ordinary man in the world. He had a round face and broad features and dull brown hair that was just a little patchy on top. He looked like the kind of guy who would spread out in later years. He'd start wearing lighter-colored shirts with a little polyester in them—for the stretch. He'd sling his belt a little lower than his actual waist. Leaning closer, Maddie decided he was the type to comb over the bald spot—that is, if Michelle would let him.

"Are you actually allowed to touch anything?"

Schilling pulled her hand away from the photo. "I could with your bosses' permission, but I'm not sure that will be necessary."

Karma shrugged and leaned over, picking up the photo. "Nice guy," she said. "Really nice guy. But even nice guys can only take so much, you know?"

Schilling nodded and headed to the door. "Yeah, I know. Thanks for your help. I'll let you know if I need to come back." She dropped one of her cards on Karma's desk. "And please call me right away if you hear from Gary."

Quebec City, 1993

They stayed in the living room. The teak table was pushed aside, but the chess tournament carried on. She sent him out on supply missions: duvets, pillows, wine, music.

"You're not a soldier." She laughed at him. "You're a flower petal, seeking light, sensation." She cradled his head in the perfumed world of her arms. Her fingers played with a tiny lock of hair next to his ear. "So sad. Your hair must be gorgeous when it's long. Curly."

Later, it was, "Tell me. Tell me where you've been."

He'd shrugged. "Not far. Saint-Jean-sur-Richelieu, of course. We went to Alberta one time, to train."

Her chuckle was low in her throat. "Alberta," she repeated. "That's as far as you've been?"

He rolled over on top of her, straddling her. Even naked she was a tangle of silk. He leaned in close, holding her arms down. "I've traveled worlds," he whispered into her ear.

"Rosemont," he said, biting her earlobe.

"Châteauguay." His lips on her neck.

He ran his tongue along her collarbone. "Longueuil."

He pressed a finger ever so softly to her sternum. "Lac des Deux Montagnes."

"Lac des Deux Montagnes?" She arched her back. "Tell me what it was like there."

And so he did.

10

"Thanks for letting me ride along," Bern said, as Schilling turned the squad car onto a wide street. The houses were set well back from the road on thick carpets of lawn. Trees on this street were strictly ornamental, pruned as carefully as prize poodles.

"It's no problem. Saves me typing up my notes for you later." She flashed a smile that made her look almost pretty, but it disappeared quickly under the fringe of straight brown hair that always seemed to hide her face.

"Holy shit!" she exclaimed as they pulled to a stop in front of a pristine home where a series of intricately carved pumpkins lined the walk. Schilling made no move to get out of the vehicle. Her dark eyes were wide as she stared at the Halloween decorations.

"Constable Schilling? Shall we go? I promise to keep you safe from the goblins." Bern stepped out of the cruiser and onto a street of nearly identical split-level homes.

"Weird," said Schilling as she joined him on the wide sidewalk. She pushed her duty belt down on her hips as though adjusting her armor and followed Bern along the flagstone path. At the top of the two steps to the front porch was a wide metal pot, planted thickly with purple mums. "Creepy. I visited the daughter yesterday. Her house is exactly the same."

When it looked like Schilling wasn't going to do it, Bern leaned forward and rang the bell. They waited. He leaned his head against the door.

"Hear that? She might be vacuuming." He glanced at Maddie. "You okay?" She was as pale as the folk art skeleton that hung from the front door.

"This is just really weird. Total déjà vu." She fell silent as the vacuum sounds were replaced by the click of high-heeled shoes making their way toward them. "I'll tell you after," she whispered.

A middle-aged woman answered the door. She was rounded in the way that middle-aged women should be, Bern thought as he gave his customary sweep from toe to head. Her outfit was not unlike his old private school uniform: charcoal slacks, white collared shirt, and light-gray cardigan. Her hair was colored blond and had been tended to with as much care as the Halloween decorations outside.

"Mrs. Forsberg?" Constable Schilling asked.

"Yes?" The woman nodded, her face deeply creased with worry.

"I'm Constable Schilling with the Kootenay Landing RCMP. I'm making inquiries about your son-in-law, Gary?"

"Yes?" she said again. She looked behind her quickly, as though she might get caught at something. Her eyes were blue and bright and tense. Her small hand fluttered to her mouth.

"Can we come in?" Schilling's voice was surprisingly gentle all of a sudden. "I've got just a few questions."

Mrs. Forsberg took a step back, opened the door wider, then hesitated. "I wasn't expecting company," she said. "The place is a bit . . . well, it's not ready for company."

Bern stepped forward. "Mrs. Forsberg, I have no doubt that your home, at its worst, is tidier than mine at its very best." He held out his hand. When she extended hers in return, he took it in both of his and shook it warmly. "My name is Bern Fortin, and I'm the coroner for Kootenay Landing." Her eyes tensed and he held her hand more tightly to reassure her. He remembered Mrs. K.'s admonishment from earlier that morning: *Mrs. Forsberg is good people.* "No, no. Don't let that scare you. I'm assisting the RCMP in their inquiries into another incident, one related to Gary's by the barest of tangents. I asked Corporal Schilling if I could come along while she spoke with you and she agreed. But it's up to you whether or not you want me here."

He let her hand go, and she let her other hand drop from her mouth. "This is—" she started. Then, interrupting herself, she said, "Well, you'd better come in."

He slid across the forty-ninth parallel and into the woods called Canada. Already the mornings were cold, much colder than even a few weeks before, when it seemed summer had come back and would last forever.

He was running out of time.

Oh, and how close he had been to something yesterday. He'd felt the trill of good luck beckoning him closer. If only the tall man had not seen him and chased him away.

Ruben reached the old woodshed where *la doctora* did her work and settled behind a tree trunk. He'd approached several times already. Once he'd even observed her working without her taking notice. It was the smell that first drew him here—hot candles and marijuana when he'd only been on the lookout for a ready crop of beans. Marijuana was much, much better.

From the outside the building was so hidden by trees that a

person less observant than Ruben would walk right by. It looked old, its grayed boards settling right into the land. Inside, Ruben knew the floors and counters gleamed and *la doctora* took great care to keep everything clean. There was no smell today, and no lights. She was not there.

And yet, the door was open a crack.

Ruben did not rush. Rather, he stayed hidden and waited. Only when he was sure he was alone in the woods did he creep forward.

The door swung silently open and Ruben crossed himself at the sight before him. Globs of hardened green cream and wax on the floor. The smell of honey, horse bedding, skunk, and fear.

Ruben stepped away and disappeared back into the woods. *La doctora's* shelves were bare. Someone had gotten there before him.

The air stung with the smell of ammonia as they entered the living room. It brought back the cafeteria of the Catholic boarding school where Bern had spent his childhood. The smell was so strong that it took him a moment to notice the actual details: the white shag carpet, the white sofas, the glass-topped coffee table. A thickly painted white mantel was mounted on a hearth of stone the color of beach sand. He wandered to the mantel to look at the photos—recent ones of a family with young kids smiling rather stiffly for the camera. One of Mrs. Forsberg with her grand-kids, a baby in her arms, a toddler leaning against her legs. Mrs. Forsberg's fingers clutched at the young girl's shirt, as though to keep the toddler's fingers from her pristine white pants. The rest of the photos looked older, and all featured the same subject: a young girl with black hair and skin the color of Mrs. K.'s sweet tea. In many of the photos she wore figure skates and a variety of brightly colored and sequined costumes and dresses. Later photos chronicled a rather awkward preadolescence, complete with an unfortunate hairstyle, a hand-knit sweater, and braces. Even later: a rebellious adolescence of greasy hair and unsmiling face with thickly lined eyes.

He bent himself in half to sit next to Schilling on a low white couch. A look at the officer told him she had not fully recovered. Her skin was pale and he noticed a few droplets of sweat on her forehead. Her notebook was open on her lap; she was taking down everything that Mrs. Forsberg was saying.

Or rather whispering. Bern leaned forward as far as he could in his seat, and still he could barely make out her words.

"Gary's just like that, you have to understand. He gets nervous. He panics. It's hard on Michelle," she said, shaking her head. "He'll show up, tail between his legs, begging her to take him back. It happens all the time."

"But from what I understand he's never been away overnight before." Schilling spoke in a regular voice, but it sounded like a shout in the antiseptic hush of the room.

Mrs. Forsberg's hands fluttered in panic. "Shh!" she whispered violently. "Sorry, it's just—" She looked over their heads to the entry hall.

"Mrs. Forsberg, is there someone else here?" Bern asked.

She looked at him wide-eyed and nodded. "My husband. He—he doesn't like to be disturbed. He's going through a hard time, since . . ." She let the words fade away.

"Since Gary disappeared?" Schilling suggested.

"No, no, that's not it," she said, with an anxious shake of her head. "He worked at the brewery, see . . ." The words seemed to overwhelm her and she gave up again.

"Ah, now that the brewery is shut down," Bern offered.

"Yes! That's just it. It was so sudden. They've given him early retirement, but it was such a shock." Her whisper faded and Bern could barely make out the last words.

He tried to keep his voice low, somewhere between the other two. "So you were saying that Gary's never been away overnight before?" He cocked an eyebrow at Schilling as he spoke. She gave a tiny nod of assent, and he edged a little further into the questioning. "Mrs. Forsberg, may I ask your first name?"

"Oh, oh, of course!" she said, with more fluttering of her fingers. "It's Holly. Please call me Holly. And I never offered you anything. How rude of me. Tea or coffee?"

Bern spoke for them both. "We're fine, Holly. Thank you. So you were telling us about Gary."

"Yes," she said. "You know, we had the shock of our lives when Michelle announced she was marrying him. We thought she was going to go off to college—she always talked about becoming a social worker, to help kids like . . . well, to help kids. Native kids." Her voice had modulated somewhat as she warmed to her story.

Bern sat back in his seat and spread his hands wide as she looked up at him with those tight blue eyes. "Please continue," he said.

"They'd been dating secretly for a year. She was too young for him at the time, though of course now it matters so little. Funny how these things don't matter after a while, isn't it?"

Bern nodded. "And yet some things continue to matter, well past the time we think they should, no?"

The skin around her eyes creased into tight lines. "Yes, exactly," she said.

"So Gary dated Michelle secretly, and then they married. When was that?"

"Well, they got engaged as soon as she finished high school. And then they got married a year later," she said. "Michelle got the job at the medical clinic—she's the manager now, did you know that? She's a smart girl. A shame in some ways that she got married so young. But of course, the children are such a blessing."

Bern smiled indulgently. "I saw the photos of you with them on the mantel. It looks like you're enjoying them." He coughed quietly into his hand. "Why do you think they would have kept their relationship a secret?"

It seemed impossible, but her eyebrows crept even farther up her forehead. "Why?" She was back to whispering and it came out as a hiss. "Because she was so young, of course." She'd been perched on the edge of a white armchair, and now she sat back and crossed her arms, staring at them. She crossed one leg over the other and the sole of her shoe peeked up at them under the glass coffee table. Bern could see it was pristine. Inside shoes.

Schilling held her pen in midair and stared at Holly with a look of confusion on her face. Bern ran his finger along the collar of his wool shirt: it was hot in there. The combination of the heat and the cloying smell was starting to get to him too.

A door slammed down the hall and Holly Forsberg jumped to her feet. Standing before them now, she played with the hem of her sweater.

"If that will be all, I really have nothing more to say." She said this so quietly Bern could hardly hear her.

When he stood as well, Schilling seemed to snap out of it. She rose just as a man lumbered into the room.

"You finally doing something about our Cindy?" he bellowed. He was a mass of a man—he seemed to fill the double doorway that separated the living area from the wide hall. He leaned against the frame in a pair of ill-fitting gray sweatpants and an enormous white T-shirt—all equally stained. Bern could not stop staring at him: such an anomaly—a dirty man in a clean house. As he lumbered closer, the smell of sweat and stale milk followed him in a cloud.

"Sorry, were you speaking to me?" Schilling asked.

"No, I was speaking to your boss," he said, pointing at Bern. "It's about time they sent someone in charge. Been talking to uniforms for years." He walked toward Bern now. "Duke," he said, holding out his hand. "Duke Forsberg."

"Bern Fortin," Bern said, taking his hand firmly. It felt sticky, and Bern had to resist the urge to rub his own hand on his pants.

Holly Forsberg came to life then. "No, no. You've got it mixed up, honey. They're here about Gary." She said the man's name meaningfully, full of emphasis. "He panicked and ran off, remember? What Michelle told us yesterday—why she was late for dinner?"

Duke grunted. "Useless pansy that one is. Don't know what Michelle sees in him, never did. Smart girl like her."

"But the children, such a blessing," Holly said. She took Schilling by the elbow and steered her firmly toward the door. "Thanks for stopping by. Sorry we couldn't be of more help. Honey, it's time for your snack, and then you can go out for your coffee." She smiled over at Bern, who had followed them to the door. "You know what men are like—can't upset the routine!"

Schilling pulled the door open, and sweet fresh air wafted over Bern as he crouched to do up his boots. He looked up at Holly.

"You know, it might really help to talk about it," he said.

She gasped. "Talk about what? What do you mean?"

"Holly!" Duke's voice hollered from the kitchen.

"Be right there!" she cried. Then whispered, "There's nothing to say."

His boots done up, Bern stood. "Oh, I think there is, Holly. I think there's something you've been not talking about for so long that everything becomes about that—whether it needs to or not."

Schilling was already outside in the beckoning air. Bern reached into his pocket and pulled out a card.

"I'm just a coroner. I can't do much of anything, but I can listen."

"Well," she said, taking the card briskly and tucking it into the pocket of her cardigan, "I'm happy to take this, though I can't imagine ever needing to talk. But thanks for the visit. Next time I'll be a better hostess and serve cake."

Bern smiled. "I look forward to it," he said. "I love cake."

With that he was outside, breathing like a starving man. Schilling was nowhere in sight. He walked along the path of pumpkins and admired the care that had been put into them. He could sense Holly Forsberg's hope in each one: if she followed the instructions in minute detail, if she were good enough, if she got it just perfect enough, everything would be better.

Bern looked at the clipped lawn, the pruned tree, the Halloween decorations and saw them for what they were: gloss over a marred surface. He could also see that, somehow, yesterday's incidents had changed everything. Gary's disappearance and Seymour's murder—they might not be related to Holly Forsberg's tragedy, whatever it was, but his investigations would surely bring to light what she was hiding.

Schilling was seated sideways in the driver's seat of the cruiser. The door was open and she gulped in the fresh air as greedily as he had.

"I just . . . I had to get out of there. The smell."

"*Oui.* It was bothering me too."

She looked at him over the car door. "It wasn't just me, was it? That *was* weird."

Bern nodded. "It was. Do you know who Cindy is?"

"Michelle mentioned her yesterday—her sister who disappeared. It was a long time ago. I'm going to request the file as soon as I get a minute." She hiked her belt and shifted into position in the driver's seat. "You coming?" she asked.

"I'd be curious to have a look, when you get that file," he said as he got into the cruiser.

"Yeah, so would I," Schilling replied. "But I doubt Resnick will let me spend much time on it. He wants me chasing after the killers in the here and now, not old stories from the past."

"You'd be surprised how much those old ghosts can impact the present day," Bern said, thinking of the soldier waiting for him at the bar the night before.

Schilling pulled a U-turn and headed back toward the station. "Just try telling Resnick that."

Kootenay Landing, 1984

The whole house was asleep. The baby—they'd named her Michelle in the end—had finally stopped crying. Holly was asleep at last, her system afloat in chemicals. Duke made a bottle, so he'd be ready when the baby woke up. He paced the hall, waiting. Cindy's door was closed but he slipped in anyway—to check on her.

Cindy's white nightgown glowed against the deep caramel of her skin. Her hair glistened—black against the white satin coverlet. She was perfect. Just perfect. He had never seen anything more beautiful than this child with her serious eyes and her delight in everything they gave her.

And they'd given her a lot. She had never had her own room before. Or even her own bed, from what the social worker said. Her eyes when she looked up at Duke—full of gratitude and as dark as the inside of a beer bottle. He worked the labeler machine at the brewery. He'd seen his share of beer bottles slide by.

His own daughter looked pale and chubby by comparison. She squealed all the time. Holly, who had been so miserable for so long with no children, had sunk into an even deeper misery now that she had two. She had closed herself off with the baby in her little chemical world. After months of not allowing him to touch her because she was pregnant, now she wouldn't even let him sleep in the same room.

By day, when he wasn't on shift and Cindy wasn't at school, he spent his time with her. By night, he paced. When he needed a rest, he'd nap in the white-upholstered reading chair in Cindy's room.

Her thin arm had snaked out of the covers. Her skin looked smooth and cool and dry. He reached out to touch her. She was going to be tall one day. Gangly. The boys would go crazy for her. One day. But for now she was his little girl.

11

They had just reached the police station when his cell phone rang.

"Bern Fortin," he said.

The voice at the other end of the line was muffled by a watery roar in the background. Bern recognized the pressurized shush of an espresso maker.

"Mrs. K.? Is that you?" Bern asked.

"Flour was on sale," she said. "Twenty pounds for seven dollars." Her voice was pitched higher than usual.

"Ah," he said. He was silent for a moment, piecing together the spaces between her words. "Your daughter," he said finally on an exhale.

He heard the espresso maker again. As far as Bern knew, there was only one in all of Kootenay Landing—besides the one in his own kitchen, of course.

"Mrs. K., I'm dying for a coffee. You didn't have yours yet, did you?"

"Huh. I just came in to use the phone. They want four dollars for a coffee here."

Bern smiled. "How about we say it's my treat? You go pick a seat for us. Pick a good one. I'll be right there."

"Huh," she said again, more relaxed this time.

"I'll just stop by the house and get my truck first, okay? That way, I can drive that flour home for you."

Five minutes later he found her at a table by the window, perched on the edge of her seat like she might bolt at any moment. At her feet lay the string bag, now filled with groceries. Next to it, leaning against one table leg, stood the bag of flour.

Bern slid in across from her, pushing back the chair to make room for his legs. There were only a few customers on hand. A small boy sat at one of the tables, playing with some toy figurines. Bern spotted Duke Forsberg hunched over his coffee cup at the table closest to the espresso bar.

A young woman with dark, cropped hair appeared before them, a tray filled with dirty coffee cups on her hip. She wore a raspberry tank top that was held up by two impossibly tiny straps. These intersected an intricate tattooed skull, complete with spiderwebs, roses, and a full set of teeth, an image that began at her throat and extended around her collarbones.

"You get that for Halloween?" Mrs. K. asked.

The girl laughed and fingered her collarbone. "No, no. It's permanent. Can I get you something?" she asked.

The lilt in her voice made Bern smile. "*Québécoise?*" he asked.

Her thin face brightened and she smiled at him. "*Mais oui!*" she exclaimed. "*Vous aussi?*"

When he nodded she put her tray down and opened her arms to him, planting a wet kiss on each cheek.

"So happy to meet you! It's been a long time since I could speak French to someone. You live here?" It all came out in a soothing babble of their native tongue.

"I live here," he said. "But have we met before? You seem familiar, but I can't place you."

"Ah, maybe? But I think I would have remembered. I usually work in the kitchen. I bake all the muffins and make the lunch orders. But Lennon had to go out, so here I am." She stopped suddenly and looked over at Mrs. K. "Do you speak French too?" she asked in English.

Mrs. K. shook her head, her face unsmiling.

"Oh, I'm so sorry. I get so excited and then I talk too much, that's what Lennon says. 'Work in the back. You're too slow when you start talking.' So what would you like?"

"What would you like, Mrs. K.?"

She waved a hand. "I don't know what it's called. A fancy coffee. Costs four dollars."

The girl smiled. "I have a specialty. Do you want to try that? I don't make it for just anyone." She put a hand on her hip. "It's a double shot of espresso, steamed milk, vanilla syrup, and then"—she leaned forward and whispered in Mrs. K.'s ear, but loud enough for Bern to hear—"I put whipped cream on top, with white chocolate sauce and a raspberry."

She stepped back and smiled triumphantly at them. When she saw that Mrs. K. didn't look convinced, she added, "And it's only three seventy-five."

Mrs. K. shrugged. "Okay, then," she said.

"Okay! One special for you, and for monsieur?"

He dipped his head at her and said, "I always have the same thing: triple espresso, neat."

Her lips were broad across the bottom of her face as she smiled. She wore no jewelry, was completely unadorned with the exception of the skeleton tattoo.

"Any food?" she asked.

Bern looked at Mrs. K. "What do you say? Can I treat you to lunch too?"

She scowled and shook her head. "My lunch is waiting at home. Yours too."

"Juste les cafés," he told the girl with a smile.

She held up two fingers. *"Deux minutes,"* she said, and was off.

The boy joined them just as the young woman came back with the coffees. He arranged a battalion of toy soldiers before them.

"Your son?" Bern asked, sticking to English in deference to Mrs. K., though she was too absorbed in the concoction placed before her to notice.

The young woman smiled down at the boy. "This is Gabriel," she said, pulling him close to her thigh and flattening his thick blond hair against his skull. "And I'm Aimée."

"I'm Bern," he said, leaning down and holding out a hand.

In place of a handshake the boy handed him a soldier made of molded plastic. He looked up with serious brown eyes. "I'm going to be a soldier," he said.

"Ah, I see," said Bern. He held the figure up to the window. "But don't copy this one. He's got it all wrong. See here?" he asked, pointing to the minuscule leg of the figure, which was crouched in a precarious lunge. "If he really shot his rifle from this position, he'd fall right over on his face."

The boy held out his hand for the figure, looking at it closely. "How do you know?"

"Because I am a soldier, *mon petit.*"

The boy's eyes swiveled back to him, wide and serious.

"Ah, don't tell him that!" Aimée cried. It came out like "dat." "Now he'll never leave you alone."

"Ça va," Bern said to her. "We're happy to talk to him."

Mrs. K. slurped her coffee and stared suspiciously at the boy. A bell jangled as the front door swung open and Aimée looked over to a group coming in the door.

"Lunch rush starting," she said. "I hope Lennon gets back soon. You okay for a minute? Gabriel, don't bug them."

Bern shooed her away. "He's fine." He patted the seat next to him, but the boy scooted off. He returned a moment later with a whole box full of soldiers, which he proceeded to set up on the table next to them.

"Do you know what happened to your daughter?" Bern asked. Mrs. K. and her daughter had been estranged for several years; Bern had never been able to find out why.

She stirred the layers of her coffee into one creamy consistency and shrugged.

"Did you phone her?" he asked.

She shook her head tersely.

"Maybe she got busy with something?" He chose his words with care. At some point they would make up, and he would be the first to forget there had ever been an argument. He had never met the daughter, but certainly Mrs. K.'s grandson, Brian, was a nice fellow.

"Maybe," said Mrs. K. Then she turned to look out the window, as though waiting to see if this was indeed the case.

The café was starting to fill with lunch customers. Duke Forsberg stayed in place, rolling his now-empty coffee cup between his meaty hands. He stared straight ahead with an intensity that took Bern by surprise. He followed the man's gaze and found it was directed at Aimée, behind the bar making a tray of fancy coffees.

Just then, she looked up at him and rolled her eyes. "Duke! You're staring again," she called out playfully with a wink in Bern's direction. "You want more coffee?"

Bern felt a tug on his sleeve and looked down to see Gabriel. The boy pointed to the soldiers, the off-kilter one now facing a squadron on horseback.

Bern shook his head slowly. "There are a few things a soldier must know," he said, seriously. He held up one finger. "He must know when to fire." Another finger. "He must know when to ask for help." Three. "He must know when to retreat."

"Retreat?" the boy repeated.

Bern echoed his solemnity with a nod. *"Retraite,"* he said, giving him the word in his mother's tongue. "Run away." He looked down at the beleaguered figure, about to be trodden into the earth by the hooves of a hundred horses. He flicked the soldier off the table with a finger, landing him in the lap of the boy's jeans. "He has to hide. It's his only chance!"

Bern started moving the galloping soldiers forward, and then milling them about in confusion.

"Where did he go? *Maudit!*" he said in the gravelly voice of the imagined commander. The boy's eyes widened even further at the French curse. "Where did he go?" With his fingers he galloped the commander over to Mrs. K.'s coffee cup, then around the saucer of his own long-empty espresso. "We lost him! *Regarde ça,*" Bern whispered to him.

One by one he set the soldiers in formation. "They can't find him. See? He's too good a hider. They are going in circles. Why? Because he went down. They are turning, turning, looking straight ahead. He went down. Or maybe . . ." He grabbed the soldier and placed it on top of the boy's head, a move that netted him a satisfying peal of giggles. "He went up, see? Now they'll never find him. Look how lost they are." He leaned sideways toward the boy and spoke very quietly into his ear. "We're laughing today, *oui*? But promise me, if you ever need to run away, you run away. Retreat. And go up."

The boy's giggles faded as he realized that the man had indeed turned into the soldier he said he was. Bern saw that the boy was afraid, but it was true: sometimes the ones in the trees survived.

"*C'est promis, Monsieur Soldat,*" he said.

Promise extracted, Bern sat back, suddenly exhausted. He shook his head. "Just Bern," he said. "Just call me Bern."

Gary made himself a brunch of cold oatmeal and water. He followed this up with another joint, which he smoked on the stoop. The only sounds under the dull sky of morning were of the birds and the stream and the occasional helicopter in the distance.

They were still looking for him. He knew that this meadow was only one of thousands of openings in the tree canopy on dozens of slopes and valleys. He could not yet light a fire, but he felt safe enough. For now, he had found his sanctuary.

He opened his palm to inspect his cut. A seam of new white skin had closed right over the slice, turning it into nothing more than a pink welt. It was healing—way faster than he'd expected—and it didn't seem to be infected. What was Seymour onto with this cream, anyway?

The thought of Seymour brought Cindy to mind, and for the first time in many years, he allowed his memory to roam freely over what had happened in this very place so many years ago.

It was the bush rave in this meadow that had bound Gary, Seymour, and Cindy on their path of teenage exploration. The rest of his high school years clearly divided from that point, like the rail line that cut through Kootenay Landing. Before the rave and after. Before ecstasy and after.

After the rave, Gary wanted that experience back—they all did. That aliveness, that presentness, the okayness of everything.

The silky softness of Cindy's hair on his forearm as they sat, the three of them, arm in arm in arm on a log for endless hours that passed like minutes. The jump and cackle of the fire kept them mesmerized. The dancing shadows, grooving with the blare of house music from someone's dad's pickup. Small-town teens, freed from a lifetime of sameness and limitation by a little white tablet.

After the rave, no matter how much pot they smoked or how many times they took 'shrooms or acid or even ecstasy, the feeling did not come back in the same way. Hollowed out, the groove of his life seemed bleak afterward. Gary wandered in a fog, though he still managed to sail through his math classes, his science classes, and even his language classes.

Cindy was always there. He first became aware of her just before the summer of the rave, at the end of tenth grade. Even though Seymour had his own locker, he seemed to store half his stuff in Gary's. And even though he had his own lunch, he seemed to need to consume Gary's as well. On this day, Cindy was at Gary's locker, eating Gary's lunch.

Seymour had his arm around her, which was nothing new— there were always girls hanging off Seymour. But this girl was dark, Native, with long shiny black hair that stretched to her waist. Tall and skinny in tight jeans, a black T-shirt, and cowboy boots. Her skin was the color of taffy. Her eyes black and distrusting. Gary looked back at her with the same distrust. He did not like her from the first minute they met. That never really changed over the next year. He didn't trust her, and with good reason: there was no limit to what Cindy Forsberg would do.

Now, as he examined their shared past, Gary could see what he had not seen then: Cindy was damaged from the start. Now Gary could see that the impulsiveness he and Seymour mistook

for wild abandon had clinical roots in brain wiring. A lack of im-
pulse control. A dangerous susceptibility to addiction.

A teenaged Gary, adrift since the death of his mother, and Seymour, who'd been lost and on the loose for as long as Gary had
known him, were swept up into the vortex that was Cindy. They
were simply along for the ride. It was a ride that, Gary could see
now, might never end. Unless he did something about it.

Bern saw the man the second he slowed the pickup to cross
the train tracks. He was seated on Bern's front steps, looking
completely out of place in his corduroys and trench coat, with a
schoolboy's satchel at his feet. Bern resisted the urge to press his
foot on the gas and hurtle down to the highway, with Mrs. K. and
her string bag in tow.

"Want to run away with me?" he asked her as he slowed to a
stop in front of her house.

"I can manage from here," she replied.

But of course he could not let her. She opened the door and
got out, tugging the hem of her town dress over her woolen
tights as she slid down from the truck. He was out the door and
behind her by the time she had pulled down the string bag of
groceries.

"No, no. Let me get that," he said, reaching for the flour.

The man was moving toward them. Bern held up a fist in a
basic military hand signal. Freeze. If there was any soldier left in
him at all, the man would obey. "Can't let him make a coward out
of me," he muttered, more to himself than to Mrs. K.

He heaved the sack of flour over his shoulder and followed
her to the back door, where she let herself in with a key that she

kept tied around her neck with a length of garden twine. He turned to survey her garden as he waited: piles of clippings that needed to be bundled, garden beds coated with a thick layer of compost ready to be dug in, stakes standing naked of their harvest, waiting to be stored away for winter. He'd have to come one day and help with the last jobs; he'd have to find the time.

"I have borscht," she called from inside. "Bread and pickles." It wasn't a question.

"I have to get back to work."

"You'll work much better with food in your stomach."

He thought of the sour pit that had had him begging eggs and a skillet from strangers the day before.

"I'll just go tell him," he called, walking back to the truck.

Though Bern knew his name perfectly well, he did not recognize the rabbit of a man who leaned against the post of his carport, waiting for him.

"Do you remember me?" Troy Thompson asked. He didn't hold out his hand, and Bern wasn't sure he would have taken it if he had.

Bern shrugged. "Not specifically. But I remember your type." Whiner. Whistle-blower. Troublemaker.

"You were my hero, you know that?"

Bern held up a firm hand to silence him. A commander still. "This is not the time."

"When is?"

"Later. When I'm done with my work for the day. I'd like to say when I'm done with this case, but I don't want you hanging around the fringes of my life until then."

"I did hear about the murder." The man paused. It was an invitation to tell the story. When Bern ignored him, he asked simply, "Where?"

"Kootenay Landing Hotel. The least you can do is buy me a drink."

"It would be my pleasure," Thompson said.

"We'll see about that. I'm not promising I'll say a word." Even if the past had caught up with him, Bern could see no reason to make things easy for this weasel of a man.

Thompson bowed slightly. "I'll be there from seven o'clock. Waiting for you."

"I'll be there when I get there," Bern said. He turned his back and went in for his borscht before Mrs. K. started fussing that it would get cold.

Quebec City, 1993

Tuesday morning he woke up alone on the floor. He'd let the fire go out, and the air, when he reached a bare arm out from the duvet, was frigid. All that was left in the space where she'd lain were her casings: a cashmere shawl, an embroidered robe, a peignoir.

He heard the click of her shoes on the marble floor and she appeared before him, all-black wool suit, black silk hose, heels that would cause her death if she walked any distance on an icy sidewalk. She held out her arms to him. In them was his freshly pressed uniform. He looked up to her face, a perfect mask of foundation and smudged kohl, her lips painted a venous red.

"Up, up," she said, not smiling. "My car will be here. And then the movers."

He stood and reached for his clothes. Her eyes moved over his naked body, appraising him as he dressed. Then they stood, together in their uniforms. He felt something in him loosen and break away—some part of him that would stay forever in the cocoon of silk and feathers they had shed.

He reached for her, but she shook her head and uttered a low growl, like a dog protecting a bone. *"Non,"* she said.

Eyes wide at the rebuke, he gestured to the duvet on the floor.

"*Laisse,*" she said. *Leave it.* "The movers will look after every-thing."

"Don't you have to pack anything? A suitcase?" he asked.

She gestured impatiently toward the foyer. "I have an over-night bag."

A chime sounded. It echoed around them as though the space had already been emptied of its furnishings. She stood taller and he instinctively offered his arm. With his other hand he grabbed his parka off the back of the couch, where it had sat, bearing witness, for two days. He escorted her to the door. She lifted her chin to the fur coat, folded over the edge of the banister.

He held it for her, and as she slid her arms in, he allowed him-self a moment to hold each of her round shoulders in his hands. Then he opened the door to the blinding light of cold sunshine. "Madame LeClerc," her chauffeur said with a bow. He took her arm from Bern's, and with that motion, the world they'd built shattered like an icicle.

The chauffeur escorted her to the car. Bern fetched her over-night bag and closed the door of the house behind him, hearing the click of the automatic lock. The chauffeur took the bag from him before he reached the street. He could see a white smudge through the darkened window, which he supposed was her cheek but might have been a reflection.

The chauffeur got into the driver's seat. Left alone on the sidewalk, Bern did the only thing he could do: he saluted and stood, unmoving, until the limo reached La Grande Allée and turned toward the airport.

12

Leigh pulled the lever and tipped a pitcher under the tap as Bern slid into his usual seat at the bar. She smiled over at him. "Served him doubles all night, only charged him for singles. He weaved his way up to his room about an hour ago—said he'd be right back, but I think you're safe. For tonight anyway."

"Thank you," he said.

She shrugged. "Don't thank me too much. I put the difference on your tab."

She placed the finished pitcher on a tray and got his whiskey ready—also a double.

He raised his glass in mock salute and took a sip. "A bargain at twice the price."

"'Kay, be right back," she said.

He watched her go. She wore faded jeans that fit just right over the round of her hips, the swell of her belly—no complicated cut or style, no bowing to the current trend, no pretending she was more, or less, than what she was. She wore a T-shirt from the Bugaboo Brewery. This too was a practicality, no doubt: until a new beer supplier came along with branded T-shirts for the bar staff, she'd stick with what she'd been given and not ruin her own clothes by wearing them to work.

He took another sip and watched her make her way through the bar, taking and giving orders with equal good humor. She put her hand on a man's shoulder, leaning closer to him to hear him. Then she threw her head back, delighted with whatever he had said. Still laughing, she caught Bern's eye from across the room.

He smiled back, then closed his eyes and looked away from her. He felt the buzz of his cell phone in its clip at his waist and pulled it up. Sauvé, the screen read.

"Oui, allô?"

"C'est Sauvé."

"Oui, colonel. Ça va?" he asked, though he could tell from his former commanding officer's pinched voice that something was wrong.

"He's dead."

"Qui?" he asked. Who was dead? Sauvé spent a lot of his time slaying already-dead ghosts.

"LeClerc. In his sleep. Peacefully. The bastard."

"You spoke to madame?"

The sigh that reached him across the ether was longer than the physical distance that separated them. "Called with my condolences."

"And? How is she?"

Sauvé barked a bitter laugh. "Madame LeClerc never changes."

"She has regrets too, if that is any help," he said. "We all do."

Sauvé grunted something.

"What did you say?"

"I said I always suspected as much," Sauvé spat. "That summer in New York? Is that when it happened?"

"Long ago now, Colonel. Long ago." Even as he said the words, something fluttered in him, a waft of perfumed softness, a giving over of himself.

"Not long ago!" Bern heard something slam, a fist on a table-top. "Don't give me that long-ago bullshit. It's alive in my life like it's happening right now. You too. Don't lie to me, Captain Fortin. Remember what I said that first day? 'Tell me the truth and we'll get along just fine.' Remember that?" Another slam, and then the sound of Sauvé's breath across the line.

Bern took a sip of his drink. Sixteen years later and Sauvé still called him Captain. Leigh was back now, drying glasses, not listening with a little too much studious attention.

"Did I lie to you, Colonel?" he asked.

"Were you with her in New York? Because if you were, that was a lie to start with."

"Then it was a lie. But not to you."

"Bastard."

"I'm not lying to you now, though, Colonel. It *was* long ago."

"Tell me it's not still with you?"

"Yes, it is. Like it just happened. But it was long ago."

"All her fucking fault."

"You can't blame her for Rwanda."

"Maybe not. But I can blame him. He's the reason I was there."

Bern shrugged at that. "Someone had to be," he said.

"But why me? And why did I have to come back alive?"

The colonel's voice broke with the question, and Bern felt a shudder in his own already weak foundation. He caught a movement out of the corner of his eye, and there was the ferret climbing onto the seat next to him.

"That is a question with no answer," he said at last. "Colonel? Are you there?"

He heard a shuffle. "Funeral is on Friday. Parade from the Plains of Abraham to the basilica."

"You going?"

"Of course. You?"

"I'll send her some flowers."

"Of course you will. You bastard."

Bern chuckled. "Speaking of bastards, I've got a sticky journalist at my side. Better go."

"Talk his ear off, but don't say anything. Isn't that what you always told me?"

"That's good advice. *Au revoir,* Colonel." He hung up before the other could respond.

Ruben saw the man as he approached the cabin. Fairly young, but old in the way that some men look old: tired at too young an age by responsibility, stress, and overconsumption. He was starting to get fat around the belly and losing hair, but maybe he was older than Ruben by only a few years. He was sitting on the stoop, smoking weed.

Interesting, thought Ruben. Perhaps there was something here. Perhaps fortune had not overlooked him after all.

Ruben made himself invisible so he could watch the man. He tucked himself around himself and became very, very quiet. When he did this he disappeared—at least for most people. Some, like the tall man who had caught him near *la doctora*'s garden the day before, had more sensitive instincts. Ruben had seen that tall man before: he wandered the woods too, and Ruben would see him at the flat rock overlooking the valley, waiting as though for something to come to him.

The man on the stoop of the cabin crushed out his joint and stared straight into the trees beyond the meadow, right where Ruben was hiding. He looked, but he did not observe, and

Ruben knew the man could stare all night and never see him hiding there.

For now, he filed the man in the old cabin away in his mind, a little piece of information, no doubt useful, perhaps profitable. He was sure, if he listened over the next few days, he would find out more about this man, about who he was and why he was in the woods.

Yes, perhaps fortune had not overlooked Ruben after all.

The man's eyes were bloodshot. His hair was a tousled mess. The skin around his artful goatee was pale and pimply with ingrown hairs.

"Let me buy you that drink," he said. His breath reached Bern in sour puffs.

Bern gestured at his almost-empty glass. "I'm about ready to move on to coffee," he said. That had always been his other piece of advice to Sauvé: Don't talk to reporters when you're drinking. "Looks like you might want to do the same."

Troy Thompson laughed, showing all the teeth crowded to the front of his mouth, glossy white where Bern expected them to be yellow.

"We've decided on coffee," Bern said as Leigh approached them. He ignored the questions he could see in the crease of her brow.

"I'll make a fresh pot," she said.

They sat and watched her. Troy leaned his head in his hands and rubbed at his eyes. Bern stared straight ahead, riding the wave of turmoil inside him. What did the man want from him? He closed his eyes for a moment, felt the wave crest and crash and subside, and in the hair's breadth before it began gathering force again, he felt a conviction: it was better not to talk. Not yet. The man could not force him, after all. No matter how far he'd come.

They waited in silence until Leigh brought the coffee. Thompson added two creamers and three packets of sugar and perked up visibly after a few sips. Bern took one bitter sip and pushed the chunky mug aside.

"You've come a long way," he said.

Thompson looked at him through eyes made glassy by the alcohol receding from his system. "I know there's a story in there," he said, pointing at Bern's chest. "I want it."

Bern's lip twitched at the desperation he sensed in the other man. "What makes you think it's yours to tell?"

Thompson snorted and tossed back the remainder of his coffee. "You're just like the rest of them, you know that? I was a soldier too." He thumped a hand on his own chest. "I was a stupid fucker in Somalia, twenty years old and shitting my pants and watching the guys take the fall for the shit the officers got us into. I did my time!"

"And then you got out."

Thompson shrugged. "I wanted to tell that story. And other stories. Tell the stories of what really happens. Make the bigwigs accountable to the soldiers, the way it should be."

He reached over and flipped open the flap of his satchel. It flopped on the seat, buckles jingling, as Thompson pulled out a glossy photo and slapped it on the bar.

Bern took one look and closed his eyes. He took a deep breath and fingered the edge of the photo. Then he picked it up and opened his eyes.

Corporal Alais stared back at him. Bern knew he had been moved to a civilian prison, which explained his longer hair.

Always a little unruly, even when clipped to regulation, it was wild now with waves of tight red curls. His skin had always been pale: Bern remembered Alais reaching constantly for sunscreen in the Afghan desert. He'd joked with his subordinate that if they survived, at least he wouldn't get skin cancer. Alais's skin in the photo was pasty from lack of sun, and doughy around the chin and neck from lack of exercise. But it was the eyes that made Bern swallow and look away. Even the last time Bern had seen them, when Alais was confessing to his alleged crime, those eyes had been full of spark and vigor and the get-it-done attitude that Bern had come to rely on. The eyes that looked out at him from this photo were vague and dull. Unimaginative.

"When was this taken?" Bern asked.

"Last month. I went to see him at Bordeaux Prison."

"They let a reporter in?"

Thompson shrugged. "We were in the same platoon at one time. I said I was an old friend."

"But you're not a friend. Not if you're going to take his story and sell it to the world."

Leigh approached with the coffeepot and refilled Thompson's cup. She raised an eyebrow at Bern's untouched mug and he shook his head. He followed the line of her hips as she walked away again, aware of Thompson next to him, emptying a fourth container of cream into his coffee.

"I don't see those two things as mutually exclusive," Thompson said, taking a sip. Now that the journalist was more alert, Bern could feel his mistrust of the man coming back. He was sly, of that there was no doubt. Even now, with his hungover, jet-lagged eyes, Bern could see the sliver of judgment that had kept him from being a true soldier. Some part of Thompson no doubt questioned every order. He'd take a moment to assess, to survey, to make his own judgment. And that moment, however fleeting, was dangerous. That moment would cost lives.

Bern locked eyes with the younger man and marveled that even the Canadian army could not reach inside some men and stamp out this will.

"If telling the truth of this story gets Alais free," Thompson argued now, "I don't really see how it matters."

Bern tipped his head only slightly, to concede the man's point.

"Look at him," Thompson said.

Bern shook his head. "I have seen enough to know," he said, and slid the photo back across the bar.

"Then you see, right?"

Bern closed his eyes and pressed the tips of his long fingers to his forehead. It seemed they were all there inside him, and with each press of the pads of his fingers they made themselves known: Corporal Alais, Colonel Sauvé, General LeClerc. Madame LeClerc was the painful spot above the arch of his right eyebrow. Rwanda he carried whole in the sagging dark circle under his left eye. Afghanistan pounded in his temple. Alais and his deeds were buried deep under the crown of his head. His own deeds were buried even deeper.

"Tell me what happened that day," Thompson said, leaning forward and breathing his creamy coffee breath on Bern.

"The events of that day are not in dispute," he said. "If you've spoken to Alais, you know that. He came across a mortally wounded Taliban soldier. A man whose breath rattled through the holes that punctured his body. A man who would have lain for hours, possibly days, before death claimed him. Tormented by the remains of life, baking in the desert sun, his bloody hole of a body filling with sand."

Danger, danger! Stop talking! But he could not. The anger shot through him.

"There is no question: Alais shot him. The question is not whether it happened. Or even whether it was the right thing to do. The question is whether it was legal."

Thompson rolled his eyes and huffed through his nose. "I didn't come all the way here for the party line," he said. He stood, collected his satchel, and left the photo on the counter. "You sit here, Fortin, as your soldier rots in a civilian jail with murderers and rapists, with Hells Angels and Vietnamese gang members. And meanwhile his wife is at home, raising their daughters alone. Do you think he deserves to be there?"

"Of course not!"

Thompson leaned close. "I may be an outsider, but I know how to tell the story that will set him free." He jutted his chin at Bern. "Think about that. And answer your goddamn phone tomorrow when I call you."

He stalked out then, a man barely tall enough to be a soldier, and too independent to follow the clearest of orders. Bern watched him go out the door into the hotel lobby. Then he watched the door long after he was gone, all the while feeling Alais's eyes, devoid of hope, staring up at him from the photo on the bar. Let him watch, goddamn it. He'd done nothing wrong.

He gestured to Leigh for another whiskey, and when she brought it, he looked down at Alais and raised his glass.

"Chin-chin," he said.

New York City, 1993

The summons came months later, from a Colonel Sauvé at UN Headquarters in New York City. Did he want to go to Rwanda, as Sauvé's executive assistant? It would be a few months at most, to oversee a peace agreement.

"Make sure everyone is sticking to the deal. Simple stuff." Sauvé's voice had a gruff certainty to it that Bern liked immediately. "General LeClerc himself said you were the perfect man for the job." Bern hung up the phone knowing there was only one way the general could even know his name. *Damned if you do, damned even worse if you don't.*

New York in July was like being wrapped in a steam room towel that hadn't been washed. Bern found his way through the warrens and tunnels of the peacekeeping office, each hallway a microcosm of some larger international conflict. He found that if he kept his mouth shut and his ears open, he could maneuver through any conversation and bring a morsel back to Colonel Sauvé.

General LeClerc, he rarely saw. Rwanda was only one of the UN missions on the table, and LeClerc was in charge of the whole patch. Madame LeClerc was in New York—this much he had been able to discern—shopping, lunching, and hosting elaborate dinners from her home base: a sprawling apartment not far from UN headquarters.

Bern worked endless days and nights in a borrowed office, sharing a desk and at times a chair with Sauvé. His long walks through the corridors, which they soon dubbed reconnaissance missions, since this was where their most reliable intelligence came from, were driven by necessity.

A few hours out of each twenty-four—sometimes as dawn was already spreading across the skyline—he'd make his way to his closet of a room in a house reserved for junior officials. His high-ceilinged rectangle of a room, barely big enough for the single bed and the wooden wardrobe, had one redeeming feature: a sash window with a dark wood frame and a tiny view of the East River in the distance. He would lie there for a few hours—he could not call it sleeping—and imagine her beside him. Madame LeClerc. Sasha. Imagine them together in the heat, free of the feathers and silk and cashmere that had covered them in winter. Free of the ornate mantel, the carved banister, the tinkling chandelier. He'd imagine them in his room with only the striped mattress covered by a thin white sheet. There was a window to open when she wanted to smoke, a water closet with barely enough room to turn around. Whatever she wore, he would peel off her, piece by piece. There would be nothing to hide.

13

Once again, Gary started his day on the stoop, smoking a joint as he watched the morning light leach its way into a sky heavy with clouds. He was cold, and yet he did not want to go inside. It felt like Cindy was there, waiting for him. Waiting to face him.

He stared out at the pale meadow. The mountains would appear soon, but for now in the half dark he could be anywhere, on any stoop, in any forest, anywhere in the world. Why was he still on this stoop, in this forest?

He inhaled again and held the smoke deep in his lungs. His already relaxed body let go even further and he felt the desire to be free of Cindy at last.

When he and Michelle had first gotten engaged, they'd gone with Duke on a trip to Vancouver. Gary hadn't known what they were in for, but Michelle must have. After dim sum in Chinatown, Duke pulled out a stack of photocopied flyers. "Have you seen this girl?" they read.

Michelle had done that thing with her eyes, and he'd wanted to do anything to help her. So he went along with it. He showed Cindy's photo to clustered groups and sleeping figures along Hastings, along Main, along Cordova. They stopped at First United Church and visited the soup kitchen and the women's center, though Gary was not allowed in there. Women only. Michelle had gone alone, and when she came out, white as a sheet, she told him what they were saying: women were going missing, and the police were looking for a serial killer.

"But have they seen Cindy?" Gary knew, even as he asked the question, that they hadn't. He'd known that even before Duke had pulled out the posters, before that first dinner at the Forsbergs' house.

"They found her backpack. In a rooming house. You know that, right?" Michelle asked.

"I know, you told me," he said. *Like a thousand times,* he thought but did not say. He just rubbed her back.

"What if he got to her before people around here even knew her?" Michelle cried out. "They think someone's been killing girls—prostitutes—for years!"

A man shuffled by, a muttering mass of torn clothing. He stopped at Gary and ducked his head in toward Michelle.

"He being good to you? He being good?"

Gary put his arm out to push the man away and his hand sank into the greasy rubble of fabric. The smell reached him—overcooked vats of soup, train grease, and underneath it all, the smell of human decay.

"I'm okay. He's good," Michelle said.

The pile of cloth swatted Gary's hand away. "Don't touch, man. Don't touch," his voice croaked from between the folds. "You be good to the lady. Find me if he's no good. I'll look after you."

"Christ, let's get out of here," Gary said.

He should have said something back then. That day. But how? After that trip had come the list.

"The police have a list, Gary," Michelle told him one night. "Of all the girls who've gone missing. All the girls they think have been killed. We've got to get Cindy on that list. Get them looking for her."

So Gary had called. To get on the list, they needed DNA and dental records. Gary had helped Michelle with those too. Should he have?

How could he not?

He had waited for years. Eight years since he and Michelle started dating. Sixteen years since Cindy disappeared. But it was never the right time to speak up.

Gary knew now that the right time would never come. If he wanted to be free of Cindy—and Seymour—he'd have to make his own timing. He'd tear off the Band-Aid in one swift motion, yes, he would. Today.

He sucked in the last of the joint and let it fall to the ground and burn out. He'd have to pick it up. He'd have to pick all of them up. He'd do that too. But first, he needed to look after Cindy. And get her out of his life for good.

They weren't really open. Not yet. But the first customer sidled in the door early, because Aimée had unlocked it early—again.

"Hey, can you come back in ten minutes?" Lennon called in his usual cheerful tone. "We're not quite open yet."

The man kept walking toward the counter. "I just need a bunch of coffees," he said. His dark hair was cropped close to his scalp in the way that appealed to balding executives. His eyes darted everywhere like he was casing the joint, everywhere but back at Lennon.

"We're not open yet," Lennon said, more firmly this time. He didn't like the guy's vibe.

"I just need some coffees."

Damn it, Aimée. How many times had he told her to keep the door locked until they opened? *Who cares, Lennon?* she'd say in that accent of hers that he used to think was cute. *They want to spend money, why make them wait for a certain time?*

"We don't have any food ready yet," Lennon said.

The guy was right up at the counter now. He looked Native, but the dark jeans and pressed white shirt threw Lennon off. The clean-cut, corporate First Nations look was not one he was used to seeing around here.

"I just need some coffees," the guy said again. Still, he wouldn't look at Lennon.

"Fine. What can I get you?"

Their eyes met for just a second and Lennon caught his breath. The man's were bright blue where he expected them to be brown. And hard. Criminal hard. Jail-time hard.

He could hear Aimée behind him, talking to a sleepy Gabriel while she made a last batch of muffins. Lennon kicked the swinging door to the kitchen shut.

The customer looked up at the chalkboard menu. "Three Americanos. All double. A large mocha. Two chai lattes. And a caramel macchiato."

"To go?" Lennon asked, trying to get his happy groove back but knowing it would take him until opening to make all those coffees. He wouldn't have time to count the float or set out the cream and fill the sugar before the morning rush. Let alone get the muffins and scones into the display case. He'd be playing catch-up all day.

But it's a big order, Lennon! Aimée would say. *Don't turn away a paying customer just because you don't like his eyes.*

Lennon lined up seven biodegradable paper cups on the

counter and started on the order. He couldn't get a rhythm going, though. First he misjudged the amount of milk he needed, so he had to steam a second batch. Then he ran out of chai concentrate and had to call back to Aimée to bring him more.

He felt a shift in the air when she came in. He turned to see the man, still as a pole, staring right at her with a light in those mean eyes that Lennon did not like one bit.

"Lennon, take it! I've got to get the muffins out," Aimée said, pushing the Tetra Pak against his shoulder.

He took the chai and she was gone. The man stood staring as the door to the kitchen swung closed behind her.

It took forever but Lennon finally got the order ready. He placed the cups in two trays on the counter, all under the watchful gaze of those hard eyes.

"That'll be twenty-two fifty," he said.

The man looked right at him then. Straight in the eye and did not look away. He lifted one tray and then the other, and stepped back.

"Take it from what you owe us," he said with a smile that twisted in Lennon like a knife. "Maybe we can work out a deal. She can work off your debt, or some of it anyway. Hm?" He chuckled as he said it, jutting his chin toward the kitchen door and Aimée behind it.

And then he was off. Lennon stood, hands raised helplessly in the air, as the clean-cut man with the eyes of a hunter walked out of the store.

"Hey!" he called after him. "Come back here!"

The man didn't turn around, just shoved the door open with his shoulder and stepped onto the sidewalk and out of sight.

Lennon ran out after him. On the sidewalk he called out again. "Hey! Come back!"

But the man was gone. Lennon was alone on the sidewalk. Somewhere a vehicle started up, the sound absorbed by the cotton batting of early morning cloud cover.

"Everything okay, Lennon?" a voice asked.

He turned to see Maddie standing behind him. She didn't look like a cop at all when she was out of uniform. He swallowed. "Yeah. Just a—Never mind. You ready for your coffee?"

"Yeah. You open? I'm a little early."

"No worries, Constable. Come on in. I've got a mudslide with your name on it."

Bern drank his triple espresso while standing on the back porch. The heavy clouds from the day before had settled stubbornly overnight and showed no sign of lifting. He stood under the overhang of the roof and surveyed his garden. What was it missing? He had turned the soil. He'd weeded and mulched. He'd cut tarps to size and secured them over each bed. The paths between were wide and tidy. Everything was square and perfect and devoid of life.

He thought back to Gia's garden. Even in almost full fallow, it teemed with life. Mrs. K.'s garden, a corner of which he could see from his vantage point, was similar: orderly yet lively. The liveliness was what was missing from his own, and he felt the hollowness of failure square in his chest. The trill of his cell phone kept him from traveling further down the road of his shortcomings.

"Fortin," he answered.

"Can you get in here?" As usual, Resnick skipped the preamble.

"Has something happened?" Bern asked.

"You mean other than the dead guy in the marsh? And the missing dad who might have killed him? Other than that, you mean?"

"I mean, are there new developments?" Bern checked his watch. "I assume that's why you're calling. It's barely seven o'clock. I've never known you to be much of a morning person."

Resnick ignored the barb. "I want you to go with Schilling and bring in the good doctor."

"Dr. Sinclair? Why?"

"You really need to ask why I want you to bring in the only witness we can find? We asked her to come in and give a statement. She hasn't. She left the scene. Do you need me to go on?"

"I'm just not sure why you want me to go with Schilling."

"Because you're the one who let her get away," Resnick said. "Now you're going to sweet-talk her into coming back."

"I need twenty minutes," Bern said.

"I can give you five."

"Well—" Bern began, but Resnick had already hung up.

He swilled the last of his coffee and ducked his head around the side of the house. Brian's bike was there. He was safe to skip breakfast and get right to work. He was about to grab his windbreaker and head straight to the police station when he thought better of it. He'd best say hello, at least.

Mrs. K. was sitting with her grandson, watching him eat. Before the gangly teen lay a platter of food: eggs and pickles, cheese, thick slices of sourdough toast. They made a perfect pair, Bern thought—Brian with his bottomless hunger, and Mrs. K. with her continuous need to love people by feeding them. The rich aroma of cinnamon and yeast told Bern that it was cinnamon bun day. Good thing he hadn't skipped breakfast.

She jumped to her feet when he came in.

"Sit back down, please, Mrs. K.," he said. "Visit with Brian. You don't need to worry about me."

"What are you going to do? Get your own breakfast?"

He shrugged. "It has been known to happen."

She grunted in that way he was beginning to know so well. "Men don't eat breakfast unless we women make them. And then they are grumpy all day long. I know this," she said.

She slid an overflowing plate of sliced, diced, boiled, and pickled food in front of him. This she followed with a cup of tea and another grunt.

Brian shot Bern a nervous look out of the corner of his eye. Bern winked at him and smiled up at Mrs. K. "We'll eat this, gratefully. But what we want to know, Brian and I both, is when are the cinnamon buns ready?"

"Ha! Cinnamon buns. You boys never change." He saw her smile with pleasure as she walked away. "They'll be too hot to eat when they come out of the oven."

"I like them hot," Brian said.

"Best like that. With the icing melting on top." Bern's phone rang as he said this and he reached into his pocket to turn the ringer off.

"You have to eat breakfast first," Mrs. K. said, pointing at his pocket. "I don't care who died."

"Rules are strict around here," Bern said to Brian.

"For good reason," Mrs. K. retorted.

She pulled the tray of cinnamon buns out of the oven and began the complex process of separating them, cooling them and icing them. Bern was dying to ask Brian what had become of his mother the day before, but he dared not bring it up. The rift in the family was just one of the unmentionable topics at Mrs. K.'s table.

"How come your garden looks like that?" he asked instead.

Her strong brows pulled together in a deep furrow. "Like what? What's wrong with it?"

"No, no, nothing's wrong. It's just that it's so lively, even when the season is done and everything is dead." Bern shifted in his seat as the phone vibrated in his pocket. He didn't dare answer it now.

"Huh."

"Huh? Is that all you're going to say?" He looked over at Brian, who busied himself with a hard-boiled egg. The boy caught his eye, hunched his shoulders, and got right back to his food.

"The garden doesn't die, that's why. You wrapped yours all tight like in a coffin. But the garden is alive. Needs room to breathe."

"So what do I do?" he asked.

She shrugged. "Try again next year." She came back to the table and stood over them, inspecting their plates. Judging that they'd eaten enough, she took them away and replaced them with a tray of cinnamon buns, hot and heady-smelling.

"These are the best. Gramma, can I ask you something?" Brian's voice was tentative.

"You ask anything. I might say yes or no. But you ask."

"My basketball team is having a bake sale. In case we make it to provincials? To help with the bus and hotel and stuff? Anyway, will you make something?"

Mrs. K. waved a hand. "Of course I make. Cinnamon buns? You want those?"

He nodded. "They'd sell for a lot. It's next Wednesday. Okay?"

"Okay, no problem," she said. She opened a grocery-sized paper bag and slid in two plastic-wrapped egg sandwiches on thickly sliced bread for the boy's lunch. To Bern, her movements seemed livelier than before and he knew she was pleased that Brian had asked her.

"My mom always goes and buys stuff, you know, from the grocery store. It's kind of embarrassing," Brian said quietly.

Mrs. K. huffed. "She never learned that from me," she said. Then she seemed to soften. "Tell you what. If you make provincials, I'll make these for the whole team. Okay?"

His whole face brightened. "Will you? That would be great."

She nodded. "I used to do that for your mother."

Brian was busy eating, so Mrs. K. turned to Bern.

"Did you talk to Mrs. Forsberg yet?" She wiped an imaginary spot off the kitchen table with a striped dishtowel as she spoke.

"I did," Bern said, fingering his cinnamon bun. "I met her yesterday."

"Didn't I say? She's good people."

"She is, but I had a feeling there was something she wasn't telling me. Did you see her husband yesterday? When we were at the coffee shop?"

"I'm not talking about him." Mrs. K. waved the dishtowel as though swatting a fly. "You should go back. Talk to her again."

Bern knew it wasn't a suggestion. "I'll try, okay?" He felt his phone vibrate again, and this time he answered it.

"I said twenty minutes, Resnick."

"And I said five," Resnick replied smoothly. "Schilling's out front waiting for you."

Bern hung up without answering. "Sounds like I need to get going," he said to Mrs. K. Between her, Resnick, and the nosy reporter, he wasn't sure anymore who was in charge of his life. It certainly didn't seem to be him.

"But you haven't touched your cinnamon bun!"

Bern slapped Brian playfully on the shoulder. "You'll finish it for me, won't you, Brian?"

The boy who would soon be a man simply nodded and waved, his mouth too full to answer.

A man in a hospital gown slept in a chair, his arm hooked to a bag of fluids, his face as gray and still as if he had died already. A red-faced toddler sat listlessly in his mother's lap. Schilling kept moving and tried not to look. Sick people made her nervous. The coroner followed closely behind. She was glad when they were able to walk straight through to the nurses' station without being stopped.

"We're here to see Dr. Sinclair."

The nurse looked up from the chart she was reading. Audrey, her name tag read. Her look said, *You can't put one over on me.*

"I'm working triage in the waiting room, so you can wait there. Take a seat if you're not well."

Thanks to the magic cream, Schilling was feeling just fine and there was no way she was going to be mistaken for a patient. She put both hands on the counter and pulled out her tall voice, the one they taught her at the police academy.

"I'm Constable Schilling of the RCMP. I need to speak with Dr. Sinclair on a matter of police business. Immediately."

Before the nurse could answer, Dr. Sinclair's face appeared from behind a partition. She had the kind of hair that always looked perfect, Maddie thought. And a body that made Schilling feel even more stumpy than usual. Her face too—even when it was pinched with exhaustion, as it was now, she looked beautiful.

"I can't see you right now. I've got a waiting room full of people," the doctor said, her voice steeped in fatigue.

"Dr. Sinclair, can we at least speak with you privately for a minute?" Schilling softened her voice this time.

The doctor's eyes narrowed as she looked from Maddie to Bern.

"I have no reason to speak to Coroner Fortin. I've been on call for over thirty-six hours and have saved three people from becoming customers of his." Her gaze returned to Schilling. "But I'll talk to you."

As Maddie stepped behind the partition, Dr. Sinclair pointed to a hospital bed. "Sit," she said. "I'll be right with you."

Schilling shook her head and dropped her shoulders. "I'd rather stand, thanks. This won't take long."

Dr. Sinclair wasn't listening. She sat before a desk, typing into a computer. An X-ray popped up on the screen and she leaned in closer to take in the details. Schilling could not tell what kind of bone it was but she looked away in embarrassment, as though she'd caught a stranger undressing. The doctor made a notation on a chart and chewed on her lip. A page over the loudspeaker interrupted her thoughts.

"Dr. Sinclair, line one. Dr. Sinclair, line one."

She grabbed the phone. "Sinclair."

She listened for a moment, and when she spoke, her tone reminded Schilling of her own mother's voice when she was in a certain mood. Maddie and her brother called it her "quiet but deadly" voice.

"Shift change? Do you think that matters to me? Last time you called you said you had a crew on the way! I'm a hundred miles from anywhere with a cardiac patient who is not going to make it to shift change. I need a helicopter and a bed."

She listened for another moment, then evidently interrupted the speaker on the other end. "You don't seem to understand. I don't need any more reasons why this can't happen. I need a bed and a helicopter. I'm getting him ready for transport. Call back within half an hour and tell me who is picking him and where they're taking him." Then she hung up the phone without waiting for a reply.

"I told you to sit on the bed."

Schilling dropped her shoulders again, her hand on her belt. "I'm not one of your patients. I came to bring you into the station to get your statement."

Dr. Sinclair put down the file she was holding. "Sit."

The constable hiked up all twenty pounds of her duty belt and clambered onto the bed. She felt like a kid up there, legs dangling. So much for being in charge.

"You are the only witness to a murder, Dr. Sinclair. You can't ignore that fact," she said, trying to regain some ground.

"Oh? Is that right?" The doctor's voice was as calm as it had been on the phone. Maddie was struck again by how pretty she was. Where most women would have looked haggard and exhausted, the stress and lack of sleep gave Dr. Sinclair an air of elegant vulnerability. "Let's look at some facts that you're ignoring. I'm the only doctor in town at the moment. Without me, some of these people will die. That's a fact."

"So you're a superhero? You've been at it for a day and a half already. How long do you think you can keep it up?"

"As soon as I get this cardiac shipped out, I'm going to take a nap for a few hours. But then I'll keep going."

"Until when?"

"Until all the sick people have been seen. Or my colleague gets back from holidays. But how about you?"

"How about me what?"

"How long can you keep it up?"

"Keep what up?" What was happening here? Hadn't she come to do the interrogating? To get a witness, and possible suspect, to come in and make a statement? When did it become about her?

"We'll need to get some tests to be sure, but I bet you feel like crap, right? Tired, run-down, out of breath?" Dr. Sinclair stood before her, inspecting Maddie's complexion. "I'm guessing anemia."

"Can you treat me if I don't consent to it?"

"No," replied the doctor. "Look up."

"Look up?" Schilling looked up. She felt Dr. Sinclair's fingers on her right eyelid. She lifted the upper lid, then after a moment let it drop.

"Any pain? Menstrual issues?"

Schilling blinked and rubbed at her eyelid. When she didn't answer, Dr. Sinclair sighed and turned away.

"You need a full workup: blood work, pelvic exam, maybe even an ultrasound to figure out what is going on for sure. But I can give you this in the meantime." She went back to the desk and scribbled on a prescription pad. "It's an iron supplement. It's not a prescription, but it is behind the counter. Go see my pharmacist at the clinic and he'll get your dose sorted out. It will take a week or two until you have more energy, but at least it's a start. We still need to get at the root cause, whether it's menses or some kind of bowel inflammation, or something else. While you're there, stop at the front desk and make an appointment to see me. I'm not taking new patients but tell Michelle you spoke to me and I said it was okay. In the meantime, try to take it easy. Not too much stress. Anything else?"

Schilling finally spoke up. "When can I tell my boss you're

coming in? Because if you're worried about my stress, that's my number one problem right now."

"Tell him I'll be in when all the patients have been seen." She was interrupted by another page. "That'd better be my bed and my helicopter," Dr. Sinclair muttered as she reached for the phone.

"I had breakfast with your mother this morning," Bern said.

The nurse paused her typing and looked up from the screen, eyes wary. They were Mrs. K.'s eyes, and Brian's, but the rest of her was all her own. She was taller than her mother, and in her raspberry-red scrubs, she was dressed more fashionably than her mother ever was. She started typing again without looking away from him.

"You're not going to wait in the waiting room, are you?"

He smiled and pulled a chair up to her desk. "I will in just a minute," he said. "Just tell me, don't you miss her?"

"Who? My mom?" A printer whirred behind her and she spun toward it.

He nodded.

"You're her new neighbor, right?" she asked, spinning back to face him. "I've heard about you." She made a note on the print-out and attached it to a waiting clipboard.

"I'm her neighbor. And the coroner."

"Yes, well, I knew that much."

"Now that we have that established, don't you miss her?" He crossed ankle over knee and sat back, waiting.

She held the clipboard upright and tapped it twice on the desk. "I'll tell you this, because I want to get rid of you, and only for that reason: my mother and I don't get along. We see the world entirely differently, and she has no room for my way of seeing things."

"She has her strong opinions, it's true," Bern said.

"It's way more than that. Different opinions don't exist to her. She doesn't like to be challenged, and I've got ideas of my own." She looked over his shoulder into the waiting room and stood. When she spoke again, it was more quietly. "Trust me. It's better this way."

"And yesterday?" Bern asked.

"Yesterday?"

"She's trying to pretend she's not hurt. But she's made a full batch of borscht and enough cinnamon buns to feed every patient in this hospital for a week."

"I'm sorry, you've lost me. Yesterday?" She walked past his chair and ducked her head into the waiting room. "I'll be with you in a minute. Please have a seat," she called out to someone Bern couldn't see.

He stood too and turned to face her. "You were going for coffee? She was going to ask you to drive her home, so she bought a bag of flour." He paused when he saw the pained realization hit her eyes.

"Let me guess. A fifty-pound bag," she said, rubbing her palm on her forehead.

He shrugged. "Twenty, but still. She called me when you never showed up. I went and got her."

She gave a guttural grunt that sounded just like her mother's. "Surprised she didn't just drag it home out of spite."

"That's something she may have been able to do once. But not anymore."

The look on her face was one of sheer misery. "I said I would go when she called and asked me for coffee. But then we got hit with a trauma—a car accident—and I had to call everyone in and stayed way past my shift. By the time I finally went home . . ." She sighed. "Yesterday is just a blur. That kind of day always is. I forgot all about meeting her until just now, when you reminded me. Tell her I'm sorry?"

"I can tell her," Bern said, "but wouldn't it be better coming from you?"

She looked lost and he felt a momentary pang that he'd upset the careful order of her day.

"I will talk to her," he said when she didn't answer.

Schilling came out then, with a prescription sheet in her hand but no Dr. Sinclair. "Let's get out of here," she said.

He handed the nurse a card. "Feel free to call me anytime. Maybe I can help somehow." He shrugged as he said it. "Not sure how. But I want to help. How's that?"

She took the card without a word. Bern glanced one last time at her familiar eyes and stepped past her into the waiting room.

"I have to go to the clinic," Schilling said once they reached the parking lot. "See the pharmacist."

"Let me guess. To get her to talk, you agreed to seek medical attention for whatever ails you."

Schilling rolled her eyes as she opened the door to the cruiser. "I wish," she said. "She bullied me into getting medical attention, then played the superhero card. Said she'd talk to Resnick when she was done saving lives."

Bern climbed into the passenger seat. Schilling's face was pale and her chin hung barely an inch over the steering wheel. If Mrs. K. still drove, no doubt she'd look like that. "I think she might have a point," he said.

"Well, whatever," Schilling said, twisting right around in her seat to check her blind spot before backing up. "I'd better get this done right away. When Resnick finds out the good doctor is not coming in, he'll put me on some shit job for the rest of the week. So do you want to wait while I go to the clinic, or can I drop you somewhere?"

Bern thought of Mrs. K.'s reminder from this morning. *Talk to her again.* It wasn't just a suggestion. "How about you drop me back at the Forsbergs'?"

"You're going to give that another try, huh?"

"Yeah," he said as she pulled into traffic. "Pick me up when you're done and we'll go back to the station to take on Resnick together."

Kootenay Landing, 1984

The need for her moved through his body. There, in the privacy of her bedroom, Duke finally gave way. It was dark. Cindy was sleeping. What harm could there be? Once again he told himself he wouldn't. He shouldn't. But this time, he slid his hand under the waistband of his sweatpants and over the protrusion of his belly.

The thoughts came but he pushed them away. Warped and perverted—yes. Beyond the allowable—yes. But he could not stop. Her delicate arm against the white bedspread; her glistening hair; her grateful eyes now closed in sleep. Her innocent perfection promised him something—a moment of joy, of forgetting. He had held back for so long. All he wanted was release.

If he had other thoughts he did not let them in. Later they would torture him. But now he closed his eyes, his hand moving swiftly, up and back, up and back. Within seconds he was beyond the stopping place—had there been one?—and he opened his eyes to find her watching him.

She slipped out of bed and stood before him: a skinny eight-year-old with teeth that were going to cost him a fortune and more scars inside her than the ones that glistened like feathers on her skin.

He pulled his hand out of his pants and stared back at her, breath short and sharp.

She held his gaze, her face serious. Then she moved forward and tugged at the waistband of his pants. He moved his hand out of the way and put it on top of her silky head. He kept his eyes open, to take everything in. Because this would never happen again. It would not. And anyway, to close his eyes would be to allow the thoughts that he could not think right now. Thoughts like, *How the hell did she know just what to do?*

14

"Hello, Holly," Bern called out. He tapped the roof of the police cruiser as Schilling drove away and stepped onto the pumpkin-lined front path. Holly Forsberg was standing in the middle of the lawn, dressed more casually than the day before, in jeans and a bright-blue windbreaker. In her hand she held a cardboard box, which she pulled back in surprise when she saw him.

"Oh! Hello there. I wasn't expecting you!"

"I just wanted to ask you a few more questions, if that's all right? Can I help you with that?" He crossed the lawn and reached out for the box.

"I was just going to put up some more Halloween decorations. Do you mind if we talk while I work?" she asked. "I like to keep busy."

"That I can understand. I'm that way myself," he said with a slight bow.

"Wait here," she said. She headed to the house and returned a moment later with a folding stepladder. Bern followed her to the center of the lawn, where she set the stepladder under a tree already bare of its leaves. He shielded his eyes against the sun pressing through the woolen clouds. This kind of dull, glaring sky always gave him a headache.

He looked down at the box in his hands to see a family of ghosts staring back up at him. Mrs. Forsberg had set up the stepladder and was about to climb up when he stopped her.

"Would you like me to get up there? I'll be able to reach the higher branches." He pulled out a ghost and held it up. It was a tiny white plastic bag, stuffed with what looked like shredded paper, held together with a twist tie and imprinted with a little smiling face. Friendly ghosts. "You can tell me exactly where to put them."

Those seemed to be the magic words. She took the box from his hands. "Start with a high one," she said as he stepped up on the ladder. "Then alternate with a lower one."

He reached up to hang a friendly ghost on a hook provided by an upper branch. "Like this?"

"Yes, that's good," she said, and handed him another.

They worked in silence for a few minutes, Bern dutifully alternating ghosts on upper and lower branches. She seemed to have forgotten that he was there to talk to her about something. Either that or she was perfectly comfortable pretending he'd just popped by to help her with the decorations.

He waited until he had to move the stepladder.

"Heard anything from Gary?" he asked as he stood back up on the ladder, reaching for another high branch.

"No, not that one. It's too close. Move it over to the right a bit." Her windbreaker rustled as she pointed.

Bern looked directly into the hazy glare of the clouds to find a branch slightly to the right of the first. He felt the inevitable headache spread under the plate of his forehead.

"That's better," she said. She smiled up at him, her features more relaxed than he'd seen before. "That's just right."

Bern hung it there, though to him it looked the same either way. "You were saying? About Gary?" he prompted.

She raised her hand up to her mouth and the ghost hooked between her fingers fluttered in the air. She shook her head quickly. "He hasn't been here."

"But this is unusual, yes? You mentioned that when he's done this in the past, he's always come back after a few hours." He reached his hand down for the ghost in her fingers and she released it to him. He found a new branch and asked, "Here?"

She nodded, then waved her hand quickly at him, her nod turning into a shake of the head. "Lower, lower. It's a low one now, right? High, low, high. Now low."

Bern took a patient breath. "My apologies. How about here?"

"Yes, better." She was back to nodding now. "Michelle is very upset. She's letting herself fall apart a little," she said with a sniff.

Black dots appeared before his eyes as Bern stepped down to move the ladder. He blinked them away, wishing he'd thought to wear sunglasses. "I wonder if it might be better if we switched places? If you go up one step higher than me, you'll reach the upper branches without too much trouble."

She handed him the box in assent and scrambled up to the top step. Once she was steady, Bern handed her a little ghost.

"You'd met Seymour before, though, right?"

"Oh, yes," she said. "I met him right around the time my girls arrived. He must have been what, eight or nine? Eight," she decided. "Yes, he's the same age as . . . well, the same age as Gary. So eight. Seymour lived in a tiny house along the highway and I used to see him standing there, watching the school bus drive away in the distance. He lived not half a block from the bus stop, but he missed it every day. Or maybe he started missing it on purpose after a while."

She sighed and stepped down from the ladder. The lines on her face furrowed even more deeply as she studied her arrangement and, apparently satisfied, moved the ladder three steps to the right.

"He was drinking a can of Coke that first day. Coke for breakfast, if you can imagine that! And that was it, his food for the day. So the next day I brought him muffins and a brown bag lunch, and after that he was there, every day, waiting for me."

Being in charge of the placement of the ghosts seemed to have loosened her tongue. She kept going with little prompting. "He was a sweet thing. Small and hungry and not very clean. I brought him clothes too, and even looked into his situation a bit, to see if there was anything that could be done for him. But they told me he was with his father, and even if I didn't think Coke was a good breakfast, it was something. There were plenty of kids who got less."

"So then what happened?"

"Oh!" She said it like an exclamation and surprised him by laughing. Her laugh was whole and open, and she quickly put her hand to her mouth as though to hold it in. "Oh, I had forgotten until just now. I was pregnant, see. With Michelle. Very pregnant. I was working at the gas company as a receptionist and it was one of my last days before going on maternity leave. Well, we called it maternity leave, but I knew I would never go back.

"And then on my way to work one day, with Seymour right there in the car . . . well, my water broke!" She laughed again, more openly this time. "Oh, poor kid. My contractions started right away and I somehow managed to drive to the hospital. I just pulled up to the emergency doors, right where the ambulance parks, and laid on the horn until someone came. And by the time they came, Seymour was gone. I didn't see him leave. He just grabbed his lunch and I bet he ran all the way to school."

She worked steadily as she talked and Bern followed her around the tree, handing up ghosts each time she held out her hand. "And then?"

"Well, then Michelle was born."

"You said girls, though. You said when your 'girls' arrived."

Her face shut like a blind and she didn't answer right away.

"I never saw Seymour again after that," she said finally. "I heard a bit about him—that he turned wild in high school and then ran away—and I felt a bit bad about that. Maybe I could have helped him more. But I had a baby of my own. Duke got on at the brewery full-time and I never went back to work, never drove that way in the mornings again."

They had done a full circle of the tree by now and the ghosts rustled in the branches, smiling down at them at carefully selected intervals.

"Do you think I could have? Done more to help him, I mean?"

Bern tried to focus on her question. He felt the pressure of the sky intensify, and his headache with it. "I don't think there's any way to know the answer to that question. Do you? There are so many influences on one person's life."

"Yes, I suppose," she said, subdued again. She stepped down to move the ladder.

Bern rustled the box. "There are still some ghosts left. Shall we do another round?" he asked.

He waited until she was back on the ladder before he spoke again. "Tell me about your other daughter." He clasped her fingers in his own as she reached down. "Tell me about Cindy."

She shook her hand free of his and raised the decoration to a branch. "Is this one high or low?" she twittered uncertainly.

Bern pushed through the pain in his skull to look directly into the pressurized sky. Barren except for the perfectly spaced ghosts, the tree was silhouetted against the cloud-bunched sky. If only the ghosts in his own life would be so orderly. "It's a low one," he said. He hesitated, uncertain whether to press her, when she started speaking.

"She was so beautiful, our Cindy. And so graceful."

The pharmacist was just the kind of guy her mother might have wanted for her—solid, plain, employed—and the thought made her freeze, unable to remember why she was there.

"Can I help you?" he asked from behind a chest-high counter. The shelves behind him were stacked with pill bottles and boxes.

She stood uncertainly in the doorway, studying him. He had almond-shaped eyes and a forehead that was growing longer as his light-colored hair receded up his head. His pointed chin and nose gave him the look of being slightly dissatisfied with whatever was before him.

He was too old for her, whatever her mother would say. He was thirty-five at least. This thought bolstered her and she stepped into a pocket-sized waiting area. "I can't help with your inquiries," he said. "I don't know anything about it."

"About what?" she asked, confused. Did no one in this business wait for you to say why you were there?

"About husbands running away," he said. "About guys getting themselves shot while a doctor looks on."

"All right, then. How about we start with something easy. Like your name."

He laughed and quickly covered his lips with his hand, but not before Schilling caught a glimpse of a mouth full of crooked teeth.

"Wilson," he said.

"Okay, Mr. Wilson. I'm Constable Schilling."

He pinched the tip of his nose. "No, no, sorry. Wilson Smith. I've never talked to a police officer before. I'm a little nervous."

"Will this make you feel more at ease?" Maddie held up her prescription like a peace offering and his demeanor changed.

He waved her into a chair and came around the counter. "Sit down. What have you got?" he asked.

"From Dr. Sinclair. An iron supplement, until she can figure out what's wrong with me." She sat in the chair he'd pointed to. It was a relief to get off her feet and catch her breath. "I went to ask her about all those things you mentioned, and this is what I got."

His laugh was almost a titter—high-pitched and girlish. "That's just like her," he said with another pinch of his nose. "You go in to question her and come out with a prescription and a diagnosis."

"Think it will help get her to talk to me?"

He was reading the scrip and took a moment to answer. "Never can tell with Dr. Sinclair. That's the thing with her: she does what she thinks is best. How much do you weigh?"

"A hundred and twenty," she said. *When I don't have my period.* "So is she usually right?"

He stepped behind the counter with his back to her and called over his shoulder, "Well, she's my boss, so I guess in that way she's always right."

"You're a better employee than I am. I know I'm supposed to

think that about my boss, but I don't usually manage." Schilling was surprised by how easy he was to talk to.

Wilson came back around the counter with a bottle in his hand. He hiked up his lab coat and sat on a stool, which he rolled up next to her. "Not like that with Dr. Sinclair, I find," he said. "She sees things exactly how they are, and she isn't afraid to say so. Even if it gets her in trouble."

"And does it?"

He shook his head. "Nice try, but I'm not going to bite. Okay, here you go." He handed her the bottle of pills. "Follow the instructions on the label. Make sure you eat lots of vegetables and fruit. And drink water. These babies tend to make you constipated." The words flowed out quickly. He'd said them a thousand times before.

She took the bottle from him. "Will they give me more energy?"

"Maybe. But if there's an underlying issue, you'll still need to get that addressed. I have no doubt that Dr. Sinclair spoke to you about that. Did she say to make an appointment?"

Schilling nodded.

"So let's ring this in and then you can go up front and see Michelle. She'll be happy to make an appointment for you to come back."

But Michelle was not at all happy to see Schilling when she approached the reception window off the deserted main waiting room.

She looked up only briefly, then got right back to her keyboard. "I don't have anything more to say." Her voice was clipped and mean.

"I'm surprised to see you at work today," Maddie said, deciding to play along.

"Dr. Sinclair needs me here." Michelle spoke while she typed. It was an impressive skill, Schilling thought. "Besides, I don't have any more sick days and can't afford the time off."

Michelle's pretty features pinched as she spoke. Schilling could tell she was close to the breaking point but saw no benefit in putting her over the edge just then. "Look, I just need an appointment. To see Dr. Sinclair."

"She's not taking new patients."

"She said to tell you it was okay." Maddie shook the bottle of iron pills to emphasize her point.

Michelle finally looked up at her. A small crease had popped up between her eyebrows and looked like it was there to stay. Red veins were showing in the whites of her eyes, and lipstick had left an uneven stain in tiny crevices that looked suspiciously like smoker's wrinkles. The veneer of perfection was wearing thin.

She turned back to the computer screen. Her fingers pecked at an unseen keyboard and her eyes stared at the screen. She pecked at the keys again, and then once more, before saying, "Eight a.m. on December fifteenth?"

"December fifteenth? That's more than six weeks from now!"

Michelle shrugged. "That's the soonest we can get you in. If you need to see a doctor sooner, you can always go to the ER. Or we could do ten thirty a.m. if that works for you." She offered up this last option as though she had found a solution to all of Schilling's ailments.

"On December fifteenth?"

Michelle nodded and smiled, confident now that she was back on familiar ground.

"I'll take the eight a.m."

"Do you want me to fill out a reminder card for you?"

Schilling tapped her forehead. "I'll remember," she said. She moved as though to leave, then leaned back over the counter. No harm in one more try. "While I'm here—any news from Gary?"

The crease between Michelle's eyebrows deepened with the effort of not looking up from her computer. "I said I'd call, right?"

"Yes, you did say that."

"Well, I will. If I hear from him, I'll call you, just like you asked. But I haven't heard from him."

"Are you holding up okay?"

Michelle looked up then. "I don't want to talk about this anymore," she said. She stood up and gathered a stack of files off the desk, hugging them to her chest like a shield. "I have nothing more to say."

With that, she turned and walked to the back of the office, out of sight of the reception window. Schilling heard a drawer open and the gentle slide of paper against paper as Michelle started on her filing.

"She was so talented—a figure skater." Holly Forsberg chose yet another branch and hung a ghost with focused precision. "She'd always skated. Even with the life she'd had, someone always managed to get her to the rink. And once she was with us, she just blossomed."

She reached down and Bern handed her another ghost.

"Blossomed how?"

"She loved to design her own skating dresses. Only bright

colors." She chuckled at this. "And a new dress for every big competition. We fought over that sometimes—those dresses are expensive. At first I could sew them myself, but later her designs got so complex, and sequins *everywhere,* so we had to get them custom-made. Oh, but it was worth it. She was so grateful to us, and never happier than when she was competing on the ice.

"And Duke loved every minute of it. He drove her all over the province to competitions, cheered from the stands, sat through every practice when he wasn't on shift. In the summers he'd spend hours with her in the backyard, coaching her as she walked through her routines and performed the same movements over and over, sometimes dozens of times. I've never seen him happier."

Bern handed her the last ghost and she took even longer than usual to find its exact placement. Then she nodded and stepped down. "It's perfect, isn't it? Just right."

"Lovely," Bern said vaguely. He couldn't fully appreciate the perfection of a barren tree adorned with plastic ghosts, but he too liked his world to follow a logical order. He thought back to the photos on the mantel in Holly's perfectly ordered living room; the sullen teenager with her eyes heavily circled in kohl. "What happened to Cindy's perfect world?" he asked.

Holly sat on the top step of the ladder and Bern lowered himself onto his haunches so she wouldn't have to crane her neck to look up at him. "She got injured. First it was her Achilles tendon. Then it was a fractured femur. It was hard on her—hard on all of us. She had a long recovery and was in a lot of pain. But she had the best care. Physiotherapy, private coaching, massages—we did it all for her. To help her recover."

"How old was she then?"

Holly sighed. "She was fifteen when she first got injured. At sixteen she had to give up skating for good. It was a fractured pelvis that finally did her in."

"And then?"

She dipped her head. "Then we lost her," she said, her voice hoarse. "It was as if skating was all that held her to us. And when she lost that, we lost her. To parties and alcohol. To drugs and boys. And then she just disappeared. She went out with a friend one day and didn't come back."

Holly stood and folded the stepladder. "We tried everything, looked everywhere. It's been sixteen years and we have no idea what happened to her." She reached out and took the box from Bern. "I don't like to talk about it. It upsets me too much." She looked away, anywhere but at him. "I tried so hard, but I still got it wrong." A tear rolled down her cheek and dropped into the box.

"How can you think it's your fault? After all you did?"

Holly Forsberg just turned away and started walking toward the house.

"Here, let me at least help you inside," Bern called after her. He reached for the stepladder but she shook him off again.

"I'll be fine," she said from between the pumpkin sentries on the path, her voice false and bright. "You have to go. Your friend is here." The fact that his "friend" was an on-duty police officer was one more mere detail to gloss over.

"She can wait while we talk." He gave Schilling a wave to let her know he'd be right there.

Holly shook her head. "I'd like to go inside now. Have a little rest." She climbed the step and leaned the ladder against the railing. "Thanks for your help with the ghosts. Come back another time."

"For cake?"

"Yes," she said, brightening. "For cake."

She waited for him to get into the squad car. He watched out the window as she waved and smiled at them until they turned the corner and were out of sight.

Kootenay Landing, 1993

Even though it was a June day, Cindy wore a heavy wool sweater. It was dark gray, the kind of sweater loggers wear. When she took it off later, he found it smelled like Seymour's house, and he wondered if she had stolen it from Seymour's dad. And then later still he wondered if Seymour's dad had given it to her—and what she might have given in return.

Seymour had it planned all along, had promised her drugs—which he'd bought by pawning some of Gary's dad's power tools. Seymour and Cindy carried backpacks as they all hiked together to the cabin in the woods. When it got dark enough that no one would be likely to see them, Cindy and Seymour planned to skip town. Head to Vancouver, where the heroin was cheap and plentiful and they could live the way they wanted to live.

They hiked up, Cindy in her tight jeans and baggy sweater walking right in front of Gary, showing off her skinny legs. But she was flirting with Seymour too, calling up ahead to him, teasing him, calling him her mountain man. Playing them both, hedging her bets.

Once at the cabin Gary felt his edginess ease as he watched Seymour prep the hits. Seymour liked to play doctor. Dealer and doctor—he'd find the heroin, cook it up, and then administer the dose. Gary and Cindy were his willing patients.

Seymour hit them all up and they lay back, piled together on the lumpy mattress in the loft. Gary gazed at the triangle made by the pointed ceiling of the A-frame as though it were the only thing in the world: the triangle as the shape that started and ended the universe.

At some point Seymour got up and left. "Going for a nature walk," he'd muttered, staring hard at Cindy as he said the words.

Gary had just been forming a thought about the triangle— something important, life changing—when there she was, above him, her long hair in his face, her skinny legs straddling his adolescent hips. She pulled off the sweater and dropped it over his face, and for a moment he was encompassed in the smell of man, hard work and wood smoke, cedar shavings and weed. When he tried to pull the sweater away she pinned down his arms with her knees.

She slid the sweater off his face slowly and he saw the truth of it: the scabs and marks down the length of her arms. Scabs and scars thinly covering pus-filled sores and abscessed skin. The tight undershirt she had on was like something a child would wear: baby blue with a dark-blue whale in the flat part of her chest between the two tiny lumps where her breasts pushed against the fabric.

She was on top of him, and despite the stink of her and the infected scabs on her arms, Gary responded.

"It's time we looked after this virginity thing." She smirked. "Chuck it out the window."

"Through the triangle," he grunted.

"Yeah, yeah. The triangle."

They barely undressed. She pulled down her jeans to her ankles—she wasn't wearing underwear—then shucked his jeans and boxers over his erection and slid them down just far enough.

She hovered over him for a moment, an exquisite image burned in his memory: the pyramid of the post-and-beam construction being held up by the triangle formed by the top of her dark head and the points of her knees, with her pubic hair the tiny beating triangle at the center that held the whole construction aloft.

The very second that dark heartbeat engulfed him, he exploded.

Afterward, he could not stand the feeling of her over him. Her hair on his chest felt greasy and he could see pus ready to explode from one of the sores on her arms.

"All gone now." She'd laughed. "Bye, bye, Gary the virgin."

He'd laughed and shifted, trying to get up, but her knees still held his elbows in place. She sat up, her butt on his stomach, and stared right at him with those dark eyes.

"Now, no matter what—no matter where I go and no matter what happens to me—you'll always remember me," she said.

He nodded, wanting her gone now.

"Say it," she insisted, pushing her knees into the soft corners of his elbows until it hurt. "Say it!"

"Okay, okay! Say what?"

"Say you'll always remember me."

He looked at her, really took her in—her ruined skin, the whale dented by the points of her breasts, the dark triangle now hidden by the line where her thighs met—and he said it:

"I will never forget you, Cindy."

15

Gary was starting to lose hope. He'd dug half a dozen holes already, but still he'd found nothing, especially using this piece-of-shit avalanche shovel.

It was the same piece-of-shit avalanche shovel he'd dug the hole with all those years ago. Back then he'd used the ax from the cabin to loosen up the soil first, then the flat-edged shovel to scoop the dirt away. Seymour had cleared off, taking Cindy's backpack with him.

Gary used the same system now, as he started on his seventh hole of the day. He didn't dare dig too deeply with the ax for fear of breaking up any remains he might come across. It was slow going—chopping a layer of soil away with the ax, clearing it with the shovel—but he'd decided to give it the whole day. What were the chances of finding Cindy's remains after all these years? Slim to none, he thought, and if he didn't find her soon, he'd give up.

Finding her felt like a way, however small, to make up for the harm he and Seymour had caused. A tiny step toward reparation. He'd have done what he could do: given Cindy's family an answer, some measure of peace.

The rest he could do nothing about. The thought of Michelle's

reaction made him groan. She would be devastated. She would
never let him see the kids again.

He hit a thick tree root with this thought and the shovel tinged
in his hands. Maybe he should take action for once. Not wait for
her to flip out but make the decision on his own. Was there any
way to live with all of them knowing the truth: that Gary had
watched their years of pain, their uncertainty, their hope, all the
while knowing that Cindy was dead? That he'd buried her himself, sixteen years ago, on the banks of this very stream?

As he scraped along the length of the tree root, Gary thought
of the endless calls to and interviews with the RCMP. They cata-
loged every surviving bit of hair, every baby tooth, every nail.
They reviewed every injury (and there had been many) listed in
her medical records. If he did dig up Cindy's skeleton today, he
knew they would be able to identify her from those records. A
femur would be best—she'd fractured both on the ice. He would
need either a femur or her skull—for the teeth. Her dental records were an inventory of early neglect.

The tree root was thicker than he imagined and he decided to
dig under it rather than try to clear the soil around it. He wanted
to stop and take a break, smoke the joint he'd rolled. But he was
afraid he'd never get started again if he took even one minute to
think about what he was doing.

Something about the angle of the soil here seemed familiar.
It felt like he was close to the right place. Even the way his feet
were anchored—one uphill, one down—seemed to awaken a
kinesthetic memory of a night he'd never forget. Even his body
remembered that night—remembered Cindy, still pliable and
warm and curled as though asleep, in the grave he'd dug for
her.

He knew he was in the right place. He could feel it. It was right near here somewhere, and he would find it if it weren't for that damn tree root.

Except there was no tree.

"Shit."

He let the shovel drop to the ground. There were trees along the bank of the stream, of course, and any one of them could have a root that stretched this far. But this particular spot had no tree.

The dirt-covered root was just the diameter of a bone.

He pushed himself through without stopping to think. He dug at the ground with his bare hands, clawing with his fingers until the impacted dirt began to pull at the edges of his nails. Then he took up the shovel again and scraped along the cold ground under and around the bone's length until finally, finally, the earth let it go.

He sat back, the bone lighter in his hands than he could ever have imagined. He could see the rounded edge of the second femur poking out from the rough soil too.

Cindy.

All that was left of her.

He thought back to that day, and though most of it was a blur, he remembered that he had laid her with her head uphill and her feet downhill, like his mother had always taught him to sleep when he was camping. So the blood doesn't all pool in your head. Because that can be uncomfortable.

Two femurs and a skull should be plenty.

He placed the first bone ever so carefully on a boulder, then shifted slightly uphill and began to dig again.

•   •   •

"Where is she?" Resnick hollered.

Schilling waited for Bern to step into the staff sergeant's office before gently closing the door.

"Was my order not clear, Constable? I told you to bring the doctor in to make a statement." Resnick glared at her from behind his paper-scattered desk.

"Give her a chance to explain at least," Bern said. The coroner pulled out one of two wooden guest chairs and sat, stretching his long legs out before him. Schilling could never imagine striking such a relaxed pose in front of Resnick.

"She's in the middle of an ER shift, sir," she explained. "There was no way to bring her in without putting some seriously ill people even more at risk." Resnick had not suggested she sit, so she stayed standing.

Her boss leaned back in his seat with a grunt. His office was standard issue—no personal effects whatsoever. Either he had no personal life at all or he wasn't staying long. Schilling hoped for the latter.

"If only all criminals had such a good excuse."

"Come now, be reasonable," the coroner said, tenting his fingers. "Why are you being so harsh with Dr. Sinclair?"

Resnick waved a hand in Maddie's direction, which she took as permission to be seated. The rickety wooden chair creaked under her weight. "We've had our eye on Gia and Lennon Hinton for ages, as Schilling knows perfectly well," Resnick said. "Lennon's dad was extradited to the US for selling marijuana seeds years ago. There's a strong likelihood that some part of his business is still being run by mother and son, but we just can't get our hands on the evidence. Yet."

He paused and rubbed his eyebrows with the tips of his fingers as though just thinking about the situation gave him a headache. "So it seems a handy coincidence that their room-mate—or whatever Dr. Sinclair calls herself—was right there with Seymour when it happened."

"They weren't together, though," Bern said. "She was alone on the marsh. She said she'd seen him before and knew his name, but she didn't say how."

"Yet another question for the good doctor, when she finally comes in." Resnick looked pointedly at Schilling as he said this.

"But draw the picture for me," Bern continued. "Why is a connection between Seymour and the Hintons suspicious?"

"You want to tell him, Constable? Show off what you know?"

Maddie bit her lip. Was he baiting her? She never could tell. "We're finding that there is no such thing as a mom-and-pop drug operation anymore," she started. "Where there are drugs, there's organized crime."

She knew she'd gotten something right when Resnick gave a curt nod. "Organized as in gangs," he added. "You can carve up the whole province according to which gang runs the drugs. Around here we're in Hells Angels territory. Overstep those bounds and there is trouble."

"So you're saying that if the Hintons are involved with mari-juana still—which is a big if, since you have no proof—they're working for the Hells Angels?" Bern asked.

Resnick nodded again. "Basically. They may not have started out that way. Probably started out as independents. But then one day some guys turn up with guns and say, 'You're working for us now.' And just like that, mom and pop are gangsters."

"Seymour was a known associate of the Hells Angels," Schil-ling explained, "so any connection between him and the Hin-tons, no matter how tenuous, is something we need to look at."

Bern gestured out the window at the cloud-cushioned

mountains. "Gangs. Not what I'd expect in this tranquil environment."

Resnick snorted and pulled a cigarette from his pocket. He sat
back in his seat, put it between his lips, and sucked on the filter.
"You know what I always say, Fortin?"

Schilling closed her eyes to keep herself from rolling them.
Here it comes. *Where there are people, there are criminals.*

But Bern surprised her by getting there first. "Where there
are people, there are criminals?" he offered. "Fascinating theory,
but maybe we could move on to the weapon?"

"Crime scene guys have scoured the marsh. No cartridge,"
Resnick grunted, cigarette back between his lips. He shifted
through the mess of papers on his desk as he spoke. "That plus the
fact there's no exit wound leads them to believe that we're dealing
with a blank cartridge, rather than an actual bullet. But of course
we'll wait to see what the autopsy results say." He tipped his head
at the coroner as he said this. "Any idea when those will be in?"

Bern ignored his question. "I wouldn't expect a blank to leave
that kind of"—his hand circled in the air in front of his face as he
searched for the word—"that kind of damage."

"You know—" Schilling began, only to be interrupted by
Resnick.

"From a revolver? Fired at close range?"

While the two men debated whether the blast from a blank
could shear a man's face clean off, Schilling sat back and waited.
She already knew it could.

"It didn't necessarily have to be a revolver," she finally inter-
jected. Her tone was certain, her voice strong.

Both men stopped talking and turned to her.

"A cattle stun gun makes that kind of wound too. If you don't
know how to fire it properly." At last, her farm girl upbringing

was coming in handy. "Not just any stun gun, though. It would have to be a Blitz. They do that if you fire them wrong."

Maddie's father had stocked the Blitz in his supply store only when farmers started asking for it. That's how her dad always worked: he wouldn't try a new product until he found out people were already ordering it off the Internet or crossing the border to the big feed store in North Dakota to get it. *You don't keep up, Dad,* she'd tell him. *Sure I do, Maddie. Sure I do. I just don't run after every newfangled thing. Let them try it out first, see if it works. If it's a keeper, I'll get it in.* The Blitz had turned out to be a keeper.

"You load it with a nine-millimeter blank cartridge," she continued. "It causes a concussion in a cow that is fatal within seconds. No exit wound."

"Huh," Resnick said, waving his cigarette toward the window. "Interesting. Farms everywhere out there."

"But the killer would've had to have direct contact, no? How would they get that close to the victim?" The coroner's curly dark hair bobbed as he cocked his head in her direction. Genuinely curious, she realized. "How do you get the cows to stay still?"

Schilling cringed. "We immobilize the cows. Hard to do that with a human, I guess. At least in the middle of a marsh. And there was no evidence of that."

"Don't be so quick to discount your own theory," Bern said. "Perhaps Seymour knew his attacker, in which case he would have allowed the person to approach."

"True," Schilling said, but the hesitancy was back, lodged under her sternum like a case of heartburn. She laughed at her own stupidity. "So we're looking for someone Seymour knows, who has access to a stun gun but doesn't know how to use it. Pretty far-fetched, I guess." She looked up to see Resnick staring hard at her.

"How far from the border to the place where Seymour was shot? On foot, I mean?"

"We could GPS it," she said. "But once you cross the river it's just a few miles—dike trails, dirt roads, the occasional driveway."

"Driveway to what?" Resnick's gaze was intense.

She shrugged. "Dairy farms, mostly."

"They likely to keep a bolt stunner handy at a dairy farm? A Blitz, as you call it? Sitting in a barn, waiting for the day they need it?"

"So Gary Dowd, you're saying," the coroner spoke up. "Not a gang war at all."

The staff sergeant rolled his shoulders back. "Major crimes officers are all over the gang theory. Somebody sending a message to the Hells by killing one of their associates. They're not going to look that closely at Gary Dowd."

"Don't you think they have a point? The Hells Angels connection seems much more likely to get Seymour in trouble than his childhood friendship with Gary Dowd." Bern leaned forward and put his elbows on the desk as he spoke.

"I have to agree, sir," Schilling said, feeling a flutter in her throat as she stood up to him. "By all accounts Gary was a dependable, predictable guy who just panicked."

Resnick shook his head. "I don't like coincidences," he said. He interlaced his fingers behind his head and stared up at the ceiling. "Here's what I want you to do, Constable. I want you to go to every house, every farm, every homestead you can find between the border crossing and where Seymour was shot. Interview every homeowner and kid and farmhand. Interview the goddamn cows, if you have to. Find out if anyone saw Gary on their property on Sunday. And find out if they have a bolt stunner. And get them to show it to you—make sure it's not missing. Got it?"

"Yes, sir." What she got, loud and clear, was that this useless grunt work was her punishment for speaking up. And for not bringing in Dr. Sinclair.

"And you, Fortin. I want you to stay out of the way. I don't want to see your ugly face until you walk back into this station with an autopsy report in your hands, you hear?"

Bern laughed and stood. "You make it sound as though I work for you."

"Well, somebody's got to keep you in line."

Kootenay Landing, 1993

"Come down here, Gary. I'm bored."

Gary lay on the mattress in the loft, staring up at the peak of the timber frame. He was trying to find his way back to the thought he'd caught a teasing glimpse of—the one that promised to make sense of his place in this life—but it was gone. The more he looked for it, the more it hid, until he just lay there, aware of the empty place in his mind where the thought belonged.

"Gary, I'm bored." The crescendo of Cindy's whine echoed off the vaulted ceiling.

He could hear her walking in circles. He heard the door of the woodstove creak open and the crinkle of newspaper. A fidgeting Cindy was a dangerous beast. If he didn't distract her soon, he knew she'd do something drastic—carve shapes into her skin or inhale the fumes from the bottle of ski adhesive they'd found in the makeshift cupboard.

It was getting late in the day and Seymour still wasn't back from his walk. Maybe he'd gotten lost or gone home. The idea of being alone in the cabin all night with Cindy made Gary sit straight up. From below he heard the scrape of a match.

"Be right down," he called. He crouched in the loft to pull up his jeans. He started to tuck in his shirt, out of habit, but then left it hanging loose over his waistband. He ran his hand along the flat of his belly, along the colony of hair that had sprouted there over the past year.

Not a virgin anymore.

The thought cheered him and he clambered down the ladder.

"Whoa, whoa, little girl," he said as he jumped down from the third rung. He took the box of matches out of Cindy's hand. In her other hand, between her thumb and forefinger, she held a lock of hair. She'd set fire to the end and was holding it close to her face, watching with intensity as it burned. Gary reached out and pressed his own fingers into the greasy black strands to snuff out the flame.

"Didn't your mama ever tell you not to play with matches?" The smell of burned hair filled the space between them.

Cindy laughed and shook out her hair. "It's your fault. You shouldn't let me get bored."

"True enough." Gary opened the door to the woodstove and checked that nothing was burning in there.

"Seymour knows better," she said.

He turned to face her and noticed her whole now. She'd left the sweater upstairs and the fading light absorbed some of the ruin of her skin. A bright curve of line formed where her body met the low angle of the sun coming through the dirty windows. She looked elegant, like a dancer.

"Tell me about figure skating," he said.

"Figure skating," she repeated. She was using a log as a chair and she leaned backward, arching her back and pointing her toes. The straps of the tank top slipped down over her shoulders as she extended her arms back in a lazy arc. She dropped her head until her hair pooled on the ground. The line of light followed, illuminating a profile of lean, graceful muscle. She crossed her hands at the wrists and closed her eyes. Gary could almost see her spinning.

Then in one motion that came from a snap at her waist she was sitting again, curled around herself.

"You're really good," Gary said.

She hugged her knees and spun on the log to face him. "Yeah, I'm good. I *was* good."

He reached forward to draw the hair from her face. She rolled her neck with his movement, exposing her cheek and then her eyes. Her real eyes, shining and clear, for only an instant, before the mask of distrust shuttered back into place.

"What happened?" he asked.

"Indian girls don't skate."

"What does that mean?"

"Have you ever seen one? Have you ever seen an Indian girl skating?"

"I just saw you! I saw you skating and you're not even wearing skates."

She rolled her head right back and laughed. Her mouth was full of fillings. "Come on, let's do another hit."

Gary looked toward the door. "Seymour has the shit."

Cindy stretched her legs out and sat forward. "I've got my own. Don't tell Seymour," she whispered.

"Your own?"

She arched an eyebrow at him and smiled. "My own source. You think I got all this on the shit Seymour doles out to me?" She gestured at her pockmarked arms.

"But how? Why?" Gary didn't know which of the questions in his head to ask first.

She stood and went over to the door to rifle in her backpack. "I don't want any more," he said. "I'm all done."

"All done? How can you be all done?"

"How can you keep going?"

"I don't want to stop."

He shrugged. "Well, I do. You guys will be gone after tonight. I'm going to need to pull my shit together."

"Poor Gary. All alone," she said.

She was back on the stump with a kit of her own. She was beautiful to him now, her hair falling forward as her fingers moved through the practiced motions of preparing her dose.

"You sure?" she asked. "I don't mind sharing."

He put a hand on her arm. "Why don't you stop, Cindy? Stop. Stay here. Finish high school. Hang out with me. Go back to skating."

Her laugh was bitter. "I'm washed up."

"You're only seventeen!"

"I was washed up at fifteen. Fractured femur. Then pelvis. Knee injury. No more skating." She rolled her shoulder in a circle. "And it hurts. All the time."

She tied off her arm.

"I thought you didn't like to do that yourself. Needed Seymour's help with it."

Her eyes flicked away from the syringe, but only for a moment. "I lied."

She found a clear patch of skin and vein and pricked the needle in. Gary could not look away.

"Who gets it for you?"

She pressed the plunger and stared straight at him, pupils lava black and empty.

"My cousin. Jared."

The shot hit home and misfired. Cindy convulsed—not a graceful skater now. She fell to the floor, tense and heavy as the log she'd been sitting on.

That's when Seymour walked in.

16

She wasn't on the porch when he drove up this time. He got out of his truck, scooping up the small brown-paper parcel in his hand. He scraped his boots as best he could on the wide planks of the porch and headed into the mudroom. If the jumble inside that room had changed at all since his last visit, he could not tell.

He knocked on the door, thinking that if no one was home, he would simply leave the parcel on the wooden bench on top of the egg cartons. Gia would figure it out, he had no doubt.

"Come on in." Her voice came strong and clear from inside.

She was seated at the table, just as she'd been the last time he was there. Except now the table had been cleared off. The whole room was spotless and seemed to glow, even in the waning afternoon light. At the center of the table stood a small appliance—an inverted stainless steel cone with a display screen and a few knobs and lights. Bern had never seen an apparatus like it.

She gave a low laugh when she saw him. "Oh, it's you."

He crossed the floor, holding the offering out to her.

She extended her hand and took it like a queen. "What have you brought me?" she asked.

She gestured toward a seat and he slid himself down while she opened the package.

"Cheese!" she cried with a laugh. Then she read the label: "Goat gouda."

"I thought it would taste good in an omelette. I used the last of your cheese the other day."

She waved this away with a hand covered with silver rings. She was dressed completely in white, or rather, draped completely in white. Her head was covered in the turban again, and a white shawl hung over her shoulders. It was clipped in front of her heart with a filigree brooch adorned with gemstones.

She placed the cheese to one side of the table. "You're just in time to keep me company while I take my medicine."

He opened his hands, palms up. "Do you need help?"

She smiled and shook her head. "It's a very passive process. And very pleasant, I might add."

"Ah, I see," he said. Not seeing at all, but willing to play along. "Am I taking the medicine too?" He looked at her closely. Under the regal demeanor, he could feel a tension in her. Her remarkable eyes were tight in the corners and had a hardness that he didn't remember from his last visit.

She pulled a velvet pouch out of one of the folds of her shawl and crumbled some dry leaves into a small black tube. As the pungent odor of the leaves made its way to him, she screwed a metal screen on top of the tube and slid both pieces into the top of the metal cone on the table. "You're most welcome to join in. I would say that showing up when you did means you need it." She gestured at her legs. "But obviously, you need it for a different reason than I do."

Although he didn't necessarily agree with her logic, he had to admit he was curious. "I have a confession to make."

She picked up a plastic bag with a black ring at its base and snapped this into the top of the machine. Then she raised one long eyebrow and waited.

"It's my first time."

She smiled at this and pressed a button that made a green light come on. The bag began to fill with air, like a balloon.

"How that can be?" she said. "You're obviously a man of the world. How did you make it into what—your forties?—without ever smoking up?"

Bern did not reply right away. They watched the balloon fill, and when the green light went off, she removed the balloon and attached a small black tube to the end of it. She lifted this tube to her mouth and sucked in the air from the bag. As she breathed out, the vapor dissipated the tension from her face. Pain, he realized.

"Tell me about this thing," he said.

She smiled indulgently. "Not until you answer my question."

She removed the tube and put the bag back on the machine and waited for it to fill again.

"I believed what I was told—all through school and military college and my army career. I believed what I was told and did what I was told."

"Your turn," she said, handing him the full balloon. He put his lips around the molded plastic tube and sucked in, then let the moist air out with a sigh. The fact that it was vapor and not smoke was a surprise. There was no coughing.

"And now?" he asked as he exhaled the last of the vapor.

"Now we relax," she said. "And talk. And so, you were told . . . ?"

"That marijuana is the devil's way of trying to lure you away from God. Either that or it was the quickest route home from military college." He was surprised at how easily the words flowed. His usual need to chase after them, rein them in, was gone.

"And you didn't want to go home?"

"I had no home to go to. I don't exist, you see. To my family."

"Funny, that. I can see you just fine."

Her face had changed again. Her shoulders, under all the layers, relaxed from her ears. Her smile—for when she looked at him now, she was smiling—reached all the way to her eyes.

"Yes, you would think so," he said.

"So tell me why you don't exist."

"For the same reason I've never smoked weed before. Though this isn't smoking, is it? This is something different." He knew he'd jumped topics but found he didn't care. It felt not like a jump but a natural step—just following where his thoughts led. "This is more like going to see the nursing sister with her eucalyptus vaporizer."

She rolled her wheelchair back from the table and started massaging her thighs, still smiling. "The medicine is different for me. I'm not as easily distracted. You can float off topic if you want, but I'll keep bringing you back. Tell me why you don't exist."

He pushed his chair back too and stretched out his legs. It felt good to move them. It felt good to breathe. It felt good to feel. Like dropping his pack after a long day of marching—realizing that the weight he carried was not actually part of him. "I don't exist for the same reason that I've never smoked pot," he repeated.

"Because of the devil luring you away? I'm not following you."

He nodded in all seriousness. "Yes. Because I'm Catholic. Because my mother was a teenager and unmarried when she became pregnant with me."

"Bastard," she said. She spat the word out, then dipped her head back and laughed long and loud.

Bern watched her and began to chuckle too. "Bastard," he repeated slowly.

"Baaaaaaastard. Like a sheep."

"Baaaaaaa—" he repeated. "Baaaastaaaaaaard."

They were both laughing now, and Bern felt the shame within him unfurl. He'd carried it for far too long, and now he felt it loosen and lift and release.

When he stopped laughing and breathed deeply again, he saw that even in the midst of laughter, Gia had not forgotten what she was about. She was lifting one leg and then the other. Massaging the muscles and pushing at the back of her calf, encouraging her knee to straighten.

"See?" she said to him. "It's just a word."

"I'm sorry," he replied. "I'm laughing and you have work to do. This is your medicine."

She tipped her head and the depth in her eyes pierced him in the newly opened place. "You're in exactly the right place and doing exactly the right thing."

"I am?" he asked. He leaned back and sighed, looking around. Outside, it had started drizzling. Inside, the simple furnishings gleamed and the whole area—living room, dining room, and kitchen—seemed to welcome him. "I think that's the first time ever."

She lifted her chin, regal again. "Feels good, doesn't it?"

He nodded. He did feel good.

"Let's go further," she said. Out of another fold of soft fabric she produced yet another pouch. This one glistened with tiny glass beads that rattled as she pulled the drawstring. The leaves were paler green this time, but the smell reached him right away. "Sit back and enjoy the ride, bastard."

• • •

Gary kept sifting through the inventory of Cindy's grave under the watchful gaze of an eagle that had settled itself on the branch of a nearby larch. He was tired now. He wanted his joint. He wanted to give up and—and what? What was left? There was nothing else to do but finish what he'd started so long ago.

It was one of those days when low-lying clouds descended over the valley and never lifted. A muted day. Still and heavy as the eagle's gaze. The kind of day when Michelle would wake up and say she had to get out of town. She'd head down to Spokane with a girlfriend and spend more money they hadn't yet made. Gary would be left alone with the kids under that blanket of sky, fighting the urge to have a nap.

A few times he'd tried taking them hiking in the marsh. He would remember the field book, binoculars, bird guide, and a bit of chocolate for a treat along the way, but he'd forget changes of socks, sippy cups full of juice, colorful flip-top containers of penguin-shaped organic cheese-flavored crackers. He'd dress himself in layers, but the kids' coats came with the fleece lining sewn right in. When Michelle bought them the newest in brand-name clothing she never thought about anything but style. Gary had found that what she would call "the *sweetest* rubber boots" had very little practical value when it came to holding out water.

After the outing when Natasha slipped on the boardwalk and broke the thin layer of ice as she landed in the marsh, Gary gave up. He wasn't sure what finally did him in: the icicles forming on the sleeves of her Dora the Explorer raincoat, the wails coming from Natasha herself, or the panic that Holly Forsberg raised when they rolled up to her house, looking for help and comfort.

A sky like this could put him in that frame of mind. By the time his piece-of-shit shovel scraped against what remained of

Cindy's skull and he extricated it from its stony grave, the sky had darkened to a soiled gray.

He sat back on his heels and cradled the skull in his palms, trying to get some sense of Cindy from it. Nothing in the rounded protrusion of her forehead or the eye sockets that swept into wide cheekbones brought to mind the tumble of black hair and caramel-colored skin that he thought of as Cindy.

He should feel something, shouldn't he? Sad or ashamed or afraid. But the days in the cabin had washed away a lifetime of feeling and all that was left was a need to take action and move on.

Gary used the shovel to push the smaller bones back into the hole and fill it over with soil. He carried the shovel and ax under one arm, the skull and femur bones cradled in front of him in his other arm. With a last glance at the eagle, he went on his way. And he didn't feel a thing, other than a certainty that no matter what happened, tomorrow would be different from today.

The cabin was abandoned when Ruben returned the next afternoon. The man—whom Ruben had nicknamed Dough Man because of his pale, puffy face—had tidied up after himself, but he'd left traces: the butt of a joint in the underbrush, scattered flakes of oatmeal on the counter, a trail of candle wax on the floor.

Ruben cleaned up without examining his reasons too closely. Mice will come, he thought first. But he also thought he wanted to give the man a break. A *leg up*, the Americans called it. A *hand*. Why he wanted to give the Dough Man a helping hand, Ruben did not know, except he had a vague idea that doing so might cause his own good fortune to make its appearance sooner.

Only once the cabin looked as uninhabited as it had when Ruben first discovered it several months before did he close the door and set off in search of the man himself. He slipped through the forest as silent and agile as the white-tailed deer he often saw. He headed away from the cabin into a strip of trees that flanked the stream. When he heard the sound of scraping, an echo of metal against wood, he crept a little closer, tucked himself behind the trunk of a fat cedar, and watched.

The man's T-shirt was stained with dirt and sweat as he stood over a hole he had dug along the stream bank. He dropped his shovel and ran a damp hand through his hair, leaving a muddied palm print on his forehead. He muttered to himself as he crouched down and dug at the dirt with his hands.

Ruben had no idea what the man was digging for—marijuana, maybe? That would be helpful. Cash would be better. As he leaned forward to get a better view, he felt eyes on him. He settled back against the tree trunk and crouched low, scanning the ground and the gaps between the trees to find the one who observed him. He kept his gaze low and gradually raised it until he found it—there.

An eagle, perched at the very top of a nearby tree. Ruben could not see its eyes from this great distance, but he had no doubt the animal had spotted him and was watching him and Dough Man with equal intensity.

At last Dough Man pulled his hands out of the hole and held up his treasure. Nothing bagged or boxed or baled, as Ruben had hoped, but a human skull, clean of tissue and stained brown with dirt.

Ruben crossed himself. He looked up to see the eagle lazily open its black wings to a quarter of their span and then settle on its perch again. Dough Man covered the hole and, filling his arms with bones and tools, set off down the mountain without so much as a whispered prayer.

Quite a procession they made, Ruben thought. Dough Man led the way, though he seemed indecisive and that slowed his progress. Ruben stole along behind, stalking from tree to tree, tracking the man along the trail from a few meters away. The eagle brought up the rear, soaring from treetop to treetop with effortless flaps of its broad wings.

Dough Man stopped at the intersection where the rough dirt road met the hiking trail. He shuffled close to an enormous cedar at one edge of the road and laid the skull and bones under its shade. The eagle landed in the upper branches, but the man seemed oblivious to its presence. Again he did not pray. He just shook himself, as a horse shakes off a fly, and turned to head back down the mountain. His steps now had a steady resolve to them that they had lacked before.

Ruben waited until the man had been gone for five whole minutes before he approached the cedar tree.

He had seen bones before—picked clean by buzzards and bleached white in the desert sun—but these were different. Preserved by the earth, they were smooth and whole. Ruben raised the skull in his hands and felt the heaviness of the mystery it contained. A movement startled him and he looked up in time to witness the gliding descent of a second eagle. It landed on the outstretched branch of a larch in full golden color, and waited.

The skull in hand and flanked by the two eagles, Ruben knew he had a decision to make. This was not about his own good fortune. It was not about the packet of money to send home. In his hand he held the remains of a person—male, female, young, old, he had no way of knowing. But this skull had once been part of a person like him.

What if something happened to him, here in the woods so far from his home? His family would survive without the packets of money, sure. But if he just disappeared? Disintegrated into this foreign soil and became nothing more than a skull and some bones? The not knowing would tear them apart.

He looked up at the eagles. They gazed out over the knitted evergreen forest, the flank of the mountain, and the marsh, the rivers, and farmland of the valley. He wished that he could see the world from their vantage point. That he could rise up and fly over not just this valley but all the valleys and know that he was nothing more than a speck among the trees with a skull in his hands.

These bones needed help. They needed a proper burial. They needed police and government and paperwork. Things that Ruben avoided at all costs. He could not help with those things. But there was one thing he knew he could do.

Ruben scooped up the two long bones and carried them and the skull up the trail. It was steep, but he ducked his head and moved in his steady, small-stepped way, the bill of his black baseball cap low on his forehead. He headed to a side branch of the trail and broke through the trees to stand at the base of a large, flat rock.

Only once he saw the eagles land in their perches in the overhead trees did Ruben lay the bones down. They made a hollow thunk against the rock and Ruben was glad to have their flinty weight out of his hands.

He had done what he could. From here it would be up to someone else. The Tall Man, perhaps, or another hiker. Ruben's job was done. Night would come soon. Now it was time to steal his way back to *la doctora*'s garden and discover what good fortune waited for him there.

The eagles seemed satisfied with his decision. When he tunneled through the trees and back onto the trail, they did not follow but kept their vigil over the bones.

New York City, 1993

His opportunity finally came: Canada Day and an invitation to a cel-
ebration at the consul general's apartment. The all-Canadian
guest list included Colonel Sauvé and his team, which, as the
colonel had spent the past weeks telling anyone who would listen, was made up of one man: Captain Bern Fortin.

"As good as he is, I need more," Sauvé kept saying. He said
it that night too, when he grabbed Bern's shoulders and steered
him through the gymnasium-sized sitting room, past the intimate
groupings of circular tables draped in white linen and set with a
confusion of silverware.

"Make way for the Canadian contingent enforcing the peace
accord in Rwanda," Sauvé shouted as the crowd parted for them.

They ended up on a rooftop terrace lined with boxy containers of scarlet and white flowers. Bern did not suggest that Sauvé
stop his griping, though he knew this was not the place to do
anything about it. These were simply overworked civilian diplomats, intent on enjoying one evening of fun. They were easily
distracted from matters of international importance by the long
buffet table.

Then there was an opening in the crowd—the parting of two
shoulders, one in dress blue, one in a light summer suit—and

there she was. She was listening to a man in a seersucker jacket and casual trousers. He wore a bow tie and tortoiseshell glasses. He seemed to be telling her something irresistible, and Bern wanted to grab the martini glass out of his hand and throw it onto the street below.

"Colonel Sauvé!" she exclaimed, and raised her cheek for him to kiss. When she turned to allow him to kiss the other one, she saw Bern standing at attention in his dry-cleaned uniform, his polished boots. With one scan of her impossibly light-blue eyes he might as well have been naked.

"And who have we here? I recognize this one. You were one of the general's men in Quebec City, *non*?" she asked, her voice light with laughter. "You see?" she said to her companion. "Canadian soldiers are serving the whole world. Showing them how it is done, keeping the peace. Colonel Sauvé is taking a team to Rwanda. Although you will probably have to look for it on a map, they are still worthy, are they not, of a peaceful life, with a little help from Canada?"

With that, the tortoiseshell glasses man and Colonel Sauvé fell into deep conversation, soon turning their backs on Sasha and Bern. The thought that the man might be a journalist, and that the colonel had had a few too many beers to be talking to the press, was pushed out of Bern's mind by the sheer presence of her.

She stood before him, in heels that raised her as high as she could go, and even then, the top of her head barely reached his heart. She wore a fitted linen suit, the color of the lace doilies on his grandmother's tea table but with none of the modesty. The skirt fell to just above her dimpled knees, fitted over the round of her hips and nipped at the circle of her waist. A cropped jacket of the same fabric lay open, its wide, short cut making the whole proportionally correct. The long legs and sucked-in cheeks of

Madison Avenue models made them look like hunted animals compared to her peach-like perfection.

The pale-pink camisole she wore under the jacket whispered promises to him, and her eyes, when he finally looked at them, spoke with equal intensity. Her fingers, tipped in the same pink as the camisole, played with the bloom of a fuchsia. The side of her jacket fell open, exposing the line of a tailored pocket.

He had been waiting for this chance and made his move quickly. He slid the note, folded around a shiny key, into that pocket in a gesture that looked like a junior officer bowing to a senior officer's wife.

She opened her lips to speak, and he leaned even closer to hear her above the hum and chatter that surrounded them. The only sound that escaped the ruby enclosure of her lips was a sigh.

"*Bonjour,* Fortin. *Ça va?*" a hearty voice said behind him. "Keeping a close watch on my wife, I see."

Bern stood to attention. "Sir," he said. "Just making sure she doesn't get trampled by hungry civilians on their way to the buffet."

"Good man," the general said as he stepped behind his wife and placed a proprietary hand on each of her shoulders. "Sauvé has told me you are an invaluable addition to his Rwanda team." And with that he began to steer her away, through the crowd of shoulders—some starred, some padded, and all of them more important than Bern.

He stepped aside and watched the crowd for a few minutes, an observer now that his mission was complete. He was grateful for the darkness that had fallen. The balcony was lit only by strings of tiny lights, and of course the lights of the city in the distance, each one a signal of a life lived, a lover embraced, a soul forsaken.

In the shadows at the edge of the patio he leaned on the railing. The fuchsia blossoms in the planter brushed his forearm, and he plucked one as he took a sip of the scotch he'd held all this time. It was warm and watery, but he drank it anyway. A luxury to enjoy while he could.

He turned the blossom in his hand and noticed the curved skirt of it, belted by sharp edges of scarlet petals. He peeled these back, exposing the stamen. With a flick he sent the blossom hurtling into the night. He took a last swallow of his drink. He wasn't hungry anymore. The laden table, the jostling line of diplomats, waiting to eat their fill—it all seemed too much somehow.

He walked inside, past the clustered diners, as though looking for the washroom. The marble foyer stood empty. Bern turned once under the medieval ironwork chandelier that hung from the coffered ceiling, then slipped into the carpeted hallway and pressed the button for the elevator. The doorman in the glowing lobby was the only one to notice his departure.

17

At some point they decided on grilled cheese sandwiches.

"See, it's perfect. You come bearing cheese, just in time to share the medicine. And now, with your able body, you can make us grilled cheese sandwiches," she said. She had stopped the exercises and was sitting perfectly still and relaxed in her wheelchair. Yet she was not slumped. Even in her relaxed state she maintained the air of the queen of the court.

He had come to question her about whether she knew Gary Dowd and Seymour Melnychuk, and about any connections between the two men. But the questions floated away before he could ask them.

He stood, feeling the lengthening in his limbs. He was lighter somehow, and taller, and it took him a while to recognize that what he was feeling was simple relaxation. "We need herbs," he said.

"Herbs? You haven't had enough? I've created a monster!"

He shook his head, serious now. And all of a sudden he wanted out of there. "From the garden. I need to go to the garden."

"Well, you know the way," he heard her call, but he was already gone. In the mudroom, boots on, and out through the back.

Rain drizzled down from the gray sky, making it impossible to guess what time it was.

He ignored the rain and began to wander through the garden, amazed at the changes since his last visit. There was still a bed of salad greens in the earth, next to a long row of carrots. This was marked at each end with a tall pole tied with a length of fluorescent-pink tree-marking ribbon. He could just imagine Gia rolling out in the snow and digging up carrots all winter long. He kneeled down now and pressed his fingers at the base of the leaves of one. With a tug it was out of the ground, the soil evidently tilled and loosened before the first frost. From the row of greens he picked the outer leaves of some late-harvest lettuce and a bunch of spinach. The rest of the garden was a picture of dormancy: beds tilled and covered in a winter patchwork of mulch.

It was an order of wholeness. Even when covered and seemingly dead, the garden had life below the surface. He allowed the words to circle in his mind before he formed them with his mouth.

"An order of wholeness."

He laughed at how ridiculous they sounded, though part of him was not laughing at all, knowing that those words held the answer he'd been looking for. Produce in hand, he started back the way he came, then froze at the telltale prickle at the base of his skull. He darted his eyes to the perennial beds at the garden's edge, where the black-eyed Susans, still in full color, stood firm against winter's slow encroachment. Past the grayed slats of the compost bins, past the thin straggle of trees that separated the garden from the adjacent grassy clearing stood a man.

Bern's instinct was on the mark. He could clearly make out his quarry—a darkly clothed, stocky man with tufts of black hair sticking out from under the rim of a baseball cap—but the man had not spotted him yet. Bern watched him emerge from the tall grasses that surrounded the hillock at the center of the clearing. He looked left and right, rustled the grasses back into place, and tugged on the rim of his baseball cap. Then he sauntered through the clearing and disappeared into the thick forest beyond.

Bern was through the garden and over the fence in a few swift, silent movements. His prey was gone, but he was more interested in whatever it was that kept the man coming back to this place. Who was he? And what was his business here? Bern pushed his way through the tall grasses and found that the hillock had been flattened out on one side. There before him was a wooden door, covered in moss.

The heavy door was ajar. He pushed it open and inched into the pitch black; the ground dropped off. Steps. He put his hand flat on the rough wall for support and stepped down. Barely a glimmer of daylight made it past the door, and in the darkness each of his other senses seemed to bloom.

The reek of skunk and damp became his breath. He could feel the rough texture of the wall under his pores as he descended the stairs. As the ground flattened out, his hand found a place where the wall of the stairwell met a corrugated metal wall. This was smooth and cool and emitted a metallic echo under his touch. He moved forward with one hand running along the wall at shoulder height, the other hand, full of vegetables, stretched out in front to keep him from bumping into anything. He slid each foot along, in case there was anything to trip him up. Moving in this way, he finally found what he was looking for: a light switch. He flipped it up.

A new world appeared before him: a hallway stretched into the distance, as white and clean as a laboratory, and as empty as the corridor of a spaceship. The dimensions took his breath away. It was as wide and long as a shipping container, and when he looked more closely, he realized that's precisely what it was: a shipping container buried underground. And not just one. He walked the length of the empty space and could see it was two containers long. To his left, four openings had been cut, and a heavy steel door had been fitted to each one. Four hallways. Four doors. All of them closed. The smell was overwhelming. And unmistakable, if only because he had encountered it just moments before in Gia's dining room.

He was standing in an industrial-sized grow op just steps from Gia's backyard. She must know about it—how could she not? What else did she know? Was this grow op linked somehow to Seymour's death? He remembered Resnick's assertion that Seymour's presence meant a major drug operation somewhere in the valley. And drugs meant Hells Angels.

Even through the fog of his thinking, Bern knew he needed to get out of there. He was in no state to investigate, and in any case, this was well out of his jurisdiction as coroner. *A soldier knows when to retreat.* Bern looked down at the greens and lone carrot in his hand, paltry weapons to fight a war on drugs.

He'd forgotten himself. He'd let down his guard. And here was the proof that even when he felt safe, things were not as they appeared.

He retraced his steps. Light switched off, he felt his way up the steps to the pinpoint of daylight outside. He left the door slightly ajar, just as he had found it, and hopped the fence back to Gia's garden. Once in her greenhouse he turned back to the task at hand and found it remarkably easy to let any other thoughts float away. The rosemary, though touched by frost, might still provide the perfect complement to a grilled cheese sandwich. He picked a sprig, along with some oregano and a few chives, and returned to the house. With the ease of a long-ingrained habit, he pushed the stink of the underground grow op into that storehouse of images he did not want to think about.

What mattered now was making the perfect sandwich, and he set his full concentration to the task.

Gary decided to risk a joint. He needed to wait until dark before he could implement the rest of his plan. And besides, he needed some time to figure out exactly what the rest of his plan was. He'd found the bones. That was step one. Once it got dark he would head into town—step two—and somehow extricate himself from his life. He had only a vague notion of how he'd go about this last part, step three. It involved figuring out what Seymour was up to and getting a piece of the action for himself.

Some part of him was convinced, despite all evidence to the contrary, that everything would be all right. He kept his mind on this as he sat at the base of a larch tree and took out the joint. He lit it and pulled the sweet smoke into his lungs, leaning back until every part of his body was touching the tree. He felt as if his spine and the back of his head were held solid and supported by the larch. He looked up at its canopy of branches, its golden needles hanging on for one last explosion of color. A larch is deciduous coniferous. He blew out the smoke and said these words out loud: "Deciduous coniferous." He laughed. They were great words. He'd learned them, of course, from his mother, who'd had deep relationships with trees, as well as with birds. He'd thought her magically gifted when he was younger. On their walks she'd stop to greet an old friend, placing her hands on a trunk, closing her eyes. "Ah, yes," she'd say, as if in reply to some news whispered to her.

Gary inhaled again. Why had he not taught his own children to speak to trees? He knew the reason well: people would laugh at them. Michelle would laugh at him and possibly run off to her parents' until he stopped acting so crazy. But it was a comfort to speak to a tree.

He blew out the smoke and felt the relaxation start to take over his muscles, his tired body. With the next inhale he imagined the tree entering him through the points of his spine and telling him what to do next. When he exhaled, he imagined the tree's strength passing through him, bolstering him.

"Thanks, buddy," he said to the tree. "Coniferous deciduous. A tree with needles that fall off every year. You won't make a good Christmas tree, hey?"

He thought about smoking only half the joint and saving the rest for later. Who knew what he'd be facing? He might need some help. But the tree made him feel invincible. The worst had already happened. Anything to come was bound to be better.

He smoked the whole thing.

He remembered a time when he'd been walking with his mom. They'd headed to a trail that was close to town, just a few blocks from their house. They could see the machines from a full block away. Aspen, larch, fir, pine, cedar. They were tearing out the lot of them, to make room for new houses. Gary was angry— he'd played in that oasis of forest for years with his friends. They'd created warrens and hideouts, a maze of trails.

"Private property," a man stepping out of a bulldozer had said. "C'mon, Mrs. Dowd. Don't make trouble. This is my land. This is how I make my living."

"Selling trees!" she'd cried.

"Selling trees is a start. But then I'll subdivide the land and sell it off. New families will move in. You'll like that, won't you, son?" he'd asked Gary.

They'd returned later, when it was almost dark and the machines were sleeping. Gary's mother had put her hands on the ragged stumps, had cradled the exposed roots gently in her fingers and wept.

He'd erased that memory from his mind. Now, for the first time, he thought of his job tallying accounts for the mill. What was he, if not a man selling trees? What would his mother think?

He reached back and patted the tree to thank it, as his mother had shown him. The tension that had kept him wired up all day was gone with the smoke and he felt resigned now. He would wait with the tree for dark to come. Then he'd head into town and find a way out of his life. And Seymour would help him.

Aimée's eyes were on him as the screen door to the café kitchen flapped closed behind him. He could hear the tightness in her voice as she said, "It's fine. I'll close up." Gabriel just ignored him, as usual. His own son had started calling him "Lennon" instead of "Dad" months ago. That was a real kick in the gut.

He threw two full black garbage bags into the back of his beater pickup and shoved a pile of empty ones onto the passenger seat, then put the truck in gear. He wanted to feel the wheels spin as he pulled out from the lane. He wanted to roar down Selkirk Street past the senior citizens on their daily walk to the diner for an early dinner. Make the accountants and bankers, lawyers and shop owners look up from their desktops and countertops, from their end-of-day routines. He wanted to yell at them, *Wake up! It's not just another fucking day!*

He didn't do it, of course. If there was anything he'd learned from his parents it was this: Do not draw attention to yourself. Conform, at least when it comes to building codes, municipal taxes, and traffic laws. The only laws they ignored had to do with pot.

But Lennon knew, more than his parents ever would, that times had changed. The players had changed. The days of honor among outlaws were long gone, and if he obeyed every law except the marijuana laws, he'd be the only one. And that would make him the biggest sucker around.

She can work off your debt. Some of it anyway.

Even in memory he could hear the implied threat in the man's words. The man, he knew, must be his Warrior contact. Jared. They'd never met in person before today, but Jared's message was clear: We'll take what we want until you've paid us back. You owe us.

Lennon pulled away from the last traffic light in town and accelerated along the flat stretch of highway that led to the mountains and home. He found a speed slightly above the limit and stuck to it, though he was tempted to go much faster.

He did owe them, it was true. He'd pay soon enough. There was never more than one crop between him and anything in the world he wanted. What he didn't know was how they had found out that everything had gone so terribly wrong.

As for honor among the dishonorable—well, they might be hoodlums, but they weren't stupid. Lennon knew more about growing pot than any pea-brained gangster wannabe in the province and they knew it. He wasn't expendable. Not yet. They'd dug the hole together, but he was the only one who could get them out.

He turned from the highway onto the trunk road and passed the police tape. He slowed and pulled to a stop, getting out of his truck and crossing the road to stand at the spot where Seymour was killed. He could tell where the asshole had fallen by the scuff marks at the edge of the marsh. Tire tracks showed where Seymour's truck had been parked. He must have been sitting on the bumper when—boom. Until now, Lennon had been too overjoyed that the jerk was dead to really think about how it had happened, but standing there was giving him some ideas.

He nodded his head and smiled slightly. Interesting theory. Quite possible that the Warriors knew all about what had happened. That Seymour's death had been payback for what he had done to Juniper, to Gia, to the plants, while Lennon had been forced to look on helplessly.

If his theory was correct, then the man who'd visited the café that morning was both more loyal and more dangerous than he'd thought.

He started driving again, not too fast but not too slow either. He pulled off onto the road that led to the dairy farm, parking in the spot he'd cleared in the brush early in the summer.

"Please, please, please," he muttered under his breath as he made his way down into the ditch, empty garbage bags in hand. *Please let the plants be good. Please let them not be too far past the peak.* It was as close to a prayer as he'd ever get.

Some days he thought of it as his trap crop. Other days, he called it insurance. Trap crop because of the placement. If this one got mowed down, he'd be warned: the cops or the Angels were close and he needed to protect his main grow. Insurance because if it survived the season, there'd be a little extra cash under the mattress come winter.

Hidden in the ditch, it got watered automatically by farm

runoff. He checked it every once in a while—a little extra watering through the dry part of summer, a little fertilizer, a mold check every so often—but for the most part he just left it alone. He didn't want to be seen there.

He slid the last few feet down the ditch and reached the first plant.

"Oh, mama," he whispered. "Look how beautiful you are."

She was a beauty too, her colas perfectly dry and lavender-streaked and stinking with ripeness. A few days late, but still plenty of goodness left in this crop. Good high. Good value.

"Beautiful mama," he said as he sliced the plant from the roots and shoved it into a garbage bag. "Beautiful mama," he said again. "Thank you for saving my ass."

New York City, 1993

She didn't come. Not after Canada Day, or Independence Day. That day he got home earlier than usual, just in case. He got home early enough to see a slice of midnight fireworks while he sipped a warm beer, standing alone at his tiny window.

She didn't come through the hot weeks that followed, when anyone who could manage to had left the city. Everyone else worked, heads down, droplets of sweat making borrowed keyboards slick, staining outdated maps, wetting the corners of correspondence.

Bern worked hard and harder, driven by Sauvé, by the internal force that seemed to overtake his commanding officer. He was vocal, moralistic, demanding: more soldiers, more intelligence, more money. Suit the operation to the need, not to the available resources. Bern followed behind, negotiating with junior staff, listening to hallway chatter, gaining, though not quickly enough, some understanding of what lay before them, of how little they could do.

With each passing week the shadows under Sauvé's eyes deepened. Bern watched this change, felt it himself. Though his own face looked the same, he felt a twisting in his belly, one that seemed to bore a hole to his core. A pit to contain the dread, the uncertainty.

One evening in early August, on the eve of a recce mission, Sauvé sent Bern home at dawn.

"Get some sleep. And for God's sake, go see something. The Statue of Liberty. The Staten Island ferry. Might be your last chance. Rendezvous at 0400. That's almost twenty-four hours."

He returned to his room through the already-warm streets. He had only the smells of piss and alcohol, of warm yeast, of frying bacon and newspaper ink for company. The smells of night mixed with the smells of morning. And then, in the narrow entryway of his rooming house, mingling with the smell of the smoker on the second floor and the sourness of leftover cooking in too small a space, he caught the scent of crushed petals and sheepskin.

He ran up the stairs.

She stood at the window, smoking, exactly as he'd imagined her so many times. She wore a black linen scooped-back dress, hemmed to a length that had been calculated to maximize her curves. She blew a ring of smoke out the window through bright red lips, and he exhaled with her. She took up so much space, there in the envelope of his room, that there was nothing to do but meld with her.

It was hours before they spoke, and in that silence, stripped bare on a striped mattress between dirtied white walls, there was nothing between them. His body was long and lean, softened at the belly from too much desk work and too many lunches on the run, too white from a summer spent indoors. Hers was soft and supple, white by design, perfumed and kneaded, waxed, and rubbed to perfection.

They slept through the heat of the day, the air motionless around them, breathing each other in. Bern woke up in the late afternoon and felt the dread before he even opened his eyes. They lay on their sides, facing each other. Her face was buried deep in the plain of his chest, both his arms wrapped tightly around her head and neck. Eyes closed, he breathed in the fullness and smallness of her, the pain and sadness, the absence of hope. He let them seep into his own pores, adding them to the dread and fear already within him.

"I may have made a mistake," she said. The first words she'd spoken.

"You? *Mais non. Ce n'est pas possible.*" Not possible.

She pushed him away and sat up, arranging the thin sheet around her torso until it hung as gracefully as a ball gown. Her eyes were too light in color to bear heaviness.

"I'm serious."

He propped himself up on one elbow and bit on his cheek to suppress his smile. "Tell me about this mistake you made."

"What I'm hearing about this mission—it's not good. I don't want you to go there, to Rwanda."

"But I'm a soldier, this is what I do. It has nothing to do with you." But even as he said the words, he knew they did not ring true.

"Ah, but it does, you see. That was my mistake."

Bern sat up and leaned against the wall. "The general knows about us. Is that it?"

She rolled a round moon of shoulder and raised one eyebrow. "He suspects."

"Suspects what?"

"That you mean more to me—"

He finished for her: "Than the others?"

She tipped her head.

"So it is because of you, because of this"—he threw out his arm in a gesture that encompassed the room—"that I am going to Rwanda? This is the reason I'm the right man for the job?"

"Perhaps both?" she asked with a purse of her lips. They were pale now—all color rubbed into his skin—but still full.

She raised herself up at that and with her hand pushed him down on the bed, backward. He stretched his legs out, feet on the pillow, and smiled up at her, hovering above him like a Venus de Milo. She arranged her draping before lying down on top of him. She took his face in her hands.

"I don't like what I'm hearing. The mission needs more troops, but it's unlikely to get them," she said.

When he did not respond, she kept speaking. "I don't want you to go there. And I wish—" Her voice heavy with emotion, she paused. "I regret that I have put you in harm's way."

Bern folded his arms behind his head and stared up at the ceiling, keeping the anger that wrestled within him from showing on his face. "It is my job. If it is to be my punishment as well, so be it. It's also my duty."

She stood then, her toga intact, and headed over to the window. She pulled a thin cigarette from her silver case and lit it, blowing the smoke out into the soupy air of the summer afternoon.

After several minutes of silence, she said, "I have no doubt you are the best soldier for the job." She butted the half-smoked cigarette on the windowsill and walked toward him, exhaling the smoke into the unmoving heat of the room. "My husband needs an operation with every chance of success." When she was a few feet from the bed she loosened the sheet until only her hand at her throat held it in place. "You'll find that Colonel Sauvé is too idealistic by far. He needs someone intuitive to pick up on the subtleties he will miss. Someone loyal and patient.

"For my own sake, I wish it wasn't you. But for the sake of my husband, and Sauvé . . ." As she took another step closer, the sheet shifted, freeing the curve of one round hip. She dropped the sheet and moved to him, her voice barely a whisper. "I'm glad they have you."

18

It took Juniper a minute to remember which futon she was on. It was the one in her office, she determined after a moment, without moving or opening her eyes. The one in the hospital lounge faced a different direction.

Still without opening her eyes, she tried to figure out what time it was. The office was silent. Definitely after five p.m. They had let her sleep, then. She'd said to give her an hour and then she'd start seeing patients. But Michelle probably opted to send them all home. Good choice, Juniper thought. Because now that she was rested she could see she'd pushed herself too far. There comes a point when you can do no more, regardless of what they say in medical school.

She opened her eyes at last. The only light in the room came from the streetlamp in the back alley. A truck rumbled past on Selkirk Street, and then there was a shout of voices either arriving at or leaving the Kootenay Landing Hotel. Late, then.

She watched a new triangle of light make its way into the room as the door opened. She still did not move. Wilson stood in the doorway. Even in the dim light she recognized him by the uncertainty of his step and the defeated curve of his shoulders.

"Don't worry, I'm awake now," she said. "They need me back at the hospital, right?"

He jumped back at the sound of her voice.

"You are here," he said. "I wasn't sure."

She sat up and turned on the small lamp next to the futon. She rubbed at her eyes and looked up at him.

"You didn't even pull the futon out," he said.

"I never do when I sleep in the office."

"But you'd sleep better."

She smoothed a hand along her hair. Were they really having this conversation? That was the thing with Wilson: you ended up talking in great detail about things that never came to mind for most people. Detail-oriented was a good trait in a pharmacist, but this quirk of his always irked her. *Let it go,* she thought. *He's good. And you need him.*

"It's just a landing pad. As good as any, and better than some," she said. "What time is it anyway?"

He looked at his watch. "Just after nine."

"So do they need me at the hospital? Did I miss my cell phone ringing or something?" She reached for it now, but the screen showed no missed calls.

He shook his head. "Not that I know of."

She waited but he said no more. "So you thought you'd just come in and wake up a sleeping doctor?"

"Sorry, sorry." He began to step back out. "I thought you said you were awake, though."

"I was kidding," she said with a laugh. "A joke. You used to get those."

His shoulders slumped a little further. "Sorry, I just—"

She took pity on him. "Come in, Wilson. Have a seat." She gestured to her office chair, behind a desk stacked high with paperwork awaiting her attention. It was the only other chair in the room. She never saw patients in here.

He picked his way through the small room and sat on the edge of her chair. He had taken off his lab coat and looked pale and weak without it. "What's on your mind?" she asked finally, when it seemed clear that he was not going to speak.

"I got a letter," he said.

She nodded slowly. "Let me guess. College of Pharmacists?"

He nodded, eyes wide. Dark-blue eyes. He would be handsome if it weren't for the pinched features spoiling an otherwise attractive face. Unfortunate, really, Juniper thought. He was a nice guy. A good pharmacist. Hard to come by a pharmacist as good who wanted to work in a clinic setting. In a rural town, no less. Most of them could make more if they bought a storefront franchise and owned and operated their own retail business.

"If I'd wanted to run a cash register all day, I could have saved myself a lot of trouble and not gone to pharmacy school," he'd said in the phone interview from Vancouver when he'd applied for the opening. "I want to practice pharmacy."

"Can you compound?" she'd asked.

She'd hired him over the phone when he said yes. As much as she didn't want anyone else involved, she needed his knowledge and skills. Compounding the hormones to the right dosage was the only part of making the cream that she could not handle herself. And he'd proved to be a hard worker. Smart, informed on current practices, and good at remembering who was boss. Not that she needed to remind him often.

"I got one too—from the College of Physicians," she said now. "What did yours say?"

He played with the letter opener on her desk. Sterling silver and engraved with her initials. A gift from Grandmother Sinclair when Juniper had opened her own practice.

"Cease and desist," he replied. "That was the essence, in any case. There was more."

She nodded. "Mine said the same."

"What are you going to do?" he asked.

She stood and rubbed her eyes again, then stretched her arms up. Dropping them with a sigh, she looked over at him. "I'm going to go pee," she said. "And then I'm going to follow doctor's orders: cease and desist."

She left the room and made her way to the staff washroom. It always amazed her how long she could go without peeing. Yet another useful skill taught in medical school. It was only as she walked back to her office that it struck her how odd it was that Wilson was still there. She ducked her head back into the room and there he sat, still holding the letter opener.

"What are you doing here so late anyway? You should be out having fun. What do you do for fun, Wilson?"

"I fish, remember? And I stayed late tonight to get caught up on paperwork so you wouldn't give me a hard time when I asked for Friday off to go fishing." He gestured around her desk. "Looks like you have your share of catching up to do too."

She plopped back down on the futon, pushing the comforter aside. "What I need is another doctor to join the practice. That's what I need."

He nodded. "Or . . ."

"Or what? Some other option I haven't thought of?"

He shrugged. "Just, you know, if you don't cease and desist? Couldn't you just do that instead?"

Up until now he'd compounded all the progesterone cream she'd asked for and had expressed very little curiosity. Had it been a mistake to involve him, even on the fringes? And yet, had she had a choice? Without him she'd have had to stop long ago.

"A lot of questions for a guy who's about to cease and desist."

He pinched the tip of his nose as though holding back a sneeze. It was a movement she'd seen him make a thousand times over his work, as though a drop of fluid was about to escape and drip out. "I just see production creeping up. You must be helping a lot of people. Progesterone cream from wild yams. An estrogen antagonist, so we're talking women, right? Menstruation? Menopause symptoms? And yet the dosage is so low that you must be mixing it with something else—"

"Why are you still here?" she interrupted, waving a hand at him. "Cease and desist. And go home."

"Just like that?"

She nodded. "Just like that."

"But what about what you've discovered? Surely there's a market for that? For all the women you're helping?"

Juniper snapped her head up. "Wilson," she said, "you're a pharmacist, not a cashier, remember? There's too much at stake, starting with your career and mine. Cease and desist. And no more questions. You don't know anything now that will get you in trouble."

He stood and made his stooped way out of the office.

"And Wilson?" she called after him. Did he know more than he was letting on? Surely she was being paranoid, but she said it anyway. "Keep it that way. It's all over. Got it?"

He blinked at her. "Got it," he said.

He walked back toward the pharmacy, presumably to get his stuff before heading home. Her own home would not see her for another day, and though Gia would surely be wondering, Juniper did not feel the need to call. Roommates, she thought. When you

take the plants and the cream away, we're just roommates. And
when you need to work late, you don't have to call your room-
mate. She turned on the desk lamp, pulled down the first file, and
got to work.

Gia watched him from the table, moving her shoulders as though
to some unheard music.

"Tell me about Lennon," Bern said.

She lifted her arms and tilted her head. "Lennon, my love
child," she crooned, swaying her arms slowly from side to side. In
anyone else he would have seen the movement as an affectation,
but it seemed to be part of her regimen. The pot allowed her to
move freely and with less pain.

He rubbed some olive oil on a cast-iron pan and set it on the
gas burner. While waiting for it to heat, he sorted and rinsed the
greens and sliced the cheese. He placed the first piece of bread
on the skillet and chopped the herbs while it browned. Gia was
silent the entire time, arms swaying. A woman at peace with herself and her home. She looked content. Trustworthy.

"If you are talking about Lennon, it's in your head. I meant
tell me out loud."

She dropped her arms and rolled her wheelchair into the
kitchen area. "Can I help?" she asked.

He placed three slices of cheese on the first piece of bread,
even though one would normally do the job. The perfect sandwich would have cheese oozing out the side, would it not?

"My neighbor thinks I'm completely incapable in the kitchen,
but that's not at all the case." He smiled down at her as he said
this. "I can see from your garden that you are perfectly capable of

doing anything, including making your own grilled cheese sandwich. But let me do this for you, just because I want to."

He turned back to the skillet to see the cheese melting over the edges of the bread and causing the pan to smoke. "Shit." He pulled the pan off the flame and used a spatula to flip the burned bread into the garbage.

He turned to her, holding the pan up. "See? Now stay out of the kitchen. How about you go set the table and tell me about Lennon while you're doing it."

She rolled away with a laugh and he started over again to the sound of her voice coming from the other room.

"He was born in 1984. Too late to be a flower child really, but we were hanging on to that whole thing. Living in the bush— well, living right here, but it was really the bush then. There was no one else around." She gestured out the window to the suburban-style homes in the distance. "This was the bush, not the suburbs."

The disdain in her voice was clear, and Bern felt himself warming to her again. The memory of what he'd seen grew fuzzy as he fell into the story and the strong, full sound of her voice.

"This was Con's property back then. He'd bought it for a song and it was quite the scene, let me tell you."

"Sorry—who's Con?" Bern asked. "I missed something."

"You don't know about Constantine? You haven't been doing your research, Mr. Coroner," she said.

He sprinkled a layer of herbs over the melted cheese and nestled a second slice of bread overtop. Then he used the spatula to flip the sandwich over. "Yes, I suppose not. Any research I have been doing hasn't extended back to a bush scene in 1984. Not yet anyway," he said, pointing the spatula at her. "Enlighten me, please."

"I suppose I think everyone has heard of Con. For me he's so much bigger than life that I can't imagine never having heard of him. And to think I came across this place by accident. I was barely twenty, tough and stringy and traveling around. Looking for adventure, I called it, but really I was escaping."

"Escaping what?" he asked. He'd fallen into a nice rhythm and kept making sandwiches, even though there were already more than the two of them would likely eat. He slid each finished sandwich onto a tray in the oven, which he had set to low. Then he brushed the pan with oil and began the whole process again.

"You know, same old. Shitty childhood. Mom's abusive boyfriend. Dead-end jobs. Never enough food or money for rent. Same sob story that everyone has."

Bern tilted his head as he slid a new slice of bread into the pan. "I find everyone's is different, actually."

She snorted. "Well, I find it best not to dwell on it. You can get stuck there and it's like you never got out, you know? I tell Juniper that all the time. Not that she listens to me—about that or anything else. But anyway, I was escaping. Didn't get far. Grew up not a hundred miles from here, hitched a ride over the mountains, and my first lift stopped right here to do some business with Con. I got out of the truck to wait and it seemed like the trees were talking to me. I was straight as an arrow too, nothing in my system. I wandered around—there was the garden, even bigger than it is now, and animals. Chickens and goats and a few cows. I'd never gardened in my life, but I walked through the driftwood arch and sat down in the earth and thought I would never leave.

"That's where I was when my lift came looking for me. There in the garden, in the sun, in my little sundress, thin as a whippet and more serious than any flower child has a right to be. And Con walked in and that was that. With his dreadlocks and lean body and small features, holding it all together—the garden and the animals and, though I had yet to see it, a massive number of grow ops in the hillsides surrounding the homestead. I took one look at him and his black eyes and tanned skin, and when my driver said, 'You ready?' I shook my head and replied, 'I might just stay here awhile.' Con nodded, like that was right, and my ride went on his way.

"The house was a hull back then: the timber frame and not much else. Milk crates for furniture and plywood countertops. There were people everywhere. Come to help. Come to get stoned and stay that way forever. Some were serious, wanted to learn the business, propagate plants, do research. Because that's what Con was all about: researching marijuana medicine, propagating seeds, selling seeds. He was developing strains for medicinal use—pot that would treat symptoms but still let people get on with life. He believed that everyone should have the right to grow weed. That marijuana should be part of every household's first aid kit. And with that one look, and a hand extended to pull me out of the dirt, he swept me fully into his world."

Bern kept his rhythm going as she spoke, making more sandwiches and sliding them into the oven. He had no idea what time it was and did not bother to look at his watch. He saw the light being let out of the sky from the window behind Gia, who was in shadow now.

"Lennon came along ten months later, and in a way that's the whole story. He was the glue that held us together, because I guess there was probably not much else. A university-educated scientist devoting his life to pot research and an abused twenty-year-old escaping poverty. I guess I was beautiful, though there were more beautiful women who came around. They swarmed to Con like the bees that we kept for a while. Con would often say I wasn't beautiful. Not in the way some of those women were. He would never lie to me like that. 'You're not,' he'd say. 'You're something more than beautiful. Be yourself. Don't try to be something you're not.'"

Bern turned off the stove. Surely they did not need more sandwiches, and in any case, he had used all the cheese. He made a tidy pyramid of sandwich halves on a large platter and brought it, along with a stack of plates, to the table to hear the rest of the story.

She clapped her hands when she saw the pile. "You've made enough for an army!" she cried in delight. "Oh, and don't they look good. Well, Lennon will be along soon. And maybe Juniper too. We'll have a feast."

She'd cleared the table and set it with woven placemats and matching napkins. She waited for him to be settled and then offered him the platter first. He chose two halves and waited while she made her selection, then poured them each a glass of water from the pitcher on the table.

"Bon appétit," he said.

"And to you," she said with a nod.

He took a bite of his sandwich. The cheese slid out the sides of the thick bread, just as he'd expected it would. The herbs added a tang to the smoky flavor of the gouda; the bread was thick and heavy. He'd created the perfect sandwich experience.

"It's delicious," she said.

He could see, in the lines of pain that had mapped their way across her face, exactly what Con had meant. She wasn't beautiful. Not in the way that people waxed poetic about. Not in the way of Dr. Sinclair, with her shiny hair, haunting eyes, and long legs that could distract any man from what was important.

If he could pick one word for Gia it would be *lithe*. Bend-able and strong, but not breakable. Even in her current state of ill health, he would call her that. And yes, he could see that she was just the kind of woman who could keep a farm and homestead running with one hand and raise a child, or a whole brood, with the other—all while her brilliant husband was off seeking inspi-ration among truly beautiful women.

"So he wasn't faithful to you?"

She rolled her eyes. "Faithful? What does that word mean? It means nothing, that's what. He was there, doing the work he needed to do on this earth. And I was there, helping him. That was my work. If he found inspiration with some waif looking for a free high, so what? Waifs passed through. I stayed. I'm still here, as you see."

"Yes, I can see that. And hungry, evidently. Please have an-other sandwich."

She obliged him. "The pot makes me hungry. Without it, I have no appetite."

"Then it's a good medicine for you. It wouldn't be right for me, though. I never have trouble eating."

"Never? It seems to me the last time you were here you'd starved yourself to the point of begging for eggs."

He laughed. "Ah, yes. Well, on occasion I deprive myself."

"Why?" Her eyes cut right through him and his walls were back up. The grow op was front and center in his mind now that the effects of the pot were wearing thin. "Put it down to human frailty," he said.

"Even our strongest are fallible," she said. "That's what I thought with Con, see? If a man has a weakness, why punish him further?"

"Indeed," Bern said. She was making sense, in a circular and rather simplistic way. Did it have to be more complicated than that? "But where is he, then? This Con of yours?"

It was the first time he saw her look uncertain.

"I'm not totally sure. He got arrested for selling pot seeds and was extradited to the US. Fifteen years ago."

"Is he still in jail?" Bern asked.

"I can only assume. I'm not his wife, not legally. What counts as common law here means little there. And he's determined that I should be free. So if he directs the prison and his lawyer not to tell me anything, they have to listen to him."

"Is that even allowed?"

"Seems to be. I write to him through his lawyer. He never writes back. I don't even know if he gets the letters."

"But what about Lennon?"

She took a breath and pushed her plate away, her second sandwich untouched. The food sat between them like something that was no longer a good idea. "Lennon was just a little kid when Con left. Ten years old and Daddy's gone. Except he never called him Daddy, always Con. He missed him at first, would ask about him all the time. Then he just got on with life, as ten-year-olds do."

"And Mountain Station?"

"We just had to get by without him, and without the seed business. Of course, some people say it's just a front." She laughed at that and held her hands out, gesturing toward her withered body. "As though I have what it takes to run a restaurant and an underground business on the side." Her eyes looked hard now and he could see the abused child beneath her regal veneer.

"Would you tell me if you were still in the pot business?"

She shook her head. "No."

"No, you're not still in it? Or no, you wouldn't tell me?"

"Both."

Now that the haze had worn off, Bern could see the care she was taking with her words. Had she been that wary the whole time?

"Why not?" he asked.

"Because some things are best not discussed. Even between friends."

"So we're friends now?"

"It suits me," she said. "For the time being."

In the growing darkness outside the window, headlights swung through the trees and approached the driveway.

"There's Lennon. Funny, I would have expected Juniper before him." She said this more to herself than to Bern. "In any case, you'd better go. Good as your sandwiches are, I've had enough of your company for today."

Bern got up. "*Eh bien.* It's good to know where I stand."

It was darker than the night inside the workers' dorm—too dark to see, but Ruben knew his way by feel.

He climbed onto his empty bunk and covered himself with the blanket that had been too warm in summer but was not warm enough now. He had no pillow, so he cradled his head in his hands and listened to the ebb and flow of the breath of the workers who surrounded him.

Once again fortune had turned the other cheek. Again he had gotten there too late.

He'd been so filled with hope when he opened the door that led underground. This time he'd been truly invisible. He'd waited until dusk, when he could still see, but it was more difficult for others to see him.

And what had he found? An underground world. Hallways lined in gleaming white; shelves that until recently had held more marijuana plants than Ruben had ever seen. More than he could even have imagined.

Before the end of the month he'd be on a bus full of migrant workers headed south. The lucky ones would go home for a few months before starting strawberry season in California early in the new year. The unlucky ones would disappear into the fabric of a big city, working for cash, barely getting by.

A few of those plants were all it would take to make Ruben one of the lucky ones. Three or four plants would never be missed, and would allow him to go home for a season.

A dozen plants and he could take more time. Stay with his family for half a year and wait for fortune to shine on him again. Perhaps it would be enough that he could invest in his brother-in-law's business and not leave home again.

But once again he had been too late. Because there in that underground world, all the plants had been cut down, their pots thrown, the growing lights smashed. The smell of fear trapped underground was overpowering and Ruben had to force himself to check every corner before retreating.

Now he huddled under the blanket. It was too cold to sleep and the cold only reminded him of what he knew too well: he was almost out of time. He had only a few more days of work here before the crew moved on. And only one more day off— one more chance to cross into *la doctora*'s world to see what fortune had in store for him.

From: chiefcoroner@bccoronerservice.bc.ca
To: bernfortin@bccoronerservice.bc.ca
Re: Autopsy Results—Seymour Melnychuk
Sent: Tuesday, October 20, 5:17 p.m.

Bern,

Please find attached the autopsy report for Seymour Melny-chuk.

   Note that we are still waiting on toxicology results, but Dr. Cooper detects physical evidence that Melnychuk was a habitual, long-term injection drug user (likely heroin).

   Regarding your question about a cattle stun gun, I asked Dr. Cooper about this after she had completed the post-mortem. Her answer was as follows:

- wound possibly consistent with a bolt stunner or similar implement;
- would depend on the type of stunner and the size and type of cartridge used;
- would account for the absence of an exit wound;
- but does not necessarily explain the missing cartridge.

I will leave it to you to communicate with the RCMP. They have been calling me as well.

Regards,
Ogden
Ogden Kumar, Chief Coroner
BC Coroners Service

19

Bern woke up early and lay in bed watching the dawn light through the slats in the blinds. He wished that they were open so he could see the sky, but he made no move to open them.

His mind wandered over the facts of the case: Seymour, dead; Gary, missing; Holly Forsberg, agitated; Dr. Sinclair, uncooperative; Gia, cagey. Everyone had something to hide. He thought of the complication brought by Troy Thompson and knew that the suspects in the case were not the only ones hiding something. He, Bern Fortin, had secrets of his own.

Bern tried to find the energy to reach for his phone and make the call he knew he needed to make, to tell Resnick about the grow op. Really, he should have phoned it in the night before. Resnick would be eager too to see Seymour's autopsy results, which were likely waiting in Bern's email inbox. All he needed was the motivation to go to his desk and turn on his computer. But his limbs felt loose and disconnected, his instincts dulled, his reflexes dead. The relaxed euphoria of the night was gone. Lethargy had taken its place.

It was only the thought of coffee that finally got him out of bed. He fixed himself a triple espresso while his computer fired up, then sipped it while he read the chief coroner's covering letter and skimmed the report. It was as he expected.

Resnick had waited this long for the autopsy results. He could wait an hour longer. Bern needed fresh air and perspective before he could face the day. He needed to move his limbs and clear his mind. There was time, he decided, to take a little hike before he called the station.

Lennon pulled out of the driveway at dawn just as Juniper pulled in. He waved but didn't stop. She was on her way home—no doubt from a night in the ER—and would get straight to work in her studio. He was on his way out, headed for a long day of manicuring after a long night of harvesting. Whoever said pot growers were lazy asses had no fucking idea.

He aimed his truck in the direction of the regional dump, just as he would on any other day. After he unloaded the two garbage bags from the café, he laid a tarp over the other bags and supplies in the back. Then he started toward town, as though he were headed to the café. As though it were any other day.

Looking around to be sure there was no traffic, he swung a left onto the trunk road that led through the farmer's field. Twenty minutes of driving along secondary routes and he was right back where he'd started—at his parents' house. This time, he went by their driveway and kept going. He passed the ditch where he'd harvested the night before and, just a short distance on, the scene of Seymour the asshole's demise. He slowed at the little bridge over the creek and took another left, this time onto a forest service road.

He needed a place to process his harvest. Of course he had his own drying and processing room set up in his main grow. He even had a crew of guys ready to help clip the bud. But Seymour had fucked all that up, hadn't he?

Lennon geared down as the road headed uphill. He thought of Aimée, how hard she was working. Hell, they were all working hard. It was just that time of year. And they'd have to keep working hard all winter too, wouldn't they? Thanks to Seymour.

Away from prying eyes, Lennon pressed down on the gas. The old farm truck shot forward. He tugged on the steering wheel to keep it in the tracks on the dirt road. It felt good to go fast, to feel the risk of the edge. The trees opened up on one side and a thin strip of brush was all that separated him from a drop down the side of a rock face. He sped up even more.

"Fuck you, Seymour." He pounded his hand on the steering wheel as he said it. It felt so good that he said it again, louder this time. "Fuck you, Seymour fucking Melnychuk!"

He spun through a switchback without slowing. The old truck roared and bucked. Lennon twisted the steering wheel until the tires jutted back into the tracks.

This was not how it was supposed to be—Lennon, by himself, drying and clipping a measly few dozen plants. This would barely satisfy that asshole Jared and subsidize the café through the winter. And the risk was high, with Seymour dead, Jared nipping at his heels, and the police and the coroner sniffing around. He needed the bud, but he needed to be out of sight. He couldn't use his usual system.

That's why he'd picked the cabin. Long forgotten except by a few snowmobilers, it would be a safe place to hole up for a day or two. Hang the plants, manicure them, and leave them to dry. No

one would know. He'd be done in time to do the weekly cleaning at the café. That would make Aimée happy. And he'd give
himself a little kick to get it done, just like the old days. A little hit
of ecstasy to make it all more fun. Because life was supposed to be
fun, wasn't it? Wasn't that what this was all about? Living a good
life, a fun life, loving people and getting what you need from the
world? Wasn't that the whole point?

Lennon twisted sharply to make the last switchback before
the cabin. The truck lifted onto the right wheels and for just one
moment he was looking down at the valley below through the
passenger window. In that moment he took in the fields, acres
and acres of them; the cows, tiny dots in the distance; a farm-
house, a barn, a highway. An ordinary life. Then he righted the
steering wheel and jostled in his seat as all four tires landed back
on the ground.

No. His life would never be ordinary. He'd never fall for that
illusion. Sure, he had to do the work of half a dozen men today.
But tomorrow, he'd take a little trip in his mind while cleaning
the café. And then, once he'd dealt with this crop, maybe they'd
take a real trip, all of them together. Close up the café and go
somewhere warm, he and Aimée and Gabriel. Have some fun
and lay low. Let the pressure dissipate. Make a plan. And take it
from there. He'd get back on his feet. He'd done it before, and
he'd do it again.

The roof of the cabin flashed up ahead and Lennon slowed
just enough to steer the truck through an opening in the trees.
He slammed on the brakes and opened the door. It took three
trips to get the bags of weed and his supplies into the cabin. Then
he locked the door from the inside and got to work.

• • •

Juniper headed straight for the converted woodshed she used as
a workspace. The wide pine boards looked almost white in the
morning light. The first two feet of them anyway. Then the mess
started. The long counters under the windows, the view of the
tall evergreens, the angles of the sun—their beauty usually filled
her with joy.

Not anymore.

She surveyed the mess only long enough to determine the
tools she would need. Once she'd settled on them, she went to
the shed to get what she wanted: a shovel, a few buckets, a trowel.
She could add any solid waste to the burn pile.

Walking back in, she almost let the sadness sweep her away.
And with it the hope she'd put into converting and setting up
her own space—her safe place to explore her plants, to explore
herself. Gia called it her lab, but secretly, Juniper thought of it as
her studio.

She tried to use her training to shut the thoughts out. She
needed to separate the destruction before her from the hopes
and dreams she'd started with: it was a matter of survival. It had
taken her months to source just the right beeswax. She'd lined
the shelves with butcher paper and stacked the bricks of wax
there—enough for a whole year. Those same bricks had been
thrown to the floor, dropped one by one from Seymour's hands
as his eyes slithered about the room. She'd stared straight at him,
crouched in the corner. She'd backed into it when he'd smashed
the door open and stomped into her space, yelling. But she held
her gaze steady and her chin high. He could do no permanent
damage, or so she'd thought then.

The pellet stove had been an extravagance, but she'd justified
it with a few extra overnight and weekend shifts in the ER. She

wanted the warm coziness of a wood fire but didn't want to fuss with chopping wood. He'd started on the pellets next.

"What do you want?" she'd asked him.

He didn't answer. Just ripped open the first bag of pellets and scattered it over the damaged wax. Then the second.

Now Juniper left the door open behind her and tried to shut the thoughts down firmly. It was just wax and pellets. That's all that was before her. Except then Seymour had taken the stockpot full of salve—two gallons of pure, hot liquid that she was about to bottle—and had poured it over the whole mess.

Taking care to avoid the slick green pools of dried salve, she scooped up the first shovelful and banged it against the bucket.

"Need a hand?"

Juniper jumped and turned. Gia stood in the doorway in old faded jeans and a turtleneck that might have fit at one time. The turban was in such contrast to the rest of the getup, it almost made Juniper laugh.

Gia held her arms out in triumph and smiled. "I came to help."

"You're having a good day, I see." Juniper kept her voice neutral.

"Yes, a good week. I didn't want to say anything, in case it was a fluke," she said. Her smile was radiant and Juniper wanted to be glad for her.

"That's great. But still, best not to overdo things."

"At least you could be happy for me," Gia said. She took a step into the room as she spoke, and Juniper moved quickly to hold out her arm.

"Careful. It's slick."

Gia shook her off. "I can manage," she said. Then she whistled.

"Wow. He really made a mess in here too." She tilted her head and held Juniper's eyes. "Won't you let me help you? I don't want you to be all alone with this."

Juniper turned from her searching look. Tears pricked at her eyes. "Well, maybe you can hold the bucket."

They worked together—Juniper scooping, Gia holding and shaking the buckets. Juniper was surprised at how fluid her friend's movements were. She'd been in and out of the wheelchair for close to a year, but for the past few months it had been more in than out.

Juniper went back to the house twice for more buckets. On her return the second time she found Gia seated on a cushion on the floor, scraping the wide wood planks with a trowel. She moved with such grace and care that Juniper stood in the doorway for a moment to watch her. She knew it would not last, and a dart of grief shot through her at the knowledge.

She busied herself by helping scoop the last of the cold salve into two final buckets, then lining those up next to the half dozen that were already by the door.

"Lennon can take those to the dump later," Gia said. "And this is coming up real nice from the floor. A scrub with superhot water and a little pine oil and it will be good as new."

Juniper found a cushion of her own and sat down on the floor next to her friend. "Like nothing ever happened," she said.

Gia put down the trowel. "But it did happen, honey. Why won't you talk about it?"

"For the same reason you won't talk about it. Or Lennon," she said. "Talking won't help. There's nothing we can do."

"Oh, I wouldn't say that. And anyway, by some grace, he's gone now," she said. "So maybe we don't have to do anything."

Juniper blinked and looked up at the ceiling to contain the

tears. "Grace? Is that what you call what happened?" She remembered the feel of his grimy T-shirt under her hands, the sound of his last moan in her mouth as she tried to breathe her life into his. She shook her head again but the tears came anyway. "Oh, dear God," she cried.

Gia's arm was around her shoulders then, pulling her down. Juniper laid her head on the other woman's lap and allowed herself a moment of comfort as Gia's fingers stroked her hair.

"Don't let him take this from you, Juniper."

"He did! He already did!"

Gia continued to stroke her hair, now with the flat of her hand. "Tell me about it."

Juniper shook her head again, but the words tumbled out. "It makes me so mad. He wouldn't say what he wanted. If he'd said he wanted the formula, I'd have given it to him. But he just stormed in here, determined to ruin it all, like we owed him something. That's what makes me mad. Like that skinny guy with his heroin addiction and those crazy bikers with their guns have a right to what we've built.

"I would have given him the formula. Who cares? It's a recipe—anyone can make it. I would have given him all the bottles in the cupboard too. But no. That wasn't enough for him. He wasn't going to be satisfied until he and his goons had ruined our lives.

"And then!" Her voice broke as she thought of it. "Then I had to try to resuscitate him. He was wearing the same shirt. Did I tell you that? Days later and he was still wearing the same shirt. It smelled like this studio, like *my* cream."

Juniper felt the tears tumble out and for a moment she didn't try to hold them back. Didn't try to hold herself together. For one minute, she let someone else be the strong one. She took comfort in the rough fabric of the jeans against her cheek and the steadiness of her friend's fingers in her hair.

"I'm sorry," Gia said finally. "I didn't know it had happened that way."

And even though Juniper knew that Gia and Lennon had been through worse—they'd had to deal with the bikers, and those guys had had guns—when she heard the words, she took comfort in them. After a moment she squeezed her friend's hand in her own and stood. She put both hands out and pulled Gia slowly to her feet.

"I'll look after the buckets and cleaning the floor. You should probably go take it easy for a bit, don't you think?"

She squeezed Gia's hands once more, watching that she was steady on her feet before she let go.

"There's more to discuss."

"I know. I know," Juniper replied. "But that's all I can take for today. Do you want me to walk you back?"

Gia shook her head and started for the door. "I'm fine, see? I'll go slowly. See you at lunch?"

Juniper nodded and watched her friend make her way back to the house, stepping over tree roots and rocks like she was skating.

Organize garage.

It was the first thing that came to Gary's mind when he awoke, cramped and uncomfortable, on a camping bed he'd made for himself on a storage shelf in his own garage. From a gap between the color-coordinated bins that were his only cover, he could see that the garage was a mess once again.

Organize garage. Replace lightbulb at top of stairs. Hose down drive-way.

The first time Michelle left a sticky note next to his coffee cup on a Saturday morning, Gary had thought it was a joke.

"What's this?" he'd asked. She was in the kitchen making him French toast, her back to him. She wore low-slung jeans that showed an inch of hip in the gap between waistband and T-shirt. The band of a flowered apron crossed that gap and was tied in a bow at the middle.

"Come here," he'd said.

"Just a minute. I'm going to burn your toast."

"Just come here."

She had finally come, carrying a plate of golden toast—three slices—and a tiny bottle of real maple syrup that they couldn't afford. Still seated, he pulled her toward him and pressed his lips into the smooth of her belly. She smelled like melted butter and sugar and mango-scented skin cream. He reached a hand back, untied the apron, and let it drop to the floor. Then he kissed her belly again.

"So what is this?" he asked again.

"What?" She tried to pull away.

"This." He held on, rubbed her belly with the whole side of his face like a cat wanting food.

She pushed his head away with both hands, scooped up the apron, and headed back to the kitchen.

"It's your 'Honey-Do' list."

"My what?" he said over a mouthful of toast.

Michelle came back with a single hard-boiled egg and a slice of dry toast for herself. She took a napkin from the ceramic holder at the center of the table and handed one to him as well.

"My mom says it's the secret to a happy marriage. I write a

list of the things that I want done around the house, and you do them." She peeled her egg as she spoke, placing each fragment of shell at the center of the napkin. "That way, we don't need to argue or get frustrated about things. Whenever you have time, like on a Saturday morning, you just pick something and do it."

"So this is what I'm doing today?" he asked.

She began slicing her peeled egg. "Just think of it as instructions for making me happy," she said. "There's no mystery to it. I just really want the garage to be tidy."

Except it was never enough, was it? Gary thought now, stretching his legs cautiously in his garage hiding place. He remembered all the times he'd completed his "Honey-Do" list and had to conclude that the system did not work. No matter how many lightbulbs he replaced, walls he painted, and cracks he repaired, Michelle was never, ever happy.

Gary did feel better after a much-needed sleep. Just a few hours, but it was more sleep than he'd had in the three days since his ordeal had begun. And here he was, right back in his own garage—the place that had started it all. *Paint the garage.* Sunny, he could tell by the windowpanes in the garage door. Cold, he could tell from the air on his face. Eight thirty a.m. Almost time for Michelle to leave for work.

Just then, the garage door jerked open. He wanted to cover his ears before the midpoint squeal that was to come—there it was—but he dared not move. *Repair garage door.* After the kids came along, he'd started ignoring most of the items on the "Honey-Do" list.

"Natasha, don't rub up against the van! You'll get your dress dirty." Michelle's voice carried a note of hysteria he'd not heard before.

"It's dirty. Dirty van."

Gary's eyes flew open at the sound of his daughter's voice. He wanted to catch sight of her. He needed a glimpse of her fine hair braided for school. She'd have spent precious minutes picking the ribbons, and suddenly he was desperate to know which ones she'd chosen. But all he could see was the side of the Rubbermaid bin that served as his camouflage. Forest green for outdoor equipment. His head pressed against the bin on the next section of shelf—red for Christmas decorations—but he still couldn't see her.

The van doors slid open and then closed. Michelle, depositing Geoffrey into his car seat and buckling him in. Geoffrey. Never Geoff, though Gary liked the short form just fine.

"In your seat and ready please, Tasha." Automatic words in a singsong voice. Secret family code: be ready when I get there or else.

Michelle's heels echoed on the concrete floor as she walked around. The clip of buckles, the clunk of the door closing. *Van for servicing.* Then a thunk as she walked into the pile of boxes that he'd let Seymour store in the garage. The boxes he planned to spend the morning searching through.

"Goddamn it, Gary!" Her voice volleyed, trapped in the three walls. He heard a shove as Michelle slid the boxes along the floor. "Why could you never clean the garage properly? Not even once?"

Gary steeled every muscle to keep from answering. The silence stretched on forever. He wanted to snake out of his hiding spot and apologize. To wrap his arms around her. He'd do better. He'd organize the garage. But he found a kernel of determination and held on to it: he'd cleaned the garage countless times. And she'd never even said thank you.

She took a deep breath now. Bull breath. They'd learned it

in prenatal class. Slow steady inhale, then long heavy exhale. The instructor shouting at them like a drill sergeant. *Sigh. Grunt. Huff. Push through the pain with determination. You are strong.*

After exactly three breaths, Michelle got in the van and backed up. Only when the garage door had progressed through its full range of squeaks and groans did Gary dare move.

This time Bern stuck to the trail, following a route less direct than the one he had taken a few days earlier. He tried to shake off the dullness as he moved, but the weed was still in his system, slowing him down, upholstering his senses—a sensation more unusual than unpleasant. His normal swirl of anxious thoughts still called, but from a distance.

The rain of the night before had passed. Tendrils of sunshine reached through the golden needles of the larches, drawing out moisture. His boots and the hems of his jeans were soon wet. He took the first switchback and the second, heading north. Soon he would reach the place where the path forked—north to the throne rock, west to the hunting cabin.

Vegetation was so thick at the edge of the trail that the sun could barely reach through. The air was moist and cold. He reached the intersection and headed north to continue his climb.

He felt a flicker of apprehension as he pushed aside the branches that sheltered his rock from the trail. A skull flashed into view and then was gone. Like a snapshot. Or a flashback. He closed his eyes to see a mountain of skulls in his mind. His eyelids flew open. Heart racing, he focused on the real picture in the fracture of sunlight between the swaying birches.

There was only one. Just one cranium, and next to it a long

bone. They sat in the center of his throne rock, as though waiting for him.

His heart returned to a more subdued rate and the images in his mind dissipated. His sole focus was the bones. He walked forward and crouched down. Stained brown, they had been in the ground for some time. Unearthed recently, no doubt, but whether by humans, animals, or a natural shift in the soil he could not tell. Their placement was no accident of nature, though— they had been placed on this shelf of rock by human hands. Perhaps, he thought, so that he could find them.

He allowed his eyes to roam the contours of what had once been a face. The crown was unmarred by bullet holes or fractures, the upper teeth intact. Plant roots grew through the nose cavity. All would be clues to an expert, which he was not. To him it was just another skull.

He widened his scan, searching for clues that might help him understand. Was the long bone a femur? It seemed likely. Bern backed away and crouched at the base of two larches that shaded the edge of the trail. As he pulled out his cell phone to call Resnick, he had the distinct sensation he was being watched.

New York City, 1993

When Bern woke up, she was gone. In the predawn light of the room he searched for some trace of her: a note, a lipstick-stained cigarette butt, a bead, a fastener, a feather. He found nothing except the sheet, rolled under the bed in a sausage-like tangle.

He brought it to his face and breathed in the very essence of her: her perfume, her skin, her summer sweat. Not her tears—there had been none of those. He scolded himself to hurry; he had no time to hang on to the shell of something gone. He had only himself to blame. As irresistible as she was, his own actions had sealed his fate. Now he must face his punishment. He showered down the hall and dressed, returning to the room only to shoulder his pack and leave.

He marched quietly along the abandoned streets, once again witnessing night and morning as they traded shifts. He arrived outside peacekeeping headquarters a full ten minutes early, and waited for what was to come.

20

He found the cell phone in the pocket of Seymour's other jeans—the blue pair, not the black pair he'd been wearing when Gary last saw him. Where the hell was Seymour, anyway? He'd said he'd come back for his stuff as soon as he got settled.

Seymour's *other* cell phone in his *other* jeans—like he was two people, not one. This second phone was the pay-as-you-go kind, not the newer touchscreen version that was permanently cemented to Seymour's left hand. Gary pressed button after button. Only when a list of recent numbers popped up on the screen did he realize this was what he was looking for.

The list was made up of only one number, both incoming and outgoing, sometimes several a day, dating back three and a half weeks.

It was a number Gary was sure he recognized.

Bern perched on a boulder uphill from the trail, bones in sight. The memory of his hands cradling other craniums pricked at his fingertips.

He waited for the forest to settle around him, but the feeling of being watched did not go away. The air felt heavy and the ground, when he slid his booted foot down to press into it, was boggy. Bern stayed as still as he could, cursing his dulled senses. The neurons fired but the processing came slowly; he wondered how long it would be before his brain returned to normal.

The breeze shifted the canopy above him and more light filtered in, revealing the bones in full sunshine. The air was sucked out of him, exposing the bottomless hole of loneliness within. The last man alive in the world. He opened his mouth and let the moan that was building inside him escape in a controlled sigh.

He'd moved to the quietest corner of the earth and yet here he was again, alone amongst the dead. How could this be?

For some reason, Holly Forsberg came to mind. He pictured the tightness in her forehead that caused her eyebrows to rise in constant surprise. What secret from her past was she still guarding so fiercely? The very act of working around the unspoken had narrowed the possibilities of her ever living a full life. He thought of Mrs. K. refusing to talk about her daughter; that too cut a wide swath between her and the people and experiences that surrounded her.

Was it the same for him? Was he destined to relive the same moment, the same view, over and over again?

He looked back at the cranium on the rock and knew that it was related to everything else that was going on. Gary's disappearance. Seymour's death. Gia on the deck with a shotgun. Lennon's shout: "The asshole is dead!" Even Holly Forsberg and her unspoken pain. They were all related—but how? And how much of it was his responsibility to sort out?

Who died, how they died, when they died, and by what manner. There was no room for doubt in the coroner's crib sheet. That Gia was intelligent and witty, that he liked talking to her and admired her garden, that he did not want to cause Holly Forsberg more pain, that Dr. Sinclair did not want to be inconvenienced—these things didn't factor in. It was a simple equation: he had to find out the truth. Everyone's secrets would come to light.

And if he was to expose their secrets, he had no business hanging on to his own.

A flicker of light drew his gaze to the golden branches of the two larches overhead and he saw that he was indeed being watched. With a lazy lift of black wings against blue sky an eagle stilled itself on its perch in the tree and stared back at him.

"I thought you were off today." Chantel Postniuk looked up as Schilling entered the station.

"And I thought you were Kelly," Schilling said.

"Good point." Chantel went back to inspecting the moons of her nails. "Kelly's got the flu. I'm pulling a double shift."

Schilling leaned against the counter. "Yeah. Well, Resnick's going to call me in anyway, so I thought I might as well get into uniform."

The receptionist picked up her emery board and made a minute adjustment to the nail of her index finger. "If you say so. Wouldn't catch me dead in here if I didn't have to be." Then she smiled. "Unless of course they're paying me double time."

"We should all be so lucky," Schilling said. "Anyway, I've had an old file on my desk all week. Might as well take a look at it."

"Yeah. Good day to catch up on stuff. What file?"

"Cindy Forsberg. Missing person case. Sometime from the nineties. You know it?"

Chantel shook her head. "I'm not from here, you know. I'm from Cranbrook." She said it like it was Paris. "And I'm not *that* old. You want to know about ancient history, you need to talk to Kelly. She knows everything and everybody."

"Ah, good to know," Schilling said. "I'll go get in my uniform, just in case."

Schilling was barely back at her desk before Chantel called her. She lifted her hand from the Cindy Forsberg folder and reached for the phone. "Yes?"

"Resnick just called. He said to call you and tell you to get your ass into uniform and then call him for more instructions."

"How about I get right on that?" Schilling said with a laugh.

Michelle had invited Wilson to dinner when he'd first moved to town. Gary stood in the middle of his disorganized garage and tried to think when that had been. Last winter sometime? Gary had trudged out in the snow to barbecue the pork chops and Wilson had stayed inside talking to Michelle, which Gary thought was weird. What kind of guy doesn't come out and stand by the barbecue and drink beer?

It was just a friendly, welcome-to-town dinner for a new co-worker, and if it'd been up to Gary they would have left it at that. But Michelle said the guy was lonely, had no social life. She was convinced that Gary should be his friend.

Take him golfing. Have Wilson over to watch the game. Wilson couldn't golf for shit—the guy liked *fishing,* for Christ's sake—and when he watched the game he had no idea what was going on. But Gary dutifully called anyway and invited the pharmacist along, because Michelle insisted.

That's why he recognized the number on Seymour's secret cell phone.

"Hello?" Wilson's voice was hushed and a little panicked.

"It's Seymour," Gary said.

"Seymour, what the—" Wilson interrupted himself. When he came back on the line he spoke in a hushed whisper. "Seymour? Is it really you? How—"

"How what?" Gary imitated Seymour's low chuckle.

"I thought you were—"

"Thought I was what? What's wrong you, man?" Pretending he was Seymour came more easily than Gary had expected. "I need to see you. Get this sorted out," he said, low and drawling, like Seymour in a bad mood.

"Um—" There was a pause on the line. "Um, okay. Come to the clinic. Tonight, okay?"

"Sure thing." His tone lazy.

"Seymour?" Wilson's voice was louder now. "You still got the stuff?"

"Sure, sure. I got it." It wasn't hard to tell one of Seymour's lies; he'd heard them all so many times.

"So we're back on, then? I'll let my guys across the line know."

"Sure thing, my man," Gary said. "See you tonight. Nine?"

"No, later! Later. Like eleven. Good? Hey, Seymour?"

"Yep, that's me." He'd heard Seymour say that a thousand times.

"Who's the dead guy then?" Wilson was back to whispering. "The guy they said was you?"

The air suctioned right out of Gary's chest. Dead guy? What the hell was he talking about? "Later," he choked out in a voice that didn't sound at all like Seymour's. He found his breath and tried again. "Later, my man. I'll explain everything."

Then Gary hung up—definitely in character, Seymour never answered questions he didn't want to answer—and went into the house in search of a newspaper.

"I've been standing here watching you for three and a half minutes."

Bern spun around at the sound of the voice. Resnick stepped out of the pattern of shade on the trail below. "I thought soldiers had better instincts."

"And I had no idea you could hike this far, let alone be quiet about it."

"Well, it's a good thing one of us has skills that are still sharp."

"Yes, evidently."

The shadows made the officer's heavy brow stand out. He looked even more pissed off than usual. "What have you found now?" he asked.

Bern pointed toward the rock, which was now in full sun. "Looks to me like a human cranium and two femur bones."

"Shit." Resnick's eyes were glassy—shining mirrors into whatever he'd been up to the night before. Bern knew that his own eyes were bloodshot versions of the same. "Did you call Kumar?"

"Twice. He doesn't want to send the forensic anthropologist over without knowing what we're dealing with. Save on the budget."

"Cheap bastard."

Bern laughed. "You've been known to be a tightwad with the RCMP budget, I might remind you."

The officer pulled a cigarette out of his breast pocket and sucked on the filter. "Right. So now what? What do you need?"

"We need to take some photos and email them to the forensic anthropologist. Bones in situ, and the surrounding area." Bern circled and pointed to the roots of an adjacent shrub. "We need photos of nearby plants and trees—see if we can match the roots to find the burial spot."

Resnick crouched down and pointed at the packed dirt of the trail. "And footprints, litter, debris. Any clues to how those bones got there." He looked up at the coroner. "So? Should we go have a look?"

Bern shook his head. "Not yet."

A dollop of sunshine reached them through the tree canopy. Resnick squinted, a rare smile playing on his lips. "Oh, I see."

"See what?"

"You're spooked." The officer stood, brushing off his pant legs. "Well, I don't think the RCMP needs to be as cheap as the coroner's office on this one. I've already called for Schilling. I'm sure between the two of you, you can find some evidence that will get your boss to change his tune."

Bern ignored the comment and crouched to look for debris on the trail. By the time Resnick had finished giving someone instructions over the phone, Bern had taken a mental inventory of fourteen items they'd need to collect—from empty beer cans to gum wrappers and apple cores. It was going to be another long day with no breakfast to speak of.

"There's something more," Bern said as Resnick finally disconnected the call. "And you're not going to like it."

"Always something up with you, isn't there?" He squeezed the unlit cigarette between his fingers. "Spill it, Fortin."

"I was over at Gia Hinton's house last night and I saw a guy just over the fence around the garden. There's a clearing over there. You ever seen it?"

Resnick shook his head.

"He seemed to come out of nowhere. So after he took off I went to have a look around. And I found an underground bunker. Huge. Made of shipping containers—half a dozen of them, at least. I only got as far as the entry area and I couldn't see much. But the smell was unmistakable."

"Over the fence? Like west of the property?"

"Yes."

"Huh. Pretty sure that's Crown land." The officer's face broke into sly smile. "Gotcha."

"Sorry, what?"

"Gotcha! And it's about time. We've known for years that they're growing pot on that property. Even with the husband put away, there is some kind of grow op happening there. We've been looking for an excuse to go in, and now we have it. You know what, Fortin?"

"What?"

"If you weren't such an ugly son of a bitch, I'd kiss you."

"Ah," Bern said, "my ugly face finally did me some good."

"So now I really need to get out of here. You wait here for Schilling. She'll look after everything."

"What will you do?" Bern asked.

"I'm going to get started on a search warrant for that property." Resnick tipped his unlit cigarette at him. "I'll come back up here this afternoon and see how you made out."

Bern pointed a finger back at him. "Just because you're out of my sight doesn't mean you can light that thing."

"Got it, boss," Resnick said, and headed back down the trail.

• • •

Gary tiptoed through his own house like the trespasser he was.

The kitchen smelled like the natural tea tree cleaner that Michelle sold as a sideline. Ounce for ounce it cost more than good wine, but Michelle insisted it was practically free after she'd wrangled most of her friends into buying from her.

"You get all these bonuses. Plus there are hair products too. Shampoo that will keep your hair from falling out. It's great! I ordered six of them."

A dozen muffins sat in the container that Michelle always kept full of home-baked goods. Carrot and walnut—Natasha's favorite—but he dared not eat one. Instead he pulled a burrito from the freezer and heated it in the microwave.

When the burrito was ready he stood over the sink to eat it. It was hot enough on the outside to burn his tongue and frozen in the middle, but still an improvement over the fruit leather he'd found in the camping supplies for breakfast.

Burrito finished, he inspected the counter and sink for crumbs, then wandered into the living room. He sat gingerly on the couch in a puff of tea tree–scented air. The couch, the carpet, the dainty cushions, the glass bowl on the glass coffee table—all felt lifeless. Aside from the photos of Natasha and Geoffrey, there was nothing in the room that meant anything to him. He'd lived in a stranger's house all these years. Lived a stranger's life.

The current edition of the Kootenay Landing newspaper was in its usual spot, on the lower shelf of the coffee table. Seymour's high school yearbook photo stared up at him from page one. Gary yanked the paper out and started reading. The article carried over from page one to a full spread on pages four and five. He read the whole thing, then closed and folded the paper and placed it back in the exact center of the coffee table shelf.

Gary Dowd. Person of interest in this case. Seymour was dead—murdered—and the police wanted to talk to *him*? He was in shit he didn't even know about. On the run. Keeping secrets from Michelle and her family. All things he'd go down for if he had to. But murder? *Seymour's* murder? They couldn't hang that one on him.

He had to get out of town. But first he needed to make this thing with Wilson work. Whatever it was that Seymour had started, Gary had to finish it.

He'd need a few urgent supplies to get by until he had some cash. Toothpaste and toothbrush from the stash that Michelle kept in the guest bathroom. A washcloth. A fleece pullover from the back of his closet that Michelle would never miss. An extra pair of socks. A shower, a shave, clean underwear—all these luxuries would have to wait. He crept upstairs to collect the basics without leaving a trace of his presence. On the way out he dug around in the odds and ends drawer by the back door until he found the spare set of keys. Then he put the key he'd used to let himself in back under the flowerpot where they always kept it.

The backyard was a minefield of disregarded "Honey-Do" jobs. He traversed the overly long grass and leaned against the paint-peeling wall of the garage. Sheltered from the prying eyes of neighbors by a tall back fence that also needed painting, he took a moment to feel the sun on his none-too-clean skin. Then he let himself back into the garage and squeezed into his secret hideout for a nap. He had hours to kill before his meeting with Wilson.

•   •   •

"Take a break," Bern said, setting aside the bag of debris he'd collected while Schilling had taken photos and emailed them to the chief coroner. "There's not much more we can do until we hear back from my boss."

"You ever worked a bones case before?" she asked him.

He shrugged and leaned back against the trunk of a nearby tree. "I guess you could say I've had a few of these."

Schilling turned her back on the bones. Her bright-yellow RCMP slicker rustled as she settled herself at the base of the throne rock. "Are they always this creepy?"

"Always."

"Those eagles aren't helping. Feels like they're staring at us."

Bern looked up to see the eagle at the top of the closest larch gazing out on the horizon. "I don't know. I find them kind of comforting. How's the investigation going? Any progress on Gary?"

Schilling blew out a breath. "Resnick's wasting everyone's time. I just spent a day and a half knocking on doors and getting farmhands to show me where they keep their bolt stunners. I know it was my idea, but honestly? A day and a half?"

"So no luck, then?"

"None. I mean, there are lots of farms. But none with missing bolt stunners. And no one caught sight of Gary on Sunday between the time he ran and the time Seymour got shot."

Bern's stomach gurgled, but he felt oddly disconnected from hunger or any sensation in his body. "You think he's barking up the wrong tree with this Gary angle?"

"He's just trying to keep me busy." She kicked at the dirt in frustration. "Punishing me for not getting Dr. Sinclair to come in. It's totally the wrong angle."

"I think he's getting clearer on that picture. Especially after what I found yesterday. Did he tell you?" When she shook her head he described the underground bunker adjacent to the Hintons' property.

"Finally," she sighed.

"If I may—" Bern started, choosing his words with care. "I think you have good instincts. You're going to make a good cop."

"You don't think I'm a good cop now?"

The hurt in her voice surprised him and he waved a hand as though to erase the words. "I've seen soldiers like you. Bristle against authority when your commander rubs you the wrong way. It'll trip you up every time."

"But he's getting in the way of the investigation!"

Bern shrugged. "Then you work around him. And you follow your instincts as best you can, when you can. Make him think it was his idea. You're good at that, Maddie. You'll go far if you figure this out. You just can't let your attitude get in your own way."

"But don't you think he's wrong?"

"It seems unlikely that Gary shot Seymour, I agree with you there. But there's no doubt Gary needs to be found. And the best way to do that—"

"Legwork. Right," Schilling said, tapping her cell phone against the yellow stripe of her uniform pants. "It's got to be the drug angle. We know Seymour was involved with drugs and the Hells Angels. There's the Hintons with their history of growing pot, and now this grow op. It's got to be drugs. Don't you think?"

Bern rolled his head against the bark of the tree, thinking back to his earlier conviction that all the incidents were related somehow. "You want to know what I think?"

"I'm asking you, aren't I?"

"Yes, you are, and so I'll tell you. I think it's extremely unlikely that two eagles would spend the better part of a day standing watch over these bones. And yet they are."

Schilling ran a hand through her mousy hair, only to have it fall back in the same place. "I don't see how that has anything to do with anything."

"Me neither. But you aren't the only one with good instincts, and here's what my gut tells me: all these strange incidents—Gary, Seymour, the grow op, these bones?—they are all tied together, as unlikely as it seems right now. All we need to do is find the right thread and pull."

Bern's cell phone rang as he stood. "Are you ready to get back to work? Here's my commander with our marching orders."

With the battery-operated trimmer, the whole thing took less time than he'd thought. He'd worked from dawn and by late afternoon Lennon started his drive back down from the cabin, crop manicured and hung to dry on a series of makeshift clotheslines in the old hunting cabin.

He hadn't gone far when a man came out of the trees and flagged him down. A police officer. *Shit.* Lennon did a quick scan of the truck as he geared down. Nothing. He was cool. He pulled as far right as he could and slowed to a crawl, but he didn't stop until the officer gestured again. *Resnick. More shit.* Lennon rolled down the window.

"Lennon, what brings you up this way?" Resnick put one hand on the edge of the window, an unlit cigarette between his fingers.

"Just checking on our logging sites."

"Logging, huh? Little late in the year for quote unquote logging, wouldn't you say?"

"Not at all. We'll be working one of those upper blocks all winter long."

"Good income from logging these days?"

"Not bad," Lennon said. "We're trying to be selective, you know. Not clear-cut the whole thing."

"Right. Keep a good cover for other crops."

Lennon kept his face neutral. "I don't know about that, sir, but it's better for the environment. And we don't want to be greedy."

"Right, right. Would never want to be greedy. So where is this block exactly?"

"Oh, way up at the seven-kilometer marker."

"You've been there all day?"

Lennon nodded. "Been up there marking trees and ribboning all day." He gestured to the bucket of tree-marking ribbon he always kept in the back seat.

"Uh-huh. You know what? I don't believe you. Not for one second. But I've got bigger fish to fry on a crime that happened before you were probably even born. So off you go," Resnick said. He tapped the window ledge with the flat of his hand and went to pull it away, then seemed to change his mind. "Say, where are you living these days?"

"Home," he said. "At my parents', I mean. Sometimes above the café. Why?"

"No reason. See you soon." He tapped the window again and really did take his hand away this time.

"Have a good night, Staff Sergeant," Lennon said as he put the truck in gear.

"You too. See you soon."

Lennon rolled down the hill, taking the turns nice and slow. He was almost back to the road before he could breathe fully again, but he didn't let down his guard completely.

See you soon. Resnick had said it not just once but twice.

STATEMENT FROM HOLLY FORSBERG

In support of our application for a peace bond against Jared John of Kootenay Landing, BC, I provide the following information:

My husband and I adopted Cindy Forsberg (formerly John) in 1984, when she was eight years old. During her short life she had been terribly abused and neglected. There were signs of sexual abuse as well, but the offender was never caught.

We suspected at the time that the offender was Cindy's cousin Jared John. This was never proven and no charges were laid against him. In the interests of helping Cindy get on with her life, we let the matter drop and focused on moving forward.

Under our care, Cindy has thrived. She is a happy, lively girl. She has always been a talented figure skater. Now, at age twelve, she has begun to compete at the provincial level and shows great promise.

Our complaint is that Jared John continues to attend every one of Cindy's skating practices, performances, and competitions. In the past six months we have traveled to Cranbrook, Kelowna, and Burnaby for competitions, and Mr. John is always in the stands. He does not approach Cindy or talk to her. He just sits in the stands, by himself, and stares at her. He always picks a very visible place high up in the arena, away from other spectators, so Cindy can clearly see him.

We believe he is stalking her and we want this behavior to stop. Given their history, we believe his presence is not in Cindy's best interests. My husband has asked Mr. John to stop attending the practices and competitions, but Mr. John refused to look at him and did not respond when spoken to.

Please find attached a detailed list of fifty-seven sightings of Mr. John at Cindy's skating practices, performances, and competitions in the past three months.

Signed: *Holly Forsberg*
Dated: February 23, 1988

21

There was only one cash register open at the first grocery store. Schilling recognized the cashier right away. The last time she'd seen her—late shift on Saturday night—the woman had been in her bathrobe and little else. She was barefoot on the cold pavement in the middle of the night, yelling at her boyfriend. He yelled back—just as drunk as she was—calling her a skank while another officer held his arms. The woman's bathrobe had fallen open and Maddie tried not to look at her breasts, which stuck straight out in perfect globes while the rest of the skin on her neck and chest sagged down.

"He punched me, that bastard! That bastard!"

Now Schilling placed each of her grocery items on the conveyor belt. She'd allowed herself one bag of chips and a plastic tub full of two-bite brownies. It was a good thing she'd added the mini organic carrots and the bag of oranges at the last minute.

Lisa, the cashier's name tag said. Schilling filled in the rest from memory: Lisa Kensington, age forty-seven, address 32 Osprey Close.

A tightness at the corner of Lisa's eyes was the only indication that she remembered Schilling.

"Having a little party?" she asked. Her enhanced breasts were buttoned demurely into her uniform shirt and she looked like just another smiling cashier. She was wearing foundation, a lot of it, and had managed to cover the discoloration from the bruise that Schilling knew must still be there.

"Something like that," Maddie said.

"In the middle of the week?"

"Well, I worked all weekend."

"Ah." She averted her eyes. "Need a bag?"

There were three aisles open at the other grocery store, so Maddie risked an extra-large bag of Cheezies and two bags of chocolate chips. The thin-crust pizzas with the fancy toppings were on sale. She bought three, along with a box of spicy chicken wings.

She picked the only male cashier. He didn't even look at her food, let alone comment on it. She need not have bothered with the head of romaine lettuce and the two still-green tomatoes from Mexico. She bought them anyway.

"Grilled cheese, *maman*?"

"*En français, cher.*" Aimée wasn't sure which she hated more: that she needed to say the words at all or that scolding her son came so automatically. She didn't want to scold him. She didn't. It was just that she was so tired. And if she didn't teach him to speak French, no one else would. Nobody else cared.

She'd carried him up the steps and now she slid him down onto the linoleum floor. The kitchen of the apartment they shared was much smaller than the one in the café downstairs. It was opposite in every way, really. Downstairs, the café gleamed with stainless steel commercial appliances, broad pine floorboards, walls painted glossy white and covered with paintings from local artists. Upstairs was so small that only half the couch fit in the living room. The other half stretched into the hallway and they were forced to turn sideways to squeeze into the kitchen. Except Gabriel. He jumped onto the arm and then leaped into the kitchen like a superhero.

"Fromage grillé, maman!" he shouted now as he flew through the air.

"Oui, monsieur," she said. She didn't have the heart to tell him to stop jumping. Isn't that what four-year-olds were supposed to do? Jump all day long if they wanted? Go to the park? Fingerpaint on big sheets of paper taped to the wall? Weren't they supposed to nap in their beds in the afternoon, and not on a cot at the back of a café kitchen? Let him jump.

Cooking for the two of them was the last thing she felt like doing after a day of cooking for the whole town in the café. Just once it would be nice to come home and find that Lennon had cooked for them. Just one time. He still had a key, though he rarely used it. He rarely slept there anymore.

She laid the cloth grocery bag on the counter and pulled out her groceries: she'd shopped from the café again. A hunk of cheese cut from the much larger one kept in the commercial fridge. A half loaf of bread from the batch of dough that she'd run downstairs to knead at five a.m., while Gabriel was still sleeping. A takeout container of Greek salad—if she washed the feta and dressing off the cucumbers and tomatoes, Gabriel might eat them. Two-day-old muffins for their breakfast.

"Fromage grillé, maman! Fromage grillé!" He was squatted on the back of the couch now, jumping down into a perfect handstand.

"Bien fait, mon petit," she said. Well done.

They'd missed gymnastics today, yet again. She'd begged

Lennon to let her sign Gabriel up, to give him something to do. Lennon had agreed, of course; he always did. He'd gone right over with Gabriel and checked it out and paid—in cash. Money was never the problem.

But after the first few times, Lennon had gotten busy. Too busy to take Gabriel to gymnastics, and too busy to cover Aimée at the café so that she could take him. What was keeping him so busy? He would not tell her.

"Hello?"

Aimée dropped the skillet on the counter at the unexpected sound of the voice from below.

"Oui?" she called back. "Lennon?"

Gabriel landed a two-footed jump onto the floor from his handstand and with a twirl was at the top of the stairs, looking down.

"C'est pas lui," he announced. It's not him. Gabriel refused to call Lennon Papa or Dad. Most of the time he just called him *lui*—him.

"C'est qui, alors?" Who is it, then?

Gabriel stood at the top of the stairs, a huge smile on his face. "It's soldier man!" he shouted.

The French man from the café, Aimée thought, and called down, *"Ah, c'est toi."* It's you.

"I brought dinner," a voice called up. A voice she didn't recognize.

"She's already making dinner," Gabriel said. *"Fromage grillé."*

"Gabriel, who is it?" She squeezed by the couch and joined him at the top of the stairs.

"The man who gave me the soldiers, *maman,*" he said.

The man was stopped halfway up the stairs, a grocery bag in each hand. She recognized the slant to his eyebrows, his dark skin, blue eyes and a smile that looked like it could turn mean at any minute. He'd been to the café before.

The awareness of what was about to happen—what she was about to do to herself—hit her when she turned on the oven. She pushed it away.

Schilling ripped the bag of Cheezies open with her teeth and pulled out a handful. She took two cookie sheets from the drawer beneath the oven, pulled open the box of chicken wings, and dumped out the contents. She slid one cookie tray into the still-cold oven, then put one pizza onto the other tray and slid that in too.

"There. Dinner," she said.

She rifled through the rest of the bags now, sorting as mindlessly as the cashiers had done. Carrots, lettuce, tomatoes—she left these on the counter. The other two pizzas into the freezer. Everything else she lugged to the floor in front of the TV. She sat down, not on the sofa but on the floor. She pushed this thought away too, and along with it the cashier's snide look.

Schilling argued with her in her head: *Your boyfriend beats you. At least I have one. And look at my life: nice house, nice furniture.*

Schilling looked around her basement suite. On a sunny day the plain white walls looked cheery, but in the fading light they seemed bland. She pushed herself up from the floor and went to change—this time into her eating pants and a loose-fitting T-shirt. The relief of the soft elastic around her waist was palpable.

There is room for me now. Room for me.

The cashier again: *Just watch you don't get fat.*

Schilling was back in the living room, TV remote in one

hand, the other tearing at packages and bringing food, unseen, to her mouth. No, there was no taste to the pink cupcakes sprinkled with sweetened coconut. There was no enjoyment in the chocolate chips, eaten straight from the bag.

Each of those bags is half a pound of chocolate and sugar! Did you know that? And fat! Look how many grams of fat!

When the pizza was ready she sliced it and put it onto a plate. First only half—but who was she kidding?

"Might as well eat it while it's hot," she said out loud to the ghost of the cashier.

The hot pizza, the warm dough with the melted cheese, was perfect. She felt the deadness growing in her and welcomed it, craved it. She chewed off another bite before the first was barely swallowed and felt it mounting in her: a wall of relief, of unfeeling.

Was my order not clear, Constable? Resnick, now. There was no pleasing the man. With him, either she got it wrong or she got it wrong.

Give her a chance to explain. Almost worse, the way the coroner stood up for her with his old-fashioned manners and his roaming, sad eyes.

She breathed between bites now, eating more slowly, though still actively pushing against that feeling in her diaphragm—the feeling of a balloon being pressed to its maximum and threatening to explode.

She got up and refilled the plate—with chicken wings this time. The spiciness of them, the hands-on job of holding them, the gnawing of the bones under her teeth, soothed her in a new way.

How is Maddie? I haven't seen her in a while.

Oh, fine. She's fine. She's around here somewhere. Maddie?

She chomped into another chicken wing and ignored the heat that burned the roof of her mouth raw.

Maddie? Come down and say hi to your uncle.

Her mother's strident voice reached her, but it was as though the thick sleeping bag she had tucked around herself back then deadened the sound even in memory. She had been hiding at the back of her closet. Just another pile of linens.

I didn't hear her go out, did you?

Since when does she tell us? Teenagers. Her father.

Eventually they would settle back in their seats, beers in hand, chips on the table, football on the TV, but Maddie stayed on the floor at the bottom of the closet. That's when she would ever so slowly open the Tupperware container filled with her mother's cookies and eat them one by one. Each one was a buffer against the past and in case of the future. In case her uncle went looking for her. In case he found her.

Now she stayed on the floor of her own basement apartment, her uncle three provinces away. She stayed on the floor through the rest of the chicken wings and the second pizza. Through the second bag of chocolate chips, the last of the Cheezies, and the three chocolate bars. She stayed there on the floor, even though the couch was right next to her. When she got sleepy she pulled a quilt off the couch and bunched it around her. It was the one her mother had made her—a log cabin pattern, the scrap of red in each square signifying the light of home. When her stomach was so stuffed she could not fit in one more thing, she closed her eyes.

The food wrappers crinkled on the floor with each movement. As she fell to sleep at last, deadened and relieved, the ghost of the cashier took one last shot.

At least I won't let myself get fat.

• • •

"Gabriel, come here." She tucked his small body behind her legs.

The man's smile widened. "No need to worry, mama bear," he said as he reached the top of the stairs. She stepped back to make room; they could barcly all fit on the landing.

He lifted a grocery bag to gesture toward the couch. "Why don't you sit down with your boy? Let me cook for you tonight."

Gabriel clung to her legs, and as she reached down to pull him up, her shoulder brushed the man's pressed cotton shirt. His aftershave was expensive and she could see he was old—as old as her father. He reached out and ran his finger along her clavicle, following the outline of the tattooed skull as though it completed a current and connected him to her.

Aimée shuffled sideways, out of the way. She placed her hand flat on Gabriel's head and pulled it down so his face covered her tattooed chest. She made her way to the couch and sat with him. Only once she was sitting did she realize what a relief it was to be off her feet.

"Who are you?" she asked.

"I'm a friend. Spaghetti okay for dinner?" He squeezed past her into the kitchen and started pulling vegetables from his bag: carrots, celery, green pepper. He opened a drawer and pulled out an eight-inch chef's knife. Lennon liked to keep them sharp, though she always worried about Gabriel getting his hands on them.

"I love spaghetti!" the boy said.

"Yes, you do, don't you?" Then she added, "But Lennon won't like it."

The thwack of the knife through the carrot made her jump. He sliced like a pro.

"Lennon should take better care of what's his—if he wants to keep it." The staccato of knife hitting cutting board punctuated his words.

She should tell him to leave. Lennon would not like this one bit. Plus she could sense this man's meanness, no matter how nice he was being at the moment. She should tell him to go.

But Gabriel would want spaghetti now. And it felt so good to sit down. To wrap her arms around her boy and, for the first time since her feet hit the ground before dawn, do nothing. Gabriel nudged his sleepy head against her chest and pulled on the strap of her tank top.

"Nou nou," he said.

She gave him a stern look. She'd been weaning him for weeks, but with little success. *He's too old to nurse,* Lennon was always telling her, but in the evenings it was so hard. Gabriel wanted to nurse, she wanted to take a break, and it was just easier. Shouldn't there be something in her life that was just easy? That wasn't a fight?

So she let him pull down the strap of her tank and latch on to her breast. If the man who'd stormed into her kitchen dared say anything, he could just let himself out.

But he didn't say anything. He just kept on chopping and sautéing, watching them from the corner of his eerily blue eyes. After a few minutes Gabriel started making that humming sound that he made when he was about to nurse himself to sleep. Aimée reached for something to cover herself with. She found a hoodie of Lennon's and was about to cover her breast with it when she looked up to see him staring right at her, as though she was the spaghetti dinner and he was a starving man.

She pulled Gabriel closer to her and covered his arm and face with the hoodie. He started a new round of his presleep grumbling hum and sigh, releasing her breast from his mouth. Aimée looked up at the man. He stared back.

"Spaghetti will be ready soon," he said.

"I think you should go," she replied.

"No," he said. His face was mean now. "Not until you eat."

She stood. "I'll just put him down."

"Leave him there."

She tilted her head and shifted the sleeping Gabriel on her hip. "I don't know who the hell you are, but this is my house. He sleeps in his bed. *Point final.*" End of story.

He smiled and his face opened. "Nice," he said, nodding. "I like your spunk."

She felt a flutter that she'd made him smile and she stomped it down as quickly as it appeared. Who the hell did this guy think he was? She'd put Gabriel down, then get rid of him.

She shuffled past him to get through the tiny kitchen to the even tinier bedroom that was Gabriel's. At least he had his own room. It was something she'd never had as a child.

She stepped into the dark room and pushed the door partly closed with her foot. She laid Gabriel on the bed and sat down next to him. He did not stir.

"*Ça va, petit monsieur. Dors, dors.*" As she spoke she pulled her cell phone out of her pocket and flipped it open. She had texted Constable Schilling only once before—it was months ago, when she'd hung out with the officer a few times. Aimée had thought they could be friends, but Lennon didn't like it. *People like us aren't friends with police officers,* he'd said.

"What are you doing in there?"

"Shh. Just getting him settled."

She scrolled through the numbers until she found the one

she thought was Schilling's. She typed, *Come to my apt. Right now. Urgent.* She slipped the phone back in her pocket.

"Come eat now." His voice was quieter, but the edge was still there.

She brushed Gabriel's forehead one last time. She'd keep him safe. No matter what. Whoever this man was—whatever happened—he would not hurt Gabriel.

She woke up with something pressing on her face. It covered her nose and mouth with a heaviness that kept her from breathing. She was frozen in place, couldn't move her arms from the weight on her.

He'd found her.

She wriggled her arms free and tugged at the covering over her face. It crinkled in response and then gave. Soft, not heavy.

Don't scream—you'll wake everyone up.

How had he gotten in? How? She pushed and pushed. Against nothing. The quilt fell away, and with it the plastic grocery bag that had tangled its way into her hair and covered her face while she slept. She could have died.

She was alone. Alone in her sad apartment. Alone with her secondhand couch. Alone on the floor. Her uncle—with his heavy weight, his breath that stank of sauerkraut and threats—was back in the past where he belonged.

But she still could not breathe. The heaviness in her chest cut off the air, and when she sat up, a sharp cramp of pain radiated across her ribs and down, where it joined the pelvic cramp that had dogged her for days. She stayed there, half lying, half sitting, taking shallow breaths. Each breath hurt more than the last. She had muted the TV but the pictures rolled on: the Gilmore Girls, yelling at each other in that frenetic way that passed as repartee. They filled her with dread, mother and daughter with their shiny hair and their tight jeans.

Through the pain of the cramp she felt tears prick at her eyes and the weight of her own body land on her. She could feel the heaviness of the skin that was now surely folding over her bra strap more than it had before she had fallen asleep. She could feel the place where her elastic waistband seemed to cut at her skin. She dreaded having to get dressed in normal pants again. Or in her uniform.

Was she having a heart attack? Maybe it was for the best. She didn't want to die, but she couldn't stop herself either. If she kept it up, she would be fat before long.

The room came into high relief then. They would find her here—but how long would it take? She wasn't scheduled to work until Saturday. If she didn't show up for her shift, they would probably come looking for her. And what would they find? Her dead body in her fat pants, among the wrappers and plastic bags.

Her cell phone pinged then. Maddie pushed through the pain, digging through the debris on the floor until she found her phone half under an empty chip bag. A text. A connection. A reason to stop.

She stood in the doorway to the kitchen and smoothed her tank top over her hips. He'd set the kitchen table and served a plate for each of them—a small portion for her, a larger one for him. He sat at his own seat and looked in her direction, but not into her eyes.

"Looks delicious," she said, though she doubted she'd be able to eat a bite. "Should we have some wine? I've got a bottle—"

"No!" His voice was angry. "No alcohol. Alcohol ruins your body," he said. "Sit down and take off your shirt."

"Sorry?" If she was hungry at one point she was no longer. Had she really let this man into her house? All for the relief of having someone cook her dinner? Maybe she was as stupid as Lennon said.

He grabbed her wrist as she walked by. In one motion he twisted it behind her back and pulled himself to standing. "I said sit down and take off your shirt." His voice was quiet and his breath hot in her ear. "Don't you listen, skater girl? I want to see your whole tattoo. And you've already shown me your tits, so what the hell difference does it make?"

She swallowed and opened her eyes wide to keep the tears from falling. Skater girl? What the hell was he talking about? And where was Schilling? Where, for that matter, was Lennon?

"Now sit down and take off your shirt," he said, his voice an invitation. His hand brushed against her hairline, under her ear. "And eat."

She sat. Her throat was so dry she could barely swallow but there was not so much as a glass of water at the table. The sauce was thick with chunky pieces of vegetable and sliced sausage. Aimée had been a vegetarian since her tenth birthday.

He sat across from her. "Good. You're sitting. What next?"

She looked straight across the table to his slanted forehead, his mean blue eyes that were focused somewhere around her clavicle. She grabbed the hem of her tank top and lifted it up. She broke contact with his stare only long enough to pull the top over her head.

She dropped her shoulders back and held her head high,

shaking her cropped hair. She could feel the fatigue of the day in the soreness of her legs and the pain between her shoulder blades. All she wanted in the world was to sit back on the couch with a glass of wine in her hand and her feet in Lennon's lap and share a toke.

She picked up her fork and swirled it around on her plate, filling her fork with vegetables and pasta, refusing to think that a piece of sausage might have got mixed in with what she was about to put in her mouth. She lifted her fork, opened her lips, and took a bite.

"Tell me the story of your tattoos," he said.

Her throat closed around her food. This was too much. She concentrated on chewing to keep from spitting her food back on her plate.

He stood again and circled around behind her. He pressed a finger against the top vertebrae of her spine, where the tattoo began. "Why a seed that grows into a skull?" His finger crawled over her shoulder and then began pressing into the muscles, sore from kneading bread. When he reached her clavicle his touch became feather-like, following the line of the skull. He pressed his lips to her ear and she cringed and tilted her head away.

Where was Maddie?

"Tell me," he said. He nibbled on her earlobe and she tensed even further. Her skin puckered into goose pimples.

"Tell me," he said again. He pinched her earlobe, his fingernails biting into the delicate skin.

She couldn't tell him the story of her tattoos, how each image marked a part of her journey and all she had left behind: her native Quebec, her native tongue, her family, and so many traditions. Each image signified the newness of her life, of finding her own way. She'd had them permanently painted onto her skin as a way to clear the path and tell the story of it, both at the same time. She hadn't told anyone, except Lennon.

There was a knock from below—the front door of the café.

"Aimée?" They could barely hear Schilling's voice through the second-story windows.

"Who's that?" he asked. He rolled down the sleeves of his white shirt. "What did you do?"

Aimée shrugged. "My friend Maddie. She sometimes stops by in the evening."

He went to the living room window and looked out. "It's that cop! I can't believe you called the cops."

Aimée shook her head. "She's my friend. Sometimes she stops by. Just like you stopped by, yes?"

Then he was behind her again, his hands on her hair, his thumbs pushing hard into the base of her skull. "We are not done," he said. And then he was gone, out the back door, the same way he had come.

"I don't want to make a report," Aimée said. She scraped the food from the plates into the garbage. "I'm just telling you, as a friend."

Schilling tried to get her head out of police mode and into friend mode. "So he just broke in and started making you dinner?"

Aimée left the room and came back a moment later, cradling the sleeping Gabriel in her arms. She sat on the couch with the boy in her lap. Her face was drawn, her olive skin pale. She shook her head.

Schilling sat next to her. "What? He didn't break in?"

"The door was unlocked. I must have forgotten to lock it."

"Okay," Schilling said. "So he didn't break in. He walked in? And insisted on making you dinner. Did he say anything threatening?"

"He wouldn't leave when I asked him to. And I didn't like the way he looked at me." Her voice was defiant. "You make it sound like it's my fault."

"Sorry, I don't mean to. It's just . . . what did he say?" She stood. "Wait, let me make you some tea." She had to turn sideways to squeeze past the couch into the kitchen. It was a house for skinny people. She filled the kettle and plugged it in.

"He said that Lennon needs to take better care of his belongings. And he made me take off my shirt."

"He made you?" Schilling chose two cups and sorted through a cupboard full of tea. She found a tea called WomanEase and decided that if there was ever a time for that, it was now.

"Well, he told me to. And I did."

"Why?"

"Because he wanted to look at my tattoo." She shuddered as she spoke. "The whole thing."

Schilling closed her eyes. Friend. Not police officer, she reminded herself. She poured boiling water over the two tea bags and used a spoon to swirl them around.

"I guess what I'm asking is—how did he make you? Did he do something to convince you? Or to force you?"

Aimée brushed a hand along Gabriel's hairline and looked down at his sleeping face. "He's a scary guy. He's just got a scary way about him. Like if you don't listen to him, he'll really hurt you."

"But he didn't. Hurt you, I mean."

"No. He just scared me."

Schilling squeezed back into the living room, two teacups in hand. She handed one to Aimée and sat back down with her own. "So basically he came in uninvited and made you dinner?" She took a sip. The tea was dark green and tasted bitter.

Aimée laughed then. "Sounds horrible, doesn't it? And I'm a vegetarian. The sauce had sausage in it."

Aimée had pulled a hoodie over her tank top, but she still looked exotic and beautiful. In her eating pants and oversized T-shirt, Maddie felt frumpier than ever. "I just don't know what I can do if you won't fill out a report."

Aimée stared at her hard and tilted her head.

Schilling tilted her own head back. This was the friendship part: she could feel it. "What do you want me to do?"

"Can you find out who he is? I just need to know. Is he a bad guy—"

"Or is he just a weirdo who likes sausages? Okay, I'll find out. Did he tell you his name?"

Aimée shook her head. "*Non.* He looks Native, like First Nations. Maybe in his late forties? He was dressed up, though—nice jeans, white dress shirt. I've seen him around."

"And Lennon knows who he is?"

"Oh, but you can't ask him! He'll just get jealous. And then he won't help in the café at all. It will be so much trouble."

Schilling sighed. "Okay, okay. I'll see what I can find out based on your description. It's a small town. Shouldn't be too hard."

"Thank you. As a friend, not a police officer, right?"

Schilling took another sip of her bitter tea. "As a friend." She said it just to see the relief in Aimée's features, but the distinction struck her as very convenient. "And because I'm a police officer."

MISSING PERSON REPORT

ROYAL CANADIAN MOUNTED POLICE—KOOTENAY LANDING, BC

MISSING PERSON

Name: Cynthia Amanda Forsberg

Alias/Street Name/Nickname: Cindy

Note: surname at birth—John

Relatives:

Duke Forsberg **(father)**

Holly Forsberg **(mother)**

Michelle Forsberg **(sister)**

Race: Native

Height: 5' 6"

Weight: 115 lbs.

Hair: Black (long)

Eyes: Brown

Sex: Female

Age: 17

DOB: January 14, 1976

Last seen wearing:

Gray wool sweater (men's)

Shirt: knit tank top, baby blue, image of whale on front

Pants: jeans, black denim

Shoes: cowboy boots

Other: thought to be carrying black backpack

Missing person reported by: Duke and Holly Forsberg (parents)

Narrative (brief summary of facts as supplied by reporting person):

Person reported missing by adoptive father, Duke Forsberg. Mr. Forsberg said his daughter was last seen leaving home on the morning of Saturday, June 19, 1993. Cindy did not say where she was going. She had been known to "hang out" with Seymour Melnychuk, also a student at Kootenay Landing Secondary School. Mr. Forsberg said it was not unusual for Cindy to come home late at night but that in the past she had always come home.

Mr. Forsberg became very worried when Cindy had not returned home by Sunday morning. Mrs. Forsberg looked in Cindy's room and noticed that her backpack and some clothes were missing. When asked if Cindy might have run away, Mr. Forsberg said it would not surprise him, while Mrs. Forsberg said she would be very surprised. Both agreed that Cindy had been "unhappy" and "sullen" for several months.

Reporting Officer: Corporal Godford
Reporting Date: June 20, 1993

22

The door swung open as Gary knocked on it. He stepped into the staff entrance of the clinic, as he had dozens of times before. To pick up Michelle. To drop off a forgotten lunch. To trade vans or exchange kids. All of it during regular business hours.

The entry was dark, but Gary knew his way. He started straight ahead to the dimly lit reception area.

The door swung closed behind him and he heard the dead bolt hit home.

Gary turned his head and caught a flash of white lab coat before the cold cylinder pressed against his temple. "Gary, you're in big trouble." There was nothing weak or uncertain in Wilson's voice now.

The vise closed around his rib cage. Gary couldn't breathe and dropped to his knees, fighting for air. He held his hands up. "Plea—" *Please,* he wanted to say, but the word would not come out. Wilson pressed the gun harder and Gary moved with the pressure until he was lying in a fetal position on the sanitized linoleum.

This was it. He was going to die right here in his wife's office. Shot. Or suffocated by his own breath.

Then the pressure at his temple lessened. "Wow," Wilson said.

"So that's what that looks like." Through half-closed eyes Gary saw the hem of the lab coat lower until its white cotton blend filled his vision. He sucked in a desperate breath. Wilson's face zoomed in toward him. "You ever think of taking something for that? An antianxiety medication—something mild that won't interfere with your day-to-day?"

Gary squawked as he laughed and inhaled at the same time. The next breath came easier. With the third one, he trusted himself to speak. "Is this what it's like to get held up by a pharmacist?"

Wilson sat back against the wall, the pistol dangling in his fingers, and giggled. That was a sound Gary was more used to hearing from him. He sat up too and leaned against the opposite wall. Wilson was nothing but gleaming eyes and white lab coat; the gun was barely visible in the dark hall.

"Were you really going to shoot me?" The antiseptic air of the clinic was as refreshing to Gary as mountain air, he was so relieved to be breathing again.

"I didn't know who you were. I just knew it couldn't be Seymour," Wilson said. "I had no idea what I'd be facing—the guys who killed Seymour come back to get me?"

"I didn't know when I called that he was dead." Gary sighed. "Do they know who killed him?"

"You. That's what they're saying anyway." As Wilson shifted, the pistol swung beneath his fingers. "But I know that's not true."

"Because you know I'd never do that."

"Something like that."

"So why'd you agree to the meeting, then? Why not just call the police?" His stomach growled as he spoke. He hadn't eaten in hours.

"You wouldn't make much of a criminal, Gary. Hunger pangs. Panic attacks." Wilson pointed the gun at him. "Michelle brought some muffins in today. They're in the fridge if you want some."

"You going to shoot me while I'm in there?" Gary asked as he stood.

"Nah. Go ahead."

The muffins were from the same batch he'd seen on his own kitchen counter that morning. He was headed back to the entry when he thought twice about it. "Want to sit in here and talk?" he called.

He heard Wilson get up off the floor. "Sure. Want to put the kettle on?" He flicked on the light switch, illuminating the sterile staff room.

Gary put the kettle on and pulled out a chair next to Wilson. Looking at the pharmacist's plain face, widely spaced eyes, pointed chin, and almost colorless hair, he realized how much the two of them looked alike. The thought depressed him.

"You still want to do the deal?"

Wilson laid the pistol down on the table and pawed through the muffins. "These aren't my favorite. I like the banana chocolate chip ones she makes."

Gary gripped Wilson's wrist. "Just quit it, would you?"

"Quit what?"

"Quit touching them, first of all. If you're not going to eat them, I am. And second, answer the question: Do you still want to do the deal?"

"The deal was with Seymour," Wilson said, pulling his hand away.

"So maybe the deal can be with me."

The pharmacist pinched the end of his nose like he was holding back a sneeze. "You got the stuff?"

Gary tossed the remainder of his muffin into his mouth and

reached into his back pocket. He pushed the pistol out of the way and placed a single jar of Victoria's Remedy at the center of the table. "This what you're looking for?"

Wilson reached forward and picked up the jar. "Did you know that Queen Victoria used marijuana to help with menstrual problems?" He twisted off the lid and sniffed as though he were testing the bouquet of a fine wine. He lifted his nose in the air and swayed his head from side to side. Closing his eyes, he said, "Beeswax is clear. Some kind of carrier oil—almond, maybe? Could be grapeseed. Comfrey. Calendula." Wilson snapped his eyes open and looked at Gary. "But what else?"

"Marijuana."

"Right. But not just any marijuana. It's a particular medicinal varietal, propagated just for this cream. Remarkably effective at treating symptoms of PMS."

Gary held up his palm. "And healing cuts. And headaches."

"Well, the wound healing is likely from the calendula. But headaches? Yes, that could be the marijuana. Unintended side effects of the main purpose: ease pain and balance hormones." He held the jar up to the light and smiled. "The wild yam is my job."

"Your job?" Gary asked over a mouthful of muffin.

"My job. I'm a pharmacist, remember? And every once in a while, Dr. Sinclair has a special job for me."

"Dr. Sinclair? Like, Michelle's boss?"

"Yes, Michelle's boss. My boss." Wilson pinched the end of his nose again. "She makes this cream. And the formula—whatever it is—involves a fair amount of progesterone cream, which I compound for her."

"Compound?"

He nodded. "The cream itself is derived from wild yams. It's been used for years to treat symptoms in menopausal women. Dr.

Sinclair needs a very low dosage, but she goes through a whole lot of it. So that part is my job. Order in the cream, and get the dosage just right for her purpose."

Gary looked down at his hand again. "And what is her purpose exactly?"

Wilson twisted the lid and put the jar back on the table. "She's never told me straight out. But I think she's found that when combined with marijuana, the progesterone cream gets rid of premenstrual symptoms. It's wildly popular anyway."

The kettle whistled behind him and Gary stood. He found a Styrofoam container of ramen noodles in the cupboard, peeled off the lid, and filled it with boiled water. "What kind of tea do you want?"

"Oh, nothing with caffeine," Wilson said. "Mint if there is some."

He rifled through the cupboard until he found a mint tea bag for Wilson and a regular tea bag for himself.

"So is this legal? What she's doing? What she's asking you to do?"

Wilson took the mug that Gary handed him and toyed the tea bag up and down before answering. "The part she's asked me to do is borderline. Progesterone cream is legal, but I need to be able to say where it's going. There have been questions."

"And this stuff?" Gary asked, picking up the jar of cream again.

"Dr. Sinclair's part in this is definitely illegal, although relatively harmless. I mean, experimenting with what is basically a homemade herbal salve is probably okay. One with marijuana, less so. But making it available, even in an indirect way, to the general population?" He took a sip of his tea. "Well, let's just say she's under pressure to cease and desist."

"So why does she do it?"

"She's very idealistic, our Dr. Sinclair. And she takes her job as a healer very seriously. I believe she has determined that the potential good of helping a whole lot of women with PMS outweighs the harm." He paused, mug of tea in his hand, pinky finger in the air.

"Okay. Let's get back to the point here. Tell me where Seymour comes in. And explain your deal with him."

Wilson shrugged. "I was curious about where all that wild yam cream was going. So I started to pay closer attention to Dr. Sinclair and what she was doing. One day a patient was listing her medications and offhandedly mentioned the cream, like it was nothing to worry about. Told me she got it from someone at Mountain Station Café and it was good for PMS. I gave her a twenty-dollar bill and asked her to bring me a jar.

"And she wasn't the only one. Other patients mentioned it. Some people came in asking to buy it from me. I put two and two together. Then I started to research the potential market value of a cream that could cure PMS. It's huge." He picked up the jar and rolled it between his palms. "This little jar in the right hands? It's worth tens of millions."

Tens of millions. Gary let that sink in while he got his ramen noodles and brought them to the table. "Millions?" he repeated. "Sounds like a stretch."

"What's across the line, Gary?"

What kind of question was that? But the pharmacist seemed to be waiting for an answer. "The United States," he said over a slurp of soup.

"Yes. And more specifically?"

Gary raised his spoon in the air. "Montana? Idaho? Washington?"

Wilson made a gun with his fingers and pointed it at Gary. He seemed to have forgotten about the real pistol on the table between them.

"Washington. Exactly. And not far from there? Oregon. And farther south still? California. And east? Colorado. All states that are working to legalize marijuana." He put down his teacup. "There are entrepreneurs in all those states looking to invest in new products so they'll be ready for market when the legislation passes."

"And these people are waiting for the package that Seymour tried to make me carry across the line?"

"Yeah, sorry about that. No way around it. They wanted a sample." He kept talking when he saw Gary's wide-eyed look. "I thought the risk was pretty low. I mean, how was I to know you were going to run away? Besides, when it came to the real shipment, I was going to take it myself. I've got it all set up."

"I can't believe you put me at risk like that." Gary shook his head. "You're a real shit, you know that?"

Wilson held up his hands. "Seymour's idea, not mine."

Gary pushed the soup away, not hungry anymore. "Seymour. It all comes back to him," he muttered. "How did you hook up with him anyway?"

"Why, at your house! I thought you knew."

Gary shook his head.

"Almost a month ago now. You had to work late and Michelle really didn't want to be alone with Seymour. So she asked me to come home with her for dinner. Seymour and I spent most of the evening talking while Michelle looked after the kids. He asked me lots of questions about Dr. Sinclair. Seemed he was working on another project and saw the cream as a sideline opportunity for himself. That dinner turned out to be the start of a long negotiation. We each had what the other was missing."

"You knew about the cream and had contacts," Gary supplied.

"Yes. I'd been going to conferences on medical marijuana. Making connections in the pharmaceutical industry. Asking around. I knew who to contact," he said. "And Seymour, it seemed, could do what I wasn't able to: get the product, and the plants, from Dr. Sinclair."

"Product and plants. So that's what you're looking for?"

Wilson nodded.

"And if I can get those for you? How much is it worth?"

The pharmacist smiled and narrowed his eyes. "Plenty." He pushed the gun aside and put his elbows on the table. "So do you know where the product and the plants are?"

Gary took a sip of his tea. "I think so. I have a good idea anyway. I just don't have a way to get them to you."

"No problem. I'll pick them up. Name the time and place."

Sitting back and crossing his arms, Gary considered his options. Product and plants. They were hidden somewhere in his house, he was sure of it. All he needed to do was think like Seymour to find them. "Okay," he said. "Let's talk money. And by money I mean cash. How much is this worth to you?"

After a day of guarding the bones of the dead, Bern found that the sight of Troy Thompson, solid and alive and sitting like a stray dog on his back step, did not annoy him nearly as much as it might have normally.

"The time has come, has it?" He stepped around the younger man and unlocked the door to his house. "See what you've made me do? Before you started showing up on my doorstep I never used to lock my door."

Thompson shrugged and slid into the house, his eyes darting from side to side, taking it all in like the robber he was. He didn't take off his shoes but walked straight to the bookshelf and started to finger the spines of the books. "Better than Alais anyway, right? His door is always locked. And he doesn't even have the key."

Bern closed his eyes and resisted the urge to shout the command that had lodged itself under his collarbone. He wanted the man out of his house, away from his one sanctuary in the world. He wondered if there was enough soldier left in Thompson to respond to a hollered command, or if he would have to remove the man by force.

"Whiskey?" he asked.

He didn't wait for an answer, pulling the bottle from the cupboard above the fridge. He came back with the bottle and three rock glasses, one filled with ice, and laid the lot on top of a coffee table book on the large footstool in front of the couch.

"Sit." He was no longer able to resist the urge to order Thompson to do something.

Troy raised an eyebrow but complied, though Bern wasn't sure if it was his tone or the sight of the whiskey bottle that convinced him. Bern took his usual spot in his armchair and left the couch for the journalist. Troy brought a book on backyard chickens with him.

"Chickens?" he asked.

Bern nodded. He poured his guest a drink and handed him the glass before pouring his own. He closed his eyes as he took the first sip, waiting for the warmth of the liquid to untangle the knot in his gut.

"There's a lot to be said for chickens." He put his drink down on a side table and crossed his ankle over his knee. "They're friendly creatures. And generous."

Thompson eyed him over his glass. "Yes, they offer up their young. Kind of like the military that way."

Bern leaned back. "That's how it's going to be, is it?"

Thompson shrugged. "Just calling it how I see it."

"How do you see it? Enlighten me."

"It's simple, really. Soldiers don't have a voice. I'm speaking for them."

"And here I thought that not giving soldiers a voice was the whole point. They do what they are told."

Thompson crinkled his nose and shook his head from side to side. A childish face on a childish man, Bern thought.

"Toeing the line doesn't suit you anymore, Lieutenant-Colonel. I can see your heart's not in it."

Bern smothered his response by draining his glass. He poured them each another generous shot.

"Tell me how it works," he said finally.

Thompson held up his glass and swirled the golden liquid in it. Bern wondered how long the reporter would be sober—how long he himself would be sober—and he decided, in that moment, to let go of his normal two-drink limit. He was drinking with another soldier, as flawed as that soldier might be.

Finally, Troy began speaking. "Do you remember when our men first went to Afghanistan? In their camouflage designed for the boreal forest? Sitting ducks, they were."

Bern nodded. "I remember."

Thompson tapped the chicken book pointedly. "Who solved that?"

"Well, it was a team effort. The commanding officer, along with top brass in Ottawa. In the end, it would have been a procurement issue."

"Bullshit!" Troy slammed his hand on the chicken book and

glared at Bern with his little-boy eyes. "You don't even see it, do you?"

"See what?" He was sitting back now, eyeing the reporter over his glass. Seeing no danger there, he finally laughed. "Evidently I don't."

"It was the media, and specifically the story *I* broke in *Soldier's Ally* magazine, that made that happen. Our soldiers had gone through all the channels. They'd spoken to their captains, and the captains had gone to the majors, and the majors had spoken to the CO. The CO even went so far as bringing it back to Ottawa, where he learned—guess what? No room in the mission budget. Meanwhile our guys were getting picked off like flies on shit. And what was the prime minister doing? Ordering new fighter bombers for the air force."

Troy emptied his glass and refilled it himself. "So they came to us. They came to me. That's what I do—watch for unfairness and abuse of power. Soldiers come to us with their stories, and we speak for them. They tell us anonymously, and then we let the shit fly. They're afraid for their jobs, their families, their pensions and benefits—or what's left of those once this government is done with them." He snorted as he said these last words.

Bern leaned forward and filled their glasses again. "So you're saying it's because of you that we got desert camo?"

"Come on, Fortin. Don't pretend you're thick. Colonel Sauvé in Rwanda used the media all the time to put pressure on the UN to send more troops. Christ, you probably booked the bloody press conferences for him. And you were in Bosnia. A major in Bosnia. Commander in Afghanistan. You're telling me you never saw the top brass use the media to their advantage? This can't be news to you!"

Bern waved a hand. "*Non, non.* It's not news. But that doesn't mean I have to like it."

Troy's eyes narrowed, and for the first time he looked like more than a petulant recruit. Perhaps he was capable of making something happen. "Is that what it comes down to? One of your captains is in jail. He could be sentenced to years. He'll likely lose his career. But you don't like the press, so you won't take a step out of your"—he waved a hand around—"your safe haven, to help him?"

"Now you're just being illogical." Bern's voice was cold. "I don't see how my talking to the press could help Captain Alais. It would only complicate things."

"You're one of the most respected soldiers in the country. What you say matters. If you speak up for Alais, it *will* make a difference."

Bern shook his head and the room shook with it. "It's not my place to speak up. And while public opinion might sway the minister of national defense or the chief of defense staff, it has no hold whatsoever on the judge advocate general. It shouldn't, anyway."

It felt like a long speech and he closed his eyes after he was done. Closed his eyes and saw Alais there, in his head. Saw the young soldier's eyes and the knowledge in them. He had done the right thing in shooting that other soldier. Alais knew that, and Bern knew it too. They both also knew that what Alais had done was illegal. Bern could not protect him from what was to come.

"What would you have done?"

The voice was so close that Bern's eyes flew open. Alais had asked the same question, and for a moment he thought his former captain was there in the room, made real by the force of talking about him. But it was just Troy, close enough that he could smell the man's whiskey breath. He refilled Bern's glass for him.

Bern drank it back and watched Thompson recede again, back to his place on the couch, next to the chicken book. Chickens. He wanted to talk about chickens. About how keeping backyard chickens was a way to build a perfect community ecosystem. About how the only way to get truly healthful eggs was to raise your own chickens or buy from a local supplier who followed strict guidelines. About how Bern had visited a chicken farm and felt—there was no other word for it—happy. Lighthearted. The chickens had made him laugh. Chickens were good company.

"It's not what I would have done. It's what I did."

The reporter had to be as drunk as he was at this point, but he seemed contained and utterly focused. "Tell me your story, Fortin. Get it off your chest."

Bern shook his head slowly. "I tell my story and they'll put me where I belong."

"And where is that?"

"In the cell right next to Alais."

A phone rang in the distance. Bern did not think he could make it there without knocking anything over, so he ignored it. Thompson stood and made his way to the kitchen counter, then came back with the receiver in his hand.

The buttons swam before Bern's eyes until he found the one that read talk and pressed it with a finger that felt slow and thick. Then he sat there, with the phone on his lap.

"*Allô?*" a distant voice said.

Bern lifted the receiver to his ear, his eyes closed. "Fortin," he slurred.

"*T'es soûl!*" You're drunk.

Bern sat up straighter. "Sauvé."

"Tabernac!"

Bern had nothing to say to that. Nothing at all.

"I went today, to see her."

An image came to him: Madame LeClerc wrapped in furs and little else.

"And?"

"And she's old. Like the rest of us."

He grunted. To him she would never be old. Never.

"Christ, you're really pissed."

"It's worse than that. There's a journalist here with me."

"Don't ever talk to a journalist when you're pissed. Isn't that what you always told me?"

Bern grunted into the phone once more.

"Give him to me."

"What?"

"Give him the phone."

Bern shrugged. "Colonel Sauvé for you," he said. He held the receiver over his head and heard Thompson's footsteps approach from somewhere behind him. Then he let himself fall, eyes closed, into the soft folds of white fur, and the hell of sleep and memory that beckoned.

Northern Rwanda, 1994

They were headed to Nairobi for meetings with LeClerc. Bern was nothing more than a chauffeur, someone who navigated roadblocks and moved corpses so they could make their way to the border and the waiting plane.

The child stepped away from the tree at the side of a road that cut through the jungle. If he was ten, it was barely. He stared at Bern and Sauvé. Bern had never seen such a look, never mind from a child. Anger, disappointment, disgust. *Why didn't you stop this?* He seemed to be shouting it without saying anything. But he was alive, and they could help him. He was the only one to have survived the slaughter that surrounded them.

"He's alive," Sauvé whispered.

The boy's eyes, round and brown, seemed to stare right through Bern, who had stepped out of the jeep to move a body that was blocking the road. *Nothing is as it seems.* The boy looked past Bern to his commanding officer in the passenger seat. The gun came from nowhere; it was a rifle, as long as the boy was tall. With an instinct born of years of training, Bern had his own weapon in his hand, the bullet out and moving. It crossed paths with the boy's at some point predetermined by chaos.

The boy's bullet shattered what was left of the windshield and entered through Colonel Sauvé's upper arm and out through his shoulder blade.

Nothing is as it seems.

"Sauve-le. Sauve le garçon!" Sauvé had cried out. *Save the boy.*

Time seemed to slow down as Bern made his way to the side of the road, sliding over corpses like so many speed bumps. He became aware of the stench and the slick of bodies. Of the buzz of flies over an otherwise heavy silence. Of the inexplicably lush green of the leaves on the trees that grew right to the edge of the road. He reached out his hand to part the branches.

The boy was crumpled at the base of the tree. Bern's bullet had torn a path through his body, but he was still breathing. He looked up at Bern, pleading with his young boy's eyes. His low keening was the only sound in the terrible silence.

That the boy was dying, there was no doubt. They were hours from the closest hospital, on roads lined and pitted with corpses. If he did manage to get the boy there alive, what could the doctors do? Their resources were stretched so thin, they were beyond being able to help.

Bern kneeled down and took the malnourished hand in his own. He was amazed that the boy had had the strength to hold up the heavy gun.

"Fortin?" the colonel called out, his voice weak. He was injured but moving. Through the foliage Bern could see him lying on the ground on the other side of the jeep, a puddle of blood growing in the dirt around him. He couldn't get up. If Bern could get him to the waiting plane, he would survive. The boy would not.

But Bern could not leave the boy there to die alone, among the dead. The blood pumped out of the rags on his chest and yet still he kept breathing. His eyes blinked. He moaned more softly now, but when Bern tried to let go of his hand he held on. He didn't speak, just pleaded with his eyes. *Take me from this pain.*

So Bern did.

He laid the boy's hand down in the dirt, then stood and pressed his pistol to that soft spot under the temple where the skin stretches over the skull.

And he pulled the trigger.

23

He knew he'd fallen asleep in the armchair, but he woke up on the couch. A stale smell clung to the air around him—the stink of his own breath. It hurt to move his head, so he stayed still, watching the sun cut lines through the spaces between the vertical blinds.

Could be the flu. Or a migraine. He'd had one once before, years ago, and he'd never forgotten the pain. But of course he knew he was fooling himself with those thoughts. What he was dealing with was a good old-fashioned, and well-deserved, hangover.

The bottle sat on the floor next to the couch; the cap was off, and it was almost empty. A glass with a few remaining drops of amber liquid was sitting on the ottoman, a book on backyard chickens its coaster. The smell of old alcohol rose up from the drops in the glass and seeped from the pores of his skin. He needed a shower, but he wasn't sure he could stand up. By staying as still as possible he could keep the pain to a minimum and the demons at bay.

The front door opened with a creak and closed with a slam that vibrated his molars.

"Pfft. Smells bad in here."

At the sound of Mrs. K.'s voice he almost catapulted off the couch, but the anticipation of pain held him back. Heart beating faster, he started devising a plan that would get him across the small house and into the bathroom.

She didn't stop to look at him but went straight to the patio door. The blinds tore across their tracks and daylight came flooding in. Bern groaned and threw an arm over his head. She slid the door open and the fresh air reached him. He sipped it in slowly at first, then more fully as his body got adjusted to the idea of something clean and nurturing.

She was in the kitchen now. "At least you usually do your dishes. What happened?" He heard the clang of a pan hitting the counter and the squeak of the cupboard door under the sink that he had been meaning to fix. It was the scrape of a knife across a plate that finally brought him to a seated position.

"What are you doing in there?" The room rocked and then settled as he leaned forward, elbows on knees, and cradled his head.

"Cleaning up. Big mess." There was a clatter of pots in the sink and the sound of running water, reminding him that he really had to go to the bathroom.

He moved from sitting to standing, hand on the arm of the couch to keep his balance. When he found a place of equilibrium he took a deep breath. He plowed through the pounding in his head and the unsteadiness, pushed past the sourness in his stomach and the accompanying roll of nausea, and made his way to the bathroom.

When he came back ten minutes later, showered and shaved and dressed, Mrs. K. slid a plate of eggs, bacon, and toast in front of him. And a coffee that looked eerily the same as the fastidious cup he made for himself each morning: a triple espresso in a stainless steel travel mug. Black. Next to this was a small brown glass jar with a white lid, which he ignored in favor of the coffee.

"This is a departure," he said.

He thought he saw her lip turn up on one side. The most response he could expect. He sipped the coffee and closed his eyes. It was perfect.

"Eat," she said.

"In a minute." He took another sip, then opened his eyes and watched her bustle in his kitchen, an unusual-enough sight to be worthy of notice. Her movements were smooth and uninterrupted. He picked up the jar and turned it in his hands.

"Who's Victoria?" he asked. "And what's her remedy for?"

"I don't know who she is," Mrs. K. said as she dried the dishes and put them away without hesitation. "But her remedy is for headaches. And cuts." She pressed two fingers to her temple. "Rub here," she said. "Then eat." She pulled a chair from the table and was about to step up onto it when he stopped her.

"Wait. I'll put those away. It's easier for me," he said, twisting the lid off the jar. "What's in this?" he asked. It smelled like bitter herbs and beeswax.

She waved his question away and stood on the chair to slide the plates onto the second shelf of the cupboard, watching him out of the corner of her eye. She nodded with satisfaction as he rubbed some of the cream onto his temples as instructed.

"What did you cook?" she asked. She was in her housedress with a flowered apron tied to her stocky waist, her legs encased in tan-colored support hose. It was a staying-at-home day. She'd not be leaving anytime soon.

He clicked through the frames of the evening before. He could not remember cooking.

"I don't think I did."

"Huh. Well, you want a new girlfriend, then. This one is not so good."

"What's wrong with her?" he asked with a laugh.

She looked at him with those fierce eyes of hers. "She's very messy!"

"Ah, I see." Bern held his cup in both hands as though it could steady him. He knew he needed to eat, and when he looked down at the eggs, his stomach stayed in place. He put down the cup and reached for a piece of toast. "Not my girlfriend," he said at last.

"Who, then?"

"The reporter."

From where she was, up on the chair again with a cloth in hand, wiping the cupboard doors, she grunted.

"Are you going to make yourself a coffee and sit with me?" he asked.

"I already had coffee."

He hardened his voice by a hair. "Come sit with me. It's hurting my head to look up at you."

She narrowed her eyes. "Will you eat?"

He picked up his fork and held it in the air. "Will you sit?"

She stepped down and pulled the chair back to the table. He took a bite. His throat closed around the hot rubber texture of scrambled eggs. He forced himself to swallow.

"Did you tell him anything?" She still had the cloth in her hand and was using it to wipe the edge of the table.

He took another bite of egg; this one slid down with no problem. He found a rhythm that did not seem to upset the delicate balance of his system and took a few more bites.

"I don't think so," he said finally.

"What does this mean, you don't think so?"

"I think if I had told him, I would feel better. Like going to confession."

"But you don't feel like you had confession?"

"No." Bern shook his head. "So I'm thinking maybe I should."

"Take confession?"

"No. Tell him."

She stopped the wiping motion. "No."

He put the fork down. "Why not? Maybe it will help."

"Or maybe it will make things worse."

He pushed the empty plate aside. "It's the only way to forgiveness. At least, the only one I ever learned."

Mrs. K. leaned forward and patted her work-worn hand at the center of his chest. Her touch was featherlight, but her expression was as serious as always.

She took her hand back from his chest and patted her own. "Forgiveness is here. Inside," she said gruffly. Before he could reply she had picked up his plate and was back at the sink, washing the breakfast dishes.

His cell phone rang. "Fortin," he answered.

"Dr. Marsha Hallman calling."

Bern sat up straight in his chair. "What time is it? I'm late, aren't I?"

"Fifty-five minutes late, yes. I've had time to reach some basic conclusions." The forensic anthropologist paused, then started in on the details in a clipped tone. "Female, mid to late teens, Mongoloid features. The bones were freshly exposed and have been in the ground for less than fifty years. Definitely a coroner's case, as I had surmised from the photos you sent. Do you plan to be here anytime soon?"

"I can be there in five minutes," he said.

"Good. Staff Sergeant Resnick already has someone searching

the missing persons' database. We may well have an identification soon."

"And then?"

"And then I'll take the cranium back to the forensic dentist in Kelowna to confirm identity. My work will be done. But you've still got the rest of the bones to locate, yes?" She hung up before he could answer.

"Staff Sergeant?" Schilling scrolled down the screen one more time to be sure, then called out louder. "Resnick? Looks like we have a match."

She spun in her chair to face the deserted squad room. Through the window to the reception area she could see Dr. Hallman with her clipped dark-brown hair and austere features talking to Resnick and the coroner.

She spun back to face the screen. First Nations, female, seventeen years old. Missing since June 20, 1993. Cynthia Amanda Forsberg (John). With a click of the mouse Cindy Forsberg's face appeared. Schilling sat back and gaped at the screen. She reached over to the file that had been sitting, unopened, on her desk since Sunday.

"Resnick!" she shouted, just as her cell phone rang. She pounced on it. "Schilling here."

"It's Michelle. You said to call if he came back."

Schilling shook her head. She couldn't stop staring at the photo of Cindy Forsberg. "Sorry, who?"

"Gary. You said to call if Gary came back?" She was whispering into the phone.

"Right. Michelle, sorry about that. Wait. Is he back?"

"No. I mean, not now. But I think he's been in the house."

"You *think* he has? Tell me what happened."

"Can you just come to the house?" Michelle's voice rose a full octave. "I'm at work right now, but I can meet you there."

"Are you okay? Is everyone safe?"

"Yes, I think so. Just come, okay?"

"I'm in the middle of something here. Give me an hour, okay? Then I'll meet you at your house."

Maddie clicked off the phone and held it in her hand, looking at it.

Cindy Forsberg. Gary Dowd.

If she were alive, Cindy would be thirty-three years old. Gary was thirty-three years old. Had they known each other? Gary had suddenly gone missing. Cindy, or at least what remained of her, had suddenly been found. Maybe the coroner was right. Maybe all these cases were connected.

Schilling looked at the screen. A sullen teenager looked back, her eyes raccoon-like with makeup, her hair lanky. But crop the hair, add a few tattoos and a take-on-the-world smile, and she'd be looking right at Aimée.

Schilling heard voices behind her. Resnick was back, with Dr. Hallman and the coroner in tow. "I think you all need to see this," she said.

Seymour had had the run of the basement, so Gary headed straight down there. The flowery smell hit him on the second step. Michelle must have brought in the carpet cleaners. The gilded fleurs-de-lys that she had stenciled on the walls were fading, rubbed down by toddlers' hands as they steadied their small bodies for the descent. *Install handrail to basement.*

She'd bought a new couch. Dark blue. Velvet. *Shit.* How were they going to pay for it? No. Gary amended that. How was Michelle going to pay for it? Getting out of his life was going to be expensive—Gary had already come to terms with that—but no way was he going to pay for a new couch when the old one had been perfectly good.

He had to focus. There was no time for reminiscing or what-ifs. All around him the pressure was building and he had one chance to get out before the whole mess landed on him.

The place was so spotless he couldn't see anywhere that Seymour could have hidden a grow op. But he would look anyway. Wilson and his contacts would make it worth his while if he succeeded. Maybe Seymour had been smarter than he looked.

He sat on the new couch. It was too springy by far. He'd never be able to settle back to watch football on a couch like that. The old one had grooves that fit his body, comforting him like a hug. Camping equipment, the old couch, and the dresser from his bedroom—these were the only material remnants of his childhood. Had she got rid of the dresser too?

He bounced up easily from the couch; it did not want him there any more than he wanted to be there. He wanted to kick it as he got up, but that would be childish. Instead, he circled the rec room, thinking like Seymour, looking through Seymour's eyes.

The grimy sheets and dirty clothes were long gone. Michelle had replaced the couch and cleaned the carpets. What was left of Seymour? The doors to the entertainment unit were glass, but Gary opened them anyway. Disney DVDs arranged alphabetically on one row. Michelle's romantic comedies took up the other two shelves. Gary liked westerns, but he'd given up his collection when they'd got rid of the VHS player. Nothing there.

The other end of the room was a mix of Michelle's yoga and

workout equipment and the kids' toys. All of it was sorted and stacked into bins and arranged on shelves that Michelle had been adding to for years. Each purchase she made doubled in price when you added in the cost of the storage unit. It all added up to whole walls of shelving designed to store and display all the stuff they had yet to pay for.

He checked the bins of pony figures with ponytails, of farm animals and hand weights. All of it emitted a smell of disinfectant but gave up no pots of marijuana cream, let alone plants.

Plants. Where would you store a plant? Wilson had said the plants would need lights, fans, and steady humidity. This was hopeless. He'd never find anything because there was nothing to find. He'd best forget the deal Wilson had promised him. Just grab his rucksack and take off. Head east, find work where no one needed to know his name or see his ID.

Tempting as the thought was, it didn't sit well with him. Michelle didn't deserve what he had done. The least he could do was stabilize her financial situation before he left.

He checked the wall closet—a regifting cupboard where Michelle put every present ever given to her. On the top shelf he found five shoe boxes. Could they be full of jars of cream? He pulled down the first box and opened the lid. A pair of impossibly high-heeled shoes stared back at him. He turned the box and whistled at the price. He couldn't remember seeing Michelle in heels that high since their wedding.

He pulled down the next box, then the next. Five pairs of designer shoes. Over fifteen hundred dollars on some credit card he didn't even know about. *Assemble shoe rack.* Enough.

He went down the stubby hallway to the bathroom. He sat on the lid of the toilet seat and looked around. *Replace linoleum.* Michelle had picked dark-purple accents to minimize the mustard-yellow fixtures, but nothing could hide the fact that it was an old bathroom. The shower curtain was a purple-and-white jacquard print. *Aubergine, not purple,* Michelle had insisted.

"Aubergine, then," he said out loud. "What the hell difference does it make?" The ceiling tile was stained from some long-ago overflow of the kitchen sink above. *Repair ceiling tile.* Michelle had been on him for ages about that. He'd started on the project, but it turned out they didn't make that exact tile anymore. He'd have to replace the whole ceiling, and the strapping too. It was a bigger job than he'd ever had time for and he'd ended up just scrubbing the stained tiles and putting them back. They were never straight again, though. One corner above the shower lifted a full inch, and from his perch Gary could see into the void between the basement and the main floor.

He almost laughed. "Seymour, you asshole!"

He placed one foot on the wide corner of the bathtub and balanced the other on the narrower rim. The crooked tile popped out easily. He waited for a shower of dust that didn't come. Someone had been there recently.

That's when he heard the squeak of the back door and footsteps on the kitchen floor overhead.

"See what I mean?" Michelle led Schilling straight into the living room and stood in front of the white couch. Schilling stepped across the white carpet in her stocking feet to look more closely. What she saw was a couch cushion. Plush, white, and plump.

"Sorry, I'm not sure—"

"This!" Michelle hissed.

Maddie leaned closer. "Tell me what you see," she said finally.

"This dent right here, and this one here. Like someone sat down on that end and put his feet up. And this"—her index finger hovered an inch above the fabric—"dirt!"

Schilling took another step closer. She kneeled on the floor, careful not to touch anything, and leaned right into the fabric. She could make out a minuscule pucker and two grains of dirt.

She sat back on her heels and looked up.

"Where are your kids this morning?"

"They didn't do this. They wouldn't." Michelle's voice was practically a whisper.

"Look, can we sit down?"

"Not in here. Let's go in the kitchen."

Schilling followed her through a swinging door into a room of immaculate marble and tile—all brilliant white. They sat at a country-style table (also white) next to a sliding glass door that looked out on a fenced backyard. Still-green grass grew long around the base of a timber-frame swing set.

"You were saying? About the kids?" Schilling asked as she fingered the edge of a plastic-coated placemat.

"I already took them to day care. Before I called you. Then I went in to work for a bit. But I really wanted you to see that."

"The dirt?"

Closing her eyes, Michelle breathed in slowly. When she opened them again there was a determination in them that Schilling had not seen in her before. "I know it might not seem like a big deal. But I know my house. I take good care of it. I vacuumed just the other day. Remember? You were here. The day that Gary disappeared."

Schilling nodded. "I remember."

"Well, after you left I tidied it all. Fluffed the pillows. I left it perfect."

"But that was Sunday. Four whole days ago. Are you saying no one has been in the room since then?"

Michelle shook her head. "No one except me. Every morning I do a walk-through and check everything. You've got to or the place turns into a pigsty before you know it. When I walked through yesterday morning, it was perfect. Then this morning I walked through again, and that's what I found."

"So you think someone came in."

"I *know* someone did."

"Is anything missing?"

"I—I don't think so. Not that I can tell. It's just that the place doesn't feel right, you know? Like someone has been in here. Has wandered through, touched things."

"What makes you think it was Gary?"

Michelle rolled the corner of a cloth napkin under her fingers. "Who else would it be?"

"I don't know. I'm just thinking of what happened to Seymour. And the fact that he was staying here."

She let go of the napkin and it unrolled itself. "Oh my God! Do you think it was the person who killed Seymour? Oh my God!" She looked down at the table and started smoothing the napkin with the flat of her hand. "We're not safe here, are we? I knew it."

"Okay, let's stay calm. We don't know for certain that anyone was here, let alone the killer. Have you checked the whole house for other signs? I mean, if it was Gary, maybe he was looking for a change of clothes or a toothbrush. Did you check for those things?"

Michelle was taking slow, deep breaths again. Schilling was starting to think it was a technique she'd learned to calm herself down. "Right. Right. Good idea. No, I didn't check those things."

"Okay, then. Let's check them together."

There was no way out of the basement except through the kitchen, and Gary could hear Michelle in there, talking to someone. He climbed down into the tub and pulled the shower curtain all the way closed around him. He hunkered down low so he wouldn't cast a shadow, and then remembered he'd turned on the lights. *Shit.*

The footsteps crossed above his head and into the living room. The rustle of the shower curtain as he stepped out of the bathtub sounded like rushing rapids to his ears. The mat slid underfoot and he pitched himself forward to keep from falling. He grabbed hold of the counter and flicked off the light, catching a glimpse of his own scruffy, wild-eyed face in the vanity mirror. Michelle really could not see him like this.

Was there a better hiding place? He might fit behind the new couch, but they could already be on their way down the stairs. He could not hear their footsteps over the ragged sound of his own breath.

He climbed back into the tub and closed the curtain in silent increments. Crouched against the porcelain, he resisted the temptation to close his eyes. *You can't see me if I can't see you.* He listened for the sounds of voices and footsteps over the roaring in his ears but heard nothing. They must have gone upstairs.

He couldn't get caught. Not now that he was so close to getting away. Wilson said he'd give him half the money for the cream and the other half for the plants. He'd be happy to find either one at this point. *Get me through this, and I'll take half. I'll get out and start over again. Build a good life that's not based on lies.*

Footsteps on the stairs. Two sets—one clunky and the other lighter. Michelle never clunked and was always telling Gary not to be so heavy-footed. She didn't like heaviness in any form.

"Do you have a spare key hiding somewhere?" A woman's voice. Definitely not Wilson.

A gasp. "Under the flowerpot! We always keep a key under there." Michelle. God, he wished he could see her.

"We'll check on the way out that it's still there. And I'd suggest you have your locks changed. Does anyone else have a key?"

"Well, Gary. And my parents, of course."

"But Gary didn't take his keys with him when he ran from the border." The woman's voice faded in and out as she spoke. A police officer? Gary imagined her ducking in and out of closets and alcoves, looking for an intruder. Looking for *him*. "What about Seymour? When he was staying here?"

"Yeah. Gary gave him a key." Fainter. Like Michelle was still on the stairs.

"Look, there's really nothing I can do. Can you call a locksmith right away?"

He heard her heavy step right outside the bathroom door. Did Michelle actually let her leave her shoes on? The breath he'd been holding was stuck in his chest. He ducked his head and closed his eyes tight and waited for the end to come. They'd find him passed out, a stowaway in his own bathroom.

And then the steps faded away.

"Take my advice: get those locks changed. Then you don't need to worry about it. If Gary comes back he can knock on the door like any other guest. Okay?"

Their voices were fainter now. Gary raised his head and managed to suck a breath into his lungs.

"One last thing."

They were by the stairs. *Go up. Go up. Get out of here.* "Did Gary know your sister, Cindy?"

And then he knew.

They'd found her.

Nairobi, 1994

The clearances were all in place. It was just a matter of getting the injured Sauvé to the border, where he could be stabilized for the already-scheduled flight.

There was no time to think. There was certainly no time to feel. There was only each action to be taken and each obstacle to overcome. Each corpse on the road to move out of the way. Each roadblock to negotiate. Each open grave and straggling parade of refugees to bypass without looking. There was nothing more to do. If Sauvé survived, he might save the lives of thousands of others. In this way and in this moment, his life was worth more than any other.

The flight was a blur. His colonel was upright, his skin pale and clammy, his jaw clenched. He did not speak, except once, in the night sky over eastern Africa.

"Did we save the boy?"

Bern looked out on the blackness and shook his head. "We'll be there soon."

He took Sauvé's good hand in his own and held it as they landed in Nairobi, and through the ambulance ride that followed. With the interminable wait in the corridor, they could have been in any hospital, anywhere except Rwanda. The halls were too clean and empty, the staff moved about steadily but without desperation; there were more living than dead, more sick than wounded, more scalpels than machetes.

He woke up to a hand on his shoulder. LeClerc.

"Va-t'en," the general said. "Go. I'll look after things here. My driver is downstairs. There's a room in Sauvé's name at the Intercontinental. Get cleaned up and rest. Someone will call you when you're needed."

24

When he finally moved, his legs were shaking so badly he could barely stand. He perched on the edge of the tub and pressed his back into the wall until he could stand up. No sounds from upstairs since the door had slammed shut. That must have been at least ten minutes ago. Time to get to work and get out of there. He was out of chances.

Gary headed back to the toy storage rack and rifled in the bins until he found Geoffrey's hippo-shaped flashlight. Open the jaws and the light shone from the hippo's mouth.

He returned to the bathroom and held the flashlight up to the space in the ceiling. And there it was: the corner of a box.

He slid the box out, then placed it on the floor and opened the flap. He lifted out a familiar brown jar with a white lid. It hadn't been labeled yet, but Gary opened it and sniffed. *Victoria's Remedy.* The same stuff from the package Seymour had tried to get him to smuggle across the border. This was the rest of the delivery that Wilson's contact would pay dearly for.

There were six more boxes. Gary took three trips, two boxes at a time, and stacked them by the back gate.

He had the cream now. For that, Wilson had promised a nice lump sum. Enough for Michelle to pay off the credit cards—at

least the ones Gary knew about. He was almost home free. Why
didn't he just call Wilson to come get it, then walk out the back
door, and hit the road?

But if Seymour had stored the cream here, why not the plants?
If Gary delivered the plant material too, he could leave knowing
that Michelle was set.

He replaced the ceiling tiles and stepped around the last box.
He checked the linen closet for a false back and looked behind
the furnace and the hot-water tank. The plants would need lights,
Wilson had said, so Gary checked around the breaker box for
new wiring. He checked every plug to see if Seymour had rigged
a grow box out of some everyday object and hidden it in plain
sight. But the lamps, TV, computer, and stereo equipment were
all as they appeared to be. The dehumidifier looked promising,
but Gary opened the lid to find it still contained the same broken
filter that Michelle had asked him to replace months ago. It was
parked to one side of the hallway outside the bathroom, its cord
unplugged and wound in a neat coil at its base.

On the other side of the hall stood Gary's dresser, looking exactly the same as it had in his childhood bedroom. He'd emptied
it so Seymour had a place for his clothes. Funny that someone
had moved it from one side of the hall to the other.

Of course.

Because there was an outlet on that side.

"Oh, Seymour. Maybe you weren't so stupid after all, huh?"

Gary had to admit that his buddy had done a good job. The
dresser looked the same as always from the front, but when he
tried to tug open a drawer it wouldn't budge. The second drawer
was stuck too. Gary shoved his hands behind the dresser and felt
a gap at the back. His fingers pressed up against hot wires.

He'd found it.

He pulled the dresser away from the wall. A plug snaked out the back and into the socket. He unplugged it, noticing the gentle buzzing sound it had been making only when it stopped. He pulled the false back off the dresser. Inside was a complex ecosystem of halogen lights, tubing, wiring, timers, ductwork, a carbon filter and fan. And three mother plants, their leaves turning brown in very dry soil.

He closed his eyes and allowed himself a moment of relief. He would get out. He shucked the plants out of their home and put the dresser back together as best he could. Michelle would find it someday, and he almost laughed to think of her adding a grow op to his list of sins. He pushed the dresser back against the wall and brushed a few crumbs of soil into the carpet. Good enough. Then he piled the three pots on top of the final box and carried them to the back gate.

Bern scanned the faces of the assembled volunteers, a squad of men and women in identical orange rain jackets emblazoned with the words "Kootenay Landing Search and Rescue." He looked over at their team leader, a wiry, craggy-faced man, and when he nodded back, Bern began.

"Yesterday, someone placed a cranium and two femur bones on this rock," he said, rolling his head toward the throne rock and the trees behind him, where the two eagles watched and waited.

"Those bones are now in Kelowna, and Dr. Hallman is working to confirm the identity of the deceased. Our job is to comb these woods in search of other bones or remains."

A young woman barely out of her teens leaned over her

walking stick, and next to her a man shifted his baseball cap to look up at Bern. He had their attention now.

"We're going to do a low-speed, small group search. Controlled and methodical—it's what you've trained for and that's what we're after today. I want you to investigate every tree, bush, rock formation, and stump.

"We do have a few clues. These bones were buried until recently, and we believe they were uncovered with human rather than animal help. So look for signs of recent digging or overturned soil. Also, Dr. Hallman has identified cottonwood or poplar roots growing through the skull. We all know that tree roots can stretch for many feet, but poplars like water: they grow in wetlands and on the banks of rivers and streams."

He paused, waiting for any groans or protests, but there were none. They were on a mountainside rife with streams, leading to a wetland and a river. There would be no shortage of poplar trees.

"Good," he said. "Let's get started."

Michelle had a desk in the alcove at the top of the stairs. He counted off three sheets of letter paper and three envelopes. He wrote as steadily as he could and kept to the point. Three letters. Three envelopes. He wrote *Natasha* on the first and *Geoffrey* on the second. He wasted precious seconds deciding how to address the third, before he settled on *Coroner, Kootenay Landing.* He'd met the man once but couldn't remember his name. *French guy, ex-army.* He added these details to the envelope and found a stamp in the top drawer. Kootenay Landing was a small town. He had no doubt the letter would reach its destination within a day.

Geoffrey's baby book was on the bottom shelf of the book-case next to a copy of Grimm's Fairy Tales. Gary pulled it out and flipped through the recounting of his son's life in page after page of scalloped-edge photos and archival-quality stickers. He settled on a flap on the inside back cover. A tidy place to store extra photos. As he slipped the letter in, his finger caught the edge of a photo waiting to be pasted into the album. Gary pulled it out and saw himself dressed for a hike, Geoffrey strapped to his back, Natasha leaning against his legs and holding his hand.

He remembered that day. It had been a disaster of wet feet, dirty diapers, not enough snacks or rain gear. But it was proof, he thought as he slipped it into his back pocket. Proof that he had tried.

He stopped in Natasha's room just long enough to put the second letter in her own baby book. Then he used Seymour's cell phone to call Wilson.

"Come now. To the back gate."

The lawn was still not mowed. The garage was still not painted. The Christmas decorations might not get put up this year. As he stood next to the back gate, waiting for the rumble of Wilson's car in the lane, he thought of how hard he'd tried. Come dark, Gary would be on his way. Headed into the unknown to make a new life.

He'd tried, but he'd failed miserably.

Nairobi, 1994

He woke up to the smell of her perfume and the touch of her soft hair on his naked shoulder. He wrapped his arms around her neck. He did not dare open his eyes in case it was a dream.

"C'est vraiment toi?" Is it really you?

"C'est moi."

Everything was white: the sheets, the curtains, the soft lamplight on her skin.

"It's a dream." He rolled to his side. Elbow bent, he rested his head in one hand. With the other he brushed his fingers along her collarbone. "It must be. How did you get in?"

"I made an arrangement with your valet."

"I have a valet? This really must be a dream."

She laughed and rolled her head to the side. He grabbed a fistful of hair and pulled her head to his chest. Her hands were on him, fleshy and warm like dough.

"You're skin and bone," she said. Something deep within him opened a crack at her touch.

"Is it as bad as they say?" she asked.

"Worse. It's worse than they could ever know." She wrapped her arms more tightly around him and he spoke into her shoulder. "Something happened. To a child. I did something—"

"Shh," she said. "It's okay. It's okay, my love." She pushed herself up and ran her fingers gently over his brow, his cheeks, his lips.

"I don't think I can go back."

"But you will go back. This is what it is to be a soldier, *non*?"

The opening within him shuttered closed at her words. He would never be able to speak of what happened. This too would be his punishment.

He shifted and rolled until he was on her. He pressed himself into her and she wrapped both arms and legs around his torso with a whimper. They stayed there, swaying slightly, moving to music only they could hear.

25

A woman in a white turban sat on the porch, staring straight at Schilling as she drove past in the police truck. The scarlet shawl draped over her shoulders almost hid the fact that she was seated in a wheelchair.

"A turban," Resnick grunted. "I never did get why she wears that ridiculous thing."

Schilling ignored him and raised her hand in a wave, and then followed the road as it curved along a rugged cedar fence. Once parked, she stepped out of the truck and trailed Resnick through a field with a grass-covered mound at its center. He crouched and parted the tall grass, pointing toward a door, then drew his weapon. Schilling followed suit.

They edged closer to the door. Resnick gestured to her again, and Schilling crab-walked behind the door and pulled it open.

"Police!" His voice echoed into the pitch black before them. Schilling pulled the flashlight off her belt and shone it into the cavern. They edged down the steps, Resnick with his weapon drawn, Schilling circling the flashlight like a beacon. There was no one there.

Resnick found the light switch first.

"Wow." She whistled.

She circled the corridor, turning lights on as she went. She counted four hallways, each made up of one shipping container and extending like a finger from the empty main corridor, which itself was made up of two more containers. It was like someone had taken Schilling's rural elementary school and buried it underground.

"I've never seen one like this," Resnick said. "I've heard of them, but I've never come across this kind of operation before."

The smell of damp skunk grew stronger as they pulled open the first door and entered the hall. Schilling flicked on the light to expose a room that had been trashed: long shelves half ripped from the walls, pots strewn, and soil scattered, sheets of reflective metal thrown to the ground. She stepped gingerly toward a pile of broken lightbulbs in one corner. Bits of broken glass and soil had been swept up in little anthills.

"Except it's not really in operation, is it? Quite a mess that someone has tried to clean up."

"Classic drug rip," Resnick said.

"Classic what?"

"Drug rip. Weren't you paying attention at all the other day?" Resnick scowled over at her. "Wherever there are drugs, there are gangs. I want you to remember that, Schilling."

She stared hard at him. "I don't need a lecture, Staff Sergeant."

He narrowed his eyes and looked around. "So then tell me what happened here, if you're so smart." He walked up to three shelves hanging under a mess of wires. They were lined with hundreds of black plastic plant pots that were filled with soil, but all that was left of the plants was a ragged stump of stem. "What's missing from this picture?"

"Oh, the pressure," Schilling said sarcastically. She poked at a pot of dried soil and the whole row of adjacent pots shifted easily.

"Let me see, we've got thousand-watt lightbulbs—all smashed—and these big fat wires to supply them. We've got hoses and fans and a stink like a wet farm dog that's been skunked." She tipped her head to the side and smiled, but her attempt at humor was completely wasted on him. "Plants," she answered finally. "There are no marijuana plants."

Resnick nodded. "Exactly right," he said. "Whoever was running this operation was involved with a gang when they started this grow, because if they'd refused to cooperate on something this big, there's no doubt they'd be dead."

"So what, then? The partnership went sour? Someone got greedy?"

"My guess is they were working with someone new. Edging in on Hells Angels territory. Then—boom."

"Boom? Could you be more specific?"

"Sure, okay. So we're in traditional Hells Angels territory here, right? But let's say this grow was started by someone else. The Angels weren't in on it, but they got wind of it and kept an eye on things. Then they waited until harvest time and came and stripped it bare—for a tidy profit, I might add. Maybe they sent our friend Seymour to do the job, hey? Took every inch of plant material out of here and smashed everything else to pieces." He was nodding away at his own theory. "So, Schilling, what questions does this raise? And what do we, as police officers, need to do?"

"Uh—" Maybe she hadn't been following along as closely as she thought. "Um, who was growing this? And we need to find evidence so we can arrest them."

"Wrong." Resnick kneeled down to examine a pile of broken glass more closely. "Come here and look at this."

She heaved her belt out of the way and crouched next to him. "What?"

He pointed with his finger but kept from touching it. "See here? Hair. And blood."

The hair was silky and gray-white; the blood had dried to a rusty brown.

Resnick sat back on his heels, comfortable, like he could squat there all day. "We already know who was growing this. But even if we can place them here, we can't bust them."

"What? Why not?" Schilling's knees screamed at her and she stood, shaking out her legs.

He looked at her angrily. "I know when you're making fun of me, you know," he said. "You don't want to follow along with the baby steps, but then you can't keep up when things get more complicated. If you're ever going to make it off the beat, you've got to think bigger, Constable."

"Sorry, sir. What did I miss?"

"You didn't miss anything. You already answered the question."

"I wish you'd just tell me."

"And I wish you'd figure it out for yourself. What did we say was missing?"

"Plants."

"Right, no drugs," he said. "I can tell you for sure that our friendly pot growers next door put this in. Think about what a big undertaking it would have been, burying six shipping containers underground. There's no way that could have been going on without them knowing about it."

"Okay, so we connect them to the grow, and then bust them for it?"

"Oh, and I thought you were onto something." He groaned. "Okay, I'm going to put you out of your misery. What grow?"

"What?" Schilling looked from side to side and gestured all

around with her arms. "This grow, right here. You said yourself it's the biggest you've ever seen."

"And you said yourself, it's missing what?"

She smacked her head with her hand. "Oh, crap. Plants."

"Right. All we've got are the roots." Resnick's dark brows knitted as he stood. He lifted one of the pots and held it in the air. "No THC in the roots. We'll never get a successful prosecution out of this."

She started pacing. "I can't believe I missed that."

"Less attitude, more focus," Resnick chided. "But keep going. What's next?"

"Oh!" She walked back to where they'd been crouched. "Well, it's not what's next, but I bet you ten bucks that explains the turban." She pointed at the hair in the glass shards.

"You're catching on. Good." Resnick's smile was more like a grimace, but Schilling felt a flutter in her chest that she'd finally said something that impressed him.

"But I still don't know what's next."

"Big picture stuff, right? What we've got here is one"—he held up his index finger—"a cleaned-out grow op, and two, a dead Hells Angel. Here's what I think happened. Some group is elbowing in on Hells territory. Whoever it is, they loaned the money to the Hintons, either Lennon or Gia—though my bet is on Lennon—to get this grow started. They were going to split the profits.

"But the Hells found out about it and sent your Seymour in here with a few buddies. They carted out every last plant, destroyed the grow, and beat everyone up just enough to scare them. They're sending a message: if you're growing in our territory, you're growing for us."

"Right. Then Seymour turns up dead. So maybe the

competition didn't take too well to him threatening their sup-
pliers?" Schilling said, finally getting the picture. "The question
is, Who has the balls to try starting up in Hells Angels territory?
That's who we're looking for, right?"

Resnick pulled a cigarette out of his pocket and stuck it in one
corner of his mouth. "Now you're getting it. Think bigger picture,
not mom-and-pop. You bust one mom-and-pop and ten more will
take their place. But what crazy motherfucker is ready to take on
the Hells? And then mad enough to kill Seymour when the Hells
don't play along? That's the guy we're looking for."

"So who is it?"

"That's the answer we're going to get out of Lennon Hinton,"
he said.

His hangover seemed to have receded—a miracle really, considering how little he remembered of the night before. A day in the
woods, with complete focus on each step, each twig, each potential gravesite, had no doubt helped. Bern had stopped only once
to drink water and apply some more of Mrs. K.'s cream.

Five hours. Yet the search had turned up nothing.

Just then, the sound of his cell phone broke the peace of the
forest.

"Fortin."

"Dr. Marsha Hallman calling."

"Yes. Any news?"

"I'm with the forensic dentist, and we can confirm that the
remains belong to Cindy Forsberg, missing since 1993."

Bern looked around at his group of volunteers, who'd proven
to be as controlled and methodical as any of his soldiers. He'd

told them to call it off but several still circled the clearing they'd already searched. Checking again. Had they missed something?

"Coroner Fortin, are you there?"

"I'm here. I met Cindy's mother recently. It's going to be very hard news for her to hear."

"Yes, I understand. The chief coroner has authorized me to come with an assistant and help with the search for the original gravesite. We hope that will speed the process, so they can plan a proper burial. Please pass that information on to the family. Along with my condolences, of course."

He disconnected the call and waited for the volunteers to gather again in the clearing. Then he led them down the mountain. He would go and see Holly and Duke Forsberg now and tell them that their daughter had been dead for sixteen years.

It was his duty, after all, to account for the dead. His duty, and his punishment.

"Duke, your wife called. She says she needs you to go home right away," Lennon said. It was sad the way the old man nursed a single cup of coffee every afternoon, hoping to catch sight of Aimée. "She looks just like my daughter," he'd told Lennon more than once.

"Yeah, time to get going," Duke repeated. Lennon offered him a hand to help balance his bulk as he stood. "Tell Aimée I said good night, okay?"

"Will do, Duke. She's gone upstairs already to get Gabriel his dinner."

"She works too hard," Duke said. "Kids need their mothers, you know? Little kids do. Makes all the difference later."

Lennon went to pat the older man on the shoulder but pulled his hand back before he touched the shower of dandruff on his dirty sweatshirt. He followed Duke to the door and locked up behind him.

Duke wasn't the only customer to come in and moon over Aimée, Lennon thought as he flipped the closed sign. He knew he should appreciate her more. He kept all the lights on and went to open the back door to let in the cool night air and let out the undertone of grease and garbage.

Lennon had been doing the weekly cleaning on his own ever since he turned eleven. He'd done it when he was half-asleep, when he was painfully hungover, when he was baked out of his mind. He'd done it on acid one time, but that hadn't worked out so well. After years of fine-tuning, he'd figured out that it was best done on half a hit of ecstasy. He took the folded sheet of paper from the back pocket of his jeans and fingered the white tablet. He toyed with the idea of taking the whole thing but decided not to.

The last time he'd done a full hit he'd become so fascinated with the sliding softness of flour between his fingers that it had taken him all night to clean off the bread board. Hours had passed like minutes—hours spent rubbing flour into his face and his arms. He'd taken off his socks and walked around the kitchen barefoot. Eventually, he'd found the presence of mind to continue his work, but he'd forgotten about his floured feet, and he left a trail of powdered footprints all through the kitchen and from one end of the café to the other. This was back when his mother still worked, and she'd come in to open up and had found him curled up on a bench, rubbing flour into his cheek, even in sleep.

She'd let him sleep, because that was Gia's way. The early customers sat away from him, so as not to disturb him. Later, when the place got crowded, customers sat all around him, enjoying their coffee, ignoring the sleeping Lennon. He'd woken up barefoot, covered in flour, and surrounded by friends.

Aimée was not like Gia. Not at all. That's why he was working tonight, even with so much happening on the sidelines. Because of Aimée's complaining. "I can't work all the time, Lennon!"

She pronounced his name "Le-*non*," with a heavy emphasis on the last syllable. It seemed to spill out of her mouth all at once and land with a plonk. Just one of the many quirks that had seemed sweet when they'd first met. But Aimée's accent never went away, and truth be told it grated on him. It stood out, always. Even when Gabriel was sleeping and Lennon and Aimée were curled up together on the secondhand couch in the apartment upstairs. Even when they were smoking a doob, with candles flickering and tunes playing, with somebody's grandmother's quilt keeping the cold arms of winter at bay. Aimée would speak, and Lennon would shrink from her. No matter how peaceful her tone or how logical her argument—no matter how right she was—her start-and-stop butchering of the English language made her sound stupid.

It made him think of his uncle, his father's brother, who got Parkinson's disease and started walking on his tiptoes and crashing into things. The more he crashed, the more determined he became; he would careen around until he got to the couch or the chair or the bathroom, or wherever he was headed. Lennon had that same feeling when he tried to follow one of Aimée's sentences from beginning to end.

Except when she was speaking French, of course. When she and Gabriel were together, her head bent toward his, she offered him the world in a melody of words. But Lennon couldn't understand one bit of what they said to each other.

He started stacking chairs on tables, and by the time he reached the front counter he'd dropped in and started on his journey. The orange scent of the all-natural cleaner filled his nostrils and lungs and brain. He imagined himself turning orange from the inside out. He became the tallest fruit of the citrus family, rolling through the café, mopping, mopping. He swayed to the electronic music he'd set to play and allowed it to bring him and the mop and the orange cleaner together into one seamless cleaning machine.

He worked from the front door to the kitchen door, careful to move each table to mop under the legs. He removed the mats from behind the coffee bar and hung them outside. It was still a little light, but he could feel the darkness moving closer when he stepped outside. The frost took hold a little more each night, and as he breathed it in, it chased away the orange. He became Jack Frost, an icicle-snowflake, shaking out the mats on the back deck. With each movement some of his frost broke away in tiny flakes, minute shavings that mingled with the dirt and coffee grinds and drifted off to become one with the pavement.

He felt the pores of the concrete opening to receive his offering. Concrete, he suddenly knew, was not the fixed, solid mass it appeared to be. It was as alive as he was, feasting on espresso grinds and dust. The tree was proof. That impossible tree that grew right out of the pavement to shade the back deck of the café.

This bore thinking about, and Lennon pulled a chair from the customer smoking table and sat down, feet on the railing. That's when he noticed the lights shimmering all around him. The light from the open kitchen door was shining out in a perfect rectangle, and he moved his chair to sit in the middle of it. The long edges of the rectangle carried the music to him, a bridge of light and music between the inside and the outside. And then the streetlight, over at the corner where the back alley met the street, joined the fray. It shone down, illuminating the pavement, that hungry creature, and showed each spot of oil, each droplet of water, each gob of spit, each pool of piss and puke. The pavement took it all in.

Above that, forming a lazy obtuse triangle with the café light and the streetlight, was the crescent of the moon. Lennon felt its magnetic pull sucking all the frost out of him, and then he was both the light of the moon and the man in the moon. He leaned the chair back on two legs. He held his hands out and let the energy of the moon fill him. He began swaying his hands from side to side, ever so slowly. Front, back, until he felt the pull of the moon magnets firmly implanted in his hands.

He dropped his head to one side and then the other. In time with the gentle swaying of his hands the sliver of moon began to move, side to side, like a kite. The moon was his marionette.

"Don't worry, moon. I know I can't hold you for long. But let's play together just for now, okay? Just for now."

He stayed that way, swaying his arms and feeling the powers of the moon seep into him, until he could move tides, whisper to crops, and pull blood from the core of women with each circle of the earth's orbit.

The red and blue lights arrived all at once. In a flashing line, not a triangle. In response the moon's magnets receded and the open pores of the concrete closed up, covering themselves in the costumes they wore for the rest of world. Just a moon, just a paved lane. Lennon felt he had dropped something precious.

"Crashers!" he cried out. "Crashing the peaceful light party!"

The lights slammed in response. Shadows walked toward him, and with each step the magic receded farther.

• • •

"Lennon Hinton?" Schilling called over the electronic dance music. Thank God she'd talked Resnick out of the siren. She didn't need Aimée to wake up and witness what she was about to do.

"It's me. Shit. Not a good time. The moon—" He sat on a chair balanced on the back legs, swaying his arms as though to wave away the flashing lights.

Resnick slammed the passenger door and stalked out to join her at the base of the steps. "High as a kite," he sniggered.

She ignored him and kept her eyes on Lennon. Bringing her friend in would be hard enough; she couldn't fuck it up by getting pissed off at her boss. She took one step up. He was on something for sure. *No sudden moves. No sense in scaring him.*

"Lennon, we're here to detain you for questioning. Can you stand up, please?" She took another step and waited.

"Sure, sure I can." He wavered as he stood, hands swaying at his sides, his calves and knees jiggling from nervous tension. *What was he on?* "The moon send you?"

"The moon," she said as she ascended the last two steps, "did not send me. I'm a police officer, Lennon."

"That's good, man. That's good." He looked right into her eyes. *Pupils dilated. Manic smile. Sweating.*

"It's not good, Lennon. We're bringing you in for questioning. We may press charges. Can you put your hands on the railing, please?"

He spread his arms wide but kept wiggling his fingers as though trying to hold on to something.

"Stay still," she said. *Don't make this harder,* she wanted to say. She glanced down at Resnick, still in position at the bottom of the steps. Ready to help, she supposed, but looking up at her with amusement.

She ran her hands along Lennon's shoulders and down the sides of his ribs. His abdomen was as firm under her fingers as she'd imagined it would be, and by the time she found the joint in the back pocket of his jeans she was blushing furiously.

"What's this?"

"For later, man. Helps me come down, right?"

"Right, got it. We'll hold on to it for now." In the other pocket she found half a tab of what looked like ecstasy, folded in a crinkled piece of paper. "And this," she added. She patted down his legs, then stepped away. "That's all we got," she called down to Resnick, taking Lennon by the arm. She wasn't sure what she would do if he resisted.

"Mudslide," he said, sliding his arm into hers as though they were taking a stroll. "Triple shot, with whip. Didn't I make it right?"

"You made it exactly right, Lennon," she said, but she couldn't look at him. "You made it the best. It's not about that."

"So it's about the moon? I was going to give it back. All of it!"

"Let's go down the steps, okay?"

"Sure, sure. Down the steps. Sure, I can."

The door. "Wait. Lennon, first you need to close up. Okay?" She led him around to the back door of the café.

He leaned right into her, then pulled away and swayed back and forth as though trying to focus. "I know you. You're straight up, right? I love those eyes. They never lie."

"Just lock the door, Lennon."

He fiddled with the doorknob and pulled it closed, and then wavered again. She caught him under the armpits just before he crumpled to the ground.

"Lennon? Can you stand up?"

His legs were still shaking but he roused himself and managed to stand. "It's all good, man. All good."

She navigated him down the stairs to where Resnick waited with the door to the back seat open. Lennon sang a dirge to the moon as he clambered up into the truck and Resnick rolled his eyes as he slammed the door.

"No cuffs?"

"I don't think he poses a threat, sir. As it is, we'll probably have to wait until morning to make any sense of what he says."

Resnick nodded and started toward the passenger door. "Let's get him in, then." He turned back toward her as he reached the front of the truck, the lights strobing off his stern face. "Not bad, Schilling. Not bad at all."

Bern was sitting on the deck with a mug full of tea when Thompson stepped through the back gate, a bottle of whiskey in his hands.

"To replenish your coffers," he said.

"We're having tea tonight. Grab yourself a mug from the kitchen."

The reporter came back a moment later with a mug full of ice and poured himself a generous serving of whiskey from his offering.

"Suit yourself," Bern said. He didn't want to look at the man in his nubby sweater and his loafers. What had they said to each other the night before? Had he unburdened himself? There was enough Catholic left in him to believe that if he had confessed his sins, even to a faulty lay priest such as this journalist, he should feel some sort of relief. But perhaps he had confessed and not been absolved of his sin?

"I've got the plan ready," Troy said.

"What plan?"

"Don't tell me you've changed your mind!"

Bern waved him off. He looked at his garden for a moment—almost a full acre that he'd managed to suffocate the life from, according to Mrs. K.

"If you're going to hold me to what I said when I was drunk, you'll have to remind me of what it was."

"You don't remember what you said over the pasta primavera? I could say anything here, couldn't I?"

"We had pasta primavera?"

"Even my cooking skills are wasted on you." He shook his head. "I made a great primavera and you don't even remember."

Bern sipped the last of his tea. "Just tell me what I agreed to."

Thompson's voice took on that whining tone that Bern so despised. "You said that if I could find a way to use my magazine—and the media in general—to get Alais out of trouble, you would tell me your whole story."

"I said that?"

Thompson nodded. "And you said you'd let me publish it. Exclusively."

"I must have been really pissed."

The reporter shrugged. "I've seen worse."

"Did I really say exclusive? It doesn't sound like something I'd say."

"I had to talk you into that part," Thompson admitted. "But you saw reason."

"Fine, then. Tell me your plan."

Bern sat back in his chair and stretched his legs out onto the deck railing. He watched the light of evening dim behind the mountains as the other man explained his plan for not only a feature in the next edition of *Soldier's Ally* magazine, but also a front page in the national newspaper on Remembrance Day.

When he fell silent, Bern considered the plan in all its detail and from all angles. He tested the sides and the middle, the way Mrs. K. might prod the surface of one of her cakes, to see if it held firm.

Thompson's anxiety made Bern extend the silence for several minutes after he'd made the decision that the proposition was sound. He watched as the mountains sucked in the last light of the sky and the two melded to form night over the graveyard of his garden.

"I will say yes, with two conditions."

Even with the darkness between them, Bern could feel the relief sweep through his companion, and it rang a little warning bell in him. What was in it for Thompson, beyond selling a few more magazines?

"Name them."

"I'll tell you my story on Saturday night at seven p.m. Here. But before I start talking, I need to see your plane ticket, proving that you're flying out on Sunday morning. After I talk to you, I want you gone. Understood?"

Thompson nodded. "And the other condition?"

"The headline," said Bern. "I want to be totally upfront with this. No beating around the bush. I want it to read 'Arrest Me Too.'"

The reporter was animated all of a sudden. "Really? That's perfect! Great. No problem. Anything else?"

Bern nodded. "Leave the whiskey at home. We do this sober or not at all."

• • •

It was late when Lennon finally came to bed, but Aimée slid over to make room for him. It was such a relief to have him there, helping around the café and being loving again. He wrapped an arm around her waist and in her half sleep she turned to him.

"Come with me, skater girl," he said. He tightened his grip around her waist.

Aimée was up like a shot. Gabriel. She had to get to him. Her legs tangled in the blankets and she fell face-first in the doorway. She heard the man's footsteps walk lazily to her.

"You used to be more graceful," he said as he kneeled down next to her. "Come."

In the dark apartment all she could see was the stark white of his shirt and his glistening teeth. He grabbed her with a rough arm and pulled her up. When she tried to run he hooked his leg around hers and steered her body into his.

He wrapped his arm around her neck and pulled her into his chest. His shirt smelled like bleach and his breath stank of beer. "Don't be afraid," he said. "I'll look after you."

She pushed with all her strength, but even drunk he was strong. "I thought you said alcohol ruins your body!" She screamed it into his chest and pummeled him with her fists.

"*Maman?*" Gabriel's voice squeaked with sleep.

"Gabriel! *Cours! Cours, mon petit!*" Run!

She turned her head so she could see her boy. The man's arms were like steel around her. She wriggled her whole body to free herself, but he just tightened his grip.

Gabriel stood in the hall, frozen in place. He wore camouflage-print pajamas that he'd picked out because they looked like the uniform his soldiers wore. Even now, he carried a handful of those damn plastic soldiers this terrible man had given him. He looked impossibly small, her little boy. Too small to be without her.

"Gabby? *Cours! Va appeler au secours.*" Run! Go get help.

For a moment they were all locked in place. The man's arms held Aimée, but she was squirming so much that he couldn't move either. Gabriel, her sweet angel, still half asleep, hesitated in the hall.

And then he ran, his little camouflaged legs gone and down the stairs. His motion brought a momentum that unlocked them, and the man twisted Aimée and crooked his arm around her neck. He steered her through the tiny living room, around the couch, and down the stairs. The blanket stayed tangled in her feet until partway down the stairs, where it let go of its grip; it too was unwilling to go with him.

There was still music coming from the café. Where was Lennon? A black car waited by the back steps. Engine running, back door open. He pushed her toward it, but Aimée hardened her body and refused to move. "Gabby?" she cried. *"Je t'aime, mon petit. Je t'adore!"* I love you. I adore you.

The man lifted her up and carried her. She kicked at his knees and shins, screaming.

He stopped and she felt her feet back on the ground. Then his fist smashed against the base of her skull. Her teeth jarred together with a sickening clack and she pitched forward. Her forehead smashed against the open car door and she crumpled to the ground.

Nairobi, 1994

"Sir? Captain? It's time to get up."

Bern opened his eyes to bright whiteness. He pushed a shaky hand along the sheets, but she was gone. He buried his head in the linens but could not recapture the scent of her.

"Who are you?"

"Your valet, sir. I mean, Captain."

He rolled over and pushed himself up on the pillows. "What time is it?"

"One o'clock, sir," the man said. He was broad-faced with black hair in tight curls graying at the temples. His voice had the friendly lilt of an African who'd been speaking English for most of his life.

"I have to get back to the hospital." He pushed off the blankets and then pulled them back when he remembered he was naked. He'd never had a valet before and wasn't sure of the protocol.

"You're to meet General LeClerc in the lobby bar in an hour. I've ordered you a light breakfast for now. I thought you might be hungry."

"The general? But my uniform—"

"I had it cleaned and pressed for you. It's in the closet, sir."

"Ah, thank you." Bern leaned his head back and the man brought a tray to the table by the window. When he opened the curtains, the room became even brighter, if that was possible.

"I think you'll be all set now, sir," the valet said as he lay a robe on the bed. "The general said two o'clock."

"And madame?" Bern asked. "The general's wife?"

"I don't know anything about the general's wife, sir."

"Thank you. I'll be fine now."

26

Between the slats of the window, he could see the moon, a shining slice of freedom.

Already he was coming down. The beautiful idea that the moon could be his marionette and the tides would do his bidding was fading as surely as the dark behind the mountains in the predawn light. But the feeling was still in him and he held it fast. They could not take it away.

It wasn't just a feeling. It was a certainty: that there was more to the world—more to life—than most people would ever know. All those half-alive people, coming into Mountain Station every morning, looking for caffeine to get through one more day at their jobs—their limitations were as imaginary as his marionette strings from the moon.

He held on to this kernel of knowledge as the boundaries of his mind began to shrink. He checked his pocket for the joint he'd prepared for just this moment, but of course they'd taken that too.

He lay across the width of the bed, his legs up the wall, his head hanging off the edge so he could see the moon, fading now in the morning light. He watched it until it was just a pale line in the sky. Only then did he close his eyes. He closed his eyes and waited for the gears of the system to churn. Waited for his mom to get the message and send her lawyer. She had a choice of several—they'd been fighting his dad's case for years. It made him laugh to think of this. How the hell did they think a woman whose only legal income was a small coffee shop and a couple of logging blocks was paying all those legal fees?

With each thought Lennon felt the doors slamming shut in the jail cell of his own mind. A prisoner of society. What the hell difference did it make if he was locked up today? It meant nothing to him. Nothing.

As the moon faded further into the morning sky, the mountains reasserted themselves as the guardians of Kootenay Landing, and Lennon allowed his eyes to close. He felt itchy on the inside of his skin. He wanted sleep. It wouldn't come for a few more hours, but he knew what to do. He'd come down hundreds of times. Smoking pot made it easier, but he could manage.

He breathed slowly and deeply. He became aware of the desire to shake, to move, to climb. He felt each door as it closed in his mind. He closed his eyes tighter and searched the growing maze of corridors until he found that kernel, the feeling of the magnetic strings in his hands, of the music, of the sway of the moon, matching his own movements.

He found the very core of the experience and wrapped himself in it until it surrounded him. His only movement was the roll of his fingertips along his palms as he held the invisible string. Breath slow, fingers moving, in that cell he was as free as he'd ever been.

With each breath, the ecstasy ever so slowly released its grip on him and he fell asleep.

· · ·

The door to the coffee shop was locked, the closed sign flipped toward him. Bern checked his watch against the times posted in the front window. It should have opened an hour earlier.

He pressed his face to the door to look inside. The chairs were upside down on the tables and the place was lit up like a suburban shopping mall. He could hear music playing. The flutter in his belly and the pounding in his ears told him that something was wrong.

"Aimée? Lennon?"

He knocked on the door. No answer. He knocked again. "*Bonjour?* Aimée?" He called.

The pressure of panic mounted in his sternum. Something was wrong. Or was it? Was he overreacting again? He pounded the flat of his hand in frustration this time. He wasted only a moment on hesitation. Better to look like a fool than to ignore his instinct, however misguided. He ran to the end of the block and circled into the back lane. Cold morning air moved through his lungs and lessened the hold of the panic. He'd never been into the lane, but the café was instantly recognizable from the back—wrought iron tables dotted the patio, which had been built around the trunk of a maple tree now in full fall color. The back door to the café hung open and music spilled from inside.

Bern took the steps three at a time.

"Aimée?" he called again. "Are you here?"

A bird squawked in the tree at the sound of his voice.

"Aimée?"

He poked his head into the kitchen. A mop and bucket stood by the door, water slopped over the sides. Wet footprints punctuated by dark splatters led through the water. He could see the outline of toes—someone had passed through here barefoot.

Shadows played at the corners of his eyes and his breath came faster. He crouched to see what the splatters were.

Soldiers. Plastic soldiers.

"Aimée? Gabriel?"

The bird's cry was deeper this time, almost hoarse. A squawk.

Bern took the stairs up to the apartment. They were littered with debris: a blue cotton blanket with loose threads sticking up like tiny caterpillars; a slipper; more soldiers; a sippy cup that had dripped water onto the steps. The air was close and heavy. At the top of the stairs Bern flicked on the light. He didn't bother calling out.

The apartment was tiny. A couch stretched from the landing through a minute living space and blocked the entrance to the kitchen. A low coffee table was covered in fat candles that had dripped over the rims of their glass holders. A table in the kitchen could seat three. The bedroom off the entry was strewn with clothing and smelled of perfume. The messy bedroom of a busy young woman. He felt a prickle at the back of his neck and spun around. The hallway, coffee table, candles looked back.

"Gabriel?"

He could hear the squawk of the bird, even from up here. There was another bedroom off the kitchen, its window open a crack. A single bed with a pillow, but no blanket. Toys organized into colorful bins, clothes tucked in a wooden dresser. But there was something very, very wrong.

"*Gabriel!*" he roared.

He could barely hear through the pounding in his ears as he raced back down the stairs. He grabbed his phone from his pocket and went out on the back deck. Who was he going to call? What was he going to say?

Kitchen mats were piled in one corner. More bare footprints

led off the deck and down the steps to the lane, then disappeared.

"Aimée?" he called again, quieter now. "Gabriel?"

He started to call Resnick, then thought better of it and dialed Schilling's number instead. He moved under the shade of the tree to try to gain some control over his senses. The phone rang and rang. Bern could hear the rhythm of his heartbeats added to the music of the café. Then he heard the croak of that bird again, followed by a whimper.

He pressed the phone to his chest. "Gabriel?" he called. Quiet now. The music from inside continued its funky beat.

"*Es tu là?* Gabriel?"

He heard breathing, quicker than his own, then a croak. Coming from above.

Go up, he'd told the boy. Bern looked into the broad canopy of the tree above him.

"Gabriel?"

"Monsieur le soldat?"

"Oui, c'est moi, petit."

"The commander didn't know what to do." The boy spoke in a hoarse whisper. "I tricked him."

Bern reached up his free hand. He still couldn't see the boy. "Well done, little soldier. Come down now."

All at once, he heard someone calling his name in the distance. He turned to see who was there, then realized it was his phone.

"Bern?"

"Schilling," he said. "I need you to come to Mountain Station right away."

"No, no, I can't. We're swamped here. No time for coffee."

"Believe me, Schilling, we're not having coffee." A skinny leg in camouflage-pattern pajamas slithered down from the tree and perched like a raven on a low branch. "Just come now. It's urgent."

He dropped the phone on the table and held his arms out to the boy. The child scrambled into them. Bern tried to hold him close, but he pushed the soldier away.

"I hid well," he said. "Will the commander come back now? With Mommy?"

Bern pulled the boy close. He was shivering. "Come," he said.

He stepped into the café and grabbed the blanket from the steps. He wrapped the boy up tight, then folded him in his lap. They sat there, two soldiers, waiting for help to arrive.

Dr. Sinclair met them at the door. The pressure of the past days had crystallized her features even further, refining her beauty to cold, sharp lines. Schilling hated to bring even more bad news to the house.

"What could you possibly want now?"

"We need to talk to Gia," Schilling said. She stepped aside to make way for Bern and the tiny, serious boy who held his hand.

"Gabriel! Are you okay?" Juniper crouched down and reached out to him, but the boy froze. "What happened? What have you done to him?"

"Dr. Sinclair, calm down. We need to talk to Gia." She knew by now to go straight to her tall voice with the good doctor.

Juniper stood again. She held out a hand to Gabriel, but he just widened his dark eyes and held firm to Bern's. "Fine, come in," she said.

Gia was seated in an armchair in the living room, her wheelchair parked at her side. She sat up straighter when they came in.

The events of the day before—the search of the adjacent property and Lennon's detainment—had taken their toll. She looked older and defeated, her white turban and raspberry-red shawl like props borrowed for an amateur play.

"Gabriel? Is that my Gabriel?" Gia's voice came out strong and cheerful as she forced a smile onto her face. "Come here, my grandbaby."

She opened the fringed hem of the shawl and the boy dropped Bern's hand and ran to her. He clambered up onto her lap and she folded his knees up and pulled off the sneakers that Schilling had slid onto his cold feet before they got in the squad car. She closed the shawl around the boy and he disappeared into the world of her arms. Then she looked up at Schilling, fury on her face.

"Explain," she said. The coldness in her eyes almost made Maddie take a step back.

"I'm Constable Schilling from the RCMP."

Gia nodded curtly. "I saw you on the property next door yesterday. And I've spoken with Lennon this morning. I know you're the one who brought him in."

"Right. So something happened at the apartment, and we don't know what. Some kind of disturbance. But Aimée is gone and Gabriel was hiding."

"What? How could this be? Aimée would never leave Gabriel. Never." She looked over at Juniper, who had taken a seat on the adjacent couch. The look that passed between them communicated plenty, but Schilling couldn't understand a word of it. Gia wrapped her arms more tightly around Gabriel. "How did you find him?"

With a cough to clear his throat, Bern spoke at last. "I went in for my morning coffee. The lights were on and there was music playing. The chairs were still stacked on the tables and it was well past opening time. There seemed to be no one there. It was unusual, so I went to the back door by the kitchen to see if I could help. And that's when I saw the disarray. The back door was hanging open; there was a blanket on the stairs to the apartment. I found Gabriel high up in the tree by the patio. He'd climbed up there to hide."

Gia seemed unable to speak, so Schilling jumped in while she had a chance. "I need to interview him to find out what he knows, or at least what he saw. Of course we need a parent or guardian to be with him for that."

"Of course," Gia said quietly. "Of course. And since you've already detained Lennon, you came here." She placed a protective hand on Gabriel's head, which was completely covered in the shawl. Schilling didn't know how he could breathe under there.

As if in response to this thought, Gia lifted the edge of the shawl to create a little space. Then she leaned forward with a look of absolute tenderness. "He's asleep. Oh, my sweet little man," she said.

She and Juniper exchanged looks again, then Gia nodded. Whatever that nod communicated, Juniper understood it clearly and stood.

"It's time for you to go," Gia said. "Constable, I will call the station when Gabriel has had some rest and some food and comfort, and you may come back then and interview him. In the meantime, I suspect that my son, who is already in your custody, will have information about what happened, and possibly why."

There seemed to be no choice in the matter. Juniper was shepherding them to the door. Schilling considered demanding to speak to the boy right away, but then she thought of her own role in the whole thing: she alone knew about Aimée's unwanted visitor from the other night. She was the one who'd taken

Lennon into custody, leaving Aimée and Gabriel alone. And the door. Had he even locked it properly? She stifled a groan.

"All right, then. We'll go—for now. We'll call you soon."

"I said that *we* will call when he's ready, Constable. Not before."

"But what about Aimée?"

"Talk to Lennon. And, Constable?" They were almost at the door, and Schilling bumped into Bern as she turned back. "When you come back, please leave the coroner behind." Gia sat so tall, she seemed to be looking down at all of them from a great height. She looked directly at Bern as she spoke the next words: "He's done enough damage here."

"I'm not getting anything out of him," Resnick said. "It's all a big joke to him." He punched the air hard, then let his arm fall. "So you two just sitting out here, watching everyone else work? There's a girl missing, right?"

Bern took a step sideways so that Resnick could pass. The officer scowled at him, stalked the two steps to the watercooler, and pulled out a cone-shaped paper cup. "Problem with you, Fortin, is that you don't have any fire in you. Know what I mean? Your clients are all dead. No hurry there." He chugged back the water and then crumpled the cup in his fist.

"Staff Sergeant?" Schilling's voice was too tentative. Bern wanted to command her to attention.

"I could take all the time in the world too, if all the criminals were dead already," said Resnick, ignoring his junior officer yet again.

Bern cleared his throat. "I can see that you're feeling the heat,

Resnick. One man missing. Another dead. A skeleton. And now a woman disappeared, possibly against her will."

"What the hell do you know about heat, Fortin?" he snapped, mangling Bern's last name, as usual. "You have only half that much to worry about, and no one's breathing down your neck."

"Ah, are there people on your case?"

Resnick started counting on his fingers. "US Border Service and the Idaho sheriff's office, for starters. 'Serious breach of homeland security' is what they're calling Gary Dowd. Then the hot-and-cold drug squad, either breathing down my neck or won't return my calls. And then there's Duke Forsberg. Wants to know what the hell we're doing about finding the rest of his daughter. Correct me if I'm wrong, Fortin, but isn't that your job?"

"Sir." Schilling's voice was stronger this time. Bern nodded at her. Better.

"What, Schilling? Make it good."

"I think we should let the coroner talk to Lennon. I'll sit in and take notes."

"Why the hell would we do that?"

She stepped forward. "Because he's good at getting people talking. Not that you aren't—I mean, you're great at it—but this has worked before."

Resnick's mouth was hanging open. He raised his hands and shook his head and just stared at them. "I can see you've talked about this."

"We're desperate, sir," Schilling pleaded.

"If you just let me go I can get her back."

Lennon was more resigned than belligerent, Bern thought.

He wore a faded T-shirt of indeterminate color with a pair of old jeans. His arms were relaxed at his sides and he stared at the table where they sat. Schilling perched in a corner, out of Bern's line of sight.

"I thought you could tell me a few things." Bern kept his tone relaxed.

"I can't tell you anything without getting a whole bunch of people in trouble."

"So don't tell me specifics." He raised one shoulder. "I'm not a police officer, remember? Just tell me enough so that we can find Aimée."

Lennon looked straight at him with eyes just as proud and certain as Gia's. "Just let me go and I can find her myself."

"You know where she is?"

"I'm not totally sure. But I can find out."

Bern raised his hands helplessly. "A slight problem, then: you're in here."

Lennon crossed his arms.

"Aren't you worried about Aimée?"

"Of course I am."

"But not overly worried." Bern nodded slowly. "Why is that?"

"Because the very second I get out of here, I can fix this. The guy doesn't want anything from Aimée. He wants something from me."

"What guy?" Schilling jumped in. "Tell us who he is or what he looks like."

Bern held up a hand to her—this needed to be handled delicately—but he was surprised when Lennon answered.

"I've seen him once or twice. That's all."

"And you think this man has something to do with Aimée's disappearance? How did you come into contact with him?" Bern wanted to shake the young man's indifference right out of him, but he kept his voice calm.

"The café. I see everyone in there."

"So he's a customer? That's a start. What else do you know about him?"

Lennon ran his thumb over a scratch in the table. "I may have been in touch with him. About a project."

"With him directly?" Bern's frustration flared at the slow line of questioning. He exhaled slowly to calm himself. He could do this, for Aimée.

"Maybe. I never met him. It was all by phone. But it could be the same guy."

"Can you tell us what he looks like?"

"Indian. Older—like forty something? Short hair, shaved. And he dresses like an IBM guy."

Bern heard Schilling shift in her chair.

"What does that mean?"

Lennon wrinkled his nose. "You know, corporate casual. Like really clean jeans and really white shirt."

"What's his name?" Schilling demanded.

"Jared."

"Last name?"

He shook his head. "Never told me."

"Jared the Indian?" she asked.

"Basically, yeah. That's all I know."

"No, you know more," Bern said. "You used to call him."

"Yeah, but he stopped answering the phone. I was trying to call him all week."

"We'll need that number," Schilling said.

"Anything else you can tell us?" Bern asked.

"He's connected, for sure." Lennon shrugged. "You'll find him."

Bern touched Lennon's thumb, still rubbing at that scratch, and held it still. "Don't you care what happens to her?"

He pulled his hand away. Bern remembered his first impression of Lennon—all fire and strength and fun. The young man before him now seemed to droop.

"Of course I do," he said. "But there's not all that much I can do from here, is there?" His eyes flashed and Bern saw that a tiny spark was still alive.

"Tell me one thing, then." He leaned close enough to smell the young man's stale breath and whispered, "Where's the first place you'd go look?"

Lennon blinked back at him. "The casino. In Cranbrook."

Bern sat back and sighed. "You could tell us everything, you know. It would help Aimée."

"I could have helped Aimée," he hissed between clenched jaws. "If I hadn't been locked up in this cage, I would have been there. This never would have happened and Aimée would be safe."

"But this is the reality now," Bern said. "Tell us what you know. It will help her."

Lennon shook his head. "I think it would just cause a bunch of people a bunch of trouble and not make any difference at all to Aimée. I know you'll find her. And I know she can handle herself until you do."

He lifted his chin and turned his head in a gesture that was all too familiar to Bern. They would get no more out of Lennon.

"I hope for your sake you're right," Schilling said, speaking the words that were on Bern's tongue before he had a chance.

Nairobi, 1994

Diplomats, officers, and journalists clustered in small groups in the lobby. Bern nodded to a few familiar faces but kept moving toward the Safari Bar. He arrived one minute late. The general was already waiting for him, tucked in a corner banquette away from the prying ears of journalists. Bern saluted and LeClerc waved for him to be seated.

"Beer?" he asked, and without waiting for an answer, he waved his hand again, this time to the red-jacketed waiter.

"They've stabilized him," LeClerc said without preamble. "Enough that we can evacuate him to Canada."

"His arm?" Bern asked.

"There's a chance they might save it. A slim one."

The waiter placed a beer before Bern and faded into the background.

"Warm as piss," the general said.

"That's how they do it in Africa," Bern answered vaguely, distracted by the thought of Sauvé going home. Who would accompany him? They had not been apart in over a year: surely he would be asked to see his commanding officer home safely. His chest fluttered at the thought of Canada. Any quarters assigned to him would seem luxurious after months of sleeping on a mattress in the besieged command headquarters in Kigali. Proper meals. Espresso. Cold beer.

He looked up to see LeClerc surveying him, as though taking measure of something. Bern squared his shoulders and looked directly back. The general's gaze hardened and narrowed, and Bern knew the decision had already been made. Wherever he went, it would be a long way from Canada, from New York, and from Sasha. His punishment was far from over; he just had to wait for his orders.

Bern dropped his gaze first and LeClerc nodded as though satisfied. "You can go see Sauvé now. And then you'll go back to Rwanda. The Hercules is headed back to Uganda this afternoon. A new mission commander will be named by the end of today and you are to be ready to welcome him by the end of the week. I have no doubt you'll be invaluable to him, as you were to Sauvé."

Bern sat stock-still and waited for more orders, but none came. He fixed his gaze past the general's left shoulder and stared hard at the glossed mahogany of the bar across the room while his disappointment settled.

The waiter materialized again, this time leaning over to whisper in the general's ear. LeClerc pushed his barely touched beer away and stood. "I have to take this call."

Bern jumped to attention.

"My driver is out front. He'll take you to the hospital when you're ready. And from there to the airport," LeClerc said as he stalked away.

Bern watched him go, and with him, his own hopes of an early return to Canada. And of ever seeing Sasha again.

27

He poked her awake. She kept her eyes closed until she couldn't stand the poking anymore—jabs to her ribs, her shoulders, her upper arms. She was cold and her head pounded with the pain of a thousand hangovers. She opened her eyes to see his mean face in a stark room with boarded-up windows.

"Get up," he said.

He was already dressed in a crisp white shirt. Same jeans. Recently shaved and just as mean as ever.

She sat up. She was on a bed, wearing only the tank top and underwear she'd gone to sleep in the night before. She pressed her palm to the back of her head and found a tender lump.

She pulled a sheet up to cover herself. It was yellow and smelled of flowery perfume. "Where am I? When can I go home?"

"You are home," he said.

She turned her head to shake it, and then stopped. It hurt too much for that. "You can't keep me here."

He smiled but narrowed his eyes at the same time. Evil. "Sure I can," he said. "I never should have let you leave."

"What are you talking about?"

His smile was easier now, more friendly, as though he'd told a joke and was just waiting for her to get it.

She smiled back and leaned toward him as though she might kiss him. When he closed his eyes in anticipation, she spit in his face. "I hate you," she said.

He used a corner of the sheet to wipe the spit away, watching her the whole time. Then, ever so slowly, he moved toward her on the bed, grabbed a fistful of hair, and pressed her face down into the sheets.

"I have to go look after some business." His voice was a husky whisper. "I'll be gone all day. When I get back, I expect dinner. I want a good dinner. A dinner for a man."

She couldn't breathe. She felt a roaring between her ears and an exploding pain where his hand pressed into the back of her head.

"Understand?" he asked.

She tried to nod but couldn't move. She kicked her legs.

"What?" he asked.

He pulled her head back by the hair and she gasped in air.

"Do you understand?" His voice was patient now.

"Yes. Yes. I'll make dinner."

"Good," he said. "Make something I like."

He let go of her head. She whimpered but dared not move. She felt the mattress shift as he got up, and a moment later a door slammed and she heard the scrape of a lock. Outside an engine started and a dog began barking.

She got up a few minutes later and wandered through the cabin. The only furniture was the bed in one bedroom, and an old dining room table with four chairs next to the living area. A second, smaller bedroom was completely empty, except for a blue foam camping pad rolled in one corner. There was a tiny bathroom that was impeccably clean, but it had only shampoo, soap, and one towel. All the windows were either boarded up or closed in with glass blocks. He'd locked her in from the outside. There was no getting out of this place.

She tried every window and crack anyway. She screamed until she was hoarse, but all it did was make the dog bark like crazy.

"I will not cry," she said. So she screamed instead. She cursed him and yelled for Lennon, for Gabby, for the police, for anyone to save her.

The dog kept barking but no one came.

She wanted to lie down, but the thought of lying on his bed made her sick. Instead she crawled under the table and pulled the four chairs in as closely as she could to make a sanctuary for herself. She lay down in a fetal position and looked up at the underside of the table. There she saw the same name, written over and over—in pencil, in pen, and carved into the wood. *Cindy. Cindy. Cindy.* A child's handwriting. *I am Cindy.*

She mouthed the words to herself as she fell asleep under the table.

"You okay? You keep sighing."

It hadn't taken them long to track down their suspect: Jared John. After Schilling put out the APB, Resnick took off for Cranbrook to stake out John's last known address with some local officers. Schilling was left behind with the coroner—Schilling to search the database for information about Jared John, and the coroner to scour the Cindy Forsberg file. They'd been working side by side for over an hour.

She sat back and sighed again. "Sorry. It's just—" She hesitated. How could she tell him? That she'd screwed it all up. That she'd failed her friend. That she should have filed a report after

Aimée called about the intruder. That she hadn't watched what Lennon was doing when she asked him to lock the door. She looked down. "It's just so hard to sit here and wait."

"Hard to believe the sun just keeps on shining out there, isn't it?" Bern stood from the area he'd cleared for himself at the corner of her desk and wandered over to the window. "Kootenay Landing, a village nestled in the mountains, picture-perfect," he said. "And Aimée is out there, somewhere."

"Resnick should be in Cranbrook by now." She stood too and rubbed her knuckles into her lower back; sore, but this time just from desk work.

"Tell me what you know," Bern said, leaning against the windowsill. "What have you found out about this Jared John character?"

"Forty-five years old. Convicted of some minor offenses—drunk and disorderly, robbery, possession of cocaine. Grew up in Kootenay Landing and lived for a time in the Shuswap area, where he served a one-year sentence for aggravated assault. Relocated to Cranbrook three years ago. Active member of the Warriors—a First Nations gang known for drug smuggling, money laundering, and prostitution."

"A guy with a past, in other words," Bern said. "And what's the link between him and Lennon?"

Schilling closed her eyes and thought. It was completely different talking over the case with the coroner. She knew that no matter what she said, he wouldn't make her feel stupid. Unlike Resnick. "Okay, so we know there was a grow op adjacent to Lennon's property. We can't link it to him or Gia right now, but I'm just going to assume for a minute that Lennon's involved, okay?"

Bern nodded.

"So he starts a grow op on an enormous scale. An operation like that takes a lot of money, so where would Lennon get it from?"

"He said he was in touch with Jared John about a 'project.' You think that was it?"

Schilling nodded. "Makes sense, doesn't it? So then we make another assumption: the Warriors, and specifically Jared John, fronted Lennon's grow op."

"In Hells Angels territory. They wouldn't like that."

"They didn't like that at all. But they waited, didn't they? Waited until the crop was ready, then sent Seymour in and ripped it. Scared Lennon and Gia real bad," she said. She pushed some papers out of the way and sat up on her desk. "And just like that, the Warriors are out a whole lot of money."

"So they kill Seymour in retaliation? It's possible," Bern said. He approached the desk and started flipping through the Cindy Forsberg file. "But then why take Aimée?"

Schilling stood again and paced the room. "That part just doesn't make sense. Take Aimée to put the squeeze on Lennon? But what does that accomplish? He doesn't have any money, and they need his expertise to recoup their losses." Schilling stopped pacing at a vacant desk and picked up a ruler, then dropped it back down. "Nope. It just doesn't add up."

The coroner riffled through the Cindy Forsberg file. "Unless we look at this from another angle. What if the connection is not between Aimée and Lennon and the Warriors? What if it's between Jared John and Cindy Forsberg?"

"I'm listening," she said. The least she could do was hear him out.

He pulled a stapled sheet out of the file. "I didn't know what I was looking at when I first saw it. But could this explain—?"

She scanned the paper and whistled. "You think he took Aimée because of a stalking complaint from twenty years ago?"

"It seems that twenty years ago Jared did not know how to let Cindy go. What if he saw Aimée—"

"And thought he'd found Cindy again?" Schilling dropped the report on the empty desk and headed to the door. "You coming?"

"Sure," he said, following her with his loping step. "Where are we headed?"

"To find out a whole lot more about Cindy Forsberg. And Jared John."

Meat loaf. Given the ingredients in the fridge and cupboards, it was her only option. A few tins of green beans and corn would be their side dish. Rather, his side dish and Aimée's meal. He couldn't make her eat meat loaf—could he?

She'd pulled a sheet off the bed and fashioned it into a toga. She was still barefoot and cold. There was a stack of logs by the woodstove. Had there been matches as well, she would have used them to set the place on fire to escape, to get back to Gabriel. That was all she could think about—getting back to Gabriel. She would cooperate with Jared only long enough to trip him up somehow so she could escape.

She set the oven to preheat, then took the pound of extra-lean ground beef from the fridge. It was red it the middle but turning brown at the sides, and the smell, when she pulled off the plastic wrap, was tangy and sour. She pressed into the back of the Styrofoam and popped the meat into a stainless steel bowl without touching it.

There were no eggs, but she added ketchup, salt, pepper, and a little dried parsley to the beef, pressing a fork into the middle of the concoction to stir it. The beef made a suctioning sound as it drew in the ketchup, filling her nostrils with the stink of rotting meat.

Aimée held her breath. She took out a second fork and pushed that in too, trying to mix it all together, but it wouldn't budge. She closed her eyes and breathed through the panic that threatened to engulf her. Think of Gabriel. She had to hold it together to get back to Gabriel.

She'd seen her own mother make meat loaf a thousand times. Reluctantly, she slid her hands into the cold meat, kneading it as though it were bread dough; it squished through her fingers, leaving trails of ketchup and slime. When she needed to take a breath, she turned her head to the side to avoid the smell. When the mixture was finally ready, she molded it into the loaf pan, then held her hands under the tap. She scrubbed her fingers with soap and hot water until they too were the color of raw meat. As she was sliding the loaf pan into the warm oven, she heard a clatter and scrape at the door. The dog was finally quiet.

It was him.

Schilling passed a sign that read John. She slammed on the brakes, and Bern braced himself against the dash.

"Jared John?" he asked.

Closer to the house, the garden beds were tended, the trim was freshly painted, and the stoop was swept.

Kelly John pulled the door open before they could ring the bell. She was wearing an old flannel dressing gown and held a wad of Kleenex to her nose. She squeaked when she saw them, and Bern thought she might close the door in their faces.

"I'm sorry!" she cried, her eyes pained and cheeks flushed as red as her nose. "I wasn't expecting company." She looked at Schilling and said, more quietly, "I called in sick. Didn't Chantel tell you? That would be so like her not to tell you."

"No, it's okay. Sorry to scare you. It's just . . . Do you remember Cindy Forsberg?"

Kelly's eyes flitted from Schilling's face to Bern's. "You're here about Cindy?"

Schilling shook her head. "Can we come in and talk? There's a lot to explain."

Kelly cleared the living room of a handful of teenagers and a basket of unfolded laundry, then invited them to sit down. Her husband tried to leave too. "Dave, you stay," she said to him. "You know more about this than I do."

Bern introduced himself to the downtrodden man. He was fiftyish and had that slender physique that looked like it came more from good genes than exercise—the kind of guy who might eat a half pound of bacon and smoke two packs of cigarettes a day and live to be ninety.

"Dave, I'm Bern Fortin. Kelly talks about you all the time."

Dave grunted. "She talks about you too."

Kelly gestured to the furniture, and once they had each sunk down into a comfortable and well-used seat, Schilling brought them up to speed.

"So you're saying that this Aimée is missing and you think Jared John has her?" Kelly summarized. "I'm sorry, but I'm not sure what this has to do with Cindy."

"Well, two things," Schilling said. "I first heard Jared John's name in relation to Aimée's disappearance. But then I finally had time to sit down with Cindy Forsberg's file—"

"And you saw his name there again," Kelly interrupted. "Cindy and Jared were cousins. Or are cousins—because who knows what happened to her?"

Schilling shot Bern a look and he shook his head once, sharply. The news about Cindy wasn't public yet.

"Right," Maddie said, nodding. "When I saw his name there—and saw that Cindy also used to be a John—I thought you might know more about it."

Dave chimed in then. "Jared is my cousin. So is Cindy." He laughed bitterly. "We're all related here."

"It's hard sometimes," Kelly said. "Some of Dave's cousins can be troublemakers—even now that we're all older and supposed to be settled down. It impacts all of us."

"Like Jared?" Bern asked.

"Jared is a bad apple," Dave said. "We never see him. He was gone for a long time—over in the Shuswap with an uncle. Working on 'projects,' he always said." Dave made air quotes when he said the word. "I don't know why he couldn't just go out and get a job like the rest of us."

"When did he come back?" Bern asked.

"A few years ago. Turned up in Cranbrook just when the casino was being built, and all of a sudden he was a 'partner.'" Again with air quotes. "I think he must have tricked someone. I don't know where he ever got the money for that."

"Has he made your life difficult by coming back?" Bern asked.

Kelly and Dave exchanged a look. He shrugged and she picked up the story. "Some local kids have talked about being in a gang. Going to Cranbrook for meetings. Wearing head scarves and getting tattoos and calling themselves Warriors."

"And naturally this is distressing to you, since you have teen-agers of your own," Bern said.

"Damn right!" Dave's resentment flared into anger. "We're trying to teach our kids the value of a good day's work. Then Jared comes along and gives them 'jobs' doing who knows what. And suddenly they've got cash and are getting into all kinds of trouble." His anger seemed to lose steam and he shook his head. "It's not right," he muttered.

"What kind of trouble?" Schilling asked.

"We just hear talk, that's all. I don't want to tell tales out of school. There's nothing we know for sure."

"How about I tell you the talk I've heard," said Schilling, "and we can see if it matches?" When Dave nodded, she continued. "I've heard of possible money laundering through the casino and drug running." She tilted her head as she spoke.

Both Johns were nodding.

"And I've heard that Jared thinks of his Warriors as a growing concern. He wants his gang to have a bigger piece of the pie, and he might be stepping on some pretty big toes—like the Hells Angels, for one, who like to think they're in charge in these parts."

Dave shook his head. "I don't know anything about that. But it would make sense. Jared has always been out for more than he should rightfully have."

Bern leaned forward and spoke very quietly. "So where can we find him?"

28

"Take it off." He looked exactly the same as he had the night he'd shown up at her place for dinner, except this time his hands were empty. No groceries, but dark washed jeans and a white button-down shirt, perfectly pressed. For sure he didn't live in this place. There was no iron, to start with.

"What?"

"The sheet. Take it off."

"But I'm cold!"

He sat at the dining room table and watched her as she went back to what she was doing. She opened the can of beans and poured it into a pot on the stove, ready to heat when the meat loaf was almost done. Then she did the same with the corn.

"I said take it off."

"And I said I'm cold. You left me all day in this freezing shit-hole. Trapped. Kidnapped, that's what I am. A hostage. And you want me nearly naked too?"

He pushed back the chair roughly and went to the woodstove. He took a lighter out of his back pocket—the right one, she noticed—and went to work building a fire. This done, he stalked into the kitchen and pulled the knot that held the sheet at her shoulder.

She clutched at the sheet to keep it from falling, but he pulled her fingers away one by one until it slid to the floor. Then he tugged on one strap of her tank top and the other. He stretched them and pulled them until her arms were free and the fabric was a tangled tube at her waist. He stared at her clavicle and leaned closer to take in the illustrations that covered her chest and shoulders.

His hair smelled like musk and he emanated an odor—no, an energy—of stubborn evil. He tilted his head and leaned even closer, his eyes tracing the rose between the teeth of the skull. He lifted a hand and pressed a finger to her sternum. She gasped in horror as she felt her nipples harden at his touch.

"You always liked that," he said with a smirk.

"What are you talking about? I've always liked that. Like you know anything about me."

He straightened and smiled at her but kept his finger in place. She stepped back, and he stepped forward. She stepped back again and felt the edge of the kitchen counter behind her. He pressed his hips against hers until she was trapped there, then began tracing slow circles around her breasts with his fingers. She reached back until her fingertips brushed the handle of the pot of beans. She twisted farther until she could grasp it. She had the pot in her hand and was about to lift it and bring it down on his head when he pulled back suddenly.

She let go of the pot and looked at him. He stepped away, staring at her breasts. She looked down to see a droplet of milk forming on one nipple. It grew in circumference, pulled away, and fell, landing on the floor somewhere between them.

"Disgusting," he said.

"Disgusting?" she asked, her voice hoarse with relief. "Yes, I agree. Disgusting little shack. Disgusting that you've locked me up here. Disgusting that you force me to let you touch my body.

In fact, I think *disgusting* is the perfect word to describe a dirty old man who—"

He slapped her hard across the face. "You never used to be so mouthy," he said. He stepped back again and Aimée used the space between them to pull up her tank top. The milk kept flowing and left two circles of wetness in the ribs of the fabric.

She folded her arms across her chest. "I don't know what the hell you're talking about. I've always been exactly this mouthy."

He pushed into her again, his hand cradling the back of her skull. "You used to think the world of me," he said. He pressed his lips into her ear and whispered, "I know it's you."

Then he was off her again. "I'll set the table."

She shook her head and blinked back the tears. She turned on the burners under the green beans and the corn, because she just didn't know what else to do. Besides, she was hungry. She'd need strength to get away.

"Meat loaf won't be ready for a while," she said. The words sounded eerily normal coming out of her mouth.

"But you forget, Cindy. I like it rare."

Kelly and Dave looked at each other again, uncertain. "He has a house on the way to Cranbrook. Big mansion with a ranch. Have you looked there?"

Schilling nodded. "Cranbrook RCMP have had it staked out all day. There's no sign of him. There or at the casino."

"I don't suppose—" Kelly looked at her husband.

He shrugged. "Sometimes that's what people do," he said cryptically.

They sat back and looked at Schilling and Bern, as though the whole thing had been decided.

"Okay, married people," Schilling said. "Translation, please."

Kelly laughed. "Ha! Sorry. We are like that sometimes. You read Cindy's file, right?"

Schilling nodded.

"Remember the letter from the lady at the school board? She said that she went to Cindy's house and Cindy's dad threw a book at her?"

"I remember," Schilling said. "Indian Road, third driveway on the left from the highway."

"Exactly. Jared moved in and lived there with Cindy and her dad. Things were pretty bad, and eventually Cindy was taken away by social services and adopted by a white family."

"What do you mean by 'bad'?" Bern asked.

"People thought the bruising was from skating accidents," Dave said. "She was a really good figure skater."

Kelly was nodding. "It was when she needed to have a physical for the skate club that the doctor pegged it. Turns out she'd been abused for years—physically, sexually, you name it. Her insides were a mess. They couldn't prove if it was her father or Jared, and Cindy wouldn't say a word."

"It was sad what happened to that girl, and a sad day on the reserve," said Dave. "In the end, we couldn't guarantee that she'd be safe again, coming back. And there was a white family that wanted desperately to adopt. They could offer her everything— skating lessons and competitions and all the dresses she wanted. And they could keep her safe. Except—" The sadness in Dave's voice told the tale.

"Except the damage was already done," Bern finished his

sentence for him. "So do you think, in a time of stress when he wanted to hide, Jared would return to Cindy's house?"

"It would make sense," Kelly said. "He lived there for a long time after Cindy left. Even after her father died, he kept living there. It's all boarded up now. Might be a good place to hide."

Schilling was already on her feet, and Bern stood as well. "Thank you," they both said at once.

"Wait!" Kelly said. "You said there were two reasons why this related to Cindy. What was the other?"

"Do you ever go to Mountain Station for coffee?" Schilling asked them.

They both shook their heads. "We're more Tim Hortons kind of people," Kelly said with a laugh.

"Well, Mountain Station is where Aimée works. If you'd ever seen her, you would understand. She looks exactly like Cindy."

Afterward he let her have a sheet. She wrapped it around herself both to keep warm and to keep her naked body from his prying eyes. And he had pried and examined every inch of her skin.

He lay on the bed watching her. She lifted the sheet higher so that only her eyes and the top of her head were showing, and watched him back.

He sprawled on top of the sheets, comfortable in his nakedness. His skin was slightly darker than hers, and completely smooth and hairless. The skin at his neck sagged a little, but he looked like a young man from there down.

"What are you thinking about?" he whispered.

"What the fuck I'm going to do if I get pregnant." She didn't bother keeping her voice down.

He sat up on his elbows. "Don't you think you'd like having a baby?"

She dropped her head and started to sob. He was up like a shot, his arms wrapped around her. She pummeled him hard with her fists, but he held her arms tighter. She bit his shoulder and he slapped her again, harder this time.

When she was spent, he backed away and they sat staring at each other, both breathing rapidly.

"What's wrong with you, Cindy? Don't you want to have a baby with me? We'll look after it together."

"I have a baby, you sick fuck. I have a baby! His name is Gabriel and he doesn't know where I am right now and he's probably scared out of his mind." She stopped talking. Best not to give him too much information. Best wait until he fell asleep. Then she'd whack him over the head with a pot. She'd take the leftover meat loaf out to bribe the dog, and she'd run. Barefoot, naked, it hardly mattered. She would get back to Gabriel.

He rubbed at the spot where she bit him and watched her with narrowed eyes. "I don't like the names you call me."

She laughed. She couldn't help herself. He lunged for her with his fists this time, and when she bent forward to protect her face and her belly, he punched her in the back again and again. She grunted as he hit her spine and cried out when his fist landed over her kidney.

Then suddenly he stopped. "Shut up," he said. He grabbed her by the hair and pulled her head onto his lap. "Shut up!" he said again. "Listen."

Breath ragged, the sour smell of his groin in her face, she listened. She could barely make it out through the roaring in her ears. The dog barking. There was someone out there.

This was her chance. She lifted her forehead up as far as she could and rammed it into his crotch. His hands flew from her head to protect himself. Freed, she jumped off the bed and ran toward the door.

They left the car at the road and proceeded on foot. Schilling was prepared: flashlight, revolver, pepper spray. With only his wallet in one pocket and his cell phone in the other, Bern felt exposed.

"Should we call for backup?"

"Let's just see if he's even here first," said Schilling.

"You don't want Resnick to embarrass you if you're wrong? Or you want the satisfaction of bringing Jared John in yourself if you're right? Which is it?"

"Maybe a little of both."

The road was so overgrown with brush it was hard to make out the rutted grooves where cars had once driven. Schilling turned her flashlight on long enough that they could see the next parcel of road in front of them.

"Look at this," she said. "Someone has driven on this recently."

Bern stepped next to her to see the flattened grass under the beam. "Well, let's go see. Then we can call for backup."

"Deal," Schilling said.

They kept walking, shuffling their feet to keep to the ruts in the dark. The night was clear, the mountains blocking out the stars in the sky. The air was crisp and cold and smelled of leaf mold and winter. They rounded a bend and Bern sensed an opening in the foliage. He spread his arms wide; no vegetation pressed against him.

"I think this may be it," he said. As he took a step into what he thought was a clearing, two things happened: a dog started barking, and Schilling turned on the flashlight.

She swung the beam in a wide arc and Bern took in the scene in increments: derelict lawn; boarded-up house; a black Mercedes sedan—an impractical car for mountain roads. The dog was as black as the night, one of those breeds that protects first. In the final swing of Schilling's flashlight, he saw its powerful limbs braced to jump.

The dog pounced, barreling Schilling to the ground. In the second before impact, she pulled her baton and the dog's jaws clamped on it. Bern shifted his feet like a boxer, circling the dog that was circling Schilling's prone body, her stick in its mouth. As he moved, Bern loosened and removed his belt. With a wide step he straddled the dog's back and clenched the animal's haunches between his knees. Then he slid the folded belt around its neck and grabbed the ends on the other side. He pulled the ends through the loop to form a noose and tugged upward, hard, while clamping his thighs as hard as he could against the beast.

Bern's muscles tensed as the dog bucked against the restraint, but it didn't release its hold on Schilling's baton. Bern could make out her pale face in the darkness, her features contorted as she twisted her head and pushed at the stick to keep the dog from attacking her. He yanked on the belt again, but still the dog didn't release its hold.

"I'm going to choke him." Bern's yelling made the dog snarl and buck even more. "When he lets go, knock him out somehow."

It took all his strength to grip the belt in one hand. With the other, he reached around, dug his fingers into the dog's thorax and squeezed. His arms ached from the effort and his leg muscles shook from riding the mastiff like a pack animal. He pressed his feet into the ground for more traction and finally heard the animal gag. He waited a second, then pulled on the noose again. The dog released the stick.

"Now!"

Schilling rolled to the side and in an instant was up on one knee, pepper spray pointed at the beast, which had thick streams of saliva coming from its jaws.

"Look away!" she cried.

Bern twisted as far as he could while still holding the belt. He heard the hiss and smelled the spiciness. The dog yelped and dropped its head to the ground, rubbing its face in the dirt. The pressure against Bern's thighs slackened and he stepped away, blinded.

"You okay?" Schilling asked. "Did I get you?"

"I'll be okay in a minute," he said through the seering blindness. The dog snuffled in the dirt, yanking on the belt to get away. "Should I let go of him?"

Schilling reached to the back of her belt and pulled out a Taser. She pointed it at the dog's neck and he was out. Bern let go of the belt.

"Couldn't get to it before," she said. "Sorry about the spray."

"I'll be okay in just a minute," Bern said, looking up at the sky to clear his eyes. "How about you? Are you all right?"

Schilling stood. "God, that's a big dog." Her voice was hushed. "He'll be down for a while. Let's go get Aimée."

Bern's eyes were clearing, but he still couldn't see properly. "We got a plan for that?"

"Oh, yeah. I'm the Mary Kay lady." She laughed.

"With a pistol?"

"Damn straight."

"You ready to call in reinforcements yet?"

"Yeah, that would be a good idea—" she started. "Oh shit! How long has that door been open?"

Bern turned to the cabin. The front door stood wide open, a rectangle of light raising the night-dark lawn to a charcoal gray. His eyes still burned from the pepper spray as he took in the blurred edges of the cabin, the Mercedes, the lawn.

A shadow moved at the edge of the lawn. Another rose up behind Schilling's shoulder.

"Behind you!" he cried.

She reacted, but not quickly enough. Through the haze of peppered eyes Bern could make out a bare arm around her throat, a dark head bobbing behind it.

"What the hell did you do to my dog?"

The pepper spray had not affected his ears. Bern could hear the menace in the man's voice just fine.

The dog stopped barking. Aimée was alone. With shaking hands, her breath ragged, she pulled on her tank top and underwear. She picked up the sheet to cover herself further but then let it drop. She couldn't stand the feeling of it on her skin, and besides, she needed to run. Fast. This was her chance to get back to Gabriel.

The main room of the cabin was lit up but empty. The dishes she'd washed and stacked in the drainer after dinner were dry now.

"You can put them away in the morning," Jared had said. "Let's go relax for a while."

Relaxing? Is that what he called what he'd done next?

The door was wide open now and Aimée could see figures moving in the yard. The wooden steps were rough under her feet. She hopped down them and moved to the side of the house, away from the light. The grass pricked her bare legs. She reached the edge of the clearing and dove into the forest, where the underbrush scratched her skin and tore at the soles of her feet.

Just a few feet into the trees there was no light whatsoever. Aimée kept her arms out in front of her to protect her face. She could hardly breathe through the fear that clamped at her chest. Cold air bit at her skin. The dark threatened to swallow her whole. There was no path through the trees and the going was painfully slow.

But she pressed forward, moving into each open space as she found it, her only thought to put as much distance between herself and Jared as she could. She had no idea where she was, so no idea which direction to take. They hadn't driven for that long, so she knew she couldn't be too far from Kootenay Landing. But she was in the woods, and in Kootenay Landing, there were woods everywhere.

There was a light ahead and she kept moving to it, her limbs slowed by the cold. But when she got to the light, she saw that she was somehow back at the cabin. How could this be? There were people in the clearing, and she could hear Jared's voice. She turned and pressed back into the woods again, maneuvering as best she could between the trees, only to end up back at the clearing once more.

She heard the thud of fists but could not tell who was there with Jared. It could be anyone. Then she heard a voice she recognized, its lilt the same as her own.

"Drop it!" the coroner called.

She remembered how gentle and patient he'd been with Gabriel. And she remembered what he'd said: *Go up.*

Exhausted, cold, and lost, Aimée did just that. She found a

solid birch tree, its white bark glowing in the dark night, and climbed as high as she dared. A crook of several branches formed a solid perch eight feet off the ground and she huddled there, waiting for rescue.

She remembered the series of moves taught in the first week of police academy—straighten and tense your arms to create space, stomp on their toes, step back, turn, jab. Schilling performed each step more smoothly than she had on her combat defense exam. With Jared John bent double, Bern wrestled him to the ground. Schilling cuffed his hands behind his back.

She pulled out her weapon and pointed it at him. "Freeze," she said.

It was textbook. And it worked. Now she just needed to read him his rights and find Aimée.

"Good work," Bern said.

She smiled. "Now I guess I'll call for backup."

"And I'll go find Aimée."

The cabin was desolate. Barren of furniture and with most of the windows boarded up, it felt heavy with trapped memories. It smelled of bad meat and sweat and something worse.

Bern stayed inside only long enough to determine that Aimée wasn't there.

The light did not extend far from the house. At its outer edge he saw Schilling, gun drawn and pointed at Jared. Beyond that, darkness.

"Aimée! Are you there?"

The black woods surrounded him. There was nothing to see, but his skin tingled with sensation. The trees drew him into their shroud; the ground beneath his feet was soft where the trees had dropped their leaves in preparation for winter. Even in darkness, he could sense the life in the barren branches.

"Aimée? *Gabriel t'attend, ma chère.*" Gabriel is waiting for you.

He held his hands before him and allowed the trunks to lead him from tree to tree. He made his way in the dark, with only the occasional brush of branches against his sleeves.

"Aimée?" He whispered it this time. "Are you there?"

There was a rustle in the tree above him, a gulp, and a hiccup. He looked up. "Aimée? Come down." Firmer this time. It was so dark he could really be talking to a tree.

"Me voici." Here I am.

He helped her down the last few branches. She was barely clothed, scraped up, and shivering. He unbuttoned his own shirt and covered her with it, then rubbed her arms to keep her warm. He murmured platitudes in her native tongue all the while: *you're safe now; there's no more danger; let's get you home; Gabriel is waiting.*

Only this last one elicited a response. "Gabriel?" she asked.

He turned her to the edge of the clearing and helped her navigate the last steps out of the woods.

"It's safe now. Come."

They stepped into the clearing to the growl of the dog. Bern saw it rise from prone to barking in mere seconds and launch itself toward Maddie.

"Schilling!" he called out.

Her shot drowned out Aimée's screams.

29

The dark made no difference to Ruben. With twenty-four hours to himself, he navigated the woods by memory and the light of the moon. The cabin waited for him. It would be his getaway from the hops farm for one night. On the outside all was the same as when he'd tidied up after Dough Man a few short days before, but on the inside things were different indeed.

Before he even lit a candle, Ruben was quite sure that his luck had turned at last. Once he had lit two candles he knew that he would be home in time to celebrate the Day of the Virgin of Guadalupe, and that he might never need to come back again.

Ruben had once worked on a marijuana farm in the hills of northern California. He knew what he was looking at. Before him, strung on clotheslines made of kitchen twine, was a treasure trove of pot plants, manicured and dried and ready for clipping.

It got better. Next to the woodstove was a cardboard box outfitted with layers of trays. The bases of the trays were made of window screen fabric. All Ruben had to do was clip the bud and layer it on the trays. The product could dry while he carried it on his way.

Ruben started a fire to keep warm and got to work. He

worked through the night, and by the first light of dawn, the box was full. He cleared away the branches and leaves, laying them in the woods to decompose. Then he tidied up the cabin so it looked exactly how he had left it a few days earlier.

Before heading on his way, Ruben rolled two joints.

He left one on the counter, as a thank-you to the person who would no doubt come back for his crop. The second he smoked while he sat on the front stoop and watched the morning give birth to the mountains.

Bern spent the day at the police station. He parked himself next to Chantel Postniuk's desk and waited. When asked, he'd share his opinion freely, but for the most part Resnick and his team ignored him while they worked.

"Just a dead dog," Resnick told him. "No bodies for you, Fortin. Go home, why don't you?"

Lennon's lawyer secured his release early in the day. The RCMP had held him for questioning for twenty-four hours but had not come up with any evidence to charge him.

Jared was another story. He would be charged with forcible confinement and assault at the very least. Schilling and Resnick went out to Gia's house to take Aimée's statement and piece together her story. Then they went back to Jared's boarded-up house to search it for physical evidence.

But no matter how many times they interviewed Jared John, they could not tie him to Seymour's death.

It was late in the day when Schilling came and sat next to Bern.

"I don't think he did it," she said simply. "He's a creepy bugger all right, and I wouldn't put it past him. But he really doesn't seem to know anything about how Seymour died."

"Did he say why he took Aimée?" Bern asked.

"It's just what we thought," she said. "She looks just like Cindy. It wasn't even to send a warning to Lennon—at least not that either of them will admit. There was no logic to it. Once he laid eyes on Aimée, she was like a lost possession that he had to have back. Never mind the fact that Cindy, if she were still alive, would be ten years older than her."

When Schilling left for the day, Bern finally went home. He was at work in the garden when Troy Thompson showed up several hours later.

"You sure we can't do this over whiskey?" the journalist asked.

Bern handed him a shovel. "Don't start renegotiating the terms now. I might change my mind." He pointed to the garden beds squared away under black plastic. "We are going to take up these covers and fluff the soil a little, then dig in a little more compost," he said. "I'll talk while we work."

"You're kidding, right? Who's changing the terms now? This wasn't part of the deal." The petulant soldier was back.

"You've booked your flight?" Bern asked.

"Yes."

"Good. The way I figure it, you want to get out of here just as badly as I want you gone. You're not going to walk away now. So dig."

Bern squatted down and peeled back the first cover. He folded it in half and then in half again, and laid it to one side. The ground took his shovel easily and he moved down the row, turning soil as he went. Troy followed, imitating his movements.

"This story starts when I was a captain. I was sent to Rwanda. It was 1994." As he spoke he turned another shovelful of soil and the garden exhaled another pent-up breath into the air. Bern could almost feel its relief at being freed. At being exposed and made whole. At being in order once again.

"I have never before told anyone what happened there. What I did when I was there . . ."

To whom it may concern:

The bones found in the woods belong to Cindy Forsberg. She died on Saturday, June 19, 1993, of a heroin overdose at the snowmobiler's cabin at Waterfall Creek. I witnessed her death and so did Seymour Melnychuk.

I dug a grave and buried Cindy. The rest of her bones are under a cottonwood tree along Waterfall Creek, in the woods about five hundred feet downhill from the cabin.

After we buried Cindy, Seymour took her backpack to Vancouver and left it in a hotel on the Downtown Eastside.

Cindy told me she started taking heroin because of the pain from her figure skating injuries. I tried to get her to stop, but she didn't want to. Her death was an accident. I did not cause it, but I have caused a lot of pain. I know that, and I'm more sorry than I can ever say.

There is no way to make up for what I have done. I have carried it with me every day since Cindy died, and now I want to be free. I'm leaving of my own free will. I might come back someday, but please don't look for me. I haven't done anything wrong. I've just had really bad luck for a really long time.

Signed:
Gary Dowd
October 22, 2009

30

On Monday morning, Mrs. K. brought the mail in with breakfast.

"I thought you died. Or maybe that reporter killed you?"

She strode past Bern, who was sitting in the armchair enjoying his triple espresso, and sniffed her way into the kitchen.

"Huh. No mess," she said. "Come eat."

Bern sighed and stood. "You know what, Mrs. K.? I'm really not hungry right now." He walked over to the tray she'd placed on the kitchen table and lifted the edge of the tea towel to reveal eggs and cheese, pickles, fruit, and a slice of homemade loaf, all beautifully arranged. "It looks really delicious. I'd like to save it for later."

She crossed her arms and stood right in the middle of the small kitchen. "Hmph."

"Hmph, what?" he asked.

"Something's different. What is it?"

"Nothing. Nothing's different," he said. "Let me make you a coffee. You want it the way they make it at Mountain Station?"

She narrowed her eyes. "Do you have raspberries?"

He raised an eyebrow. "Frozen okay?"

She tilted her head in response.

He patted her shoulders and pushed her out of the kitchen. "Go sit down. I'll bring it to you."

He delivered her coffee a few minutes later, complete with the raspberry on top. "Maybe not as good as Aimée makes it," he said, placing it before her.

"But not four dollars either," she said. "How is she?"

"She's going to be okay, in time. I'm going out there to see her this afternoon."

She nodded and took a sip of her coffee. "I hope she's back soon," she said. She waited until he sat down to start on the real reason for her visit. "So did you tell him? The reporter? Did you confess?"

Bern sipped his coffee and nodded.

"And?"

He put his coffee down and leaned forward to look her in the eye. "I feel good," he said. "Better."

"I don't see why."

"No," he replied. "Neither do I. Except that I kept it secret for so long. It's good to have it free."

Mrs. K. shook her head. "But what is he going to do with it? With your secret—whatever it is?"

"He's going to put it in the paper," Bern said with a shrug. "He's a reporter. That's what he does."

"So what did you do yesterday that you didn't go outside all day and didn't eat anything?" she demanded.

"I slept."

"Again?" she asked. "You slept it off?"

"No, no. I just slept. Like a baby. Most of the day," he said. "I woke up and ate some soup and then went back to sleep."

"Are you sick or something?"

He was saved from answering by a knock at the door. Schilling came in a moment later. She handed him a bottle of chocolate sauce and a can of whipped cream. "Café is closed all week. You've got the only other espresso maker in town," she said.

He laughed. "Join the club. You need help?" He followed her into the kitchen. "Milk's already warm."

"Believe it or not, I worked in a coffee shop once. After a week I decided I was better off working at the feed store." She prepped a double shot of espresso as she spoke.

Bern picked up the pile of mail that Mrs. K. had left on the table. The usual bills. A few garden catalogs making a pitch for his Christmas spending. One letter addressed to "Coroner, Kootenay Landing, BC. French guy. Ex-army."

"Amazing how this makes its way to me," he said, holding the envelope up for Schilling to see.

"You going to eat something while you're in there?" Mrs. K. called from the living room. "There's enough for her too."

"Ah, Mrs. K.," he said. "Always looking after everybody." He used a kitchen knife to slice open the envelope.

"That's my job," she said.

Bern paused and looked at her, his words stopped by the sound of Schilling steaming milk.

Mrs. K. met his eye and then looked away. "Hmph. You going to open that letter or what?"

He sat across from her again and took another sip of his coffee before pulling the sheet of paper from the envelope. Schilling joined them with her own concoction of whipped cream and chocolate sauce.

Mrs. K. eyed it with suspicion. "How much does that cost at Mountain Station?" she asked.

Schilling shrugged. "It's around five dollars with the tip."

Mrs. K.'s eyebrows almost flew right off her face. *"Tip?"*

Bern had been following the interaction and reading the letter at the same time. It took a moment for him to understand what he was reading.

"Schilling, look at this." He laid the paper on the coffee table so she could read it.

"Oh my God," she whispered.

"Dr. Sinclair? So sorry to call on your day off."

"Michelle?" Juniper hitched her cell phone between her shoulder and chin as she finished cleaning the cupboard doors. "Everything okay at the office?"

"Uh, I think so. I mean, no emergencies. Nothing like that. It's just—" She paused, and Juniper could hear her talking to someone in the background. "Sorry about that. Just had another one."

"Another what?"

"Another patient looking for a prescription. I'm sending them to the pharmacy downtown. It's the only thing I can think of. Just a sec—"

Juniper swung the cupboard door closed and circled the studio while she waited. Everything gleamed, clean and new. She'd spent two days scrubbing and wiping every surface so that no trace of her former occupation remained. No trace of Victoria's Remedy, or Seymour.

"Sorry. I'm back."

"Michelle, what is going on there? Where's Wilson?"

"That's what I was calling to ask you. He's scheduled for today, but he's not here. Did he call you?"

Juniper leaned her shoulder against the window as she tried to digest the words. "He asked for Friday off. He said he was going fishing—"

"Right. But today? I've never known him to miss a day without calling."

"And you called him?"

"Well, that's the weird thing. I called his cell and it's saying his mailbox is full. And I went by his apartment—"

"And let me guess: he wasn't there."

"Right. How did you know? No one around and the neighbor hasn't seen him in days. And with everything else that's been going on . . . well, I guess I wondered if I should call the police."

"You didn't, though, did you?"

"No, not yet. I thought I'd call you first."

"That was good thinking," Juniper said. She closed her eyes and leaned her forehead against the cool glass. *Wilson. She should have known not to trust him.* "Do you think he might have had a family emergency or something?"

"Um. He never mentioned anything like that. But he's pretty private that way."

"Yeah. So maybe he just needed a bit of time, hey? Leave it with me. I'll look after it."

"Okay. That's great. Thanks. So what should I tell patients?"

"Tell them to go to the pharmacy downtown. Better yet, put a sign on the door and lock up, since you're the only one there. How are you holding up, Michelle?"

"Me? Oh, I'm doing okay."

"Of course you are. You're the strong one, right? We all count on you. But how about you take the rest of today off? And tomorrow too?"

"I don't have any time left. I'd rather work, if that's okay."

Juniper shook her head. "Take a few days, Michelle. Paid."

"Really?"

"Really. Go look after your family."

"Okay. And Dr. Sinclair?"

"Yes?"

"Thanks a lot. I won't forget this."

"You're welcome. Bye, Michelle."

Juniper disconnected the call and turned to face the cabin, sliding down to sit on the floor.

She wouldn't see Wilson again, that much she knew. Victoria's Remedy would resurface somewhere—her formula in a different package, under another name. What could she do about it? Call the police? She almost laughed at the thought.

She surveyed her former studio. The wood floor gleamed. She'd cleaned and polished the pellet stove. The cupboards, lined with shelf paper, were ready to hold someone else's belongings. A blank slate.

It was not her studio anymore. Just a beautiful cabin in the woods that would make the perfect home for Aimée and Gabriel. Nothing more.

And she was just a family doctor. Nothing more.

After processing Gary's letter, Schilling circled the streets of Kootenay Landing on patrol. "Go catch some speeders," Resnick had told her. "Then take a few days off." She did two lazy loops around town, then headed for the marsh to revisit the scenes of recent events—Gary's disappearance, Seymour's murder, the busted grow op, Aimée's abduction. She had just pulled off the highway onto the trunk road when she saw Lennon's truck. As she passed the marsh trail and the scene of Seymour's murder, he pulled off onto the forest service road. She slowed and gave him a minute's head start, then pulled in after him.

She couldn't get far in the patrol car. After only two switchbacks she pulled over into the brush and continued on foot. The road was steep and she was breathing heavily before long. But the damp air felt good on her skin, and despite her labored breathing she moved on. When was the last time she'd actually been outside for a walk? She couldn't remember.

She passed the place where Cindy's bones had been found. Two switchbacks later, she finally saw Lennon's truck at the side of the road. Off to the left was a rough-hewn cabin. She could smell weed, and she found Lennon on the front step, smoking a joint.

She shook her head as she walked up to him. "Scooch over," she said. She sat next to him on the step and looked out at the meadow and stream in front of the cabin.

"You want a toke?" Lennon asked.

"No. I'm trying to decide whether to bust you."

It was his turn to shake his head. "A lot of trouble to go to for one joint."

"Exactly what I was thinking. That's all you've got?"

"I'm all cleaned out," he said. His voice was quieter than usual. "If I had more, that is. And I'm not saying I did."

"So what are you doing here, then?" she asked.

"Nice place, don't you think? Good spot to get away for a few minutes. A little peace and quiet. You should try it sometime."

"I am," she said. "Right now."

"No, you're not. You're too busy wondering if you can bust me for something. How about we call a truce? For five minutes, we'll just sit here. Don't say anything. Don't arrest anyone. Think we can do that?"

"Sure," Schilling said.

It seemed much longer than five minutes. At first all she could feel was the hard board under her and the pinch of the waistband of her pants. Then she heard Lennon's exhale and smelled the smoke as it melded with the aromas of the forest. She heard the call of birds in the trees, the clean sound of the stream rolling down the mountain, and the honking of geese headed south for the winter. And then it was over.

"That wasn't so bad, was it?" Lennon asked.

Schilling stood. "Not so bad."

"Where are you headed now?"

"To your mom's house," she said. "Going to go say hi to Aimée. A social visit. Don't worry—I won't arrest anyone."

His smile, when it came, was missing its usual spark. "Tell her I'll be home soon."

The house was deserted. So was the studio. Bern went back to the garden, but still he did not find Gia.

He stood next to a bed of winter kale and watched as a flock of geese headed toward the US border. The landscape had changed in the days since he'd last been there, and now, through the thinned leaves on the trees, the door to the underground grow op stood out clearly. Open, where it should be chained and bolted by the police.

He hopped the fence by the compost and circled the grassy hill. The door gaped open, the lights on in the cavernous space below. Making his way down the steps, he found Gia in the second of the four corridors. She was filling small pots with soil from a large bucket and lining them up on a shelf. And she was standing.

"There you are," he said. "I've been looking all over for you. Where are the others?"

"Juniper took Aimée and Gabriel for a hike," she said. She shifted her footing and aimed her rifle at him. "Don't come any closer."

He lifted his hands helplessly. "Here we are again," he said with a smile. "Just like when we first met."

There was nothing between his chest and that bullet except an electrician's nightmare in cabling that hung from the ceiling.

She stood a few feet from him, clear-eyed and alert, and aimed the rifle at his core. "Difference is, I'm not going to back down this time."

He shrugged and took a step closer. "I was prepared to die by your hand then, and I'm still willing." He nodded at her legs. "You can walk."

"Yes, yes," she said with a wave of the rifle.

"Since when?"

She smiled at him. "You know, it's amazing the assumptions people make when you're in a wheelchair."

Anger slashed through him. "People tend to believe what you tell them," he said. "Especially when you appear so trustworthy. But you're just a liar, aren't you?"

She shrugged. "And you're very sensitive, aren't you?" She shook her head and her turban wobbled. "I'd have told you if you asked. But even you, observant and curious as you are, never asked. You just assumed."

Bern leaned on one hip as though relaxed, but his senses were on high alert. "Perhaps I thought it rude to ask. Perhaps I thought it would be too intrusive," he said.

He could pick up the very scent of her, of amber oil and earth. He could sense each palpitation in the triangle of space between her, the weapon, and himself. In the smell of skunk and damp that permeated the underground air he reached a certain conclusion: she would not shoot him.

Standing, she was shorter than he would have thought. Even if she could walk a bit, the illness had gnawed at her muscles. Her limbs were wasting away. All he had to do was wait her out; she would not last long.

"Everyone thought that," she said. "It made my job easier."

Even with the weapon in her hands, she emanated the same contained calm he'd come to expect from her. Only the indentation on her right cheek hinted at her anxiety. She was a cheek biter.

He rubbed his hip in the place where his service weapon should be. All he felt was the soft fabric of his faded jeans. "Interesting role reversal here, have you noticed?" he added.

"How so?"

He pointed at the rifle, which she raised in response to his movement. "You've got my tools. Which means I've got to use yours."

"And what are my tools?"

He had expected her to lower the gun by now. He looked away as though thinking about her question and did a peripheral scan for a weapon of his own. Brand-new bags of soil, boxes of lightbulbs and light fixtures still in their packaging were piled in a corner—nothing useful.

"Communication. Nurturing. Care. Consideration." He counted them off on his fingers.

"And yours?"

"Threats and weapons," he said. "Destruction, when all else fails."

She nodded. "I'm discovering after a lifetime of using my tools that yours are much more effective."

"More expedient, perhaps. But not necessarily more effective. Will you put the gun down so we can talk?"

She lifted it higher. "We can talk like this. Besides, I have nothing more to say."

"Ah, I see," he said. "Well, I have some thoughts, if you don't mind." He crossed his arms in front of his chest. She adjusted her aim with his motion. "We were wondering how the killer got so close to Seymour. The kind of weapon—a bolt stunner or something of that sort—requires close contact."

"But if the killer posed no threat . . ."

Bern dropped his hands and nodded. "Like a woman you think is disabled. A woman usually in a wheelchair."

She smiled. "I'm glad you didn't call me old."

He tilted his head. "You're nowhere near old. And you are beautiful still."

"Not beautiful."

"Beautiful in your way. Regal."

"A regal killer." She laughed. "That's me."

"So you pretended to be a sick old lady and then you shot him with something?"

She nodded. "Pretty much." She dropped a hand into one pocket and pulled out a short stick. It had a black handle and a metal barrel. A metal wire connected the segments of the barrel, several of which looked like they could be unscrewed.

"What is it?"

"It's called a bang stick," she said. "It's for hunting alligators.

Con got it on a trip to Florida one time. Then he modified it—
cut off most of the length to make it pocket-sized. Kept it handy
when he was in the bush. Bears, you know. They usually stay away
from humans, and Con knew how to handle himself, but he liked
to have a few tricks up his sleeve in case he ever ran into one."

"And now you use it."

She smiled and looked at it almost longingly. "Yes. This is
my way out. When it gets too much—when I can't handle the
pain—this is my way out."

She shifted on one leg and the barrel of the rifle flagged; it
was no longer pointed directly at his chest. Bern stepped forward
to take it from her, but she rallied. She slid the bang stick back in
her voluminous pocket and held the rifle steady with both hands.

"You would kill yourself with that?"

Her look was hard. "You don't understand much, do you? For
all your careful manner—for all your listening and deep looks—
you really know very little of the world."

He bowed his head. "Yes, it's true. I understand little of the
world. But I have a job too," he said. "It is to tend to the dead."

"Even if they were evil in life?"

He scanned the room again. There was a shift in the light, an
angle that had changed from a few minutes before. Something
was different, though Bern couldn't pinpoint what it was.

"No matter who they were in life," he said. "That's the part
that makes it work sometimes."

"Why do you do this?" she asked.

"That's my question for you too." He took a barely perceptible step to the side as he spoke, closing the distance between
them while edging out of the direct line of fire. "Why did you
risk so much? Your family, your property, your friendships, your
very life. Why?"

She raised her head in that queenly look he was coming to know so well. "That's what we're left with in the end, isn't it? Asking why?" She held the gun steadily now. "Stop moving. I can see what you're trying to do."

He could feel a telltale prickle at the back of his neck. Something was about to happen. He needed to keep her focused on him. "Are you going to tell me?" he asked.

She smiled. "I'll tell you if you tell me. But you need to go first."

Bern leaned back on his heels as though telling a story to a friend. He used the movement to check his peripheral vision for weapons or means of escape. He saw neither. "It's simple, really: it's my duty. I have nothing else. I carry so many dead with me and I can do nothing for them. But those who die here, in this small patch of the world, I will account for them. Whoever they are."

"Until you're one of them, and then who will account for you?" She stepped toward him as she said this, so close that if he extended his arm he could reach the rifle.

"My death would matter little," he said. "Now your turn. Why did you kill Seymour?"

With her free hand, she gestured around her. "To protect my property. Isn't that reason enough?"

"It hardly sounds like you. Flower child. Earth mother. Murderer."

"See, that's just it. I feed the earth, and the earth feeds me and my family. If it was just between me and Mother Earth, there'd be no issue."

"But then people get involved."

"Exactly! We just want to grow some plants in peace."

"Illegal plants."

She shot him a look of total disdain. "Think about that for just a minute, would you? Can you really make a plant illegal?"

"No, of course not. But you can make growing it and propagating it and selling it and consuming it illegal. I hardly need to tell you the law."

"But the plant itself? Try telling it not to grow."

"So you're just helping it along?"

"Yes. Until people get in the way."

"Government. Police."

"You'd think so, wouldn't you? But these days our trouble comes from criminals."

"Other criminals, you mean."

"See, that's where I have a hard time agreeing with you, Mr. Coroner. I'm not a criminal. I'm a gardener."

"You grow an illegal crop."

She nodded. "And now we've come full circle. Because how can a plant be illegal?"

"I think you're being overly simplistic."

"Do you? Consider this: there are criminals—real ones—in this business now. They don't care about the plant. About how it can help people who are suffering. They don't care about anything but selling it for the highest price."

"People like Seymour?"

"Seymour's just a small fish. The real sharks are still out there."

"Are you going to kill every one of them?"

She was starting to flag. The effort of holding the rifle while standing for so long was too much. The weapon was now pointed somewhere at his knees.

"Seymour was out to destroy us. All of us. It was his whole purpose—beyond stealing our crops, that is." She gestured to the room that surrounded them. "That part he managed quite nicely, and the police finished the job. But the other stuff he did was optional—the humiliation, the threats, the pain."

"And you? What about you?" he asked quietly. "What did he do to you?"

She held her head high and, with one hand still holding the rifle, pulled off her turban. Soft tufts of gray hair had grown in, but whole patches of her scalp were still scabbed over.

"He and his thugs sheared me like an animal when they found out I hadn't cut my hair in twenty years."

Bern felt the pain on her behalf. This regal woman, humiliated.

"Do you see?" she whispered. "I thought that my ways would protect me. Protect all of us. They asked, 'Why do you wear that on your head?' And I used my tools—words and care—and I told them. I laid myself open and they mowed me down like a blade of grass.

"A few days later, I was looking out the window with my binoculars. I was watching the geese, cheering them on. I saw Juniper walking on the marsh. And I saw Seymour pull up in his truck. I knew he'd come back to hurt her again, to take more from her, from all of us. And as soon as I saw him, my decision was made. It was like I had killed him already, just by deciding. All that was left was to take the steps.

"I drove out there. I parked behind him and walked to where he was standing. I called him closer, speaking softly so he had to lean in to hear me, and then—bang!—that was it.

"My only regret is that Juniper found him. I didn't mean for that to happen. She doesn't usually double back like she did that day. I'm sorry for that part only."

Bern turned to the side and picked up a plant pot from a nearby shelf. He held the edges of the pot and rolled it between his palms.

"Stay still," she said.

"Why?" he asked with a smile. "This is getting tiresome, don't you think? I might understand why you killed Seymour, but are you really going to keep going? You're going to kill me, and then who else?"

She gave in then. He saw it—or did he? Her head tipping to the side, the rifle wavering—she would not shoot him. But then the light shifted and she looked at him, steady and proud.

"Drop it!" a voice cried from the door. "Police! Drop the gun!"

Bern dove to the left as Gia pulled the trigger. The bullet tore through his right arm as he flew through the air. As always in that moment of crisis, his thoughts and senses were at their sharpest: the clarity in Gia's eyes; the smell of gun smoke; the echo that shut out all other sound. Bern landed with the thought that for once, Schilling had not been tentative.

The pain in his arm registered as he hit the floor, but more painful still was his knowing how the story would end. A soldier's instinct is a terrible thing, as is a police officer's. At a certain point, training takes over. It's not a choice. Society depends on this fact.

A second blast followed immediately after this first, this one from a pistol. In its terrible echo, Gia was thrown back. Her legs crumpled like sticks. Her wasted body seemed to hover in the air before landing in a heap.

His own injury forgotten, Bern pulled himself along the dirt floor to reach her.

"Gia!"

Schilling stepped over him to secure the rifle. Training first. He heard her on her radio, demanding two ambulances, though he knew perfectly well that Kootenay Landing only had one.

"Get Dr. Sinclair," he croaked.

With his uninjured arm he pulled Gia to him, cradling her head on his lap. Her eyes were open, but he couldn't tell whether she was seeing him.

"Gia," he whispered.

The shot had pierced her chest and exited through her back. He balled up the ends of her shawl and pressed them uselessly into the wound. Her breath whistled.

He raised the hand of his injured arm to the soft tufts of hair that had started to grow back in and stroked gently; he had never felt anything so soft.

"Gia," he said again.

Her eyes snapped into focus. "You are kind." Her words were a gurgle of breath and blood. Her gaze became vague again, off somewhere beyond his shoulder.

"Gia?" Juniper Sinclair's voice came from the doorway. "I heard shots."

"Mom?" Lennon was there too. And Schilling was right behind, pulling Bern away.

"We've got to get you looked after," she said.

Bern turned back to Gia. She needed help much more than he did. But Juniper and Lennon had closed around her, leaving Bern outside the circle.

31

He woke up to the sound of women arguing.

"He'll have to change the dressing twice a day. He needs a nurse for that. He'll have to come in." He did not recognize the voice.

"Nurse? I can be his nurse. What he needs is rest. And good food. He doesn't need to be running in here two times a day like a sick person." Mrs. K. No doubt there.

"Mom, don't be difficult."

"I'm not being difficult. I'm just saying. I can change a bandage and keep his wound clean. It will be better than him running all over. He runs around too much as it is."

They fell silent. Bern opened his eyes just enough to see the standoff at the side of his hospital bed: Audrey in her raspberry-colored scrubs and Mrs. K. in her going-to-town dress, both with their arms crossed.

Mrs. K. conceded first. "You want me to do it a special way? Just show me. I'll do it any way you want."

Bern smiled and closed his eyes again. He felt like he could sleep for a week. Perhaps by then they would have it sorted out.

• • •

Bern stood in front of the medicine cabinet and looked at himself in the mirror. His skin had faded somewhat from the Mediterranean darkness he had taken on after a summer in the garden. His skin tone was just one mystery in his life. His mother's whole family was fair-skinned. Dark-haired, like he was, but with lily-white skin. And light eyes too, which tended to blue and green and combinations of the two.

His almost black eyes stared back at him now, their origin a mystery. He looked into his own eyes as he would those of a new soldier. He saw something there—a glimmer of independence that made him smile. He wouldn't make a good soldier anymore.

He squared his bare shoulders and the pain at the movement reminded him of his failure. Yes, he had done his job. He had accounted for the dead. The bones in the woods indeed belonged to Cindy Forsberg. Dr. Hallman had come back, and with the search and rescue volunteers and the clues in Gary's letter, she had tracked down the rest of Cindy's grave. Holly and Duke Forsberg would finally be able to bury their daughter and perhaps find some measure of peace.

Gary's letter had answered many questions, but it raised so many more. That their son-in-law had known, all those years, that Cindy was dead; that he'd married their other daughter in an effort to make amends—it was a lot to forgive. Despite many attempts to find him, Gary seemed to have disappeared off the face of the earth. They might never know what had become of him.

Bern rolled his right shoulder forward and back. The bullet had merely grazed his skin, but it hurt like the devil. He welcomed the pain. It was but a fraction of what Colonel Sauvé had suffered in Rwanda. The colonel had lost his arm; Bern merely had a wound to tend to, and he had Mrs. K. making sure he did it right.

He plugged the electric shaver into the outlet next to the light switch and raised the coiled cord until the implement was close to his head. He had performed this task thousands of times, but never with only one hand—and his left hand at that. Normally he could give himself a number two buzz cut without a mirror. Today he would need all the help he could get.

He started at the top and worked his way down the left side. The action made him think of Gia, like so many things did these days. There too he had performed his duty. He had found Seymour's killer, but at what cost? Gia was dead, and the pain of that would be with him forever. Yes, she had killed, but Bern believed she had been pushed too far. And those who had done the pushing? Seymour was just one bad seed of many.

Schilling was on leave after the shooting. She'd gone home to Manitoba and would be out even longer with surgery to repair the condition that was causing her so much pain. Bern knew he would have to face her someday, but he was glad it wasn't today. She thought she had saved his life by shooting Gia. What she didn't understand was that he would have died gladly.

Many things in his world had changed, but the shape of his head was the same as ever. The shaver found its way through his curls to his scalp. The wiry curls felt soft as they rolled down the long plane of his naked shoulders and collected in tufts at the towel wrapped at his waist. From there they tumbled to the floor.

As the familiar shape of his own skull emerged, he saw the light in his eyes deaden and fade away. Perhaps it had only been an effect of light and shadow. Or perhaps he would still make a good soldier after all.

It will grow back, he told himself as he looked down. It seemed like each step forward, each change, each seedling lay in clusters on the blue tiles at his feet. It was like starting over again.

The silent partners in this tragedy were the gangs at work behind the scenes. The master puppeteers. Their fingerprints were
everywhere, they were to blame for everything, and yet they remained invisible. Perhaps he could find them while there was still
something of a soldier left in him.

He nodded to himself and the grim-eyed soldier in the mirror nodded back. If the opportunity to find justice for Gia presented itself, he would act.

His cell phone buzzed on the kitchen table. Bern brushed the
last of his curls to the floor and stepped into the main part of the
house. He caught the call on the last ring.

"*T'es dans la merde,*" Sauvé said. You're in deep shit.

"So you read the paper," Bern said.

"How come you had to go and say something?"

"I didn't want to keep quiet anymore. And it was the right
thing. For Alais."

"Yeah, well, it looks bad on all of us, going to the paper like
that. And the national paper too. *T'es dans la merde, c'est certain.*"

"*Je le sais, commandant,*" Bern replied. Don't I know it, Commander. "Did you go to the ceremony on Parliament Hill?"

"Yeah, they rolled us out to parade around like they do every
year. But at least they paid for lunch."

"Mine's starting here in a half hour. I have to figure out how
to put on my uniform with only one arm."

Sauvé cackled with laughter. "You're something else, Fortin,"
he said. "Off you go, then. Knock 'em dead."

"I will. And Colonel?"

"*Oui?*"

"Will you still stand by me?"

"You know I will, Lieutenant-Colonel. *C'est certain.*"

Bern disconnected the call. Still smiling, he got himself

dressed as best he could manage. Ten minutes later, when Mrs. K. came to get him, he was standing in the living room, his dress shirt hanging open. He'd managed his pants, shoes, and undershirt, but the shirt, tie, and regimental jacket were beyond his one-handed skills.

She was in a dress of soft blue wool that he'd never seen before. She even had matching blue tights, a change from the tan ones she normally wore.

"I don't like your hair like that," she said. "You look like you might trick someone."

"Is that a new dress?" he asked.

She shrugged. "Audrey wanted to get me a present. I couldn't stop her."

"You tried hard, I bet."

"Stay still." She buttoned his shirt—though he insisted on tucking it in himself—then started on his tie. "Sit so I can reach," she commanded.

"I want you to tell me someday how it is you know how to tie a tie," he said with a smile.

She shook her head and stepped away. "I know lots." She held out his jacket to him. He stood up, then ducked down to her height to slide his arms in.

She narrowed her eyes at him and nodded her approval.

"Okay?" he asked.

"Just right," she said. "Let's go. I want to be in the front row so I can see."

Acknowledgments

The team at Simon and Schuster Canada has been a dream to work with, showing both excellence and good humor at every turn. Thank you to Kevin Hanson, the one and only Alison Clarke, Felicia Quon, Sheila Haidon, Loretta Eldridge, Brendan May, and all the others I haven't met yet for the fabulous job they do. Special thanks to Amy Jacobson for so patiently teaching me it's never rude to say, "Let me check that with my publicist," and to Paul Barker for nailing the cover.

Editor Janice Weaver is so quiet and unobtrusive when she climbs inside my head that I hardly know she's there, and yet she doesn't let me get away with much. I'm very glad we had the opportunity to work together again. Thanks as well to copyeditors Martha Schwartz and Peg Haller, who did not miss a trick.

I'm very grateful to my agent, Sally Harding, and her colleagues at the Cooke Agency, who together do an extraordinary job of tending to the big picture while looking after all of the niggly details.

When it comes to research, the questions I ask can only be called bizarre. Thanks to the experts who took time away from their real work to answer my hypothetical questions so openly: Chief Constable Wayne Holland of the City of Nelson Police

Department; Brenda Clark, anthropology instructor at Camosun College; forensic expert Bob Stair; emergency medical responder Jason Deatherage; and family physician Dr. Erik Paterson. I save my oddest questions for Renaissance man Bart Bjorkman. Thanks to Dr. Carrie Armstrong for once again checking the medicine and to fellow crime writer E. R. Brown for sharing his research on grow ops. My dear friend Dr. Rachel Eni shared her knowledge of social work in First Nations communities and connected me with Jenny Wastesicoot in a moment of serendipity that I will long remember. A shout-out to Eagranie Yuh, whom I forgot to thank last time for helping me with chemistry. Any errors are my own.

Huge thanks to the local yocals: Luanne Armstrong, Angie Abdou, Marilin States-Grahn, Alison Bjorkman, Lorne Eckersley, Anne de Grace, Pamela Clausen, Lisa Cannady, the Nelson Public Library, and the Kootenay Library Federation. Alison Masters handed me the seeds to this story, Michelle Mayer told me about the stolen wedding beans, and blog reader Renee Phypers gave Gia her name. I am so grateful to these inspiring women who use their creative superpowers to do good in the world: Sat Kaur, Susan Merz-Anderson, Bessie Wapp, Miriam Needoba, Lisa Menna, and Deirdre Collier.

For all their evil-mindedness, crime writers are a warm and welcoming bunch. I'd like to thank Hilary Davidson, Ian Hamilton, Robert Rotenberg, Louise Penny, Julia Spencer-Fleming, Peggy Blair, Vicki Delany, C. B. Forrest, Anthony Bidulka, Linda L. Richards, and the incomparable Jungle Red Writers for making room at the table. Special thanks to Robin Spano for the ongoing conversation across multiple platforms and for her valuable input on several chapters.

My mom, Carol Collier, has hand sold more copies of my

books than any bookseller and she reads all the reviews so I don't have to. She also edits, checks my French, and most of all, listens. Thanks, Mom. Thanks as well to Joanne Dale and Larry Heald, and to my sister Stephanie Collier-O'Donnell.

Every day I get to do the work I love, in the place I love, surrounded by the people I love. To me, this is the very definition of good fortune. The place is Nelson, BC, and I'm so very grateful to this community for offering daily inspiration and just the right amount of kookiness to keep things interesting.

And the people: my husband, Ron Sherman, is every bit as funny, understated, and handsome as when he asked me out for coffee over twenty years ago. He is never offended when I wander off midconversation and knows it's a very good sign when I forget to make dinner. All that, and I still can't beat him at backgammon. Our sons, Graeme and Eric, have been nothing more, or less, than *themselves* every moment of their lives. They are my daily reminders that this is what the world needs from me and, indeed, from all of us.

About the Author

DERYN COLLIER is the author of *Confined Space*, which was shortlisted for the Arthur Ellis Award for best first crime novel. Originally from Montreal, she is a graduate of McGill University. After a short career as a federal bureaucrat she ran away to the mountains of British Columbia, where she has been ever since. She lives in Nelson, BC, with her family and welcomes you to visit her at DerynCollier.com.